Kakigori Summer

Also by Emily Itami

Fault Lines

Kakigori Summer

かき氷の夏

Emily Itami

MARINER BOOKS

New York   Boston

KAKIGORI SUMMER. Copyright © 2025 by Emily Itami. All rights reserved. Printed in the United States of America. No part of this book may be used or reproduced in any manner whatsoever without written permission except in the case of brief quotations embodied in critical articles and reviews. For information, address HarperCollins Publishers, 195 Broadway, New York, NY 10007.

HarperCollins books may be purchased for educational, business, or sales promotional use. For information, please email the Special Markets Department at SPsales@harpercollins.com.

The Mariner flag design is a registered trademark of HarperCollins Publishers LLC.

Originally published in Great Britain in 2025 by Phoenix Books, an imprint of The Orion Publishing Group Ltd.

FIRST US EDITION

Library of Congress Cataloging-in-Publication Data has been applied for.

ISBN 978-0-06-343216-1

25 26 27 28 29 LBC 5 4 3 2 1

ペイン家へ

I

Takanawa Rei

高輪　令

There's an argument that I should have seen it coming. Well, maybe not this specifically, but something. My sister has been sending me death-based texts for a few weeks now, which never bodes well, does it.

The first message arrived when I was sitting in a client meeting watching my colleague Jasper present his slides, and noticing how inconsistent his use of full stops was. It's not that I give much of a shit about full stops per se, but Jasper had told me that morning, with no irony whatsoever, that he was a 'pretty detail-focused bloke'. So.

Did you know that in Korea they say Anyoung Haseyo when they see each other in the morning?

I dropped the phone surreptitiously into my lap. It was just past 1am in Tokyo. I could see the three dots, Ai typing.

It means 'youre healthy!' because everyones so pleased you didn't freeze to death in the night.
Thats a real example of glass-half-full thinking, isnt it.

When the meeting was over, I messaged her that this was news to me, and thank you for the everyday education, and sent her the video of the cockatoo pushing everything off the kitchen counter and jumping around in celebration of his own bad-assery.

How are you meant to know that's the beginning of something? Ai's like a volcano – calm for aeons at a time, with occasional geysers sputtering up, or rumblings that turn out to be nothing at all. You can't evacuate every time there's a burst of hot air.

I googled.

She messaged me two nights ago, late, asking if I could send her a photograph of a Waitrose aisle. Nothing bad can ever happen in Waitrose. All the Waitroses I looked up were shut, so I sent her a Google Images photo of the Queen in the cheese aisle. She didn't reply.

2

When Kiki calls, with her usual impeccable timing, the ambient airport noises on my headphones are turned up full blast, and I only answer the phone in order to silence it. My boss, Llewellyn, has just told me I have three hours to put together a presentation that requires at least a week of prep. Llewellyn has spent our entire working relationship making wrong assumptions about me based on my Asian face, and I have never done anything to correct him. I definitely do not have time for a heart-to-heart with my sister.

Kiki starts talking with no preamble, but her words are lost, because the paralegal in the office opposite has just taken a personal call, and when I remove my headphones all I can hear is her announcing to somebody that Bloody Vagina has gone and done it again. From what I've learnt from her calls, Vagina is her father's newest wife. Meanwhile, Hikaru is talking over Kiki at her end, an insistent and rhythmic 'MaMA, MaMA, MaMA' that I don't understand how Kiki can tune out. I have no idea why she can't text me like a normal person. I go to close the door, and manage to drop the phone so it skitters across the corridor.

'Turn on the news.' The dictum floats up from the floor, the voice of a disembodied oracle.

I grab the phone before anyone hears anything else they don't need to.

'What do you mean *turn on the news*?' I hiss, crouched down in front of one of the enormous flower arrangements that bloom incongruously across the office. 'I live in London; I don't have terrestrial television.' Japan has twelve channels, and getting access to internet TV is like trying to break into the Pentagon. I think it's a form of mind control.

'Well, go to the digital news outlet of your choice, then.'

'I have no digital news outlet of choice. The choice is liars or doomsayers so I've stopped paying attention. What is it?'

'It's Ai,' Kiki says, and my stomach drops. I should have paid closer attention to the messages. 'She's become a national disgrace and lost her job.' I've always admired that in Kiki – her ability to make all pieces of information sound equally neutral and matter-of-fact. *I think the set lunch comes with a side salad. I think the person you were hoping to see is already dead.* Sweet relief washes over me, followed quickly by irritation that my workday is being interrupted for someone who is still alive.

'Don't be over-dramatic.'

'I'm not being over-dramatic. If you turned on the news you'd see.'

'For fuck's sake, Kiki.' I look up to see one of the banking interns walking past, clutching coffees. 'Unless she's orchestrated a terrorist attack or murdered the emperor, the BBC is not going to be covering a story about a pop talent from Tokyo.' I get up to return to my office.

'She's not a talent, Rei, she's an idol. She's everywhere online. There are videos of them hanging around outside a brothel.'

'A brothel? Who?'

'Her and Ichiro,' Kiki says. 'Well, maybe not an actual brothel.'

'Who the hell is Ichiro?'

4

'Don't you know anything?'

'Nothing current, as we've already established.' I sit back down at my desk.

It turns out our little sister, to the pearl-clutching horror of the Japanese public, has been caught doing the walk of shame with a married man. Not just any married man, but Suzu Ichiro, the president of Kansas Records, the biggest record label in the country, and my sister's possibly erstwhile employer.

'Is he even hot?' I ask, like it matters.

'No, obviously not – Hikaru, if you keep doing that, you're going to shut your fingers in the drawer, and it will hurt – I mean, not that bad, for a suit. I guess the power might be attractive? He has quite nice eyes—'

'It was kind of a rhetorical question.'

Hikaru lets out a blood-curdling howl.

'It's OK, Hikaru, come here,' my sister says, the tone of her voice changing not one iota. 'Oh dear, does it hurt?' I hear kisses, crooning noises that are almost obliterated by his fire-engine wails.

'I have to go, Rei,' Kiki calls over the noise. 'Google it!'

Maybe it's no bad thing that at that moment, Llewellyn sticks his head into the office and says that, actually, the client report needs to be ready in one hour, not three, and we're presenting to the senior managers after lunch. I could swear he smirks as he says it. As he closes the door, my watch, an activity tracker that is never satisfied, orders me to 'Move!' with a smiley face.

3

It's disappointing to discover that, unfortunately, Kiki wasn't being entirely over-dramatic when she said that Ai had become a national disgrace. I hold out on googling my sister until after the client report deadline. As I hand the document to Llewellyn, with next to no fucks given about whatever holes it may contain, which I consider a win from a personal-development point of view, he tells me he hopes I haven't forgotten about the meeting with the Chinese clients first thing on Monday morning. He has definitely never mentioned the meeting before.

I decide to exit the building in an attempt to calm myself with the Zen tranquillity of central London. On my way out, I'm accosted by Jasper, who is in no way my senior and asks me to do him a favour which has nothing to do with my job title. I smile and agree. I might even say it would be a pleasure. If ever I doubt the Japanese portion of my blood, there it is in all its inconvenient glory.

As I wait for the lift down to the lobby, I scroll back through the messages Ai sent me before her Waitrose photo-shoot request.

Remember in Troy when Brad Pitt said the gods envy us because were mortal?

We watched *Troy* the last time all three of us were together, sprawled on the futon, each with half an eye on the laptop sitting on Ai's knees. I think it must have been a pirated version, because the Japanese subtitles kept referring to Achilles as 'John'. I messaged her back that I couldn't remember, and she maybe needed to have a word with herself about which films she stores in her head verbatim and which ones she filters out.

Do you think its true? That everything's more beautiful because it ends?

My answer:

You cannot go into a depression based on a line delivered by a Hollywood actor. No matter how great his abs.

The lift seems to be taking a stupidly long time, and I press the call button a few times more for good measure. Looking at the messages now, I'm thinking that, given the family history of unstable behaviour, I clearly should have followed that up. But, to be fair to myself – and I'm trying to take the therapist's advice here, despite the fact I happen to think he's lacking as a human being – in the rear-view mirror everything's always clear as daylight, and what, anyway? What should I have done?

Exiting the Silverman Sayle building, I'm confronted with a picture-perfect view of St Paul's. Some days it's a great comfort, to think that place has seen it all before, but today all I can see is the Gherkin poking up behind it like some obscene photo-bomber. The therapist said it was important to remember that you couldn't control other people's behaviour, only your reaction to it. I didn't tell him I thought that was a defeatist attitude. I haven't been back since.

I sit down on a bench in a leafy square and put Ai's name in the search bar of my phone. I'm immediately bombarded with outraged headlines and grainy images, the same few moments shot from different angles. A girl with a curtain of dark hair, her face variously obscured by the man pressed up against it, his businessman's suit incongruous and inevitable. The articles are sparse on information but strong on shock and horror, roaring at the young starlet's impropriety, the demise of her career, the scandal of it. The location is apparently the Paradise Love Hotel in Shin-Okubo, discreetly located above Ten Sluts lap-dancing bar. The married company president is named in each article once, as a sort of accessory to the story, an incidental bystander.

Ai started her singing life in Loupie Lou, one of those mega-bands with a million members all dressed in matching outfits, doing endless performances in shopping centres and at local festivals. To be honest, I hoped and assumed that this weird moment of her life would fade out when the band went bankrupt or the sleazy manager got bored. Ai didn't write any of the songs, they all sang them with faux-American accents – which is actually quite hard to achieve in Japanese – and every single one was accompanied by dance moves like an earth-bound synchronised swimming routine. For ages, the band was mainly known for creating shockwaves with their risqué chewing-gum commercial (it involved them passing it mouth to mouth in their teeth, like an unhygienic relay), but somehow, by the time I went back to Japan last year, Loupie Lou had exploded – they were all over the J-pop charts, the only band you heard in shops, selling out stadiums all over the country, performing on every breakfast and music and chat show going.

Then, in a move that was classic Ai, in being complete-ly unexpected, she propelled herself out of Loupie Lou and formed her own rock-folk-pop band, Kabuki, where she writes all the music and seems to have masterminded all their outfits and mad staging. The whole thing is like being caught in some kind of psychedelic trip where you can't really get your breath. At least that seems a little more true-to-form.

It's not even clear from the photos that it's definitely her. I zoom in closer and closer on all the pictures and it could be anybody. Well, almost anybody – any young, pretty haafu caught in a scandalous situation. I lean back on the bench and sigh so loudly that a pigeon relieves itself just next to my foot, blinking in surprise. It's not that anyone gives the smallest of shits who Ai sleeps with. She's welcome to shack up with the Dalai Lama if she fancies, and I imagine that in some respects that would suit them both very well. But the deal is meant to be that everyone does what they need to do to keep things ticking along. We eat our greens, breathe deeply and don't make life decisions likely to derail our tenuous grasp on sanity. In that, I think it's fair to say that Ai has fallen short.

I, for example, do not take mind-altering drugs. I get enough sleep. I try not to listen to love songs, or songs in a minor key. As well as never watching the news, I don't read books in which anyone dies. Or loses their job. Or breaks up with anyone. Or that feature animals of any kind. Ever. It means my cultural diet mainly consists of Dolly Parton's '9 to 5' and books about town planning, but in this way I attempt to keep my mind running smoothly along its rickety old tracks. In the same spirit, my sister should recognise that sleeping with a married man, or becoming the subject of a tabloid scandal, or somehow managing a well-executed conglomeration of the two, is likely to result in her feeling slightly out of whack, with all the inevitable consequences, and is therefore to be avoided. I dig the heels of my hands into my eye sockets.

Going back to the phone, my finger brushes against a video thumbnail and the last notes of a Kabuki song crackle out. Even through the tinny speaker, competing with the sounds of

London traffic, Ai's voice gives me goosebumps. I'm surprised every time I hear it, since I always convince myself afterwards that I must have been feeling over-emotional that day, and she can't, surely, be that good. She is, though. When she sings, the sensation is physical, the purity of the high notes like the finest froth, swimming down the octaves like cream, with a bass like the darkest alleys of your heart on its most beaten-up days. It's a sound that caresses your memories, plays your feelings like they're keys on a piano.

The song ends and Ai speaks into the mic, cradling her guitar like a child. She sounds more confident, more forceful than I've heard in a while. The timestamp says the video was uploaded a month ago. She thanks the crowd for coming. Then she thanks her bandmates for the music, and then she thanks the universe. The universe, she says, gave her the music, and the music reminds her that we are all connected, all one.

Kiki picks up on the first ring.

'What the hell has happened to her? Why is she being so woo-woo?'

'What do you mean?'

'*We are all one? The universe gave me the music?* Is she on drugs?'

'Rei, she's always been like that. Anyway, it's not a totally unreasonable idea, is it?'

'Are you even sure it's her?' I say, ignoring Kiki's last question. 'How can they prove it? The picture quality is shit.'

'I don't think she's denying that it's her.'

'Idiot child.'

'For doing it, or for not denying it?'

'For not hiding it better, obviously.' A squirrel running across the path stops to give me a hard look. 'And for doing it,' I add as an afterthought. 'Why would she go to a love hotel?'

'Where else was she meant to go?'

'Uh, anywhere? At least a classy place. Somewhere not in

Tokyo? Somewhere without pay-as-you-go dildos and spunk-encrusted sheets?'

'Don't be revolting. There's probably spunk encrusted on the sheets in the Grand Hyatt, too; it just isn't advertised in the name.'

I pull the phone away from my ear to take another look at the picture.

'Why does anyone even care?' I snap at Kiki finally, like maybe this reaction is her fault. 'She never claimed to be a *nun*.'

'She kind of did, actually. It's in her contract,' Kiki says. 'Idols are supposed to be single. How else are all her fans meant to imagine they have a chance? She's meant to be an incorruptible fantasy.'

'She signed a contract about her sex life?'

'Either way,' Kiki says impatiently, 'we live in Japan? I don't know if you've heard about the importance of keeping up appearances? Everyone's concerned for the morality of the *nation*, frankly. There they were, worshipping Ai in all her lily-white perfection, and it turns out she slept her way to the top!'

I flinch. 'She didn't,' I say automatically. It wouldn't occur to her.

'No,' Kiki agrees. 'Not on purpose, anyway.'

'Is she OK?'

'What do you think?'

I curse under my breath. 'Is she still in the share house?'

'I think. She's being cagey and not very coherent. I told her to come stay with me, but she hasn't answered.'

I have an unwelcome vision of Ai at sixteen, standing abruptly in the middle of lunch, her mouth still full of rice. She said she'd just remembered she'd left her phone in the freezer at the grocery shop, and then she left the house and didn't come back for two days.

'Why didn't you tell me?'

'Tell you what?' Even pissed off, Kiki's voice is even. 'That it's like keeping watch on an un-defused land mine? Every day a marvellous surprise? That's business as usual, Rei.' There's a one-second silence during which we both don't swear at each other. Sometimes, I marvel at our maturity. 'So when are you coming?'

'When am I coming?'

'Yes,' Kiki says patiently. 'When are you coming to sort it out?'

When Ai did eventually come home, two sleepless nights later, about a minute and a half before I ordered a nationwide manhunt, she said without explanation that she'd been in Osaka, as if she'd just been away on a planned holiday, and then pretty much went back to normal. Figuring out how Ai is doing at any given moment, or how she's going to be tomorrow, is a stab in the dark. There's one part of my brain where a fire alarm went off the moment Kiki called this morning. It's the other part that answers.

'She's twenty-one, not five,' I say. 'So she slept with some disastrous man. Who hasn't? I'm not flying ten thousand miles to commiserate.'

Kiki tuts. 'She's your sister. It's on the *national news*, Rei. That means Obaachan will have seen it too.'

Invoking our great-grandmother is a dirty trick. I refuse to react.

'I have a *job*. I basically have to learn Mandarin by next week.' I can practically hear Kiki rolling her eyes. 'Why can't you sort it out? She's your sister too.'

'Since when has she listened to anything I say? I don't have the bossy-eldest-child authority you do.'

'And I have Charlotte's wedding this weekend.'

'Charlotte's getting married? Is it to a lord? Please say it's to a lord.'

'What the fuck, Kiki—'

'Do you even know his name? Are you abandoning us to go to a stranger's wedding? Is Sath going to be there?'

'I'm hanging up. And I'm going to call Ai. But I am not coming to Japan.'

'She won't answer,' Kiki warns, and then hangs up before I can.

Kiki's right, again. I let the phone ring twenty-five times. Nothing. I try again. And again. And then a fourth time, because that will make it a neat hundred rings that my sister has ignored. It's late evening in Tokyo. I wonder what she's doing, if she's eaten dinner. If she's huddled in a futon somewhere seeing my name come up on her screen and silencing her phone, or if she's so busy weeping and being blanked by her bandmates that she hasn't heard it at all.

It's a grey day in London, the flat light and low clouds threatening rain, if they can be arsed. The buildings around the little square I'm sitting in are historic, grand, the trees well established. I picture Shin-Okubo, the Korean neighbourhood in Tokyo where Ai lives, vibrating with shops blasting K-pop, peddling thousands of collectible cards featuring its hot young things, barbecue restaurants and skincare stores jostling for space. It seems even further away than usual. Something occurs to me and I google 'Anyoung Haseyo'; the internet says it means 'hello', or 'peace'. I suppose linguistic accuracy isn't really the point. A black cab chugs past, carrying someone sleek and harassed-looking, and in my mind's eye I see the Tokyo equivalent, New York-style saloon cars in fluorescent oranges and bright greens. I think of Ai when we first visited Tokyo together, after our mother died. I can feel her little hand in mine. She was learning to read kanji, misunderstanding the flashing symbols on the front of the taxis – the letter for 'sky', 空, is the same as the letter for 'empty' or 'available'. All those sky-cars driving around Tokyo. She was so small.

4

Takanawa Kiki

高輪 清美

A good thing about working in an old people's home is that generally speaking the residents (or inmates, depending on how you look at them) are much more interested in things that happened fifty years ago than they are in current reality, so you can form your own views about the world today without being unduly influenced by other people's ideas. Also, it puts into perspective just how serious anything that's happening really is – not very, usually.

When I arrive for my shift on Saturday, the day after speaking to Rei (late, because the washing machine gushed grey water all over the floor just as we were trying to leave, and Hikaru wanted to have a forensic discussion about how old Santa Claus is at the door of his kindergarten), it's to find Hoshino-san crying her heart out in the corner of the games lounge. Nobody is paying any attention to her because there's an argument brewing about what channel the TV should be on, and most people are either involved or spectating. Sato-san is insisting on repeat – and with real venom – that only plebs watch anything other than the news, and Kanta-san is determined to watch the Olympics. He means the 1964 Olympics, and he only wants to watch Takao Sakurai win the boxing. Hoshino-san is often sad, because she thinks she's been left all alone and nobody ever comes to see her, and she wants to go home. She can't go home, because she kept wandering out of the house in her nightie, or leaving the hobs on, once starting a major fire in her building. Her son comes to see her every single day, and every single day she forgets he's been as soon as he walks out of the door. Luckily, she forgets her woes just as easily, and once I've convinced her to let me wash her hair, and sat her in front of the mirror to style it the way she likes, she's cheerful again.

I'm just brushing Hoshino-san's hair out, clean and dry and snow white, remembering when we were small and I used to make Ai play hairdressers with me (Rei flatly refused), when I hear our family name from the television. I step across the corridor back into the lounge, where Sato-san, having wrested the remote off Kanta-san, is standing ten centimetres away from the screen clutching the controller possessively. Kanta-san is sitting by the window in his wheelchair, looking defeated.

'Sato-san, you'll hurt your eyes, watching the TV from so close,' I tell her. I'm a professional, so I don't point out that she should probably just refrain from being kind of a bitch.

'Your vulgar little sister was on again,' she spits at me, looking gleeful. 'She's a home-wrecker!'

Sato-san must be having a good day, if she can remember Ai. She saw her on the New Year's Eve music show that the residents stayed up to watch and has had it in for her ever since.

'Is she?' I ask in my most patient, patronising voice. One of the great boons of being a single mother, and there are lots, is that after a while, other people's opinions about your life become white noise.

Sato-san frowns and clutches her walking stick. 'Why are you asking me?' She tuts loudly, her eyebrows knotting together. 'Who are you talking about?' Maybe not such a good day, then.

You could say that it's a perk of the job, to see the potential pitfalls of longevity. It sucks, no doubt about it, that our mother only made it to the grand old age of thirty-five. But in the moment I see Hoshino-san heartbroken, or watch five different confused personalities wash across Sato-san's face, or hear the way Kanta-san's language has reverted to something more primitive than Hikaru's at eighteen months, I think maybe it's a blessing that our mother will never get there.

I'm just about to go back to Hoshino-san when I hear Ai's name on the TV again. I've never gotten used to it, finding her smiling at me from magazines or billboards, winking about curry roux and showing her dimples, emoting in the rain to screaming crowds. I recognise her features, but she's not someone I know – this immaculately constructed, quasi-religious J-pop fantasy. My sister the epitome of purity, essentially a singing saint. Only now, it's my sister the scum of the earth, lower than a toe-cheese bacterium and in league with the devil.

On the TV talk show, a presenter with a quiff and round neon glasses is making loud noises about how 'not kawaii' Takanawa Ai has been. Takanawa Ai is not a collectible to hang off the end of your Sharpie, or a fluffy sticker for your iPhone, I want to tell him. I switch the channel over before Sato-san can latch on to it again, and consider the fact that, maybe, it's no bad thing that Rei isn't here to see all this. When the story first broke, I actually considered not telling her about it. The thing about Rei is that she might radiate calm – calm to the point of steeliness, in fact, so that if she wasn't my sister, I'd probably avoid her – but the truth is that the inside of her head is like the final note of some operatic calamity vibrato-ing without end. I really wasn't sure if bringing Ai's extra-marital activity to the party was going to be that helpful. Although I suppose, given Rei approaches her entire existence as a 24/7 life-or-death activity anyway, you could say it's a service to give her something real to chew over, and save her self-combusting over nothing. Hikaru and I watched *Ice Age* at the Oimachi kids' cinema club the other day, and I was so pleased to discover Rei's spirit animal. You know the squirrel, the one who's obsessed with finding and chasing his nut, quivering with anxiety from beginning to end? That. That's her.

I wonder how long it's going to take for Rei to back down and come home. I'd say two days – three at most. I wish she'd hurry up.

The situation follows me around all day. I'm doling out the daily portions of medication into pill trays, when my ear tunes in to the topic of discussion on the radio news – how ungrateful Takanawa Ai has been for the devotion of her followers, and how betrayed Kabuki's fanbase feels by her behaviour. At lunch in the staff kitchen, a paper has been left open to an article speculating as to how long Ai's torrid affair has been going on, and whether she would even have become the frontwoman for the band if Suzu Ichiro hadn't been totally pussy-whipped. Not in those exact words, which wouldn't really translate. The article wonders if Ai is even a very good musician.

Maria, my Filipina colleague, pats my head as she passes and tells me in English how beautiful my sister is. Ai is gorgeous, an objective fact. I try calling her again, but get sidelined by a phone survey that pops up like a whack-a-mole, wanting to know if I think fans should be refunded their tickets to Kabuki's next concert. I send the link to Rei. Ai doesn't pick up, naturally.

Sato-san deteriorates throughout my shift. She starts bellowing at me that I'm a hussy when I try to cut her toenails, so Maria says she'll take over. Maria thinks Sato-san is hilarious, and the ruder she is, the harder she laughs. Sato-san doesn't get any visitors, even though all the bills are always paid on time. I heard a rumour that her son stopped speaking to her when she disapproved of his marriage to a champion figure skater. It could all be total rubbish – the staff make stuff up to entertain themselves. When you're on your eighth nappy change of the night or Kanta-san has spat out all his pills, leaving you to scrabble around on the floor for saliva-covered blobs while he stares out of the window like it had nothing to do with him, it helps to think about what they were like in their prime. Maybe it isn't that her son isn't speaking to her, maybe he's dead, and the bills are being paid through something he organised in his will. I hope so – not that I want him to be dead; I just think that would be preferable to someone never visiting their mother. Or Hoshino-san, so sweet and bewildered, blinking politely and asking a hundred times a day where she is, listening earnestly and nodding, only to forget again thirty seconds later – what I think of is her looking after her son, kissing his round baby cheeks and holding his tiny feet in her hand. It's only in my head, but it makes it easier to be patient answering her questions over and over again. It's the least we can do, really, isn't it, to treat the oldies as well as they treated us.

After my shift, I stop off at the conbini to buy Hikaru a dorayaki. When I get to the childminder's, Hikaru rushes out, brandishing a picture proudly in my face. It's a large felt-tip circle, painstakingly coloured in yellow, with an ominous scribble at the centre. 'What a lovely picture, Hikaru,' I say, breathing in the smell of the top of his head. 'Is it the sun?'

'It's a burglar sitting in a lake of wee. He is alone, but not lonely. Did you bring me a snack?'

It's too much, really, to say the love of your life is a five-year-old; too needy, arguably not even good parenting. And yet – that feeling, like you need to be near someone more than you need to breathe; I've only ever felt that for one man in my life, and it's the little one with the pot belly and the taste for dorayaki.

Hikaru unwraps the dorayaki carefully and takes my hand to start the walk home.

'Hikaru, when I'm old and living in a care home, are you going to come and visit me?' I ask him.

'No,' he says blithely. 'I'll build you a little cave at the bottom of my garden and feed you strawberry shortcake.'

5

Takanawa Ai

高輪　愛

'I think it would be fair to say she isn't at her best.'

I heard Kiki say that to Rei once, when she thought I couldn't hear. When people talk about me – and there's a lot of people doing that, especially recently – it feels like they're talking about somebody else. They *are* talking about someone else – Takanawa Ai, this manga character I see on adverts sometimes. She's like a friend I admire, but who scares me a bit. Some days I don't really understand her at all.

When I hear Rei and Kiki talk about her, though, I know that's me. They've known me longer than I've known myself. They tell me things sometimes from when I was little, things I can't remember at all. I like hearing them talk about someone solid. I think of Kiki's words now, every time things start to go slow around the edges and I know the blinds are about to close. I'm not at my best. Even though I'm not sure what my best is. I know I was different; last week, maybe. Or last month. Then I was Takanawa Ai, that confident, energetic singer everyone was crazy about. How I felt then seems impossible. Like the only way to feel it again would be to die and get born again as a completely different person. Just imagine Rei's face, if I said that to her. You can't say the word 'die' without her suddenly becoming really busy. Kiki told me she doesn't even have cut flowers in her apartment, only living plants in pots.

I've been in this room for a while now.

Under the desk, actually.

It's good having a lid on top.

When I first got to the share house, I thought it wasn't a very nice room, but now I don't know why that matters. It has all the stuff a room is meant to have: a bed, this desk, a light, a wardrobe. There's a window, but I'm keeping the curtains closed.

There's a book on the desk about Buddhism. I've tried reading it, but my mind keeps sliding off the page. I love reading, sometimes, and other times I can't make the words be anything except black squiggles on a page, no matter how hard I try. I got the book from the library because of this priest who came to the Loupie Lou fan café one time. We were talking about how music connects everybody, and he told me that's what Buddhism says, too, that we're all connected and self is an illusion. I like that idea, that there's no me. That's why I keep the book where I can see it, even though I can't read it. There must be a huge fine on it by now.

The last few months play through my mind a lot. I don't want them to, but it's like a video on a loop that won't stop.

Imagine being the kind of person who could do the things Takanawa Ai did.

I can't.

The roar of voices as every concert began – it was like thunder.

I can feel it: the sound, the vibration of it in my bones. The first slow beats of the taiko drums were the sound of a threat approaching, and as soon as they heard it, the crowd was quiet. Spotlights rose out of the smoke to illuminate podiums around the stadium and the girls with sticks in the air like weapons, drums gripped between their legs. The crash when they brought the beaters down: that was the sound that creation was born from.

The rhythm sped up, and the heartbeat of the crowd was in every strike, faster fasterfaster

drumming up a fever.

The very first Kabuki song arrived almost a year ago, in the middle of the night. There had been sparks in my head for a few weeks before, like flares, so I knew something was coming. Before the song arrived, I told myself that, this time, I was going to go slowly. I know, I always know, that if I go through the storm I can only be spat out the other side. But once it starts, once the music's arrived, trying to go slowly is like trying to hold back the sea. I almost didn't catch the first song, because I couldn't get the headphones to work, and I knew Arisa was going to be mad if I started playing the keyboard out loud at 2am. Arisa has been in bands the longest and is the scariest one in the share house. I put the keyboard on the quietest setting and ran to the bathroom next to the kitchen. I got the ending first, pinning down what I could hear so it couldn't get away, then all the rest of it in a rush. The kanji for music is 音楽: fun (楽) noise (音). That made me so happy, that the fun noise was coming my way. In the morning I took it straight to Sakamoto, the manager of Loupie Lou.

I knew it was good. That wasn't arrogance or conceit: I didn't write the song, I pulled it out of the air like a gift. Sakamoto tried to pretend he wasn't sure; he said it wasn't the Loupie Lou sound. He was right about that – in Loupie Lou, we sang upbeat songs we could choreograph group dance performances to. This song needed something else. At first I tried to be polite and patient and wait for Sakamoto to come round, but it was making me crazy, like watching a sloth in slow motion. So I went to the head of the label.

I wasn't nervous for a second, because I knew I would make it happen. This is the first song, I told him, but I could feel a whole load more already, waiting, the rock and pop and folk all coming together. All I needed was for him to say we could record one song, on whatever budget he wanted, and if we could do that, the whole thing would fly.

He said yes, obviously.

The first song was massive, like I knew it would be.

We need taiko drummers, I told the label head. An army of taiko drummers, and they all need to be girls, and tell the costume department it's traditional dress but cool, jinbeis in neon and layers of kimonos, the kind of thing Empress Masako wore when she got married, but we'll cut them short and wear them over Levi's. And everybody was saying yes

of course they were, because yes was the only answer.

I said, there's the light show to think about, and maybe fireworks

and I'm thinking bonfires on stage as part of the finale

and I'm checking out enormous fire pits, five metres across

and the bassist's going to need a kabuto helmet

and we need to figure out how he's going to hold his head up.

Doesn't the Queen of England have some kind of a system for that? For when the crown's too heavy for her ninety-year-old neck?

My brain's this superpower figuring everything out, and I have hours in my day because I don't need to sleep. Why would you sleep, when all the colours are so bright they're ululating, and being awake is like a trip? There isn't time to explain it – I'll just do it, I'll do all of it and you'll see. I can see all the decisions in front of me – not just the one that needs to be made now but fifty after that, laid out like dominoes, and it's such a simple thing to knock them all down and reach the end.

23

Every show, I'd rise from below the stage on a hydraulic lift, on a cloud of smoke. As soon as I saw the crowd in front of me, it was like I disappeared. All I was was a figment of their energy and expectation. I put the mic to my mouth and sighed out the first melody like water. The music billowed, a blessing, and all of us were hypnotised by the spell it cast.

Those nights, we were all in it together, out of our minds on rhythm and harmony.

Chords tumbled down like lightning, the pulse of the crowd thrummed like rain

and I was in the centre of it, conducting the storm.

It was so beautiful, while it lasted.

6

Rei

令

I've done everything right and I'm still awake. I got in my exercise for the day early; I have eaten a salad containing fish and leafy greens so I am up on my omega-3 fatty acids, folates and magnesium; I have not partaken of caffeine since 1pm, or sugar and alcohol at all. Charlotte's wedding present, a set of hand-carved candlesticks made from sustainably sourced wood, is wrapped up and sitting on the table in the hall ready for tomorrow, next to my wheelie suitcase. The flat is immaculate, as always, so clutter cannot fuck with the juju of my mind. By rights, I should be in a deep, smug sleep, ready to wake up refreshed and dewy-skinned. But I am awake. And furious. Again.

Ostensibly, I'm worrying about the state of the planet, haunted by the image of Hikaru living in a pile of motorhomes stacked on top of each other to keep out of the floodwaters. In my 2am megalomania, I'm somehow culpable for it all; if only I recycled more and had a job in conservation instead of finance, I could single-handedly defeat global crisis. There is the glaring probability that this self-flagellation is nothing more than a distraction from the damn voice in my head telling me I should have left for Japan yesterday, which in turn is a good way to avoid thinking about the possibility that Sath will be at the wedding. This says disappointing things about my character and priorities, on many different levels. He won't be there; he was never even friends with Charlotte. I am going to kill Kiki for mentioning it.

I continue to lie very still with my eye mask on and my earplugs in, teeth gritted and brow furrowed, in that attitude well known to be conducive to peaceful slumber. Oddly, sleep is still elusive. It comes to me in a pang that I don't actually like sleeping in a bed; those edges you can fall off, so finite. I think of futons in Japan, everyone in a cosy pile. It's not helpful. I turn on the light and reach for my glasses, then go to the kitchen for whisky.

I call Ai again, hoping that the light of a new day will have cheered her up, willing her to have gone over to Kiki's, for the three of them to be eating breakfast in Kiki's apartment with the door open to the tiny balcony, the washing fluttering outside. She doesn't pick up. I push myself up on to the kitchen counter to sit cross-legged on the marble, put Ai's name in the search bar and flick through until Google runs out of damning headlines and starts showing me pictures of Ai in her glory days (the day before yesterday) instead.

As the frontwoman for Kabuki, Ai's giving me fuck-off looks from a million different angles, smashing a chord on the piano with her hair flying, eyes closed, frowning into the mic. A few pages back and she's part of Loupie Lou, a completely different person, peering coquettishly from behind a fringe, smelling a bouquet of flowers, wearing some kind of ruffly pink skirt and sparkling silver platform boots.

Why is your Loupie Lou wardrobe a cross between our American Pageant Barbie and the Bee Gees?

I start to message her, but I don't want to tip her over the edge.

26

Ai looks a lot like our mother. I remember holding Nozomi's face in my hands when I was small. I must have been smaller than Hikaru is now, because part of the reason I was holding her face was to keep her attention, which kept drifting over to Kiki, crawling around on the floor and threatening to go straight off the side of the engawa, the wooden terrace that wrapped around the perimeter of the house. The other reason was that I loved my mother's face, the way her eyelashes fanned out against her cheekbones when she looked down, the symmetry that made me feel calm. I've read since that babies are more likely to smile at someone attractive, which seems deeply unjust, and consistent with everything to do with nature. Nozomi's even features were a gift from Obaachan, our great-grandmother, who was apparently considered a real catch back in the day. Their physical similarities are probably partly why Ai is Obaachan's favourite. Ai's hands are the elegant, long-fingered ones Obaachan had before arthritis transformed them into gnarled claws, and she has the same defined cheekbones.

Ai also has perfect eyes, it turns out – on the fourth page of results is an article on a fan site that says scientific investigations have shown that Takanawa Ai's eyes are the optimum width apart to connote both cuteness and sexiness. Like a baby panda crossed with a siren. It's interesting to note that even with the same eyes, Obaachan doesn't look anything like a baby panda or a siren.

I usually avoid looking at Ai in her celebrity guise, or even thinking about it, if possible, which is easy in London but less so when I'm in Japan. The last time I was in Tokyo, I was walking past a Bic Camera, the display of flat-screen televisions all tuned to the same channel, when suddenly there were eight Ais, in different sizes and picture quality, perched at the bar of a ramen counter with a sumo wrestler, in ecstasies over the noodles, washing them down with oolong tea. *Drink Oolong Tea!* the advert implored as Ai sashayed her slender silhouette out the door. It melts away fat so you too can eat ramen all day and still be a svelte member of a girl band!

Sath was eating ramen from the Ippudo that had opened up near our flat, unselfconsciously and with great enjoyment, at the exact moment I realised I had to break up with him. It was because it suddenly became clear that I couldn't possibly let someone who could get so much uncomplicated joy out of a bowl of carbohydrates spend the rest of their life dealing with my shit. If he's at this damn wedding tomorrow, it'll be the first time I've seen him since we broke up, a year after moving to London together when we finished university. Neither of us was employed when we graduated, which Sath said was freedom and the next great adventure beckoning. I told him that sounded like a euphemism for death, and he said I was being kind of a downer. I did him a huge favour, if you think about it, saving him the trouble of having to end it himself.

I drain the last of the whisky and put the phone down on the counter just as it pings with an email from Llewellyn. Over the years I've been grateful to him for making my working life such a twenty-four-hour psychodrama, leaving no head-space for anything else – mergers and acquisitions as a form of corporate meditation. The email is forwarding a message from the Chinese clients, scheduling our Monday meeting at lunchtime for them, which means 6am for us. As a little PS, Llewellyn adds that he thinks it would be useful if I included in the presentation data points and analyses from the last five years as comparisons to the current status quo.

When I told Kiki that Sath and I were breaking up, I told her I'd looked into the future and it wasn't good. It had become apparent that I could keep up a facade for so long and no longer, and my time was up. I needed to leave immediately, like excusing yourself from a party when you realise you've had too much to drink and are no longer adding value.

Kiki said there was an argument that terminating our entire relationship was an over-reaction to watching somebody eat noodles. And that it was a pity, since, in her opinion, Sath was a first-class specimen. I said he was not a frog I had brought into the lab for dissection and, also, that that was precisely the point.

In the five years since, I have not thought about him every day.

7

I'm almost late for the wedding because I'm cleaning. I'm considering the fact that if I leave it long enough, my embarrassment at my tardiness will mean I have to invent a terrible stomach flu, and then I can spend the rest of the evening scrubbing the window frames with bleach instead of sharing hors d'oeuvres with people I don't know, or possibly hiding in the toilets.

I realised just this morning on Google Maps that the wedding is taking place only a mile or so away from where our supposed father, Richard, now lives with his new wife and their kids, in an enormous house with a circular driveway, and those gold decorative bars across the bottom of each stair to hold the runner in place. I messaged him when I found out, wondering if he'd like to have coffee, or if perhaps I could come in and say hello. The millisecond after I pressed 'send' I wondered what the hell was wrong with me, and in what ways Kiki would kill me if she found out.

We used to visit England quite a lot when we were small, and then Richard got us over a few times after Nozomi tapped out, but he was always awkwardly polite and didn't really know what to do with us. By the time our mother died, our parents had been living on different continents for five years but were still married, something which displays entirely consistent levels of inertia and disengagement. We stayed that first summer with our English grandmother, Richard visiting at weekends. It was a bad summer, but that wasn't Granny's fault. I remember her pulling us all in for a hug when she first saw us. She smelt of talcum powder and Chanel No. 19, something I discovered recently when I walked through Liberty's perfume floor and experienced an unpleasant time-warp sensation. 'Oh, my poor darlings,' she said. Nobody ever called us that; you wouldn't, would you, in Japanese. I dug my nails into my palms and stared at Kiki and thought how annoying she was, because if I didn't, I would start crying and I didn't know if I could stop. Our whole world that summer was her house and her garden, huge, with a sloping lawn and an orchard, and flowers we never saw in Japan – larkspur and lavender, foxgloves and alliums – living on raspberries and potatoes instead of water-melon and rice, and it was so much easier not to think of our mother when we were there. After Richard married Gina, we stopped coming to England, and now he has two blond sons you would never guess are related to my sisters and me. I've only met them twice, and on neither occasion did they give any indication they knew who I was.

Kiki and I have this theory that, actually, Nozomi only hooked up with Richard to spite her parents, and all three of us are just the products of a giant revenge joke. Or else I was an accident, and then they had to have Kiki to make it seem deliberate, an idea Kiki has issues with since it means she owes her entire existence to me. I tell her there has to be some compensation for being the eldest – we get all the bullshit, so maybe it's fair we get all the ego as well. That Ai was definitely an accident is not discussed, but also not contested, by anybody.

I take a cursory look in the rear-view mirror of the car before I get out. No smudged make-up, and the earrings that Ai and Kiki gave me for my twenty-first birthday, from our favourite, too-expensive shop in Tokyo, hammered gold and green onyx the colour of the sea. I get to the church just in time to squeeze into the last pew on the bride's side, without a moment for seeing who's in the congregation, or having to make small talk with anyone.

The service, in the ancient chapel of gold-coloured stone, festooned with bouquets of wildflowers, is beautiful. This figures, since Charlotte's been planning it for at least a decade, long before she met the groom. A quartet plays Pachelbel's Canon as Charlotte appears, flushed pink, her father patting her hand in the crook of his elbow. I stare straight ahead as her brother reads the first letter of St Paul to the Corinthians and wonder if anyone on the planet has ever managed to live up to his unrealistic definition of love, and how much they got taken advantage of if they did.

I asked Sath once why he wanted to get married. He shrugged. 'Maybe just to think,' he said eventually, 'that somebody would do that for me.' Wrap themselves up like a present and then demand that everyone turn up and clap for the big reveal; create endless lists and cake-based tension; make a promise there's statistically only a 66 per cent chance of your being able to keep; spend an entire day feeling the absence of your mother like a malevolent presence? Till death do us part, Charlotte repeats after the vicar, and I can't believe how morbid it all is, for a day of joy. I would have done it for him, though. We stand up to sing 'Dear Lord and Father of Mankind', and my eyes do a surreptitious sweep of the heads in front of me. He isn't here, of course.

The ceremony finishes, everyone whooping as Charlotte and her brand-new husband beam their way back down the aisle, a feeling of collective achievement and strange relief even though all we've done is sit here and watch. People start to wander out of the church, clustering together to debrief and catch up. That's when I see him. It's almost out of the corner of my eye, and I stop before I look again, because there is absolutely no need to over-react. He's standing at an angle so I can see his profile, the straight nose and heavy brow that make him look so serious, listening to someone who could be Charlotte's grandmother with intense, cordial concentration. He smiles when she says something, that smile that's so at odds with his brooding atmosphere. She's charmed by him, enraptured.

It's immediately clear that five years of being away from Sath hasn't done anything to make me fancy him any less, which is a shame. As if he feels me watching him, he turns his head, and time speeds back up in an unforgiving instant. He doesn't look surprised, just guarded, almost belligerent, and I turn away, suddenly engrossed in my order of service. It says the groom's name is Benedict Mortimer Gibson-Yonge. Not a lord, but worth reporting to Kiki.

We're herded to a stately home a few minutes' walk down a country lane: champagne and canapés on the lawn, and hordes of people I haven't seen, haven't even thought of, in so long. I drink too quickly, not waiting to see if the booze is going to cure me or push me over the edge. I'm talking to a man I mainly remember for not infrequently dancing naked in the college bar, who's now an eminent human rights lawyer, when someone next to me moves and Sath is suddenly right there. He smiles stiffly, and at that moment the human rights lawyer spots his old roommate by the ornamental fountain. There's a one-second silence, which I am congenitally obliged to fill.

'I didn't expect you to be here,' I say.

'Sorry.'

'I didn't mean it like that.'

Sath looks at me coolly. 'I thought you'd probably be here,' he says.

'Oh.' I wonder if he thought about it fleetingly and moved

on, or if the idea made him groan inwardly, and which would be worse. 'It's nice that you kept in touch with Charlotte.'

'I haven't, really. I mean' – he frowns at the bubbles in his glass – 'when I met her, I realised she was your Charlotte, but it's Ben I know. I guess you guys have stayed close.'

The truth is, we haven't either. It turns out that in some ways, I've inherited Obaachan's Buddhist practices – I concentrate on what's in front of me. That makes me the worst at staying in touch, shrinking my friendship group to whoever I happen to see regularly. For the past five years, then, that would be mainly Llewellyn. 'How do you know Benedict?' I ask, putting an end to that train of thought.

He sips his drink, still distant. 'We used to work together.'

Doing what? I almost ask, but it seems so rude, to have known him so well that the minutiae of his day were tied up with my own, how he slept and what he dreamt and which particular article he read in the morning in his boxers while he chewed on the dry toast he was weirdly partial to, and now to have no idea what he does for a living. It's harder than you might imagine, to cut a person out of your life, to make sure reminders of them can't leak out of the internet or the mouths of friends who don't know any better. An achievement, arguably.

'That's nice,' I say instead.

He drains his glass and smiles at a passing waitress. She tops up his glass, then mine, like an afterthought. He's looking at me, his glass halfway to his mouth, and suddenly his mask slips.

'Are you *smirking*?' I demand without thinking.

He shrugs. 'It's good to see you. You look good in the dress.'

'What dress?' I ask like an idiot, looking down at my clothes like I'm under the impression I came to the wedding in a tracksuit.

'Hello, Sath.' A girl with red lipstick cuts between us. It's hard to tell who I hate more: her for appearing at that moment, or myself.

'Oh, there's Veronica,' I say, gesturing at nobody. 'Nice to meet you, bye.' Sath smiles at his feet. He knows there's no Veronica.

I sit with people who roar a lot at dinner. Even though Sath isn't at the table and I don't ask, I learn that he's put his engineering degree to good use, that he's created some kind of pioneering, eco-friendly heating system that's currently being rolled out in new-builds across the country. He's recently won some prestigious award and has just started selling the system overseas. This is all information I don't particularly want to have, though I'm happy for him. I think of one of the first conversations we had, when he told me about his parents, who immigrated from India before Sath was born, and his brother, who dropped out of school to deal illegal substances. That left the sum of his parents' hopes and dreams on Sath's slim shoulders, which must have been a great weight, but when I said that to him, he said he tried never to let it show, because his parents were unrealistically nice people. They must be proud of him now. I down my drink and focus on trying to remember the names of the people around this table instead.

After speeches, and chocolate ganache, and port, everyone wanders off, to drink more or to dance. I'm just thinking there's a chance I could sneak back to my hotel room without anybody noticing, when a message from Kiki pops up on my phone: a bar chart telling me that 87 per cent of respondents to the survey think that tickets to the next Kabuki gig should be refunded, given Takanawa Ai's renegade behaviour. I'm just stabbing the swearing red-faced emoji back at Kiki when I see Sath walking in my direction. Because I am a socially inept buffoon and my head is scrambled by a Japanese soap opera playing out in real time, I stand up, as if he's royalty.

'Nice wedding,' he says, pretending not to notice, and we look out at the crowd together like crumbly spectators at Ascot.

'Yes.' In all the world, I can't think of a single thing to say.

'Aren't you going to dance?'

I open my mouth to answer, then close it again. Dancing gives me hives, not that there's any reason Sath would remember that. We once accidentally ended up at a bar that was having a salsa night, where the host kept lifting up my arms for me, telling me to let go and be myself. I told him I did not want to let go, and myself has nothing to do with lifting my arms in the air, and then Sath and I had to leave. The only thing to be said in defence of dancing with other people is that it's less awkward than dancing alone, probably the most horrific activity imaginable. I turn to look at him, and Sath is smiling with his mouth shut. He remembers.

'How's work?' he asks.

'Fine. You know.'

Sath thought working in the financial services was a terrible idea. He said I would be surrounded by psychotically competitive, money-driven people with no interest in reality, and it would take over my life. So he does know.

'How's yours?'

'It's great,' and he says it so easily I believe him.

'I heard that you might be selling your system overseas,' I say.

His eyes crease at the edges. 'Do you actually know what I do?'

'Yeah,' I scoff. 'Heating.'

He laughs into his chest like he's sharing a joke with himself, the way he always used to laugh at me.

'I'm setting up in the States,' he says. 'I'm moving there.'

'Forever?'

36

'I don't know. I have contracts that should take a few years at least.'

There's a pause that I leave half a second too long. 'Your parents will miss you,' I say finally, and I think of his mother in their tiny, immaculate house. She thought it was a personal affront that I'd been deprived of parents, and that feeding me might alleviate the situation. Even before Sath and I got together, he was turning up resignedly at the door of my university bedroom loaded with Tupperware boxes labelled with freezing and cooking instructions in his mother's careful handwriting. His dad, an aeronautical engineer who worked for British Airways, would appear periodically and fix things I didn't know were broken: the loose curtain rail, the weird noise my bike made. After we broke up, I spent a long time wondering if I should write to them and apologise.

'They've gone back to India,' Sath says now. 'Dad has MS.'

'Oh,' is all I can say. Does MS kill you? I think of Sath's dad, slim and regal, straight-backed. The only thing I know about MS is what I saw in a film about Jacqueline du Pré that Kiki and I watched once, and how much the actor playing her shook. I feel like Sath's dad would just refuse. 'Shit. I'm sorry.'

Sath shrugs. 'He's good. He can still walk, just about. It's good to have a million relatives around. Mum's excited to come to the States. She reckons we're going to do a road trip.'

'She'd be the best road trip buddy. She'd bring all the food.'

He smiles, like he's surprised to remember I'd know that. 'All the food,' he agrees.

I almost ask him to tell her I said hi, but I don't, because I'm not sure what the point would be. I figure there's a high chance she's been sticking pins in voodoo dolls, which is what I would do if any girl ever broke up with Hikaru. I want to ask him if he had a girlfriend when he found out his dad was sick. I hope that someone was there when he couldn't sleep with worry but couldn't say it, and waited for him after the doctor's appointments, even if it wasn't me.

There's a sharp click just in front of us and we both look up, startled. It's the girl with the red lipstick, holding one of the Polaroid cameras that have been scattered across the tables.

'You both look so sad,' she says accusingly.

Sath makes a little galvanising movement and turns towards me. I think he's about to tell me he's leaving. I don't want to look at his eyes because I have a sudden insight that if I do I'll cry, and then I'd really have something to chew over in the morning. I'd have to explain that it isn't him, it's my job and my stupid father and my sister in Tokyo. It isn't him at all.

8

Ai

愛

If someone hadn't taken the picture, none of this would have happened.

They only took the picture weeks after the unfortunate incident with Ichiro. It was just bad luck that we were standing outside a love hotel right then. Everything was already finished, no one knew anything about it, and Ichiro and I had gone back to our original relationship, him being a suit and me being a tarento and us not talking to each other. Things could just have stayed that way, stayed normal, if Ichiro hadn't decided to kiss me again.

We'd been walking away from the Kansas Records office, where Sakamoto had yelled at me for not turning up to a meet-and-greet. I didn't mean to forget. I would never. It just leaked out of my mind like so much other stuff lately. I was walking to feel better and Ichiro said he'd come too. I was walking a lot those days, because staying still made me feel like I'd swallowed too much sweet potato too quickly. Like the ones we used to get in winter, wrapped up in newspaper, from the man who sold it door to door from his cart with the burning coals inside.

Ichiro said my name, so I turned towards him. Over his shoulder, I could see a billboard of Kabuki with me in the middle, looking at the camera with narrowed eyes. I was thinking I didn't even remember that photo shoot, when suddenly his mouth was on mine, our noses bumping. It only lasted two seconds, and in that time I thought, I wonder why he's doing this, and also, Don't people's eyebrows look weird from this close up.

I guess it's not that surprising that there would be paparazzi all over Shin-Okubo, given all the fan cafés around here. I don't know how we didn't notice the guy with the big camera, though. At first there was just him, then another from the other side of the street, and then people walking past joined in, taking photos on their phones. I spent a few seconds standing there like a fool. I kept thinking that all I needed to do was explain the situation clearly and then everything would be fine. Ichiro hailed a taxi straight away and took me with him, which was good, because I left, but not, because he grabbed hold of my hand, which made bad visuals. I've heard a lot about bad visuals in the last few days.

Just for a second, as the taxi door closed, when the only thing I could hear was muffled shouting and all the cameras thudding against the glass, I felt a giant flood of relief. 'There.' I could almost hear someone saying it, one of my sisters, or both of them. Done and dusted. I could see a patch of blue sky above all the heads, and a fat little sparrow. The electric sign at the front of the car flickered and switched, from an empty car, 空車, to an occupied one, 賃送, or a sky-car to a wage-escort, depending which way you felt like reading it. I felt like the letters were in on some cosmic joke, and I suddenly remembered Rei bringing me to Tokyo when I was little. She never told me that I was reading the signs wrong, and I spent ages trying to figure out why the taxis were called that. I thought that maybe under very special circumstances they flew, and the memory made me want to laugh.

Then that bubble of joy burst as fast as the ones we used to blow when we were little. Ichiro dropped me off at the share house. He said he couldn't believe what I'd done to his life, and also that I was absolutely forbidden to leave the house. I went into my room and stared at the ceiling. I thought about the things that made me feel better before – playing the piano, or the guitar, and while I thought of it, the piano keys all turned to Velcro, and my fingers did too, sticking together.

That night the dream started again, always the same one. I'm in this elevator going up, and there's nothing I can do to stop it.

At the end the elevator always goes shooting off its axis, spinning like it's falling upwards,

and I can feel the emptiness of space

crushing me like a vice.

9

The other girls in the share house aren't that sympathetic. I didn't really think they would be, but I was hoping they might surprise me. In every corner of the house, I can feel whispering, and when Arisa catches sight of me in the corridor she drops her eyes.

It's a few days into my new life, the one where I've become a prostitute and a *One Piece* villain combined, and I'm finding myself messaging Rei, which is good. Rei and Kiki have both been calling me, but I haven't known what to say. I know they're discussing me. Usually, that makes me feel more solid, like proof I exist. Recently, though, their words have been like a too-bright beam of light I don't want to step into. The day after the story broke, Rei sent me an audio clip of 'The Show Must Go On', Freddie Mercury so earnest it sounds like it hurts him. Isn't it weird how sometimes, when you love someone so much and you can feel how much they love you back, it actually makes you feel worse.

Just when Rei's answering my message, and I'm feeling happy to see her typing back, a call from Sakamoto comes through. He keeps calling me, everyone keeps calling me, but the phone calls don't really seem to solve anything, just make the people on the other end even angrier. There are problems with brand endorsements and venues and ticket sales and press coverage and I watch myself looking at the phone and not picking up. Instead I turn it off and shove it behind the new rolls of toilet paper in the bathroom.

Arisa and Mako stop talking mid-sentence when I go into the kitchen, and Mako puts her phone straight into her pocket.

'A package came for you,' Arisa says awkwardly, motioning to a food delivery box on the table.

'Thank you.' I pick up the box. The handwriting on the label is Kiki's.

'Aren't you going to open it?' Mako sounds like she's about to tut.

'Later,' I tell her, because I think if I open it I might cry, and I don't want that to happen in front of her and Arisa.

'We were never in that love hotel,' I say instead. I press my thumbs to the tips of my fingers, trying to keep them in place.

Mako's eyes open a little wider and she nods without looking at me, like I'm forcing a confession out of her.

'When they took the picture, nothing happened,' I try again.

'But the kiss . . .' Arisa says. I hate that word. 'Chu'. It sounds like steam trains and Minnie Mouse's eyelashes.

'He kissed me,' I say, and I wish I wasn't speaking in Japanese. I feel like there are so many more ways I could get it across in English.

'Oh really?' Arisa says, turning back to her cooking, like I've just told her that turnips are out of season or that I might start using a new brand of tissues.

I start to say it again, but every time it sounds more and more like I'm lying, plus I can't truthfully say that nothing happened ever, so I go to my room to pet Coco instead.

Coco is a Roborovski hamster, the size of a mouse, or one of the fancy grapes we sometimes get sent in expensive fruit baskets. Band life isn't as glamorous as you might think – no matter how well the shows have gone, when they're over there isn't anywhere to go. It's in the contract. So it's the adoration of ten thousand fans, and then just me and Coco bonding.

I open the door to Coco's cage, calling to him because sometimes his nose comes twitching out of his bedding when I do. Then he'll sit on my hand and wash himself. I told Arisa that once, and she looked at me politely and said hamsters aren't intelligent enough to come when you call. He doesn't come now, and stupidly that's the thing that brings tears to my eyes.

I search the whole cage, even tip it all up so the floor's covered in sawdust. He isn't there. I guess I didn't shut it properly. I screwed up, again. I wonder where he could have gone, if he's electrocuted himself chewing a wire, and if he's going to get dust in his eyes. I have to sit really, really still to make my head not explode.

When it gets dark outside, I lie down on the floor again. I haven't been able to sleep for ages, so I try out new locations to jazz things up. Different patches of floor, sometimes the futon cupboard. Once in the bath, but only once because when I woke up Arisa was staring at me. If I keep not picking up the phone, I guess soon I won't be able to carry on living in this house, either.

I hear a car alarm, or someone screaming. Either of those noises would be pretty normal in London, outside Rei's apartment, but not in Tokyo. I lie there for a long time, trying to figure out if the sound is in my head.

Nobody in the house gets up or moves around.

Rei always tells me that there's no objective truth, just the reality that you choose. What if you don't get to choose, though? What if you're stuck with the one you're in, like psychedelic lenses in glasses you can't take off?

Once, at the beginning of Loupie Lou, I yanked my back during some dance routine and for a week, every time anyone came near me, the fear that they might brush against me sent my whole body into spasms, so that pain shot in waves along my arms and legs. It was only my reality, but I couldn't change it.

It will pass.

That's what you have to think.

Rain, and I'm stuck underneath it; traffic, and I'm standing in the middle of it; and either way, it won't last forever.

That's what I have to believe.

10

Rei

令

I peel open my eyes in a room in a country hotel, a fug of alcohol, weak grey light filtering through a gap in the curtains. Something very heavy is lying on my soul like a baleful dog. I close my eyes again, contact lenses scraping against the lids like dried-up papier-mâché, and scan my mind for how bad it really is. When I remember, I sit up immediately. That cannot have happened.

Sitting up is a terrible mistake. The light in the bathroom is still on, the door half open. Sath is notably not here. A feeling of fumbling against a wall, his hands in my hair, sliding up my thigh. My heart seems to be pounding inside my head, and I think of my brain, so dehydrated it's trying to pull free from my skull. I can feel the roughness of Sath's stubble against my cheek and taste his kiss. The sheets smell familiar. The thought of him creeping out quietly, trying not to wake me, is so shameful I actually get out of bed and stand next to it like someone at military camp. I would laugh at myself if I didn't think that would roll my head off my neck. Stupid old me, always snoring away while the important people sneak out in the night.

As I stand there, staring at my clothes and shoes strewn over the diamond-patterned carpet, my phone beeps. I reach for it, carefully, not lunging, not hoping – for what? It's Ai.

46

Do you think death is like getting a filling or a labial piercing?

It's nice, really, to have something else to think about.

In what sense? I text back. Are you OK? Are you going to Kiki's?

In the sense that you dread it deeply, but once its done, its done.

I type back:

Don't ignore my other questions.

Ai's online status disappears, my answer to her unread.
I mean, not really, I add for clarity, in case she comes back: CALL ME
This is exactly the kind of shit that happens if you take your eye off the ball, even if it's only for one badly judged night.
Before I can stop myself, in a maniacal need to salvage something productive from the day, I message Richard again.

Just wondering if you got my message
As I'm going to be passing your house soon!

I press 'send' and then wonder if the exclamation mark might actually be the worst thing that's happened so far. The two blue ticks appear straight away. I focus on packing up my stuff, unsurprised to discover that I can't find one of my earrings. I have just about enough dignity to get in the hire car as if I'm too busy to wait for Richard's reply.

Richard lives in a part of the English countryside so picturesque I'm always convinced afterwards that I embellished it in my memory. It's what Obaachan imagines all of England to look like, and when I'm still a few minutes from his house, almost far enough away to pretend I'm not waiting for him, I pull up in a lay-by. Out of the window are fields in shades of yellow and mauve and green, a village with a stone church nestling in a valley. The light filters through the silver birches lining the road, liquid gold and white and the damp olive of forest floors. The hangover makes everything deeply significant. There's a word for the light dappled through the trees in Japanese and the thought of it, the sound of it in my mind, makes me feel like someone is watching the light with me, someone who watched it and loved it long enough to name it. Komorebi.

Richard replies:

Not a great time im afraid, lots on ! Best

I look at the message for a fraction longer than it takes me to read it. My parents met in a bar in Roppongi, which is an embarrassment for being such a cliché: a wannabe artist and an undemonstrative risk analyst, everyone in suits with padded shoulders and perms, flashing the cash like it was going out of fashion. Which it was, as it turns out. When I've gone out there as an adult and seen the white guys and Japanese girls hooking up, a gargantuan part of me wants to tell them to cut their losses and end it now. Leaving aside the issue that the Western guys who hang out there are not invariably but frequently weird and want to mansplain Japan to Japanese people, communication issues are bad enough in people who have been brought up in the same country speaking the same language. I always wondered what brought my parents together. They were about as mismatched as you could possibly imagine.

It's unheard of, in Japan, to do what my mother did – for the wife to keep her surname, and pass it on to her children. Maybe she knew things were going to be hard enough without throwing an unpronounceable surname into the mix. Or maybe, in her heart of hearts, Nozomi knew from the off that

Richard Hebblethwaite was going to turn out to be a total flake.

My watch vibrates, a peculiarly aggravating jiggle. 'Relax, breathe with me?' it asks. I wrench it off my wrist and consider throwing it out the window, but I don't, because that would contribute to the plastic pollution of the countryside. Instead, I pull myself together and text Lee, my personal trainer. I can sweat it all out, cancel the hangover, pretend it never happened. I put on my sunglasses and drive too fast back to London, straight to the office and the attached gym.

'Focused aggression, Rei-chan,' Lee says, winking at me, adjusting his grip on the boxing pad and checking himself out in the mirror. -chan is the suffix for someone you know well, or for someone cute or young. Lee learnt it when he visited Japan once. He also explained to me in detail just how uncomfortable futons are, how in Japan they expect you to take your shoes off when you go in anywhere, and how unreasonably wound up people get if you don't want to. Then he gave me a lecture about the twistedness of the sex bars in Akihabara and how, in his opinion, Japan is going to have to open up, as a country. There's an argument that inciting feelings of extreme violence in his clients makes Lee an excellent boxing instructor.

In my sightline, a woman with a bottom like two smooth spheres is flicking kettlebells, and I find myself enraged that she has nothing better to do than perfect her arse. Then she gives a little Wimbledon-sex-grunt as she throws her arms higher and I wonder if the capillaries around my eyes are going to explode. The sensation isn't improved by me trying not to think about the fact I got so drunk, or slept with Sath, or thought for a minute that I cared that he's moving thousands of miles away. Or wonder why I do such a stupid, pointless job, or let myself be needy in front of Richard, or have no idea what I should do about Ai, but most of all, why the fuck I think the things I

49

think and have such a hateful, ungenerous heart. Lee hangs up a punchbag and I go at it fast, faster, harder, chasing the high that will melt all the anger away.

Hikaru comes to mind, his furious, indignant face. A couple of winters ago, Kiki put him in a hand-me-down snowsuit she was given by someone at work with an older daughter; pink, with turquoise and yellow hearts. Hikaru consented to be bundled into it, even made it outside, before having a King Kong meltdown. I think it was when he saw other children going by, not wearing pink snowsuits. 'This,' he said, glaring at Kiki with tears rolling down his cheeks. 'Is not. What. I want. To look like!'

You and me both, Hikaru, and it's thinking of him, my sweet, lovely nephew, that drops my heart rate just enough that I don't feel I'm about to die of unspecified rage. This is not what I want to be like, at all.

II

Thank god the flat is clean. I've always thought it makes good sense that the word for 'clean' in Japanese is the same as the word for 'beautiful'. I am also scrubbed down, lathered in Cowshed products from the gym, smelling of rose geranium and linden blossom, and everything is therefore totally fine.

One of the most unacceptable consequences of the last twenty-four hours is that, seeing Sath again, memories I have painstakingly consigned to blurry oblivion have raised their heads. Sometimes, towards the end of our being together, it was hard to breathe. I've googled the symptoms since then and discovered that thinking you're going to die is a completely normal part of a panic attack. I usually managed to make it to some windowless bathroom before it got really bad. They were offensive, those times, trying to hyperventilate as quietly as possible, wishing that my last moments on earth didn't have to be spent looking like a hysterical Victorian in a too-tight corset. The memory makes me grind my teeth with embarrassment.

While the kettle's boiling, I deal with the Sath problem. I changed my number and deleted his years ago, as soon as we broke up, so all I need to do now is scramble the passwords to all my social media accounts to remove any temptation to access them. It's amazingly easy. There are clearly ways of getting round this, but I won't, because although I may have had a moment of weakness fuelled by alcohol, I am still hard as nails and deeply in control.

Just for a second, when I open the fridge, Tokyo surges up. It happens sometimes, a parallel universe, a burst of colour, like something I could hold on to if I tried hard enough. Maybe it's the exact bright white of that new fridge light. Efficiency, modernity, comfort, a blast of calming cool in what would be stifling heat. Sometimes it's the scent of something salty and sweet at once, sticky and hot, a chord in a bubblegum pop song. Standing somewhere between a Parco and a record store, glass buildings on all sides lit up with window displays that look like a catwalk, the barely contained energy of a million well-behaved people looking for a well-deserved good time. Sometimes, weirdly, just the sight of my own legs in shorts, for a millisecond disembodied, reminding me of my sisters, other Japanese girls, somewhere that isn't here. Then it's gone before I can catch it, a gust of wind.

There's a sudden ringing like a fire alarm, Kiki calling. I'm flooded with tachycardiac guilt.

'What?' I bark.

'You have to come – the hamster's missing.'

'What hamster?'

'Ai's hamster. You know, the one Chihiro gave her.'

'Who's Chihiro?' I ask pointlessly, rubbing my temples. I go to the corridor to get my laptop.

'The only bandmate Ai liked, as far as I can tell, but she's left now – actually, I think she got kicked out for being too old. We met her after a concert one time – super glamorous. She'd just done the iced matcha advert, so she gave us a whole load of them? We were drinking iced matcha for, like, six months. Remember?'

'Oh yeah.' I don't.

'Don't you know anything?'

'No, nothing. Why do you keep calling me when I'm working to tell me I don't know anything?' I open the laptop on the kitchen table. 'So the hamster's missing, so what?'

'So, it's tipped her over the edge. I went to see her and she's basically stopped talking. Why are you working? Isn't it Sunday?'

'Money never sleeps,' I intone, logging on.

'That literally doesn't mean anything.'

As the laptop comes to life, digital sunlight shimmers through a sea of cirrus clouds, a scene from an aeroplane window. 'Silverman Sayle Stands By You', it tells me.

'We need to go to her,' Kiki says.

'This is not the fucking closing scene in *Gladiator*. I have to give this nightmare presentation in, like' – I glance at the phone – 'fifteen hours. I do not have time for this.' I try not to engage too much with the possibility that if I'd just paid more attention to Ai's messages and smoothed this out before it bubbled over into extra-marital sex, Ai would now be sending me dancing cat videos and the tabloids would be at their natural Bennifer ground zero. 'How over the edge is she?'

There's a beat while Kiki gathers her resources. 'She's like an egg that has been cracked on the floor. The share house is swarming with paparazzi – it wasn't so bad when I went, but in the pictures now it looks like a total shitstorm. She doesn't listen to me. She listens to you.'

I can see the text of the first email in my inbox preview panel. It's from Jasper, regarding the work I did for him, staying late in the office to finish it. It says 'thx'. I turn my head to lay my ear carefully against the cool, non-judgemental wood of the kitchen table. From this angle, I notice some debris that spilt out of my bag as I extricated the laptop. The cloakroom tag from the wedding. A bit of the red foil wrapper from a packet of cinnamon chewing gum. I never buy cinnamon gum, only Sath. I bet in America they have multiple varieties, entire tasting menus of cinnamon gum.

'Fine,' I say, without moving my head.

'You'll come?' Kiki sounds pleased. 'Oh, good. You're turning into a real pushover. Is there something wrong with your sinuses? Your voice sounds really weird.'

'I have to go now.'

'Can you come, like, tomorrow? Bring Twiglets. And PG Tips. And something Obaachan will like. English soap or something. She'll slag it off, but bring it anyway.'

I'm suddenly very alert. 'Why would I need to bring anything for Obaachan? We're not going home; I'm coming to Tokyo.'

'Well,' Kiki says ominously. 'It's always best to be prepared.'

I hang up at the same moment that my phone chirps like it's presenting me with a wonderful surprise. 'You have a new memory!' it tells me, before running through a slideshow of babies I have never seen before in my life.

The memory is overlaid with cello music. I rouse myself just enough to send an email to Llewellyn, telling him that something's come up, and I'm going to have to take some time off.

12

Kiki

清美

Most mornings Hikaru's awake before me, staring into my face from about a centimetre away with an intensity that would definitely get anyone else arrested. 'Mama,' he says the morning after Rei's agreed to come to Tokyo, the second I open my eyes. 'Do you want to buy a bunny from my best shop? It's a green bunny, because green is your favourite colour.'

I tickle him and squidge his cheeks and kiss his round tummy to hear him giggle, something he does with his whole body, like the joy and hilarity is too big to be contained. It feels like someone hasn't been paying attention – Rei or Obaachan or some other well-meaning killjoy – because how is it even allowed, this much happiness every single morning?

'Hikaru, it's time to get dressed,' I tell him in English eventually. This happens every time I talk to one of my sisters, particularly Rei: I restart my campaign to teach Hikaru English. Even though they've never said a word about it or spoken to him in anything other than Japanese, and Hikaru reacts to my efforts like they're a violation of his human rights. True to form, he looks at me warily. 'Look, your clothes are here. This is your favourite fire engine T-shirt!' I sound like an AI.

He edges towards me, trying to figure it out. 'Mama, I need

to wear my police car T-shirt today,' he says in Japanese. 'Kohei and me promised to match.'

'Let me find you your police car T-shirt!' I say in English, bright and clear like a television presenter.

Hikaru's face puckers and he comes right up to me. 'No. English,' he says, just as clearly.

At least that's in English.

I fully intended for Hikaru to speak both. I figured we'd use English at home and it would work like magic. Sadly, my brain was so frazzled by the early days of motherhood I just forgot. You'd think the sight of this almost Scandinavian-looking kid would bring out a Western language, but when he was tiny it was a win if I strung a sentence together at all, never mind which language it was in. I guess I just went with the one that the world around us was speaking. I thought an Anglophone nursery might solve it, but the prices are exactly what you'd expect for places marketing themselves to ambitious parents who will eventually send their bilingual children to private schools – not me, then.

Everyone is impressed when Hikaru opens his mouth, since it's well known that your ability to speak Japanese is defined by the colour of your hair and the flatness of your face, but it's one of the few things that can keep me up at night, the worry that he's growing up monolingual in the wrong tongue, too tall and too fair not to be a freak here. He's like – we're all like – one of those dogs that's been brought up by a goose, and gets a terrible shock when it catches sight of its reflection in a puddle. It's the same when we see ourselves in photographs – Rei says she wonders who the Asian in the picture is every time.

I manage to keep up the English through breakfast and packing our lunches, Hikaru and I with matching obento at institutions serving both ends of the human life expectancy. He glares at me at the entrance to his kindergarten as I tell him to have a lovely day, and at work I find myself thinking in English more than usual. This is useful, because the English me is quite a lot more bolshy than the Japanese me, so it's easier to ask for the rota swaps and the day off I need to have time to deal with my sisters. I'm granted the holiday, albeit with shock-waves of bewilderment and disapproval – most of my Japanese colleagues think three consecutive days off outside of public holidays is basically giving up on life itself.

I even remember to take the English up with Hikaru again when I collect him, to his dismay. He's mute with irritation all the way through our trip to the supermarket, even though it's usually something he loves, bouncing up and down in the trolley requesting different foods like a small potentate. I buy the mentaiko I know Rei loves with rice, and you can't get for love or money in England, and daifuku, so she can have it with tea the afternoon she arrives. I wonder if Ai got the food package I sent her. I hope she did.

When we get home, Hikaru rushes up the steps before me. Standing in front of the door, he holds up his hand like a traffic controller. 'English people are not allowed in this house,' he says, scowling at me.

'But Hikaru, Auntie Rei is English, and Ai,' I cajole, trying to ignore the fact that I've managed to turn my son into a racist in under twelve hours. 'What are you going to do if you can't understand what they say?' Or anyone else in the whole world, I don't tell him. You're going to need to know how to order Scotch eggs in pubs, and watch *Withnail and I* without subtitles, so the two of us can spend holidays in England again like I've been wanting to do since you were born: winters in cottages with a fireplace, punting in summer, like the times I went to visit Rei at university and she was happier than I'd ever seen her. I put the key in the lock and open the door, the shopping bags banging against my calves.

Hikaru glares at his trainer, tapping his heel to make it light up. Then, very loudly, he says, 'I will just say to them, PLEASE SPEAK IN JAPANESE!' He rushes into the apartment and throws himself flat on to the tatami.

I finally get him back on side by reminding him of the existence of *Peppa Pig*, which we can get in English on YouTube. Slightly mollified, he consents to sit in front of it while I cook dinner. I can hear him chortling to himself, and it lifts my spirits. Clearly, he understands more than he lets on. Turning down the gas on the oyako donburi, leaving the egg to cook to a comforting golden stodge, I stick my head over to the sitting room to see what he's watching.

'This is so funny, Mama,' he giggles. 'Daddy Pig is so silly. I like English.'

I smile indulgently and ruffle his hair. Peppa speaks, her familiar reasoned patter. It's in Russian.

13

Rei

令

I want Ai not to be over the edge. That's what I'm thinking as the plane takes off, a wish so strong that it almost cancels out the wave of guilt and self-loathing it's mandatory to experience every time I get on a plane, our mixed-race heritage drowning the planet in jet fumes. I looked up routes to Japan overland from the UK – it would take roughly a fortnight.

It's Ai I'm thinking of as the whir of the engines reverberates through my skull, still thinking of later when a female flight attendant with the flawless face of the wooden kokeshi dolls my mother used to collect, smiling beatifically, serves me oolong tea and an osenbei in a rice-paper packet decorated with tiny flowers. It says, *You can eat comfortably without feeling anxiety anything.* Ai would have loved that, last week or last month or whenever she was last herself. I want her to be fine, and stable, and maybe even a bit boring, if that would help. Not for the first time, I wish that she wasn't such a good musician, that her talent just extended to a bit of friendly amateur choiring, rather than a career with highs and lows guaranteed to bring out the crazy in the most balanced of people. So I basically wish for my sister to be a fundamentally different person, Kiki clarified, when I said that to her. Not different, I said, just not so . . .

Mental? Kiki suggested, which I told her was categorically not helpful.

Out of the window beside me, storybook clouds stretch in all directions. As always, I picture the plane plummeting straight down through them like a ball dropped from a great height. I don't like flying; it's too much like the experience of being alive. It doesn't help that Obaachan has never been afraid to air her opinions on plane travel (or on anything at all, in fact) – that it's self-indulgent and above the station of a human being, and doing something so unnatural and self-aggrandising is basically *asking* for curses to be rained upon you. I wonder if she's seen the news about Ai. Obaachan is so unprepared to entertain things that exist outside her version of reality that it's never entirely clear if she repels unwelcome information through force of will, or knows exactly what's going on and just refuses to discuss things she considers below contempt. The only thing she's ever said about Ai's career was at the very beginning, when she told me Ai was going to end up stabbed to death in a hostess bar.

The pilot takes to the tannoy, his Japanese formal, his voice a low, calming purr. I take a sip of the tea, the ice cube knocking against my teeth, and open the packet of osenbei. The smell cuts through the plastic air of the plane; sharp soy saltiness and the smoky grain of the rice cracker. The smell, the sound of Japanese being spoken, the exact colours and lettering on the packaging, and a physical sensation like a giant exhalation washes over me. Whatever the reason, I'm going home.

14

Ai

愛

I think Kabuki would have broken up anyway, but if I hadn't gone with Ichiro that night, at least it could have finished without everyone yelling so much.

They got the cause and effect the wrong way round, though. The story is that Takanawa Ai is having a breakdown because her relationship with Suzu Ichiro has been found out, but Suzu Ichiro is barely even a walk-on part. Way before that night, I started sputtering like a broken motor, messing everything up. Like I knew I would, in the end.

I think the train goes so fast because it knows there isn't much time.

It feels, when you're on it, like it's going to last forever, that you're always going to stay soaring high, when really, the reason you can't sleep, that you have to do everything so quickly all the time without stopping, is because there's so much to do before the lights go down. Write the songs, make the band, do the gigs, all of it.

And then in the end the wind drops, of course it does, and you can't do anything. Midway through a conversation with someone, I suddenly discover, like waking up, that my smile is a rictus on my face and I'm not sure what the other person is talking about. I come away from conversations with people and I hear my own voice, wonder if it was too loud, if I talked too much. Or I catch sight of myself in the mirror and, just for a second, it's like the weight of the brakes catching up, and gravity has pulled every contour of my face down to the floor.

Sometimes that's just potholes in the road, a pebble to stumble over before I take off again.

But nobody stays up forever. In the end, you always have to come down. I wasn't flying any more by the time Ichiro happened. I'm not sure I was even walking. The world got so loud, and it wouldn't stop. All my filters were broken, the ones that told me what to feel about things, and how much. The earth was screaming and I didn't know what to do. All I wanted was quiet.

And then it was quiet, everything reduced to a ringing that didn't touch me.

After months when all I could see was
sky
I was down on the ground with my face in the dirt.
Stupid Icarus, every time.

15

Rei

令

I almost want to close my eyes to savour it. The passengers and crew are moving through the airport in a smooth upbeat rhythm, nobody's presentation mussed by a trifling matter like thirteen hours in economy, and it would be letting the side down if I prostrated myself and kissed the floor. I know full well the time will come, when all the conformity and rule-following, the little things like the politely mystified look the white-gloved customs official gave me as he combed through every single one of my belongings, will make me want to perform a bellowing war dance, but not yet. At this moment, the sounds of the airport are providing an almost ecstatic background soundtrack and I, pulling my wheelie suitcase along, even more anally re-packed by the customs official than it was the first time round, am just about to walk through the door into the arrivals hall at Haneda airport.

Ai, who's travelled endlessly over the last few years, recorded these exact sounds for me one journey, when she was sitting in Departures for too long with nothing to do. It was a joke, after I waxed a little too lyrical about the nirvanic joy of airports. She doesn't know that I've looped the recording, and listen to it through headphones at work. The quiet chatter of thousands of people, excited to be going, excited to be coming back; meeting someone, returning from an adventure, starting a new life or leaving an old one. In all cases, happy anonymity, and possibility, renewal, the chance to make yourself afresh. Then the particular joys of Haneda airport – the rising, bell-like tones preceding an announcement, the courteousness of the staff. Even in the case of a problem, always regret and concern, never accusation. Everyone contentedly absorbed, like Hikaru with his model Shinkansen.

The door to Arrivals slides open, revealing the sea of expectant faces, and I feel a sudden swoop of shyness. I straighten my back against it and charge forward as a mounting storm hurtles towards me. The storm throws itself against my legs, making it difficult to hug, so I'm tousling a caramel-coloured head before I can let go of the suitcase and pick him up.

Hikaru locks his arms around my neck, not speaking. He's heavier, possibly even more cuddleable than he was before. He smells like grass, and the shampoo we used as children. Kiki hurries over to grab my suitcase and usher us away. 'Oh my god, stop attracting attention to yourself,' she whispers in English, squeezing my hand hello, 'you've only just got here,' and the familiar sight of her is such a relief I'm glad I'm holding Hikaru, and can wipe my eyes on my sleeve as if it's his hair in my face that's irritated them.

'I have a present for you,' Hikaru whispers into my ear. He opens the pocket of his shorts with one hand and reaches in with the other. Carefully, he retrieves what looks like a squashed piece of brown paper and places it in my hand. 'It's a leaf that has never touched the ground,' he says.

'He caught it right after you left last year,' Kiki tells me, and the realisation that that doesn't have to make me sad, because here we are together, makes me squeeze him closer.

'Thank you,' I tell him, and speaking in Japanese again feels like a colour I'd almost forgotten lighting up inside my head. 'It's the best present anyone ever gave me.'

'Careful,' Hikaru instructs, when I eventually put him down. 'Don't squash Kimchi.'

'Kimchi?'

'My dog.'

I look around. 'Imaginary dog,' Kiki mutters quickly. Then, watching me grinning at my surroundings, at the women at the information desk with their chic little pillar-box hats, the posters of maple leaves, the concession stalls selling intricately wrapped sweets, 'You look like a stoned frog.'

'I'm so happy right now.'

'Good.' And then, because we have been at least partly brought up by Obaachan and taught never to let down our guard by enjoying the moment, she adds, 'Savour it, because it might not last.'

'Mama says you'll want to go to the conbini before we even get home,' Hikaru says confidingly on the train to Kiki's. 'She says you'll be jet-lagged, which is like having a two-day drunk.'

'A two-day drunk?' My Japanese vocabulary is rusty, misfiring with sleep deprivation and lack of use.

'A hangover,' Kiki supplies in English.

'Mama has them sometimes, like after the care home summer barbecue.' The train comes to a stop and Hikaru puts his hand in mine. 'Mama, you take Kimchi's lead and I'll walk with Rei-chan.'

Lawson's is like a long-lost friend: the clean lines, the candy colours, the tannoy informing me of the thrill of two-for-one matcha cheesecakes and suggesting I try the limited-edition pear jelly. I fill my basket: onigiri with flaked salmon; white-bread sandwiches with the crusts cut off, each quarter with a different filling; steamed pork buns; the cone-shaped Apollo strawberry chocolates I coveted as a child.

'God, you really are jet-lagged,' Kiki remarks, as the checkout lady arranges my purchases in a bag with geometric precision. 'I thought you were a vegetarian.'

'Leave me alone,' I tell her. 'It's three a.m. in London.'

We emerge into the street, the first time I've been outside since checking in at Heathrow eighteen hours ago. The light. The heat. I always, always forget. In the brightness of it, it seems impossible that England could exist at all, the muted sky, the stone of the buildings, a place that has already taken on an aura of Mr Banks in *Mary Poppins*, a rousing rendition of 'Jerusalem'. I tear into a pork bun with my eyes closed against the dazzling sun, the rich sesame smell of the broth from the noodle shop next door wafting out as someone enters.

'It's too hot!' Kiki scolds, pushing me towards the alley on the other side of the street, shaded by its narrowness, lined with carefully tended geraniums in pots outside flimsy front doors. 'Your aunt's been in London too long,' she explains to Hikaru, who is examining his chocolate-filled koala biscuits as he trips along beside us. 'She thinks melting in the sun is a novelty.'

I spend the rest of the day on the floor of Kiki's sitting room willing myself to stay awake, clutching a cushion like it's a lifebuoy and watching Hikaru like a television. The flat is one room with a sliding paper divider, a tatamied sitting room section where you can sit on the floor in the day and put out futons to sleep at night, and a kitchen with a table. The full-length windows to the minute balcony are open, sunlight streaming in through the mosquito net, its glare tempered by bamboo blinds shading the top quarter. The view is of a low-rise neighbourhood, two-storey modern box-houses jostling with older ones with proud pagoda roofs, the train track in the distance a tangle of cables. I've brought presents: a small Paddington Bear with wellington boots and an openable suit-case ('He likes to keep marmalade sandwiches under his hat,'

66

I tell Hikaru. Hikaru's eyes melt with admiration. 'I love him so much, Rei,' he says reverently) and food – Twiglets and PG Tips, as requested, also cheddar cheese, chutney, Maltesers. Kiki holds the packet of Twiglets up against her cheek and sighs contentedly. 'I knew you were going to make my life better,' she says.

'Mama says tomorrow we are going on a rescue mission,' Hikaru announces between puffs of breath, skipping across the room for the benefit of Paddington, propped up on the kitchen table to watch. He has space for three short gallops before he hits the wall and turns back.

'Let her have a one-night grace period before you accost her,' Kiki reprimands.

'What's a grace period?' Hikaru wants to know, at the same time that I ask, 'Have they let up?'

'Who?' Kiki asks.

'People. Social media, the news.'

Kiki shakes her head, kneeling on the floor to retrieve something from the freezer drawer. 'The other members of Kabuki did some press conference about how ashamed they were. You know that awful girl, Mako?' She looks up from her rummaging, holding a packet of frozen fish. 'Of course you don't. One of the taiko drummers. She was the winner of the Cutest Schoolgirl in Japan competition. She spent the whole interview covering her mouth in a little "o" and blinking really fast.' Kiki tuts in irritation. 'Ai said that the manager was always trying to get Ai to copy her habits, so she would look more Japanese. Then the fans could relate to her more.' We look at each other. Loupie Lou spent most of their time with their hair dyed blonde, wearing blue or green contact lenses.

Kiki turns her attention back to the freezer; like a conjuring trick, with a noise of satisfaction, she pulls something out and hands it to me.

'Oh my god' – and I'm too tired to be cool about it – 'is this a Calpis ice lolly?'

'Don't get emotional over a frozen drink,' Kiki says briskly, handing one to Hikaru, too. 'It'll be fine once we get her out. We just need to help her find something else to do.'

For a moment, all three of us suck our ice lollies meditatively. 'What's the other thing she's going to do?' I ask eventually, not looking at Kiki.

'I thought you wanted her to do filing in an office or something.'

'Doesn't mean she will, though. She'd probably go mad if she did that, anyway.' I twist the lolly to catch the drips forming along the bottom. 'Differently mad,' I clarify.

Kiki rolls her eyes. 'I am one hundred per cent certain that someone who's managed to turn herself into a national icon—'

'National disgrace—'

'—by the age of twenty-one is capable of finding a way to pay the rent. She can stay here for a bit. She can be with Hikaru while I'm working.'

I can cover her expenses while she's here. I've tried to give Kiki money in the past – a balancing tax, I told her, to make up for the fact she works a good person's job and gets paid nothing, and I move things around and get paid a lot – but she won't hear of it. Maybe paying for Ai will be a good way in. I wonder how patient I'm going to be with Ai, and the thought makes me feel very tired.

'Or she can go back to Ikimura,' Kiki says carelessly. The name conjures up the sea, the deliberately nasal singing voices of the traditional performers in the Obon parade, twirling their umbrellas and smiling out their pride in their hometown. Our hometown. 'Then she wouldn't have to pay rent at all.'

'She could get a job bowing to the customers at Marusho.' Marusho is the department store by the town hall, selling house dresses and orthopaedic flip-flops, unchanged since before we were born.

'Actually, she probably couldn't. Those bowing jobs are very sought-after by retirees.' Kiki catches me looking at her with disbelief. 'I'm serious. Anyway, imagine the penance Obaachan would make her do after this performance. She'd have to dress like a nun and home-pickle things for the rest of her life.'

In the evening, I climb into the bath with Hikaru, the water boiling, the tub tiny, like voluntarily getting into a giant saucepan. Hikaru's face is pink, his hair curling in the steam as he explains earnestly and in great detail about his favourite episode of *Anpanman*, the superhero with the red-bean-filled bread head, which he feeds to children in times of crisis. Kiki gets in after us, and then Kiki and I sit cross-legged next to the open window, our hair in towels, drinking cold beer. Dinner is hot udon that Kiki cooks, the salty-sweet, chewy softness of the fried abura-age bean curd a homecoming homily, and I crawl into the futon next to Hikaru. Kiki slides the paper screen shut and turns on the television in the kitchen, and I can hear her washing up to canned laughter. The noodles are warm in my stomach and exhaustion has wiped all nuance from my arsenal of feeling; Hikaru is holding my fingers, still wearing the superhero costume complete with padded pecs that he refused to remove before bed. It takes me about three seconds to fall asleep.

16

Kiki

清美

We go to the share house the day after Rei arrives. I told myself I could just go again without her, but now she's here, I'm finding out that I really, really didn't want to. I can conduct my entire properly employed, safely housed, socially functioning single-mother life without her, but there are some things that are just better with two.

The rescue is kind of fine and kind of hilarious and kind of a nightmare. To get to the front door, we have to make our way past the press, who have multiplied from the one or two who were here when I came, and are now a swarm, lurking outside like hangers-on after a party who just won't leave. As we try to slink past, they lift their cameras and edge towards us. I pick up Hikaru, and he buries his head in my shoulder; the men are so close I can smell their breath, the stale cigarette smoke on their clothes.

'Are you related to one of the members of Kabuki?'

'Can you tell us anything about the involvement of Takanawa Ai with the president of Kansas Records?'

'Are you aware of the rumours that Ai-chan has committed suicide and her bandmates are hiding the body?'

'Don't call her Ai-chan,' Rei growls at the man who asked

the last question, putting her hand over the lens of his camera and pushing it away. He looks thrilled.

The Cutest Schoolgirl in Japan lets us in; she looks about Hikaru's age, and blinks at us suspiciously when I tell her who we are. She shows us upstairs and points us towards Ai's room.

'Mako's going to make some iced tea now,' she announces, and skips off in the direction of the kitchen.

'Is she talking about *herself*?' Rei hisses. 'This is why Ai has lost the plot. She's surrounded by people who think they're cartoon fucking bunnies.'

Just before we open Ai's bedroom door, Rei looks at me. For a moment we're both small again, seeing our mother crying and not knowing what to do. We remember we are not small and stand up straight just as we hear this weird whirring sound, like an actual chainsaw.

Rei flings the door open. The room is dark, but in the light from the corridor we see scissors next to a lump on the carpet. It looks like a hank of human hair. Hikaru's hand squeezes mine tightly, and I think it may have been a terrible error of judgement to bring him here.

'What the fuck is this?' Rei's voice is low and threatening. In the gloom, I can make out Ai, covering her face with her hands, two girls kneeling on either side of her like scheming handmaidens. One of them is holding the whirring device, which, on closer examination, turns out to be an electric razor.

Rei pulls Ai to her feet and shoves her into the hall. The light falls on Ai's head, her hair crudely cut and lopsided, one patch of it shaved where they started with the razor. The sight of it releases Rei's fury like the backdraught of a contained fire. She whips around and addresses the darkened room, her face contorted. 'You wanted to *shave her head*?' she spits. 'Are you living in the fucking Dark Ages?!'

71

She manhandles Ai down the corridor, going batshit in English in ways that must be very novel experiences for the girls who stick their heads out of their rooms to see what's happening. In among the swearing, she tells them they have no solidarity and deserve to be cursed, that they should be ashamed of themselves, that they've failed as people and particularly as women. I've always been impressed with Rei's articulation in rage. I can't decide if it's lucky or a pity that the girls probably don't understand anything she's saying. I glance down at Hikaru to see if he's upset, to find he's gazing at Rei, rapt and round-eyed.

As we leave, Rei wraps her cardigan around Ai's head to protect her from the onslaught of cameras. She hauls her out of the share house like she is actually trying to carry out a kidnap, swearing at the press like it's an art form. Thank god Hikaru refused to learn English. I flag down a taxi with the coolest driver in the world, who makes no comment on what's happening, just waits for me to throw everyone in, then drives away smoothly like this kind of shit goes down every day. Ai cries and cries and cries.

17

Ai

愛

I can't remember whose idea it was to shave my head. Maybe it was my idea. Maybe it was a practical joke, or something like the hysteria that happens in *The Crucible*. I read that on a rainy day on our last visit to our grandmother's house in England, bundled up in eight jumpers on the landing by the window on a tatty Persian rug. A lifetime ago.

Anyway, the plan, wherever it came from, was that all my hair would come off and we'd make a video saying how sorry I was. My head was so heavy I felt like I could barely keep it on my neck. I just wanted to lift off the weight. I remember thinking maybe it would help me reach enlightenment.

Rei appeared out of nowhere. I heard her voice, the way it gets when she's so angry she sounds like a terrifying man, maybe a yakuza boss. Nobody else swears in English the way she does. It felt like I'd been falling and someone had put out their hand to catch me.

And then, one second later, I realised she'd flown all the way here from her scary, important job in England where she lives in her own apartment because I'd screwed up so badly, and I was so embarrassed

and she sounded so cold and furious

and I felt so bad for fucking up her life

that I wanted to die.

18

Kiki

清美

In the taxi, Rei is still going berserk. 'Why would they shave her head?' she snarls. Then, in Japanese, in a totally different tone of voice, she says to the driver, 'Could we please open the windows?' As if he can hear her when she says things politely but not when she's spitting.

'Would you prefer me to turn the air-con up?' he asks, going along with the charade. 'It's very humid outside.'

'That would be perfect, thank you so much.' She swaps back to English, and her voice falls by an octave. 'It's something that was a shit and sexist thing to do hundreds of years ago. We are living in the twenty-first fucking century. And I don't see the married boss-man getting strung up, do you?'

It's not that I don't agree with her. It's just that she's talking the way Western Twitter talks, which has nothing to do with Japan, especially the way Japan idolises its (female) idols.

'Maybe they thought a public apology would sort things out,' I say. 'They're probably thinking about the reputation of the band, too.'

Her head snaps towards me. 'Why are you talking like it might have been a reasonable reaction? Why haven't you chucked a Molotov cocktail into the fucking share house?'

'Well, until three minutes ago, our sister was living in it.'

Rei turns to glare out of the window. Her fingers are moving, touching quickly against her thumb. She's playing the piano, one of the pieces from when we were teenagers. I've never seen her sit still and not do it. Not since she broke up with Sath, anyway. We're going through Ginza, one showy spectacle of a building after another. The neon signs are unlit, the back-street bars still sleeping, ground-floor department stores and first-floor patisseries catering to a classy daytime clientele.

Ai says nothing, Rei's cardigan still covering her head. Her skinny legs stick out from her shorts. She shivers, and folds herself a little further into the corner of the taxi.

'She isn't wearing any shoes,' Rei says to nobody in particular.

19

Rei

令

In the night, Ai has wriggled free of the covers; she's now lying with one hand resting picturesquely under her cheek, the other curved around the wooden base of a small paper lamp at the head of the futon. I know that feeling, waking up in the night like a car crash, finding wood to touch to keep the monsters at bay.

It's been over a year since I saw her last, the madness of work making a trip back seem impossible. In the clear Tokyo light, promising another sunny day, I think about the Chinese clients – a thought experiment. They're difficult to hold in my mind. Our three futons are laid out side by side like they've always been, with Hikaru squeezed in between us. In sleep, Ai looks the way she did when she was five and I first started watching her. In those first few months, I used to wake three, four times a night, heart racing; I'd cosy up to Ai lying flat on her back like a starfish, frowning with dreams, trying to match my breathing to hers.

'Why is Ai so sad?' Hikaru asks with interest at breakfast, an extravagant assortment of every type of bread they had in the bakery. By the time they opened, I'd circled the block three times. Ai has woken up and conceded to keep her face uncovered, but is still lying on the futon, staring at the ceiling like a corpse. Kiki has put the television on next to her, carefully tuned to a chat show hosted by the jolliest comedian on earth.

'She made some bad decisions,' I say, tearing into a melonpan and handing half to Hikaru.

'Oh, shut up,' Kiki says to me. She looks over at Ai. 'Come and eat breakfast,' she calls with no conviction whatsoever. Ai doesn't move. Kiki takes a bite of her cheese brioche. 'Mm, this is so good. It's still warm.' She chews thoughtfully. 'I mean, I get that it's a disaster, but you have to eat. I was always so jealous of her when we were kids. Skinny like a sylph.' She sighs, her cheeks full. 'I'm so unromantic; I can always eat.'

I don't get a chance to reply because at that moment I hear my own voice, raised and angry. There's a confusing second when I both know and don't know – Schrödinger's unhinged voice. Then my blissful ignorance ends and I see myself on the TV, the huge foreigner manhandling the weeping starlet past the shocked expressions of the other girls. The footage is excellent, taken from low down, in Ai's bedroom, presumably from a phone propped on a table or on the floor.

Ai sits up like the Bride of Frankenstein rising.

I turn off the TV when the segment cuts to the studio and even the jolly comedian seems at a loss for what to say. The damn melon bread is congealing in my mouth.

'You didn't tell me you were filming it,' I say to Ai, and hate the deadness of my voice.

'You didn't give me time to talk,' Ai says. It's the first thing she's said to me since I arrived.

'It wasn't really a forum conducive to a considered discussion,' I snap.

'It was going to be an apology video,' Ai says, and the quaver in her voice makes me want to spit. 'Where they shaved my

78

head and I said sorry. I didn't know they were going to leak it, the way it turned out.'

There's a moment of silence as we all reflect on the way it turned out.

'I guess you make a good distraction from her sex life,' Kiki says eventually. 'Now Ai can be the sad victim of a crazed sister instead of an evil adulteress.'

I open my mouth, then close it again. Everything is fine. Here I am in sunny Tokyo and everything is fine. Better than fine, because I've inadvertently taken one for the team, according to Kiki. Which is great, obviously, exactly what I came here to do. And now I can go back to London again and leave them to it. I try to concentrate on the delight of the polar bear and the little girl enjoying ice-cream sundaes on Hikaru's cup. I am going to wash up. I am not going to think about how unacceptably, screamingly unfair it is that my nasal hairs have been given a public airing and all we saw of Ai was her perfect tragic profile. It doesn't matter, because I will be leaving in a week. This may be big in Japan, but it will not exist in the world of Silverman Sayle. Nobody in the UK has even heard of Kabuki. Hopefully. The polar bear cup slips out of my hand and bounces along the floor.

'I'm going out,' I announce. Because I am the big sister, the bigger person, big enough to understand that the video is not, technically, Ai's fault, I turn to her. 'Are you coming? Fresh air is very good for you.' There's no movement from the futon. 'I'll lend you a hat and some sunglasses.' It's like I'm talking to a rock. 'You can stay here and do impressions of the corpse bride if you want, but I'm not sure it's going to achieve anything.'

Ai doesn't reply.

'I'm coming,' Kiki says hurriedly. I want to hug her, and also smack her because she thinks I need rescuing. 'I'll drop Hikaru at kindergarten, then I'll meet you.'

'Fine.' In Kiki's flat, there isn't even another room you can stalk into to get your dignity back. I open my suitcase and stare for a moment at the contents – neatly folded clothes, arranged vertically, the stack of rectangular packing cubes along one side. Emissaries from a different planet.

20

Ai is still horizontal in her futon when I leave, and as I close the door behind me, making a monumental effort not to slam it, I find myself wondering in an unhelpful rush if she would have the luxury of being this miserable and floppy if she'd been the one who had to feed everyone and get them off to school, and how nice it must be to assume that someone will look after you. I go stomping down the metal staircase leading from Kiki's door, thinking what a shame it would be if I started screaming in the middle of this lovely peaceful street.

Then I hear the cuckoo call of the level crossing, and I'm instantly distracted. I hate my sister, maybe, but here is Tokyo, and all the things I think I'll never forget, that hit me like a reproach every time I come home. The fascinator-style decorations on the telegraph poles, like something off a geisha's headdress; the pristine canvas bags from upmarket grocery shops that women carry like a badge of honour. I watch a lady with a dog the size of a kitten wait patiently for it to wee against a lamp post before hosing down the puddle with bottled water. On the market street, the fishmongers unload icy polystyrene crates from the back of a lorry, and the grocer sets out piles of earthy burdock root and small, bright melons. A middle-aged woman in an apron is beating the shit out of her futon on her balcony and I rally, because although I may be a natural bitch the way some people are natural swimmers or artists, I do try. I take a deep breath, and to kickstart some kind of human empathy I think of Ai's face when I found her on the floor with the razor. Then I think of her filthy laugh when she's well, how she'll do anything for you; and then I remember how, when she's in that state, everyone else in the entire country adores her, too, and can't get enough of how she's so talented and so stunning and so special, and the thought that was meant to cheer me up ends up making me stop so suddenly in the middle of the street that a man on a bicycle has to swerve to avoid me, bowing apologetically as if the almost-collision were remotely his fault.

There's a conbini in front of me so I go in to get plum chewing gum because maybe that will make things better. Inevitably, I catch sight of Ai's weeping, distorted visage, one hand rising to shield her face, splashed over the cover of a tabloid magazine. In a circle in the corner is a gurning person with hair like Einstein, showing their molars. Is this not quite the cover shoot you had in mind, I hear Sath asking. Suzu Ichiro is nowhere to be seen, naturally. The conbini bloke in his regulation blue bomber jacket is paying no attention to me whatsoever but, still, it's an effort not to sneak out of the shop like I have something to hide.

I board the metro on autopilot and stare vacantly at a poster hanging in front of me for a full five seconds before realising it's Ai, holding a bottle of whisky to her face as tenderly as if it's her child. I lean my head on my arm, hanging off the hand strap dangling from the train ceiling, and close my eyes.

I wonder if Ai would have joined Loupie Lou if Nozomi had still been around. I wonder if I'd have moved to London, or if Kiki would have finished school. For half a beat, I imagine her here now, knowing what to do, providing a harbour. A place to rest your weary head. The thought almost makes me laugh out loud, and my eyes open. As if. She'd be having a bad spell, probably, and be all sharp angles and freaked-out eyes. No help whatsoever.

I'm still ruminating when I emerge from the bowels of the metro into the sunshine. It's the heat of a summer holiday, too hot to work, too hot for anything, but that doesn't stop anyone in Tokyo putting up their sun parasols and tripping from one air-conditioned shop to another. I wander past Louis Vuitton, where lilac-haired angel avatars advertise handbags; past the queue for Australian chocolate that always snakes down the road and round the corner, full of groups of girls retouching each other's make-up and giggling. I turn down one of the maze of side streets and pass another queue of customers, all wearing bunny ears without irony or explanation. I admire the hand-painted skateboard shop with beautifully graffitied walls, and a shop the size of a telephone box selling the world's most beautiful miniature terrariums, and the artisan perfumery next to that, with smells so botanical and intoxicating they take all my concentration. At the corner of the street, a girl in a bonnet with a blue crinoline skirt and lace gloves taps away on her phone. The phone cover looks like it's made of an actual stuffed rabbit. Round the next corner, the street so narrow my shoulders brush the shrubs growing outside houses, I have to turn sideways to avoid parked bicycles. A coffee parlour serves drip coffee in chemistry flasks, with a sign that says, *A coffee was perfected by your pleasure and love*, a sentiment that makes it hard to stay quite so pissed off. Next door, staff in pale-pink lederhosen man the hairdryer hoods in a German-themed 'hair and make'. By the time I catch sight of myself in a gallery window, the stupid events of the morning and my frustration with my sister have just faded into facts about the world; two more of a million things to be annoyed about that you don't engage with on a day-to-day basis. Two tortoiseshell cats sleep on top of each other in the window, in front of an exhibition of crocheted petits fours.

I sit down at the garden café in Daikanyama to wait for Kiki. The café is in the courtyard of an interiors shop, a metal-and-glass construction selling minimalist design objects that make me want to fly back to London immediately so I can pour concrete over my floor and paint everything white. Pots and planters explode with greenery, the velvet faces of hundreds of tiny pansies turned to the sun, Tokyoites in structured clothes with black-framed glasses visible through the foliage. I examine the menu, which tells me that my coffee will 'soothe my soul and enrich my senses'. One girl with a perfect fringe is working on sketches on a sleek silver laptop, a poster girl for urbanites everywhere. I watch her over the menu, admiring the grace of her movements, the way she makes pushing a strand of hair behind her ear look like a ballet move, while I think about whether I want bubble tea or coffee jelly.

'No,' says Kiki, appearing out of nowhere and sitting down opposite me with no fanfare.

'What do you mean, *no*?'

'That woman. You can't have her life.' She indicates the girl with the laptop.

'She's not a woman,' I scoff. 'She's a girl.' I hand Kiki the menu. 'Why not? I could get her clothes. I could get that haircut. I could get a design job.'

'You don't have the temperament,' Kiki says, studying the menu. 'You'd be sitting in a café supposedly working but having a secret heart attack about the fact the Wi-Fi might cut out. Are you hungry? I might get the cod roe spaghetti.'

'Obviously I'm hungry.' Kiki is depressingly correct. 'Instead of taking smiling phone calls and enjoying my coffee, I'd have to have a Xanax.'

'Which isn't even available in Tokyo.'

'And I could never be tiny like her, so instead of folding myself winningly into my chair while I was on the phone, I'd dangle galumphingly.'

'And none of the clothes would actually fit. You'd get extra extra extra large and the T-shirt would be like a cute little armband.'

There's nothing to take personally in this. Kiki and I are exactly the same size – that is to say, the size of ordinary Westerners. Towering Olympic shot-putters by Japanese standards, then.

'Though it's not so bad as when we were little,' Kiki concedes. 'Haafus are quite trendy now. Lots of models and TV presenters. Have you seen all those girls in the toilets of clubs gluing threads to their eyelids to make them double-lidded?' She sighs. 'Can you imagine going to that much effort over anything?'

'What happens if you're a haafu who doesn't look like a model or a TV presenter?' I ask.

'You're a failure,' Kiki says automatically. 'Again. What do you reckon a Yakult frappé is like?' Without waiting for an answer, she smiles down the waitress, who practically runs over in her effort to show willing to serve us.

The waitress takes Kiki's order, and then turns to me and falters. Her eyes travel from me to Kiki and back to me again, as she makes a characteristically Japanese stuttering sound in her throat. She just about manages to scribble down the order, then bows deeply, her head nearly touching her knees, before rushing off at speed.

'What the fuck?' I ask Kiki, trying to ignore the ominous feeling that I know exactly what the fuck.

'I think she recognised you.'

'Are you kidding? I don't look anything like I did on the

news. My hair doesn't look like I just stuck my finger in a socket.'

Kiki shrugs, but her nonchalance is a little guarded, and she turns away from the other waitress, who is definitely looking at us with intent.

'Why did Ai have to choose a career that made us into tabloid fodder?' I ask, crunching the ice in my water. It tastes medicinal.

'You told her to be the best at whatever she wanted to be. She's just following your advice.'

I stop crunching. 'I did? Why would I say that?'

'Yes. Don't you remember?'

'No. Sounds like the kind of thing a dad in a bad American soap would say.'

'You were like that sometimes. Not in a bad way, though.'

I don't remember ever acting like an American dad. All I can remember is permanently being about to sink, always rushing to cook or to clear up or be somewhere else. I remember doing my homework late at night after Kiki and Ai had gone to sleep, loving the exquisite silence and that there was an answer to the questions in the textbook, the sound of my pen scratching the page.

'I didn't mean she should be the best at wiggling her bum,' I say grumpily.

The waitress is now whispering to her colleague with no subtlety whatsoever. 'Is it always like this?' I ask Kiki.

Kiki frowns thoughtfully. 'Kabuki's pretty big now. Even Hikaru's nursery teachers started hyperventilating when they found out. I should have changed his name.'

'Nobody gave me any grief this morning,' I say, looking at the waitresses.

'Well, it's probably because there's two of us. We're attracting attention to ourselves. Like, if you see one lion in a field of sheep you might ignore it, but once you see a herd of lions they really stand out.'

I stare at my sister. 'That is a shockingly shit analogy. Clearly, if you saw one lion in a field of sheep that would already be a fuck-up. And it's not a herd, it's a pride. And we're not lions.'

'Whatever. You know what I mean. We are now a herd of haafus.'

I slouch down in my seat a little, to put an explosion of purple-and-yellow violets between me and the waitress.

'I don't understand why somebody nobody knows yelling at a bunch of photographers is a story anyway,' I hiss at Kiki, like this is all her idea. 'Don't they have anything better to talk about? Whether or not Tokyo is going to get the Olympics?'

'Nobody yells,' Kiki points out. 'Especially not in English. And you're not a complete unknown. You're the sister of Takanawa Ai. That makes you, like, Justin Bieber's mum, or something.'

Justin Bieber's mum?' It comes out as a yelp and Kiki tuts at me. 'She isn't like Justin Bieber,' I whisper peevishly.

'Not physically, no,' Kiki agrees. 'You've been gone a whole year, Rei. Longer.'

I'm getting that that is long enough for someone to become really famous in Japan.

The waitress comes back with our food. She's gone bright red, and bows eighteen times while she puts the plates down, never catching our eyes.

'There must be somewhere where no one cares who she is, or what she did,' I say to Kiki.

'It's probably better out of Tokyo,' she says. 'Like in Ikimura – places where there are only five people, so it's no big deal even if they do all have an opinion.'

'I'm sure she'll be fine,' I say hurriedly. 'No one's saying we have to leave Tokyo.'

We collect Hikaru on the way home, and when we get back, Kiki's flat is dark. Ai is still huddled in her futon.

In a different country, not one that tells you your moods are all about self-control, maybe Ai would just pop a couple of pills and be fine. Although I'm not sure which country, or which pills. Ai pointed out when she was little that the letter for medicine, 薬, actually reads fun (楽) grass (艹). I thought of that in London, a long time ago, when I went to see a GP who looked like she couldn't really be arsed with yet another weeping patient. She told me I should try being less stressed, then prescribed sleeping pills. Some fun grass for sleeping. I took them twice but never again, because they fucked my head in the morning; also I was afraid I'd go mad and eat a handful, or forget how many I'd taken and accidentally wake up dead. There were pills Nozomi took; I don't know if they helped. She still ended up dead.

'Can you get gyoza skins from the shop, for dinner?' Kiki asks me with her head in the fridge. 'I knew I was going to forget something.'

'I'm coming with you, Rei,' Hikaru says. It's dusk, the sky tinged pink, a crow cawing. From a neighbour's house there's the sound of a door opening, a father calling his arrival, feet running to greet him.

I see him the moment I open the door, standing at the bottom of the stairs, sucking his nicotine-stained rodent teeth, pointing a phone in our direction. As soon as I catch sight of him, I realise he followed Kiki and me home from the station, that I clocked him but ignored him. My brain flashes forward: tomorrow a few more greasy weirdos with cameras, a whole blur of them the day after that, Hikaru trying to leave for kindergarten amid all the flashing and the shouting.

Hikaru almost falls over with the force of me shoving him back into the apartment.

'What's that man doing there, Mama?' he asks, and Kiki catches my eye. It's suddenly abundantly clear that Ikimura is calling after all. I'm not going back to London next week.

21

Leaving Tokyo isn't altogether straightforward, because, unfortunately, it means Kiki has to quit her job. She initially phones the care home to explain the gist of the situation and ask for more leave – the advantage of her tiny flat is that I can hear the intractable noises the man makes on the other end of the phone, polite but immoveable, a Japanese trait I've always admired and found infuriating in equal measure. I'm disturbed and impressed to find out that in the years I've left her in Japan, Kiki has mastered polite but immoveable, too.

'I quite understand,' she says, with the appropriate level of concern and sincerity. She leaves an eloquent pause. 'Unfortunately, I'm still going to have to take the time off.'

There's demurring like a constipated donkey on the other end of the line.

'Of course,' she says soothingly. 'In which case, I'm going to have to ask you to consider my contract with the company terminated.' Even on the phone, she bows slightly. 'I have been indebted to you,' she says, the formal phrase for ending a period of work. She sounds completely unperturbed. 'Goodbye.' She hangs up.

'Did you just resign?!' I ask her.

'They wouldn't give me any more holiday,' she says, like that explains it.

'Aren't you completely freaked out?'

Kiki looks at me. 'I don't know if you've heard of the ageing population? I am extremely in demand.' She puts the phone on the table. 'It was a freelance contract, anyway. And, unlike you, I have experience being unemployed.' She catches sight of my face. 'Don't try to infect me with the way you feel about it. I need to pack.'

We leave Kiki's flat at four in the morning to avoid the phone-wielding rodent, sneaking out as if we're the ones doing something to be ashamed of. I imagined we'd be carrying Hikaru out fast asleep, but he's awake and wide-eyed, thrilled by the secret escape, the magic of watching the sun rise.

Inspired by Kiki, I email Silverman Sayle on the train, though I can't quite bring myself to be as balls-to-the-wall as she was. I'm glad it's HR I'm messaging, and not Llewellyn; I'm pretty sure HR can't legally sack me for needing leave because of a family emergency, no matter how much he gnashes his teeth about it. I say I'll be back in a fortnight, a length of time I pluck out of the air, and deliberately write the email as quickly as I can, pretending I'm somebody fundamentally different, maybe someone British of Ai's age who thinks work–life balance is a human right, or a man.

It takes us seventeen hours to get back to Ikimura, longer than it takes to get to London; three trains and a two-hour wait for the boat that comes only twice in a day. Ai is quiet on the journey, her face obscured by a baseball cap and mask, going where we tell her to, keeping her eyes down or staring vacantly out of the window. The seats on the ferry have been newly upholstered – or at least 'newly' since I last rode it. We're on the second crossing of the day, and there are only a handful of other passengers, who must be residents – we don't get visitors, really, and none who would arrive in the evening. Two old ladies in hiking kit sit down and carefully unwrap their obento, then pop open a small beer each to cheers. They look so pleased that I avert my eyes.

Kiki is watching them too, and she nudges me with her shoulder. 'Imagine,' she says. Imagine if that was your grandmother instead, she means. I imagine someone who'd look delighted to see us, and listen to our woes with her head cocked on one side, and pinch our cheeks and tell us everything was going to be just fine. Kiki catches my eye and smirks.

It's dark when the boat pulls in. Instead of the usual screech of gulls around the harbour, all we can hear is the erratic lapping of the waves against the stone. The smell of the sea, this sea, is like a breeze on my skin, pins and needles and armies of thoughts and sensations I've lulled into careful slumber stirring. I have an almost physical sensation of slotting into my place on a map.

Now Hikaru is asleep, curled up with his cheek pressed against the window, barely waking when Kiki lifts him on to her back, so we decide to take the taxi, even though it's only a few minutes' ride. As we walk to the rank, Hikaru holds Paddington so precariously by one wellington boot that even Ai is shaken out of her detachment enough to rescue the bear. The only taxi in town waits, has always waited, outside the hospital. I know that hospital well; apart from anything else, it's where Ai was born, and Kiki, too, even though I don't remember that. Before them, our mother was born in this town, and our grandmother. Obaachan, our great-grandmother, was born in Hokkaido and sent to find her husband at a train station, armed with nothing but a small suitcase and a black-and-white photograph. It sounds like a socially awkward horror story, but in the end they were married for almost half a century – an unexpected romance or a case of two practical people behaving exactly as society stipulated, depending on who you ask.

The taxi is a black limousine that smells of lemon, with doilies on the seats and the driver reading a newspaper in the front while he waits. He does the taken-aback look, the one people always give us, for being too tall, too foreign, too many, and we pointedly don't react. We set off up the hill, past the shopping street, where we used to drink melon sodas in the café and collect our mother's fabric orders from the haberdashery and stand in the bookshop reading the next issue of our favourite manga serial until the guy behind the counter politely chucked us out. Most of the shops are shut but I can make out a couple of lights still on: the red lantern of the ramen stall, the warm glow of the three bars, no more and no fewer now than when we were teenagers. All the time I've been away, pretending this doesn't exist, and it's been chuntering along without even the grace to change a little. It's almost offensive.

It's only as the car is climbing the steepest curve of the hill, nearly home, that the driver says apologetically to Kiki, 'But, miss, your Japanese is so good.'

He's too polite to phrase it as a question, so Kiki, exhausted under the weight of a determinedly sleeping Hikaru, just says, 'Yes, isn't it,' in a way that isn't Japanese at all.

22

My key still fits in the lock; of course it does, but it seems surprising. It hangs alongside all my other keys on the silver Tiffany keyring I got as a gift from Silverman Sayle when I qualified. For the longest time, I thought of it as my home key and all the others as imposters, but now it feels weirdly light and small in my hand. It's been almost five years since I last opened this door.

Kiki kicks off her shoes and peels off Hikaru's, then carries him straight up the steep wooden stairs to the bedroom above us, as if we've simply come in from a day out. Next to the stairs is the entrance to the main room, a square archway obscured by a blue linen noren hanging halfway down from the top, printed with woodcut waves along the bottom. It's always been there, and yet I feel like I've never seen it until now. Instinctively, I glance under the noren, still looking for my mother after all this time.

The smock we wear for cooking hangs by the door; the photographs I know by heart on a low chest in the gloom of the living room. I pull the cord for the light in the kitchen. It grumbles then flickers to life, illuminating small white tiles and wooden cupboards underneath, a steel sink with large windows on either side, overlooking a narrow alleyway planted with bamboo. Open shelving along the walls is neatly stacked with aluminium pans, and magnets on the fridge hold up instructions for local rubbish disposal. The kitchen runs along the back of the room, a small dining table in front of the work surface, scrubbed clean but still notched with years of pen and glue, opening on to the sitting room, a low zataku table with four floor cushions around it, indented in the middle as if their occupants have only just got up. I cross the room, the hay smell of the tatami, the old, cold smell of a house that was clean but has been waiting too long filling my nose, the smooth even weave of the tatami familiar beneath my feet. The paper shoji doors slide open easily, leading on to the engawa. I roll up the bamboo blinds, unlock the glass doors on to the garden and slide them open. The room breathes out, all its waiting evaporating, the heavy night air and the melodic, melancholy notes of the evening higurashi rushing in.

I turn on the paper lamps and lie down flat in their warm glow, staring up at the latticed ceiling. Through the section above the shoji where chrysanthemums have been carved out of the wood, I can see the clear night sky beyond. It's a world away from the plastered, curlicued ceiling of my Victorian flat in London.

I hear Ai make her way up the stairs. This is where I met her for the first time, back when she was small enough for me to hold in my nine-year-old arms. This is where Kiki and I, coming home drunk from separate places, used to share 3am ochazuke, in a wordless synchronicity of making tea and finding the furikake and salted plums. The bathroom on the other side of the corridor is where all three of us used to sit in the bath playing out the ongoing drama between the Licca mermaid doll and the Rilakkuma the Bear bubble-bath dispenser, pink-cheeked from intense concentration and being so poka-poka warm. This is where I've watched all their ups and downs – my mother's, Ai's – so crippled with uncertainty over what I was meant to do about it, and then with the certainty that I'd done it wrong, that in the end the only thing I could do was leave.

Every time Ai was going through a bad patch, there was the part of me that wanted to follow her everywhere. She'd leave after spending hours getting ready, changing her clothes, dropping her keys, forgetting what she was doing and turning the house into a bombsite, then walking out the door with one shoe on. Don't go, I wanted to say every time, but I didn't, because that's tempting fate and not tenable, and once you start down that route the only conclusion is that we should all hang out in one room being mad together, and that isn't going to help anybody, is it. 'Have fun,' I'd say instead and wave her off, then close the door behind me without looking back. She was just going out for a couple of hours and she was fine, and there was no need to be making the song and dance about it, as our mother used to say in English. I close my eyes. This time, too, the storm is going to blow over and Ai is going to be fine.

I wonder if Obaachan is awake; if she's noticed the lights coming on in our house. If she has, I wonder if it's a respite from her lonely life and she's excited at the idea of seeing us, or if she's dreading the upheaval and the noise, the disturbance to the peace she's finally won herself after all those decades of drama. Tomorrow, we'll find out, and she can cast her verdict, her thumbs up or down on all our life decisions to date. I can't wait.

23

In the morning, in the second between being asleep and awake, I hear my mother's voice whispering in my ear. 'Kon-kon,' she says softly, sing-song. 'Knock-knock.' She's happy, and when I open my eyes she'll brush my hair back from my face, and ask if I think it would be a good idea to eat breakfast on the beach. Then I remember, like I always remember in the end, and I keep my eyes closed so I can fix my mind before I open them. I bet if she were here, she'd be doing something annoying, anyway, and I wouldn't be dreaming of her when I was little. I'd be irritated by the tone of voice she used to disagree with my opinion on something I'd read. She'd be put out by the fact I wasn't planning on coming home for New Year for the third time in a row. Our present problems would be too pressing for either of us to be reminiscing.

'Remember when Mama knitted us matching sailor jumpers out of that pink wool that shimmered in the sunshine?' Kiki whispers from the futon on the other side of Hikaru. She sounds wide awake, and I'm glad I've kept my eyes closed.

'No,' I mutter, sounding sleepier than I am. I lift my arm so I can put my face into the crook of my elbow. I remember how thrilling they were, sparkling like something from the television, and we all played that we were Himitsu no Akko-chan, the bright-eyed girl from the cartoon who could turn her-self into anybody by using her magical compact mirror. We played ironically to start with, for me, and then I forgot to be ironic and was surprised when Nozomi called us in for dinner, because we'd been somewhere else completely.

'Liar.'

I open my eyes and roll over so I'm facing her. A shaft of sunlight cuts between us from a gap in the shoji covering the full-length windows on both sides of the room. The wooden lattice makes a grid pattern in the light that falls across the tatami and the futons, and I think, seeing it, that it might be my very first memory. Paper screen doors divide the half of the room where our mother used to sleep from ours. Last night, too tired for discussion, we laid our futons out right next to each other on our side and I'm glad. 'How the hell do you remember about the sunshine? Why do you even remember the jumpers? What were you, six?'

Hikaru is still asleep, his arms folded possessively around Paddington. Kiki puts her hand absently on his chest, watching it move up and down. 'Of course I remember,' she says softly. 'I wonder where they went.' She turns her head in the direction of Obaachan's house. 'If we don't go over there basically now, our lives are not going to be worth living.'

'Before breakfast? Can't we even get coffee?'

Kiki sits up and looks at me. 'That would be living very dangerously,' she says. 'Imagine if someone saw you walking down the street and told her about it before we did. It would be the end.'

She's wearing the jinbei pyjamas all three of us have, dark blue splashed with carp and kanji in white, stolen from a ryokan we went to together on a one-night break in the Loupie Lou touring schedule, twenty-four hours of hot springs and beer, Ai so happy and full of energy.

98

'How can she get mad that we've arrived without telling her, when the only way of communicating with her is by post?'

'Or her landline.'

'She never picks up. Literally never.'

Kiki stretches, waking Hikaru, who goes from sound asleep to wide-eyed and bolt upright in half a second. 'I'm not saying it's reasonable of her,' Kiki says, pulling Hikaru in to cuddle him, 'I'm just telling you what's going to happen. Did you sleep OK?' she asks Hikaru's cheek.

Behind Kiki is the mural Nozomi never finished. She must have started it when Kiki and I were tiny, because I don't remember the room without it. The mural is of the beach (the long beach, thank god, not the little cove), the ancient wooden shops and the jetty with the fishing boats, the colours definite, a technicolour world that stops halfway across the wall. I wanted to paint over it but Kiki bawled and told me I wouldn't even notice it after a while. That has turned out to be not entirely true, but we haven't discussed it since.

Kiki, Hikaru and I get dressed; we don't disturb Ai, who may or may not be asleep but is lying in her futon next to Hikaru's with her eyes closed. When we get downstairs, Kiki sets Hikaru up at the zataku table, laying out felt pens and some egg boro biscuits she finds in her bag. Hikaru sets to drawing and munching immediately.

'Hikaru, you stay here, OK? Ai's upstairs. Rei and I are just going next door; we'll be back in a bit.'

Hikaru nods, absorbed and unconcerned. 'I am drawing a mouse's house,' he says.

Obaachan is complicated enough without Hikaru there, blond and fatherless. Kiki told me that the first three times Obaachan met Hikaru, she asked whose baby this was, like if she kept asking she might get a preferable answer – and if anyone thinks that's an indication of dementia rather than denial, they have fundamentally misunderstood our great-grandmother.

'And now I am drawing a man with a Molotov cocktail. He is going to blow up the mouse's house.'

Kiki gives me a dirty look. 'This is your fault,' she says. 'He definitely didn't know the word "Molotov cocktail" last week.'

'You're welcome,' I tell her.

When we slide open the front door, the light is blinding. It's already hot, the sun gearing itself up for another day of ganbaru, of doing its absolute gut-busting best, shining as bright and hot as it can. The cicadas are mumbling, not yet up to their full insistent chorus of the day, and above them I can hear seagulls. Morning glories cover the front of the house, a flamboyant waterfall of purple that's wound its way around the letterbox, and around Nozomi's bicycle, now a rusting art installation impossible to disentangle from the greenery. Chibi, the stray black cat that Nozomi started feeding, stalks haughtily around the corner and past us into the house, without even a glance in our direction.

'So sorry to bother you,' Kiki says to him.

'Isn't he, like, four hundred years old by now?' As we shut the door, Chibi flicks his tail at us, as sleek and disgusted as ever.

'So, are you just *gagging* to see her?' Kiki asks conversationally as we walk the few steps to Obaachan's house. 'Do you think she's going to open her arms for you to run into?'

'Obviously. Isn't that what she did last time you saw her? When did you see her last, actually?'

Kiki squints up at the sky, trying to remember. 'Last year, I guess? Just after you left, I think. We stayed in the hotel, though, because it was only for two nights.'

'You are a good granddaughter,' I tell her formally.

'Good great-granddaughter,' Kiki corrects, ducking under the Japanese holly that spreads its branches like a provocation, the greenery around the house emulating its occupant. 'We are not that closely related. And yes, I agree, there is a place for me in heaven, and I have no idea why I do it.'

Obaachan's house is the one next to ours, on a larger footprint, the two separated by the bamboo alleyway. There are two entrances: a latticed wooden door in the garden wall topped with a small pagoda roof, for guests, and the commoners' entrance, which we take, a gravel path to the front door. We rattle open the door without knocking, the familiar guttering sound as it slides in the wooden groove the same noise ours makes right next door. The sound of frenetic childhood, dashing from one house to the other, clattering off shoes and rushing to play, to fetch someone, pick up something you forgot, everything with urgency.

The genkan is cool and dark, inlaid with pebbles, a high step up to the polished wooden floor of the rest of the house. All the surfaces are as militantly clean as ever, and on top of the shoe cupboard next to the entrance is a careful stem of campanulas in an earthenware vase. I have a sudden memory of being small, sitting directly in front of the electric fan in the sitting room one hot afternoon, seeing how long I could keep my eyes open against the breeze. Our mother was still alive then.

Kiki calls out the greeting everyone uses when they let themselves into someone's house without knocking – neighbours, delivery men, great-granddaughters: 'I'm making a nuisance of myself!'

There's a shifting sound, like someone getting to their feet, then silence. Kiki looks at me. It isn't beyond the bounds of possibility that Obaachan's ignoring us. Kiki's shoulders move up and down in a delicate, almost inaudible sigh, then she calls out again. 'Obaachan! Tadaima! We're home!'

The squeaky slide of the sitting room door, careful footsteps, and then she comes into view around the corner. She's older, maybe a little smaller but not frail, her hair still grey rather than white, compact and upright. She says with studied disinterest, 'Kiki-san. Rei-san. I didn't know it was you,' as if she'd just walked into the sitting room to find us watching TV, rather than not having seen Kiki for a year, me for nearly five. I realise with a stab of disappointment that despite knowing what to expect, there's always a part of me hoping that since the last time I saw her, she'll have undergone some miraculous epiphany. She'll see how I've grown, what an adult I've become, and it will inspire her, in the moment it takes her to decide on her greeting, to alter the habits of a lifetime. I like to set myself up for disappointment, apparently. It's bollocks, anyway, that she didn't know it was us, with her guarded, almost disdainful expression. If she'd thought we were delivery men, or neighbours, she'd have had her outdoor face on, delighted, and been bowing as soon as she turned the corner.

'It's been a long time,' I say, smiling, finding the words coming out in dialect, like hers do. As usual, natural words fail me at the crucial moment. Fortunately, Japanese has planned for that, with stock phrases that could keep you going forever, perpetually making polite noises and saying nothing at all.

An expression crosses her face, and for one sick moment I wonder if dementia or something else has got the better of her. Then she speaks, decisively. 'You got fatter, Rei.' She turns and hobbles back into the house.

Kiki looks sidelong at me, her mouth twitching. 'Did you miss her?' she whispers, as we kick off our shoes and pair them up neatly. A decade ago, the comment (and she made them then too) would have brought tears to my eyes, drowning in shame. Now it doesn't mean anything; I'm not fat. And if I'm fatter, really, who gives a shit? I'm over aching to be minute and perfect all the time. I am not a chihuahua, or a miniature pig. My few steps from corridor to sitting room are so self-congratulatory for this amazingly balanced reaction that by the time I sit down on the floor at the table, I'm jubilant.

'You want tea, don't you,' Obaachan says, a statement more than a question, and it's only the slightest bustle as she takes the tea bowls out of the ceramics cupboard that hints she might be pleased to see us. The water is already hot in the caddy, and she sets the bowls down, then bends almost in half to put her weight on the table before lowering herself on to her floor cushion. She lands more heavily than she used to, with a little wince of discomfort. If she were a different grandmother, Kiki or I might rush to help her, suggest we sit somewhere else, exclaim over her flexibility, but we can both remember the iron grip of her fingers in the soft part of our arms between wrist and elbow, the daggers that told us appearance was everything, and we were getting all of it wrong.

'Kiki, the extra zabuton are in the cupboard.' Kiki has already failed. 'I'm not one of those people who leaves things lying around when they aren't using them.'

Kiki gets up and hands me a floor cushion, woven silk with tassels.

'Thank you for looking in on the house,' I say.

Obaachan tuts, picking up the lacquer pot of matcha. 'It needs an airing from time to time,' she says. 'Since you girls are too busy gallivanting about to take care of it. Don't expect me to clean it, though.' She takes the dainty, long-handled spoon, and places a tiny mountain of green powder in the bowl. 'It's really falling down. You don't seem to have any understanding of how to look after things properly.' This doesn't seem to require an answer, so Kiki and I say nothing. The sight of her gnarled hand on the button of the hot-water caddy, her fingers bent at an angle away from the palm, is at once so familiar and so far away from my London life that it feels like waking from a dream.

'Ai's here,' I tell her. 'She's next door. She's not that well.'

Obaachan picks up the bamboo whisk and begins to froth the tea, a delicate action that blurs her wrist. It's not immediately clear if she's heard what I said, but then, 'It's to be expected, if you spend all your time prancing around without any clothes on,' she says, not looking up. Kiki and I look at each other, unsure if that's an oblique reference to the Ichiro situation, or Obaachan's usual stance on illness in general. Neither of us asks her to elaborate and she continues frothing the tea, making rhythmic susurrations under her breath. Obaachan used to be a tea ceremony teacher, holding classes from a room in this house, a sparse, tranquil space with a calligraphic scroll hanging in the tokonoma alcove and a special bamboo sink. She started learning when her husband died, since he wouldn't let her while he was alive, and the tea ceremony room is her single act of rebellion. She doesn't teach any more, because arthritis means she can't kneel for long periods of time, but she sleeps in that room now.

Mid-whisk, she stops, her whole body alert. 'What time is it?' She gives me a filthy look, as if I have personally timed our visit to screw with her day. 'We're missing the sumo!'

She reaches for the remote, peering contemptuously down her nose at it in the manner of long-sighted people everywhere. As the television flickers to life, I think for one second that this could be the perfect opportunity for a family conference about the Takanawa news-circuit debut. Then I remember how once she saw a clip of me in a Silverman Sayle promotional video and told me that cameras accentuate my pores and awkward mannerisms. I keep my mouth shut.

'Hawaiians!' she snarls as the camera pans across the line-up of wrestlers. '*Bulgarians!* They don't even *look* Japanese. They'll never make yokozuna.' There's a slapping sound of flesh on flesh as two wrestlers charge into the ring. 'Look at the meat on Enho-san,' she says with pride. 'Magnificent. The other one's all white and dimply.'

Kiki takes cover under the sound of the television, and the fact that Obaachan isn't looking at her, to say, 'Hikaru's here, too,' quickly, like it's a dare.

With her eyes still on the screen, Obaachan picks up a packet of kuri manju, small pastries filled with chestnut white-bean paste. For a moment, it isn't clear if she's heard Kiki. Then, 'Poor little boy,' she says with feeling. Before Kiki has a chance to react, Obaachan turns to stare intensely into her face. 'You look exhausted. You're going to age very badly if you let yourself get exhausted.'

'I have a full-time job and a five-year-old,' Kiki says neutrally.

Obaachan sighs. 'All these modern conveniences and young people still insist on being over-tired. I don't suppose I would have been tired if I'd had a washing machine. Or a rice cooker.'

Even after such modern conveniences were available, our great-grandfather refused to let Obaachan use them, on the grounds that things tasted better and came out cleaner when everything was done by hand with wooden utensils and heat from the fire. There's an irori sunken hearth right there, under where Kiki is sitting, although it's been covered now so it's just a wooden square on the floor. Presumably, he would have liked it even better if Obaachan had had to go out and harvest the crops herself, and grind the flour by hand.

Obaachan takes two cakes shaped like chestnuts from the packet, and hands them to me. 'Put these out,' she instructs. 'I don't eat these any more, but they'll like it.'

I'm glad to have an excuse to get up. Standing on the stool left there for the purpose, I put one of the cakes in front of the Shinto kamidana, a small, minimalist shrine made of light wood and flanked by two white vases of sakaki leaves, high up in one corner of the room. The other goes on the butsudan, the Buddhist family altar, on a deep shelf built into the other corner, mahogany with gold trim, a Gothic extravaganza of intricate carvings. I set the cake carefully on the offering plate and place a stick of incense upright into the container of sand, then light it and tap the stout metal stick against the brass bowl on its silk pouffe so it reverberates. The sound, the smell: huge temple halls, wooden floors so dark and polished they gleam like black ice, the soft padding of a priest's feet in his split-toed socks. I think of Kiki's hichigosan ceremony when she was three, long before Ai was born, so small in her kimono, her hair up in a bun and decorated with silk flowers, a silver butterfly on a pin, her anxious moue as, just as we were reaching the shrine door, our parents began to hiss at each other. I don't know if it was that night that Nozomi cut up all Richard's suits with the kitchen scissors and put them in the bath. The bath detail always interested me – did she think that if she didn't soak them in water, he might sew the whole lot back together again? Was it just a moment of practicality mid-rage, a way to stop the shredded fabric trailing fibres all over the house?

The portrait of my mother, gazing at me from the gallery wall of the dead next to the butsudan, gives me pause. It's a new addition. I rarely look at photographs of her, and this one, grainy in black and white, doesn't look anything like her. She looks meek, keen to conform, and whatever else she was, she wasn't that.

I put my hands together and bow my head, thinking of all the people in the butsudan, the ones in the photographs and all the ancestors before them. 'Hi, guys,' I say to them in my head. 'I'm back. Enjoy the cake.'

24

Kiki

清美

Here we are, home again home again, in the house made of paper with Granny the xenophobe. When Hikaru first started talking, Obaachan pretended for the longest time that she couldn't understand anything he was saying. It was like the more extreme version of the reception my sisters and I get in shops all over Japan, where people talk to us in broken English for entire conversations we're having with them in Japanese, the audio-visual disconnect too major to be overridden. It always makes me bad-tempered, but when Obaachan did it and Hikaru, oblivious to her mind-fuckery, tried harder and more earnestly to tell her what he meant, my feelings towards her became so violent that I had to put major distance between us immediately. I swore I'd never speak to her again, and yet here we are. It's absurd just how much slack genetics cuts people.

'I'll make a list,' Rei says as we come back into our house. Of course she does; she makes a beeline straight from the front door to the drawer in the kitchen table and retrieves a pen and paper, which she probably left there specifically for this purpose last time she was here. Ai still hasn't come downstairs. 'Coffee, milk, bread, honey, barley tea,' she says as she writes.

'Natto, vegetables,' I add. 'Get a lot of garlic. Shall we have gyoza tonight?' We didn't get to in Tokyo, I don't say, since we had to do a runner across the country instead.

Rei nods, writing. 'Bean sprouts, spring onions . . .'

'We don't even have rice. Or miso. Can you get Yakult for Hikaru? And Vermont curry. And the watermelons are good now.' I open the fridge. It's completely empty, except for a lidless Tupperware box in the back on the bottom shelf that I've never noticed before. I pull it out. It's carefully stacked with packets of soy, wasabi, Bull-Dog sauce and gari ginger saved from shop-bought sushi and takeaways. 'Has this been sitting here since we were children?' I ask incredulously. Rei shrugs and keeps writing, muttering the shopping list to herself. She went into total admin overdrive after Mama died – it felt like I blinked, and all the evidence that she'd ever even lived in this house had gone. Except, not all of it, it turns out.

'I'm so glad you haven't thrown these away,' I tell her. 'This is just what we need for that huge party we're planning, where we serve our guests off condiments.' I peer inside. 'This might be the most Japanese thing you've ever done.'

'. . . washing powder, fabric conditioner,' Rei finishes. 'OK, we can get most of the stuff on the shopping street.' She frowns at the list. 'Aeon would be easier, though.'

'Car's not working,' I say, examining a packet of soy sauce for any evidence of a use-by date. 'It started making a weird noise last time I was here and I only just managed to park it before it gave up.'

Rei gives me a hard look. 'And you didn't do anything about it?'

I shrug, shoving the Tupperware back into the fridge. 'You'll get it working,' I assure her. 'I believe in you.'

'You are objectively the most annoying person that has ever lived.'

'You can use Obaachan's wheelie shopping trolley for now — it's in her genkan, just borrow it.'

Rei huffs. 'Maybe I don't want to wander around town like Urashima Taro,' she says, but she's heading towards the front door, and her shoes. 'Looking like I've aged a thousand years since I've been away.'

'I'll come with you,' I tell her. 'So I can explain to everyone that you're not as ancient as you look.' I call to Hikaru, then twice more, before he finally makes his way down the stairs.

The hydrangea bushes that line the front of the house have exploded out of control, a furore of blue, each bloom obscenely large and pleased with itself. The heat sits in the air, so humid you could taste it if you tried, leaving the nape of Hikaru's neck damp, his hair curling so he looks even less Japanese than usual. Our street is halfway up the hill, forest and shrine above us and the town and the sea below.

'So, from here,' Rei says, putting on her sunglasses and heading off in the direction of the steps leading down to the shopping street, 'how many places can you see where you've been amazingly drunk and made out with inappropriate men?'

Hikaru has run ahead of us, making a jerking movement and telling Kimchi off for pulling on his lead. 'There really weren't that many inappropriate men available,' I say. 'That was kind of the problem with Ikimura.'

Rei looks down. 'You did ferret them all out, though. Rooftop of the school judokan. Pier, obviously. Rail track, sometimes. God, I hated it when you went there.'

'You know that rail track is disused, right?'

'Still,' says Rei, frowning. 'And all the places we can't see. Mani-san — I never got why you were OK with that. All those kitsune statues watching you from the undergrowth. So creepy.'

Mani-san is an abandoned shrine on the outskirts of town,

perched at the top of a steep stone staircase. 'Sucks to be you. I always felt like they were watching *out* for me.'

'It's haunted,' Rei says decisively.

'I didn't know you believed in ghosts.'

'I don't. I just don't believe in taking chances.'

'It's not like you were teetotal all your life,' I say accusingly.

'Sure,' Rei agrees. 'But I wasn't making out with the leader of the bosozoku motorbike gang from Akaishi. Or the visiting psychiatrist from the hospital.'

'Urgh, him,' I say, remembering. 'Like kissing a purse.' Rei makes a face. 'He was just a junior doctor, anyway, not some old Freud lookalike.'

I spent the years between my first drink, maybe a year after Mama died, and getting pregnant with Hikaru trying to find a storyline suitable for a rock song and pretending my family didn't exist, both of which are quite hard to do in a town as small and upright as Ikimura. It was exhausting. Sometimes I think about the contempt my teenage self would heap on my existence now, my thriving career in an old people's home and the glamour of my social life, my single-mother status putting my desirability in the dating pool somewhere below an insolvent alcoholic with a criminal record. I smile to myself to think how impossible I would have found it, to be told that it turns out the cure for all the existential angst I was feeling back then is taking care of old people and small people. Who has time to feel sorry for themselves when there are constantly urgent, immediate demands on your attention – a catfight between two centenarians, say, or the need to know immediately and with absolute accuracy if Komodo dragons prefer to eat tulips, onigiri or people's brains?

We reach the steps down to the shopping street, the metal handrail running down the middle smooth and rust-coloured from use. The steps are shaded by chestnut trees, their leaves bright green and singing with cicadas, except for a strip in the middle where the shade doesn't meet, and the stone seems to burn white-hot in the sun. On the other side of the road, opposite the steps, is a huge stone torii gate, twice as tall as I am, signposting the way to the ancient shrine in the forest behind the house, up a hill. The steps into the forest are spotted with lichen, the hinoki cypresses so tall they seem to reach right into the sky. Hikaru crouches down to examine a column of ants making their way across the dusty path into the forest. In the distance beyond him, I can see the top of our secondary school, its off-white clock tower, practically hear the class bell ringing, smell the chalk and the lemongrass in the cleaning sprays we used to scrub down the floors every afternoon.

Left down the stairs, and then into the shade of the high street, the pavements covered by a permanent awning and mosaicked with images from myths, the story of the rabbit in the moon and how Ikimura came to be, separated from the road by green metal fencing in the shape of ginkgo leaves. On the corner is the hairdresser's, with its spinning red, blue and white cylinder outside ('Remember Ai's shit fit, the first time Nozomi took her for a haircut?' 'Obviously.'), then the Japanese curry house ('I swear, this lunchtime deal's been the same price for the last two decades.' 'The price of thirty-five minutes of your Saturday job money.' 'Exactly.'), and the dusty alarm-clock shop ('I've never seen a single customer in there, have you?' 'No, not one. Do you reckon it's a front?'). We pass the stationer selling ornately calligraphed envelopes and hand-cut stamps to be used in place of signatures, and the florist's where the huge medallion arrangements look like the peacock displays of a showgirl at carnival.

We keep walking, past the obento shop where the window display showcases layered lacquer lunchboxes with sakura flowers inlaid in the lid. Rei made our lunches, mine and Ai's, every time we went on a school trip, something I haven't thought of for a decade. I remember one trip when I was a teenager, on a day after I hadn't come home the night before, just rolled in long enough to put my uniform on and roll out again: next to the tamagoyaki and the asparagus, she'd used nori on top of the rice to spell out 'fuck you' in English. I've always respected her for that.

'Let's not go to the conbini next to the old-lady clothes shop,' Rei says. 'I asked them for a job once when we were teenagers and the manager said he doubted they could give it to someone like me.'

I stop walking. 'You never told me that.'

'Wasn't worth it,' Rei says, shrugging.

I guess part of the reason we speak English fluently is because of people like that; sometimes at home, Rei and I used to refuse to speak anything but English, a tragic rebellion against all the people in the outside world who told us we were foreign weirdos. Mama always spoke in Japanese, but she could understand us, and she didn't mind. We must have spoken both languages from the start; I can't think of a time I didn't know either. Richard was there at the beginning, even though I don't remember it much. He must have taught me to read, because I could, devouring the chapter books Granny sent us from England. I wish he hadn't, because I'm not really prepared to concede that he did anything for us. Maybe it was Rei who taught me. It's more than possible, given her extraordinary bossiness.

I think it made us feel important, having a secret language, a code that only worked between us, and for the videos we borrowed from the library. Since we've been back together, we've been speaking our mother tongue – a pidgin hybrid of both – and I have the feeling I always do, that the rest of the time I'm trying to say what I mean with only half of my vocabulary.

There's no exact translation for 'cosy' in Japanese, like there isn't for 'yorimichi' in English, a word that gets translated as 'detour' but suggests the places you go when you don't want to go home and you're wandering to find an excuse to stay out, or 'waku waku', ostensibly the onomatopoeic sound of your heartbeat, but adding this excitement and uncertainty and wide-eyed coyness that doesn't really come across when you say 'boom boom'. I dream in Japanese and I reckon Ai does, too; but I think Rei might dream in English, now. Little by little we're leaning in those directions and, if we stay like this, when we're old ladies Ai and I will be wearing indigo-dyed smocks and eating pickles and neko-manma, and Rei will be dressed in cardigans with pearly buttons and bake crumbles. As if – Rei will be a terrifying wiry old ramrod running some huge corporation to the end.

We pass a news-stand and Hikaru's eyes go so circular at the children's magazines – so loaded with the bits of cardboard and stickers you need for the craft projects inside that they're tied together with string – that I'm compelled to buy him one. As I'm paying, I catch sight of a magazine emblazoned with a picture of Kabuki without Ai, which declares that they'll be resuming their concerts with treacherous Mako as the new lead singer. Rei and I stand in front of it for a moment in silence.

'Can they do that?' I ask eventually. 'Ai wrote all the songs. Did they even *tell* her?'

'Sh,' Rei commands, holding up one finger. 'I'm sending Mako doom vibes.'

I would be very afraid of doom vibes from Rei, rolling across the country. I consider feeling bad for Mako and then decide to absolutely not bother. She smiles flirtatiously down at me from the magazine cover, standing in Ai's place. I try, and fail, to imagine what Ai is going to do instead.

'Mama, can I pick a song?' Hikaru wants to know, tugging

at my hand. The Ikimura jukebox is on the bridge just beyond the news-stand, an ancient machine where you can choose a patriotic dirge to ring out through the shopping street's tannoy system and really get the mood pumping. The old man behind the news-stand peers down at Hikaru, taking in the foreign boy speaking Japanese with not unfriendly interest. I don't think I've ever seen a blond adult man whose mother tongue is Japanese, or a haafu old lady. The mystery is what any of us are going to become.

25

Rei

令

It feels like we've gone into every single food-related shop in Ikimura by the time we get back: the grocer's that's good for vegetables, the fishmonger's, the seaweed shop, the baker's, the miso shop, the other grocer's that's good for condiments, the other one for fruit, the omochi and dorayaki shop, just because I wanted to. The idea that in my other life I order everything I need on my phone and have it delivered on a Saturday morning while still in my pyjamas seems like a laughable fantasy.

You should never shop hungry, so we've eaten along the way: a bowl of hiyashi-chuka cold ramen, savouring the tang of the sesame and the bite of the noodles, a kakigori shaved-ice dessert we shared, supposedly for Hikaru's benefit, from the wooden stall with the distinctive, cheerful flag that sets up every summer by the river, next to the wooden bridge where the koi carp gather. Three straw-spoons and one mountain of snow, and we couldn't really pretend it was for Hikaru because we got matcha flavour, piled with adzuki beans and condensed milk, served with three chewy, spherical rice cakes on the side, the taste of summer, of festivals and beaches and yukatas and your only concern in the world being that your sisters might scarf more than their fair share of the sugar syrup.

Chibi is lounging on our front step as we approach the

house, giving Hikaru the side-eye. The cat gets up and stretches, waving his butthole at us as he stalks away. 'Remember that cat you drew that day when it was raining, and Nozomi totally loved it?' I ask Kiki. I can hear Nozomi's voice, how she praised my sister, telling her it was so full of expression.

Kiki drags the front door open and heaves the shopping bags on to the floor above the genkan. 'No, what cat?'

'I don't know, it was kind of a yellow cat. And then Nozomi started talking to it, super casual, saying how the cat wasn't going to be able to wear the waistcoat it liked to the party, but she could suggest a lovely necktie instead.'

Kiki makes a thinking noise. 'You and me were falling over laughing,' I hear myself saying, even though Kiki obviously doesn't know what I'm talking about, 'and she was just carrying on like it was no big deal. Remember?' My voice is plaintive.

Kiki looks at me, sympathetic and also distracted: the worst, most patronising combination. 'Rei, I don't remember. Hikaru, didn't you say you needed the toilet? Don't forget to wash your hands.'

I am never going to talk to Kiki about our mother again.

I scoop an armful of shopping out of Obaachan's trolley and go to dump it on the kitchen table, a riot of spinach in bunches, loose persimmons, jars of tobanjan, wax-paper packages of fish. In the bright afternoon sunlight from the window, filtering through the bamboo, I can see the slits in the surface of the wood where once upon a time Nozomi stabbed kitchen knives into the table, presumably during arguments with Richard. I'd come down in the morning sometimes to find them embedded there, like a misguided art installation. I remember telling Sath about it, something I'd never told anyone, to test him.

He cocked his head, like he was considering it. 'I mean, it's a bit much,' he said. 'I'd probably get arrested if I did that. But I get where she's coming from.'

'We need to wash all the crockery and sort out the kitchen equipment,' I hear my voice say to Kiki, a pathetic vengeance for her not remembering the cat. 'Figure out which stuff's still working.' I wonder in what ways I would have needed to be a different person, for Sath and I never to have broken up.

There's a sad pile of futon in the corner of the living room, which I assume is our sister. We've brought Ai the tacoyaki she likes from the shop next to the sake store, still warm, and a crème caramel purin, because who doesn't like purin, no matter how badly you feel things are going? Kiki walks over with the bag and stands with one hand on her hip, looking at Ai like she's some kind of crime scene that needs clearing up.

'We brought you tacoyaki,' she says.

There's no reply. Kiki tuts. 'And purin,' she says, squatting down and holding out the carton, the way you'd offer a banana through the bars of a cage.

'To give you vim and vigour,' I say.

The heap seems to pull back from Kiki, like a mollusc retracting, and what washes over me isn't a flood of empathy, which would be nice, but that instantaneous combination of aggravation and disappointment specific to childhood temper tantrums, so intense it gives me a head rush. I want to pick Ai up, fold away the futons and have it be over.

Kiki puts the purin and the tacoyaki down on the table.

Kiki and I have never talked about it, the fact that our mother not being well started when she was pregnant with Ai. She mainly spent the pregnancy crying, or sitting on the tatami staring at the wall. Or huddled up in a ball, just where Ai is right now. At the time, it was hard to decide which the bigger problem was: the truth about procreation and birth, which someone in the playground had taken it on themselves to graphically enlighten us about, so horrific it was like reality itself had shifted; or the fact that our mother appeared to be unfixably broken. We pretended none of it ever happened, and Ai arrived by stork, fully formed. Ai did just about save the situation, this uncomplaining little thing with spherical cheeks that pushed her mouth into a pout, staring at me with her grey-blue eyes and kicking her tiny feet with joy whenever I went near her. It's a physical pain, just now, to think of that jolly round baby. Clearly, Richard had nothing to do with her name, and even though Nozomi seemed better when she wasn't pregnant any more, when she told us what the baby was called, it was obvious she'd lost the plot. There were Kiki and I with our neat, unremarkable names, Rei and Kiyomi, and then, like a bomb in the middle of the family, the baby named Love. And Nozomi told us like it was normal. I remember, even as a nine-year-old, thinking it was very bad.

I open a crockery cupboard and start pulling everything out, to wash a year of dust off rice bowls and soy sauce plates. They make a satisfyingly grating rattle as I place them in the sink. Hikaru is sitting at the kitchen table with a bowl of the little grapes you pop into your mouth out of the skins, each tiny berry an explosion of deliciously sweet, tangy squelch, cold on your tongue.

'Kohei had these in his obento sometimes,' Hikaru says conversationally. 'He shared them with me, but only when we used to be friends.'

'What do you mean, *used to be*?' Kiki demands.

'We're not friends any more, because I sold him.'

'You sold him?'

Hikaru nods. 'For ten sticks.' He carries on popping grapes into his mouth, appreciative and unconcerned.

I concentrate on moving the bowls from counter to sink, sink to drying rack. Here is Hikaru, cheerfully selling his best friend for sticks, and over there is a cloud of doom, ruining everything. Just like Ai was here, younger than Hikaru is now, small and bright, and our mother drifting away from us, no matter how hard we tried to anchor her. I don't want to remember Nozomi's papery skin when she was sick, the blankness of her eyes, the musty smell of the clothes she didn't wash.

Kiki gives Hikaru a long look, then opens a cupboard to put the groceries away. 'So,' she says to me, 'you haven't told me about the wedding. How was it? Was he there?'

I pull a stack of side plates down on to the counter. 'Yes.'

Kiki turns around, a packet of wakame seaweed in her hand. 'And?'

'And nothing. Charlotte's dress was very pretty.'

'Charlotte's dress?!' Kiki repeats. 'Rei, who cares about Charlotte's dress?!'

I squeeze the sponge carefully, noticing how pretty the droplets of water are as they run on to the soapsuds in the sink. 'Did I tell you I started cycling to work?'

'No. What does this have to do with the wedding?'

'Cycling in London is so vile, honestly. All the men in super-tight Lycra with their gonads bouncing around and these ergonomic helmets that look exactly like penis heads.'

'Rei . . .' Kiki stops, then starts again, utilising all the skills she's learnt from years of dealing with toddlers and unreasonable geriatrics. I let myself wallow in it momentarily, the luxury of knowing I'm behaving badly. 'Why did you start cycling to work? Did something happen?'

'I thought I saw Sath on the train.' Probably it wasn't even him; just the nape of a neck that looked familiar through the crowd. A few months before the wedding. I got off at the next stop without looking up, and started cycling to work the next day; anything to ensure I didn't bump into him ever, including avoiding a transport system that carries four million passengers daily and which I used every day for five years without a single sighting.

There's a pause, and I know the look that Kiki is giving me. 'Oh, I get it,' she says, not unsympathetically. 'You think Ai hasn't tried hard enough to keep the show on the road.'

That is exactly what I think. At this moment, it feels very much like she has failed to understand that a uroboric repetition of history is not a desirable outcome. And yet, hearing Kiki say it so baldly – I think this is exactly the kind of conversation that makes my self-loathing entirely justified, actually.

'Mama,' Hikaru says to Kiki, handing his plate of grape skins to her and standing up, 'we're playing the baby cat game.'

'Who?'

'Me and you. I'm the baby cat in a nest and you're the mummy dinosaur and you have to find me.' He runs off.

I dry my hands and squat down to open one of the cupboards under the kitchen counter.

'Did she absolutely have to sleep with that guy?' I blurt out from inside the cupboard. 'Wasn't that like pulling the pin out of the grenade?' I start hauling things out: a tabletop cooker for okonomiyaki and yakiniku, the oven-toaster that used to sit on the table and grill endless cheese slices on to toast. 'Maybe she didn't actually have to do that. Maybe we didn't all want front-row tickets to the Takanawa Ai self-destruction gala.'

Kiki lowers her voice. 'For god's sake, Rei, give her a break. She's twenty-one. Her entire career's gone to shit. I think she's allowed to be sad for a while.'

I look over at Ai, a puddle. 'I don't know if sad is the word.'

Kiki puts Hikaru's plate in the sink, and stands there for a moment before she speaks. 'Rei, Ai isn't Mama.'

'I am aware of that,' I snap. I'm also aware that Kiki and I have different ideas about exactly what Nozomi was like. I stand up and plug in the tabletop cooker. Nothing. I remember coming back from school one afternoon, upset because some girls in my class had spent the day conferring behind their hands on my terrible foreign state and hilarious, disastrous wavy hair. Nozomi had listened and nodded and suggested bombastic ways to exact revenge, while making Mickey Mouse-shaped hotcakes on the cooker for a snack. She could be cool and funny, solid as a rock just when things were going badly, and other times, even if she'd had a promotion at work, or one of us had just shown her what we could play on the piano, doing our best, she would cry with no explanation for hours at a time, still cooking, still putting the washing on and running the bath, eyes leaking and us with no idea what to do. Remembering is a knot in my stomach, something I swear I could feel if I put my hand just above my belly button. I pull the plug out of the socket and look over at Ai. Through a gap in the top of the futons, I can see a tuft of her hair.

The thing that sucks is that she was our only mother. Not like a husband, someone we could swap out if the shit really hit the fan. There is no ersatz parent.

'Hey, this rice cooker's still working,' Kiki announces from the other side of the kitchen. 'It must be, like, thirty years old.'

'Isn't it one of those Elephant Label ones?' I ask. The effort required to make my voice chirpy, to think about rice cookers instead of about Nozomi, and Ai, feels physical. 'They're meant to last a lifetime, right?'

'Mama!' Hikaru's shout is enraged. 'Why aren't you looking for me?'

'I think so,' Kiki says, turning the rice cooker around to look at it. 'I guess it did.'

26

Ai

愛

I know Rei doesn't like coming home. If I hadn't messed everything up, she would never have had to come. I roll myself up tighter under the futon. If I open my mouth, snakes shoot out like the serpents on a gorgon's skull. When I keep it closed, though, they're roiling around in my stomach, surging up my throat. I have this feeling that I have to stay still, because I'm lying at the edge of a cliff and it would be so easy to fall off and into nothing. Every time sleep is about to come, that's the rush that wakes me up, stepping back from that darkness where I won't stop falling.

I wish the thing with Ichiro never happened, or at least the picture never got taken. Without the picture, even if I felt bad, I could do it alone, without dragging everyone else into it. I only slept with him because I wanted to feel something. It wasn't because I fancied him. How do you sleep with someone by accident? It's not like slipping on a banana skin or knocking over a cup of coffee. Though I guess you could say I joined a seventeen-member girl band kind of by accident, or got that vintage Buick imported from America by accident. Living by reaction rather than intention, Rei says. Typical youngest-child behaviour.

Kabuki was so popular I was never alone. There was no time

in the day: breakfasts with journalists, rehearsals, recordings, performances, travel. All my free time was spent in rooms without windows: basement dressing rooms or backstage in stadiums. I'd been the ringmaster of something beautiful but it had started to look like a freak show, never leaving me alone. The music had been so alive, and now it was just these extremely loud noises. My ears wouldn't stop ringing, and my skin wouldn't stop prickling, like a fever, or a bad omen. I could see people's mouths moving, and I felt like I should be able to hear them, but it was like being underwater. I could hear my own breathing, shallow in my ears. I wished things could be quiet, outside, inside, but on they went, on and on and on just shut up

shut up shut

up shutup

shut upshutupshutup.

The show we did the day before Ichiro felt like a clamp closing around my neck. Afterwards, I hid in the wings for a while, because everyone was rushing round onstage taking stuff down and clearing things away, and that meant I could be almost alone back there. I was standing staring at a fire door, at a sign that reminded everyone to be quiet in the wings and thanked them for their co-operation. Co-operation, 協力. Ten (十) strengths (力), and then more strength. You need so much strength, to do a good job existing with other people.

On the way out of the venue I fell down the fire escape stairs and bit my tongue, but it didn't hurt. I thought I should feel stupid for slipping, but I didn't. After I got up, I bumped into one of the drummers, and she was crying because she'd just heard that her father was sick. I made all the right noises, but I didn't feel anything. I thought what a horrible person I was, but that didn't really make me feel anything either.

The day Ichiro started showing an interest, I woke up and couldn't feel my fingers. I dug my nails into the tips, and it reminded me of running a knife down the edge of a frank-furter. We ended up in the car together after a photo shoot that involved the band playing our instruments in rain produced by giant showerheads, which seemed especially stupid in the middle of the monsoon. There was a bit of it when we weren't playing at all, just pretending to, while the photographer took pictures, and I could feel something like sandpaper in the part of my head behind my eyes. When I got in the car, I was concentrating on that feeling, hoping it would stop. Ichiro was all right, I think; quite symmetrical-looking, not very smiley. That's basically everything I know about him. He became the CEO of Kansas Records just after I'd jumped ship from Loupie Lou to make Kabuki.

Being with Ichiro was like passing stationary monsters in a very slow video game. He took my hand and I remember thinking it was quite weird, that there must have been some kind of vibe between us that I'd missed completely. I thought I should do something, maybe move my hand, but that seemed rude, and I didn't really mind that much because it distracted me from the sandpaper feeling.

Might as well turn on the TV.
Might as well go to bed.
Might as well sleep with the boss.

I'd never been to a love hotel before. It was one of the ones where reception can't see your face and hands you a key through a little hole. I didn't think those really existed. I thought it probably shouldn't be called a love hotel – probably more like an intercourse inn, or a sex station. Japanese vocabulary is quite limited like that. The most often-used word for sex is 'ecchi', a Japanesified way of saying the Roman letter 'H'. It stands for the first letter of the word 'hentai', which means kinda perverted and weird, not that there's any reason anyone would ever write it in English. That's what I was thinking about, that and the label on the disposable hairbrush in the hotel bathroom that said, *There's something different about your hairs!*

It wasn't that bad. I haven't had all that much sex. Sometimes it's great, but sometimes it's just repeatedly rubbing body parts against each other in a way that seems unnecessary. He asked if I was bored halfway through, which I found kind of heartbreaking, so I tried to put on a good performance. I liked Ichiro while we were having sex, the way he was sweeter than you'd expect. Post-coitally, he behaved exactly as you'd expect. Grunty.

When it was over, I started calculating how long was long enough before I could politely get dressed. I thought about when I was small and Mama used to make me count to twenty with my shoulders under the bathwater to warm up before I got out, which is almost the only thing I remember about her. That didn't seem good, to be thinking about my dead mother while I was pressed up against a naked man. I wondered what I should have done to stop it before it started.

27

Kiki

清美

It's easy, over the next few days, to stay in Ai's orbit without anyone saying that's what we're doing, so we can check on her, and take her drinks she doesn't drink, and plates of onigiri and osenbei and fruit. It's been seven years since all three of us were here together, before Hikaru was born. Wi-Fi is sufficiently patchy that we struggle to get much up on our phones, even if we wanted to. We are cut off from moral outrage, and it's very relaxing.

It's taken almost no time for the people around us to start acting like we never left, and are going to be here forever. The very first time the tofu guy comes to Obaachan's – the same guy who's been doing it all our lives, looking exactly the same as he always has, sinewy and indeterminately old – he takes in the sight of us, says nothing, wraps up four more slabs of tofu and makes that his regular delivery. Kanagawa-san, the smiling lady who lives across the street, starts waiting until she sees Hikaru every morning to take the walk she goes on with her daughter around the block. Which is interesting, because Kanagawa-san has dementia, and trouble remembering anything – she asks us every day with great curiosity where we're from, and then tells us that she got a little lost on the way home, but this nice girl is helping her find the way back. It's one of the things I noticed at the care home – that the older people get, the more and more like themselves they become.

'That does not bode well for any of our futures,' Rei says, when I tell her.

Obaachan says nothing about Ai, as if it's unremarkable that someone would turn up to visit and then lie in bed for twenty-three hours at a time. Sometimes I catch her frowning at the garden with her lips pursed, but that could be about any number of things.

You turn up at home with your sister in a state, on the run from the world at large, so what do you do? You salt plums, obviously, and make plum liqueur. What else?

In the garden, the plum tree has spat its fruit in every direction, like Hikaru throwing his toys out of his buggy, which is why we're getting away with doing something that could arguably be labelled a leisure activity – it can almost be filed, for Rei's benefit, under tidying up or housework. The garden is mossy rocks and shrubs, with a gravel patch in the middle; waxy-leafed azalea bushes and hardy camellias and the ginkgo tree, which is such a vibrant yellow but stinks like nothing else in the autumn. Explosions of water irises poke out from between everything else, their purple-and-yellow petals bright and expectant. The rocks are so soft and bouncy with rich green moss that Hikaru strokes them like pets. There's jasmine growing along the back wall that Mama planted, a dense net of tiny white stars, and an osmanthus bush, with its flowers the colour of chewy peach-flavoured sweets. Along one section of bamboo fencing, tomatoes and cucumbers, snow peas and summer squash have overgrown into a knot of tough, yellowing leaves, and cosmos have sprung up all over the place in pink and white clouds.

I get the extendable ladder out of the old lock-up shed down the side of the house, perch it against the lichen-spotted trunk of the plum tree and start to fill the plastic bowl from the bath with unripe plums for the umeshu, the plum liqueur. My T-shirt is sticking to my back with the heat, and the air thrums with the orchestral drama of the cicadas and the familiar jerky trill of the uguisu.

'Don't fall and die,' Rei says curtly, sitting in the shade on the engawa, organising ingredients. Chibi sits next to her, licking himself with great tenderness. Rei looks just like she did when we were small, when she spent busy hours setting up the medicine shop of shampoo bottles, or the art gallery, or the toy stall, and then Ai and I would come and be her eager and only customers and she would take all our pocket money. Or just mine, actually, come to think of it. 'It would be such a downer.' She counts the Mason jars in front of her.

'You can't make umeboshi with split plums,' Obaachan says for the hundredth time. She's sitting on a floor chair, with her legs straight out in front of her like a jointed doll, fanning herself with a promotional paper fan from Marusho. She's talking to Hikaru, who's collecting the ripe, fallen plums for salting, but hasn't actually addressed him yet, and scowls into the middle distance. 'The usual sloppiness won't do. The ones that are split go in the green waste bag.'

'OK!' Hikaru agrees happily, squatting on the gravel. Obediently, he carries as many broken plums as he can – two – to the green waste bag open by the ginkgo tree.

'Why can't she just talk directly to him like a normal grandmother?' I sing at the tree in English. It's very useful that Obaachan doesn't understand one word of English, and pretends not to hear us when we speak it.

'Don't take it personally,' Rei advises. 'Or at least, not personally to him. She never liked us much either.'

'Did she like Mama?' I wonder.

'Probably not,' Rei says. 'Nozomi didn't really behave the

way a good granddaughter was meant to, did she, running off to Tokyo. Although at least she wasn't fathered by a white cretin.'

I don't think Mama would have come back to Ikimura, in an ideal world. She went to design college in Tokyo, secretly, because her father had given her the money for a secretarial course and wouldn't have carried on coughing up if he'd known she wasn't using it to learn touch-typing. I never met him, but all evidence suggests my grandfather was a very traditional man. Being old-fashioned and traditional excuses misogyny and xenophobia.

Mama never finished design college. She was knocked up and married, in that order, within six months of locking eyes with Richard, and safely back in Ikimura by the time Rei was a few months old, because her father had had a stroke. If you're first-born in Japan, or an only child, even now, the force of your parents' expectation is a magnetic field you can't escape. Rei should be grateful, really, that the family death rate is so high there's no one left who can tell her what to do.

Mama always said it was the horror of the white guy in his house, this house, that killed my grandfather off so quickly. I remember her pressing her lips together to stop herself sniggering about it. Dear old Richard, unemployed when he married Mama, having abandoned his post in the UK to stay with her, didn't do much, I don't think, to improve my grandparents' view of gaijin as either actual cannibals (Mama said that her mother told her with absolute sincerity that the Americans ate the Japanese during the war) or, possibly even worse, untidy unreliables with no work ethic. Lucky for them, they died within a few months of each other, an aggressive colon cancer killing Nozomi's mother unexpectedly, so that neither of them lived long enough to see how really useful Richard turned out to be, moving to Tokyo for work when I was a year old and essentially not coming back. I think my grandparents would like him better now, living in his big house with his neat children, even if it is all in the wrong country and the children have nothing to do with them.

The sound of someone practising the violin floats out of an open window, competing with the cicadas' energetic complaining.

'We didn't bring your piano music,' I say to Hikaru, remembering. Hikaru has lessons at kindergarten, like every kid there.

He sighs deeply, gazing at the shiny skin of a plum. 'Don't worry, Mama. I couldn't practise piano here anyway.'

'Why not?'

'Obaachan's piano makes my teeth itch too much.'

Rei looks up. 'Do you reckon Nakamura-san's still teaching? Maybe she could give him a few lessons.'

Nakamura-san taught piano to Rei and me before everything went tits up. She was a friend of Obaachan's, and a Christian to boot. The Christians in Japan take it deeply seriously, since it's not like they were born into church on Sundays followed by a roast and can take or leave the religion bit. So even though most of our extracurriculars were unceremoniously abandoned when Nozomi left the session, Nakamura-san carried on teaching us piano for free, as a Christian act. We'd all troop over to her house on a Saturday after school, and whichever of us wasn't having the lesson would wait on the lace-covered chairs in the genkan with Ai and pore over the manga Bibles Nakamura-san left out for us.

'I think she might be disappointed,' I say, feeling disloyal to Hikaru. He is objectively the worst at piano in his class, which tracks, given how often he practises and also who his is.

'I don't know,' Rei says. 'I think Ai was quite shocking to

her. I don't think she expected her charity to result in a girl-band-scandal-megastar.' This is true. One cannot imagine that singers in pastel-coloured mini-dresses were the teaching outcome that either Nakamura-san or Jesus had in mind. I wonder what Ai would be doing now instead, if Nakamura-san hadn't been a Christian.

For a while, all that Ai was getting out of our piano lessons was an encyclopaedic knowledge of the New Testament and a clear image of Jesus as a hot teenage cartoon character. Then one day, just as we were leaving, Nakamura-san turned to Ai and said, 'Ai-chan, are you going to learn to play the piano one day?' in the way that adults do to kids, just making noise, not meaning anything. And Ai went, 'Yes,' marched up to the piano and played the piece I had been learning from beginning to end with no mistakes. It was awkward for everyone and frankly kind of insulting for me; I'd already been learning for about six years at that point. We'd never even heard Ai touch the piano at Obaachan's house. I remember the look of disbelief on Rei's face.

Nobody is saying that Ai is a prodigy; the party line is that she watched me play it so many times she learnt it by heart, and Rei says she is also prepared to grant her an effective ear. Nakamura-san thought it was the second coming, and agreed (or rather insisted, since Rei was being appropriately Japanese about it) to teach Ai to play, something it took Ai approximately six months to master. I mean, I wouldn't say she was Mozart in six months, but not far off. She'd hear tunes she liked, then start banging pretty convincing versions out on the keyboard at home and singing along to them in pitch-perfect imitations. Rei carried on doggedly learning music by dead Europeans, practising on Obaachan's real upright piano next door, but I pretty much gave up after that – I stuck to finding the hardest, weirdest songs I could and bringing them back to see if Ai could play them, even though Rei said she wasn't a circus animal and I shouldn't encourage her. I was glad our house was full of music again.

The violinist has gone as far as they can with the piece and stops abruptly, practising single repeated phrases. The plastic bowl is piled high with green plums and my arm is aching.

'Your shorts are too short, Kiki,' Obaachan declares. 'You might think you can get away with it because you're a foreigner, but you can't. You're too old for shorts like that.'

I take a deep breath and start to lower myself down the ladder, but Rei exclaims and comes running over to hold the bottom.

'I said *don't* die,' she says tetchily. 'And ignore her, obviously. Your shorts are fine. You have lovely legs.'

'That's probably the nicest thing you've ever said to me.'

'Well, it's true.' Rei reaches up to take the bowl of plums from me. 'Is it weird that we haven't heard a single thing from anyone in Kabuki?' she asks as I climb down with exaggerated care, for her benefit. 'Not from her manager, or the other band members, or anything?'

'How would they contact us?' I ask. 'I don't think we're on their radar.'

'They could be trying to get in contact with Ai.'

'She doesn't have her phone,' I say, stepping down on to the gravel. 'And I don't know how it would go if we tried to get her to remember her email log-in details.'

'Look how many I collected, Mama!' Hikaru's bounty is a pile of yellow-faced plums, some of them blushing pink. He carries them carefully over to Obaachan. 'I did it how you said. None of them are split, look.'

Obaachan peers inside the bowl with her hands folded in her lap and her mouth turned down. She nods once. 'That's good,' she tells him sombrely, and Hikaru beams.

'I have the shiso, and salt, and shochu, and rock sugar,' Rei says. 'Do we need anything else?'

'Are we going to do honey umeboshi?' I ask. 'Ai loves those.' Just like Mama did.

'Let's do half and half,' Rei decides.

28

Rei

令

'The Miffy books!' Kiki cries out in triumph from behind me. I'm standing at the engawa with my coffee, appreciating its specific home taste and looking out at the green profusion of the garden. 'Rei, this is amazing. I thought you got rid of all this stuff.'

So did I, is the truth. Kiki and Hikaru have braved a trip up to the attic, a Stygian space full of dust and nail heads sticking spitefully up from the floorboards, and retrieved a box full of picture books from when we were small. Nozomi must have put it up there, because I'm pretty sure that any-thing memory-inducing that was still in the house when she died is now in landfill somewhere. There have been moments, in the years since, when I've felt bad about having got rid of it all, but thank god for Marie Kondo, because − were those things ever going to spark uncomplicated joy? I think not.

'Oh my god, Rei, look, our old piano books,' Kiki croons. I hear her snorting. 'Look at this note you've written for me: "Practise five times per day, no mistakes."' She's quiet for a second. 'Rei, I actually think if anyone was paying attention, they should have been quite worried by the neatness of your handwriting. Surely it's not normal for a kid to be that anal at the age of – what, eight? Why were you writing me commands, anyway, instead of Nakamura-san?'

'I obviously felt that Nakamura-san was a bit lax,' I say, not turning around.

I remember the look on Nakamura-san's face when Ai played that first crazy piano piece, and the feeling that Ai was suddenly really far away. In a way it was amazing, but it was also kind of disturbing: the first, but far from the last, time I looked at my sister and wondered where the hell this alien had actually come from. Not having a clue how things work and watching them perform mind-boggling feats is fine if you're talking Pepper the SoftBank robot, but a lot less fine if the thing in question is the child you're supposedly in charge of. In my experience.

I blow on my coffee and notice a ripped panel in the shoji between the engawa and the sitting room. On closer inspection, loads of them are ripped. Some through age, some that look suspiciously like the work of a bad-tempered cat who shouldn't be able to get into the house while we're away, but is probably capable of it. I remember crouching behind this shoji screen when my mother brought Ai home for the very first time. I don't know why I was hiding. I was excited about the novelty of the new baby, a new sister – I was only two when Kiki was born, so Kiki was already there in the very first moments I can remember; the wonder of the world, and then this slightly annoying appendage. Kiki was patently not a proper little sister, more an irritation that was always in the way when I wanted to do things, a constant note in the background music. I had high hopes for the new one, though. She'd look up at me adoringly and know that every single thing I said or did was right. I'd educate her in the ways of the world and we'd always be together. More like an imaginary friend than a real person.

The day my mother came home from the hospital, it was still

warm, even though summer was over, and the leaves of the ginkgo tree were turning yellow. She put the bassinet down on the engawa and called to Kiki and me. Obaachan had nominally been looking after us, which meant we were expected to go round to her house for dinner, and keep out of trouble the rest of the time. Recently, I've been wondering how Nozomi got back, if she took the bus or splashed out on the taxi – surely she can't have walked up that hill in the heat three days post-partum carrying the bassinet. Richard hadn't been back for months. I felt weirdly shy when she called; I didn't say anything, and when she went to look for Kiki and me, I crawled out from my hiding place and peered in to look at Ai. She blinked at me, deceptively earnest. She seemed to carry her own world around with her like a bubble, a world that consisted of the clean white inside of her basket, and anything else that came within ten centimetres of her face. My mother said that by the time she and Kiki got downstairs, I'd taken Ai out of the basket and was holding her in my lap. I don't remember that bit, which is odd; I just remember thinking I was nine years old, basically an adult, and it was pretty clear it was going to be up to me to take good care of this tiny little thing that had just arrived and couldn't even hold up its head.

'I'm going to get paper to fix the shoji,' I tell Kiki now, draining my coffee.

'What, now?' Kiki asks, not looking up from the picture book she's poring over with Hikaru. 'Do you ever have, like, a one-second gap between thought and execution?'

'No,' I tell her, putting my cup in the sink. 'Do we need anything else?'

'Maybe bulbs. The light on the stairs isn't working. I don't think the one over the sink in the bathroom is, either.'

Two women are standing on the pavement on the other side of the street when I open the door: an old lady of about

136

Obaachan's age whose straight back looks almost unnatural, holding the arm of a younger woman still old enough to be my grandmother. The younger woman looks at me, recognition passing over her face even though I don't know who she is, and I know what a loathsome person I am because I stare with intense concentration at my phone, at nothing at all, and walk off towards the shopping street as fast as I can. You can never be alone here, and in a brief rush I miss the anonymity of London, the tacit understanding that we are all antisocial and should ignore each other pointedly if we happen to meet on public transport. I slow down when I'm far enough away that she can't call out, wondering why it would be so bad to exchange pleasantries with someone who's probably known me since I was two. In London, I'm nobody's daughter or granddaughter and the stories I tell myself and how I tell them are nobody's business but mine. It's hard to go back to living carefully, once you've got used to that. I tell myself I'll start tomorrow. Tomorrow, I'll be a nice person. Although I suppose that might require a fundamental personality change.

I think of the time I had, for a variety of reasons, to leave a party Sath and I were at to go home and stick a pillow over my head. Even though I'd expressly told him he shouldn't, Sath followed me home, and we argued and I asked him from under the pillow why he thought I needed a man to save me.

Sath laughed then, a proper belly laugh, and said he wasn't mad enough to try to save me, and his gender had nothing to do with it, so then I asked him why he thought we should stay together.

He said it was because I was smart and funny and he loved me, like I was stupid for asking, which showed he was a bigger person than me, since if he'd asked me the same question at that exact moment, I would have told him that I didn't, that actually I would have preferred to share my life with a bag of slightly past-it salad leaves than with him.

I never told him I loved him. I occasionally regret that now. It couldn't last, obviously. It was over as soon as I asked a question that needy. Anyway, there's only one person you can expect to love you unconditionally, and that's your mother.

On the way to the pedestrian arcade that cuts off the main shopping street, I pass a pharmacy, its green cross on a white background. In the window stands a sun-faded advert of Loupie Lou members pouting some kind of flavoured lip gloss. The thing I don't understand (apart from any of it) is the connection between Ai being a small piano maestro and ending up on that advert, her personal life legitimate public property.

Her success, if you can call it that, was incremental: she won regional piano competitions that turned into national piano competitions that turned into festivals and getting an agent and starting to play music that alternately made me feel like I was drowning and on drugs, and dressing like god knows what, an intergalactic stewardess in purple patent leather one week, Marie Antoinette as imagined by a manga artist the next. I admit that in hindsight it's clear that at this crucial juncture, it would have been helpful if someone had been paying more attention.

I should have stayed in Japan, probably. I should definitely have come back after I finished university, probably. At the time I left Ikimura, I'd stuck around for three years after finishing school, doing extra school leaver qualifications in Japanese and in English, and being a good homemaker until I was feeling like I might disintegrate. England wasn't a choice; it was the only way to survive. I picked the university with the shortest terms and came back every holiday, and I told myself Ai was fine. And then she suddenly announced she was moving to Tokyo because she'd been offered a slot in a girl band.

The pedestrian arcade is narrow, and bustling. If the rest of Ikimura hasn't changed since we were small, the shop owners in this arcade have made a collective decision to pause time in 1950. I pick my way past displays of onsen-style bath salts, the hand-thrown chawan bowls outside the tea ceremony utensils shop that Obaachan used to frequent; breathe in the round, sweet smell of the fish-shaped taiyaki cakes mixed with bicycle oil from the repair shop. An ancient mannequin modelling a traditional kimono stands next to a rack of yukatas, determinedly coquettish.

Right from the beginning, it felt like I'd truly fucked it, like I'd sold my sister into the sex trade (or the reverse sex trade, it turned out, judging by her fully bonkers contract). Not that I would ever say that to her, clearly, and I have to agree with Sath who said, when I said that to him, that maybe what I felt about it wasn't the point, and that Ai never belonged to me to start with.

I don't know what our mother would think of any of it; if she would have thought it was Ai going on a journey and no problem at all, or if she would have been disappointed that I let that happen to her. It's not like she gets a say, is it, given that she left us to it, but still. I pass the umbrella repair shop, brightly coloured umbrellas festooning the ceiling, and hear a huge sigh escape me. Did we want the baby to be singing songs about her broken heart in leather hot pants? Or being put about publicly as having such dubious taste in (married, older) men? The whole thing gives me a headache just thinking about it.

'Rei-san?' A man passing by, our shoulders almost touching, has stopped abruptly. My instinctive reaction is wary, still wrapped in my reverie. He's taller than me, tanned and lean, dressed in builder's clothes, navy canvas trousers that balloon out and taper at the ankle, split-toed boots, a paint-spattered T-shirt. He raises the construction helmet he's holding in his hand like a greeting, and it's when I see his smile, the way his eyes disappear, that I know who he is.

'Youta!' I feel an answering smile spread across my face, the effect he always had on everyone around him. Youta, who lived in our neighbourhood, and went to our school, and we spent entire summers with, sleeping at each other's houses. Last time I saw him was before I left for England, when he was still a gangly teenager, totally in love with Kiki, who was either oblivious or purposefully ignoring him.

'Rei-san,' he says again, drawing out my name, the intonation of it subtly different in dialect, a sing-song sound I'm so happy to hear. It's been years since anybody's looked this pleased to see me. 'You're back. It's been so long.'

'I heard you left town,' I tell him.

'I was living over in Akaishi for a few years,' he says. 'But I've come back to help my old man.'

'He's still running the construction company?'

Youta nods. 'We're building the hospital extension,' he says. 'I'm on my way there now.' He makes a shucking sound with his teeth and looks bashful. 'You're so glamorous; I could see you weren't from here from a mile away. I didn't know it was you, though.'

It's a compliment, the way he says it, but I don't know how to reply.

'How long are you in town?' he asks. 'Is Kiki here?'

I nod. 'And Ai. And Hikaru.' It's out of my mouth without a thought and then I feel suddenly, weirdly awkward, even though Kiki and Youta never got together.

'Kiki's son?' Youta asks easily, and I remember that was always one of my favourite things about him, his ease, a counterweight to the high drama and perpetual offence of our teenage life.

A man hurries past us, checking his watch, and Youta starts.

140

'I have to go, I'm late,' he says apologetically. 'I just saw Masato and Daisuke.' I remember the boys from school, one tall, one small, still children in my mind's eye. 'We were saying we should go to Uradome this year.' Uradome is beautiful, a beach an hour away that we used to get up early to catch the bus to. 'It would be nice to go together.' He looks suddenly shy, blushing under his tan. 'If you guys have time.'

'We'd love to,' I tell him sincerely. Ai clouds my mind but disappears just as quickly at the sight of Youta's smile. 'Can I give you my number?'

I feel restless after we part ways, a little hyperactive. I get a paintbrush, paper, glue in the paper shop, and then take the long way home, to walk it off. The level crossing on the old rail track has been primped by guerrilla gardeners, lined with pots containing a truly impressive display of chrysanthemums in pinks and yellow and white. Obviously I'm glad – given that Kiki used to actually sit on it with her delinquent friends and drink – that it's disused, but I think how different Ikimura must have felt when the train ran here. It would have been such a scenic route, along the coast, and it would have felt so much less cut off. This route takes me past the hotel, where Sath and I stayed when he came to Japan. We visited Ikimura because Sath wanted to see where I was from, but I said we should stay in the hotel rather than at home, a decision I feel bad about when Obaachan is a theoretical old lady, and fully justified in making when confronted with her in reality.

Sath said he loved it here, but for me the trip wasn't uncomplicated. I didn't know, until after we'd arrived, that I was waiting to introduce him to my mother. Obviously I knew I couldn't; she'd been dead six years by the time Sath and I met, but when I was away from it, Ikimura seemed like where she was. I found myself telling Sath stories about her, but they didn't really seem to translate. She was so funny, I tried to tell him. You would have liked her. And I thought of how hospitable she would have been, and how impressed he would have been with her elegance and her intelligence, and then I remembered that they wouldn't even have been able to speak to each other.

I come to the ojizo-san on the roadside, three sanguine statues with eyes closed, wearing red hats and capes. Sath greeted them every time we passed them, when we were here. Someone's placed a child's windmill toy next to one, and it spins and stops, a blur of colour.

He still had it. At the wedding. The haughty girl who interrupted us positioned herself near him all night, graduating to putting her hand on his arm as everyone got drunker. The truth is, I always liked it when he'd move away from me, and I could watch people coming on to him and him flirting back just enough to make me want him even more. And then the way he looked at me later, with a face so unguarded I used to put my hands over it so I couldn't see, because what idiot goes around wearing his heart on his sleeve like that? As if anybody could love him enough to protect him from all the heartbreak that much feeling was going to get him into.

I told Sath that my mother had been ill, which wasn't inaccurate. He knew she was dead, but he didn't probe the matter because he isn't an insensitive psychopath. It's not something that naturally crops up in conversation, and I liked not thinking about it, playing the version of my life where it didn't take centre stage. Eventually it did come up – or rather, I brought it up, because it wasn't like I was trying to keep it a secret. At the time, we'd been sleeping together for a few weeks and being near him was still the most exciting thing that had ever happened to me; I was torn between being on my best, most attractive behaviour and starting to want to poke whatever was between us, to find out how strong it was. We'd been discussing the fact that English seaside towns often made you feel like the apocalypse was either around the corner or had recently taken place, wind whistling till it hurt your ears and the horizon an existential crisis. I said it was weird how even though Japanese seaside towns were also often full of old people, like Ikimura was, they didn't give me the same abandoned melancholy feeling that English ones did. Japanese old age didn't seem very tragic, actually; it seemed industrious.

Sath said, like it was interesting, that he hadn't realised my town was by the sea.

I made an assenting sound. We were lying top to toe on the sofa in my university room, our knees hooked over opposite arms. I'd been pretending to work when he came in, Frank and Cartwright's *Microeconomics and Behaviour* face down on my stomach. I told him about how it was quicker to get to Ikimura on a ferry, because the roads are so winding and hilly the bus takes forever and makes you puke.

He nodded like he was imagining it.

Actually, I said, like it was an unexpected historical fact about the town we came from, my mum drowned herself there.

He stopped nodding.

I hadn't meant to hide it, but I hadn't necessarily meant to bring it up just then, either. I find my own conversation thrillingly unexpected, particularly when it comes to things that matter and if I'm momentarily comfortable; usually I'm pretty good at my own image management, then once in a while, with no warning, words just spill out and we look at them, me and my conversation partner, wondering what to do with them and equally surprised by what they reveal. What I'd just said sounded so unbelievable that I carried on.

At the seaside, I told him. Then it occurred to me like a stroke of genius: It was a seaside suicide.

He looked at me for a second, like he was checking if I was

joking. I told him I wasn't, that that would be a weird thing to joke about. Did he know, I asked, that in England suicide used to be considered not only a crime against God but also against the Crown? Eating swans and killing yourself, all the ways you could offend the Queen. Who knew. Or that if you jump in front of a train in Tokyo, your family has to pay for the clean-up, and the compensation for delays? So, you know, thank god for small mercies.

I didn't say to him then that she'd already ended up in hospital once, a few years before, from taking too many pills. Obaachan wouldn't let us go and see her but I went anyway, sneaking in after school one day without checking myself in at the hospital reception, avoiding the staff who thought they knew her and would try to tell me what time I could visit. Well or ill, she was my mother. Mine. She wasn't herself, then, not my sarky mother who put on rude voices for cartoons she drew of people we reported were mean to us at school, and played Nagabuchi Tsuyoshi's harmonica solos so loudly the floorboards in the engawa shook and Obaachan rushed over to shout at her. I was glad that Ai and Kiki weren't there, didn't even know what had happened. She said how sorry she was. I believed her.

Shit, Sath said first. Then eventually, he said: That must have been really hard. I found that remarkable about him, that he knew it was OK to spend a few seconds deciding what to say. It was the most accurate thing anyone has ever said about it.

I went back to that beach a week after it happened. By the time I had swum the length of it fifteen times, the sea didn't feel malevolent any more. It felt neutral, maybe a little resigned. It took two and a half hours, which I think is a massively efficient way to have solved that particular problem. Nozomi's body was never recovered.

I've reached the top of the hill. I stand for a moment at the end of our road, looking down towards the sea. I'm glad to see

Chibi stalking in my direction and pick him up, even though I know he hates it. He flattens his ears and flexes his claws into my skin with deliberation, eyeballing me the whole time. 'You're a psycho-cat,' I whisper at him in English before he does a flying leap out of my arms and hotfoots it.

Approaching home, I pass Obaachan's house first. I notice, in a way I didn't before, how tidy it is, each of the plants demure and carefully pruned. Comparatively, ours is an uproar of colour, the morning glory tangling with the hydrangeas, rogue cosmos holding insurgent meetings with the geraniums along the bottom, their faces pink with determination. I remember how Nozomi tried to grow spider lilies in pots, her favourite flowers, even though Obaachan said they were bad luck. She would have liked all this colour.

'Guess who I just saw,' I call to Kiki when I get in.

'Leonardo DiCaprio,' she calls back from the kitchen. 'Taking a stop on his luxury cruise.'

'Better,' I tell her. 'Youta!' It suddenly comes to me. 'You know, Youta that you married. We made the broken mosquito net your veil, remember?'

She ducks out under the noren, wiping her hands on a tea towel. 'Obviously I know which Youta.' She frowns slightly, remembering. 'I didn't actually want to marry him. You just bossed us into it. As usual.'

I sit down on the genkan step, still holding my bag of paper and glue. 'Remember how cute he was when he smiled? How you couldn't even see his eyes because they'd disappear?' I demonstrate. 'He looks exactly the same. But maybe kind of hot now. Those builder's costumes are good, right?'

'It's not a *costume*, Rei. He's a builder?'

Before I can answer, the door rattles open and Obaachan stands before us, glowering.

'Why are you *shouting*? I was just walking past on my way

to classical music appreciation and all I can hear is you girls *shouting.* This is a nice neighbourhood.'

'Classical music appreciation sounds interesting,' Kiki says neutrally, at the same time as I say, 'Nobody is shouting.'

Obaachan holds up a finger. 'I want you to pay close attention to the way I close the door. There is no need to slam it the way you Westerners do. I don't want our houses falling down because you are so . . .' She waves her hands in front of her erratically and makes a face. 'Watch.' She closes the door behind her with exaggerated care, so it shuts in almost perfect silence, and then opens it again immediately, just a crack, so she can whisper through it. 'Like that, do you understand? Not all huge and clumsy. That's how we look after our houses and be considerate towards each other.' She closes the door again, and disappears.

Kiki puts her hand on my arm. 'So I've been thinking,' she says seriously. 'When one of us ends up murdering Obaachan in a rage, we should meet at the car park around the back of Aeon so we can get supplies before we go on the run. The one who didn't do it should bring the car.'

'I thought our meeting place was happy hour at the Dean Street Townhouse.'

Kiki gives me a withering look. 'Rei, that's only for when *you* murder someone in London.'

'Oh, OK,' I say. 'Thanks for the forward planning.'

29

Kiki

清美

Hikaru has spent a happy afternoon singing into the electric fan and rolling about with laughter when it distorts his voice so it oscillates like an ambulance siren. Obaachan is sitting next to him glaring at a newspaper and giving off a psychologically complicated vibe. We've been here over a week, and it's impossible not to notice that she eats almost nothing compared to when we last saw her, and winces every time she moves. Rei has tried pointing this out to her, only to get a lecture about how inflexible and fat she is. So relaxing, hanging out with family.

Obaachan gets herself up to go and do something – plot a Japanese supremacist takeover or peel onions – unfolding one leg at a time and pushing off the floor with her hands flat. I'm reading *The Confessions of Lady Nijo*, which I assumed was one of Rei's school texts, staid and serious, but I'm now thinking probably wasn't, since it reads like a post-watershed soap opera, a riot of drinking and lovers and weird court games. My main take-home is that in thirteenth-century Japan, you could shag whoever you liked as long as you wrote them a poem the next morning. Rei is sitting cross-legged by the shoji, fixing one of the panels using specially bought paper and glue, the occasional YouTube video and sheer bloody-mindedness. The only place she's lived since leaving here that hasn't looked like a picture-perfect showroom for an interiors magazine is the apartment she shared with Sath. I think it was the happiest she's ever been. By the end of the day, she'll probably have a second career in traditional Japanese home restoration, a thought that makes me want a beer, or possibly some Class A drugs. I would have ignored the holes.

Despite the shoji, Rei is actually doing a sterling job at living with our lack of a plan. She does chores from morning till night, which is pretty much what she's always like, and we don't discuss what day it is. I guess she'll go back to London when Ai is better, although no one's talking about what 'better' means. Being up and about in daylight hours would be a start. Eating with us. Talking. God, poor Ai. I wish I could make Ai herself again, and I also wish Rei could stay here, which is wanting two opposite things at once, like Hikaru always does. The tip of Rei's tongue sticks out from between her teeth and her eyebrows furrow as she tucks the paper neatly into the corner of the wooden frame.

I think of Youta in a builder's costume. When Rei told me about him, I had such a clear picture in my head: the way I'd open the door on a summer holiday morning to find him standing there with a serious expression, and then he'd look up at me and smile, just the way she described. He was so stoic at our wedding ceremony, in the shirt she made him wear – one of hers, because she felt he should have a smart white one. She told him not to mind about it being a bit ruffled and lacy.

'Mama,' Hikaru says, frowning at the page of a picture book he's picked up from the stack. 'This book doesn't make any sense. Lemurs only live in Madagascar and there are no lions there. And if lemurs and lions lived together, the lion would eat the lemurs.'

'Maybe he just ate,' I suggest.

'But the lemurs would be like finger food for the lion,' Hikaru objects.

'Where did you learn the word "finger food"?' I demand.

Hikaru looks at me like I am extremely slow on the uptake. 'I just know things,' he says.

I know Rei is looking at me, her lips pinched together to stop herself laughing, even though her face doesn't move. She picks up the glue and paintbrush and walks over to the sink just as the five o'clock chime rings out its tune over the tannoy. Hikaru lifts his head like a dog that's seen a squirrel. 'Can I watch *Together with Mother*?' he asks, hurrying over to the television on his knees.

Ai comes shuffling into the room, her hair in disarray, wearing the same T-shirt and pair of Rei's running shorts she's had on for days. Rei and I studiously ignore her, the way you'd ignore a wild animal you were trying to tame if it came near you to eat the food you'd left out. She pours herself a glass of water, then stands for a second looking at the glass, like she doesn't know what it is.

'Can you believe this show hasn't changed its format one little bit since we used to watch it?' Rei says from the kitchen.

'It has,' I tell her. 'Now instead of morality tales with life-size penguin puppets, it's life-size cat puppets. Hikaru, come back from the TV.'

Hikaru obeys, shuffling backwards. The programme opens with an educational few minutes on the natural world, and we see some elephants playing near a waterfall, sucking up water in their trunks and spraying it over each other.

'I forgot to tell you, Youta said do we want to go to Uradome with him,' Rei says, watching the elephants.

We used to spend days at Uradome when we were kids, jumping off the protruding cliffs into the sea like our parents told us absolutely not to. Youta never talked it up the way the other boys did; he just gamely came along, then, while we were all standing around freaking each other out and not jumping, he'd sail off the top with so little fanfare you'd wonder where he'd gone till you heard the splash at the bottom.

'Oh, for god's sake,' Rei growls, just as I'm about to answer her. Hikaru looks up, perturbed. Rei is glaring at Ai, who has sat down at the kitchen table facing the television, tears pouring silently down her face. I look back at the screen to try to work out what's upset her. The elephants are still nuzzling each other. One of them eats a leaf frond. There is no mention of girl bands, fame, death, sex, music, careers, social media, or in fact people or anything related to them, at all.

Hikaru gets up and goes over to Ai.

'If you're going to behave like this,' Rei says, 'you're better off not coming downstairs at all.'

'It's OK, Ai,' Hikaru croons, patting her head. Ai puts her hands flat over her face, the tips of her fingers against her eyes, like someone in a mime. 'Mama says it's OK to cry if you're sad,' he tells her. She takes a shuddering breath.

'Get up,' Rei says, her voice gentler than the command suggests. Ai stands obediently, her hands still over her eyes. Rei takes hold of her arm and guides her out of the room, leaving Hikaru looking after them. I motion to him, and he climbs into my lap. We sit in silence for a minute, watching the segment I always find strangely touching, where a different child every day puts on their pyjamas to the putting-on-your-pyjamas song, or brushes their teeth to the brushing-your-teeth song. Sometimes they can't quite manage the buttons, and a parent has to come in from off-stage to help them out.

'Was Ai sad about the elephants?' Hikaru asks. 'Sometimes it's sad when you know you can't really be friends with an elephant.'

Before I can answer, Rei has come back into the room. 'You should be careful what you put on that thing,' she says.

'It's not like it's a documentary about abattoirs, Rei.' I know she hates it when people put her name at the end of a sentence. I have been vetting the TV meticulously.

'Maybe it reminded her of Coco.'

'The hamster? Are you serious?!'

Rei shrugs.

'I didn't even know you knew its name,' I tell her.

After that, Ai doesn't come down again for three days. Rei redoes all the sealant in the bathroom, and weeds and prunes the vegetable patch with terrifying aggression, so that the plants get the memo and stand to attention along the newly erected trellis behind them. She fixes the handle on the toilet door and decides that the gravel in the garden needs replenishing. The car is still broken and no matter how long she spends with the hood up and the internet open, she can't figure out what to do with it. So Rei makes friends with Kanagawa-san's daughter, borrows her bicycle, cycles to the gardening centre on the outskirts of town and comes back with two 10kg bags of gravel tied to the back of the bike with string. She then spends a tranquil morning raking it as meticulously as any monk, so we all enjoy it for six minutes before Hikaru runs across it. He has the grace to apologise afterwards, looking guilty, and says it was because Kimchi was chasing a sparrow and had to be caught.

On the fourth morning after the elephants, I hear Rei hissing on the landing as I'm clearing away the plates from breakfast. It isn't entirely clear if she's talking to Ai, or to herself, and I don't go upstairs to find out. 'You are free to spend your life doing exactly what you like,' she says, and I marvel, like always, at how scary Rei is capable of sounding, 'so there is absolutely *no excuse* for the unproductive morbid sulking.' It amazes me that that doesn't get Ai up and about toot sweet. I see that Rei's phone is open on the table, to a search about mental health services in the area. She was sitting outside on the front step earlier, waving her phone in the air – I thought she was just trying to email work. I could have told her there are no services in Ikimura, or in a much wider area outside it, and I know what the trusty Japanese internet will say: if you feel low, perhaps you could take a walk, or maybe a bike ride.

30

Rei

令

Ai is just on the other side of a paper screen, and also a world away. I lean my forehead against the bedroom door.

In the weeks after we knew Mama was gone, something settled on my diaphragm, just under my ribs. If I concentrated on what it felt like, I could almost forget about what caused it. Something too big to fit in my chest, heavy, making it harder to breathe, but almost sympathetic, like a weighted blanket. I carried it carefully, because it was something I could take with me, something that didn't leave me. I can feel it now, as if it's been there all this time, just waiting to make itself known.

Out of the landing window, I can see our route to school, the clock tower, the top of the hospital, even Youta's old house. Our entire childhood world. The only thing that's out of sight is the little beach. None of us saw Nozomi leave that morning, which was normal – once Richard went back to England, she started work at the hospital before we woke up. I wish I could remember something significant about the night before, but there's nothing. I can picture her sticking her head round the door when I was doing my homework, saying she was amazed because she could never get to grips with maths at all, but that could have been any day that year. There must have been some indications, surely, but no more than any other time, ups and downs we were used to and tried to ignore because what else could we do? We were children, something I've reminded myself of every day since she's been gone.

Maybe she went in the middle of the night, or just as dawn was breaking. She loved the early morning. Sometimes I imagine she looked at the world and said goodbye and was glad; sometimes I think she was just chasing delirium, the way you track down another drink when you're already smashed. Mainly, I try not to think about it.

That morning, like always, we bounced out of our futons without putting them away, ate hundred-yen sweet red-bean rolls from the bakery while we walked, even though we knew we were supposed to have toast at home and sit down to eat it. I threw Ai at the kindergarten section of our school before Kiki and I ran for the entrance to secondary, just making it before the bell. We let ourselves in after school, and she was late back, but that was fine, not unusual. I made supper, rice and miso soup and potato salad, exactly the same as she would have, and ran the bath, and put Ai and Kiki in it, and Ai was asleep before Kiki said that Mama was even later than usual.

That was more than a decade ago now. No matter how far I've gone from this house, it's never stopped feeling like yesterday.

31

Kiki

清美

We don't necessarily mean to go to the cove. We say we're going to the firework shop, but just when we'd need to turn left down the stairs to the shopping street, Hikaru's run on ahead of us, shouting at Kimchi, and instead of calling him back, we just follow.

'So I've made Obaachan a doctor's appointment,' Rei is saying. 'Even though it's kind of hard to tell if anything is actually different from usual.'

'As in, she's only as random as she's always been?' I ask.

'Exactly. And she still has plenty of energy for telling us off.'

'She doesn't eat much, though.'

'And she moves really stiffly.'

'Maybe it's just a symptom of being almost a hundred,' I say. 'What did she say about it?'

'The appointment? Obviously I haven't told her,' Rei says. 'I'll tell her just before.'

'Like someone on death row in a country with no human rights?'

'No,' Rei corrects me. 'Like not giving your pet an opportunity to run away when you're taking it to the vet.'

'What if she won't go?'

'Of course she'll go; it would mess with her good-citizen

track record if she didn't. I just want to minimise the time I have to spend listening to her telling me why I've done everything wrong.'

'So . . .' I've avoided asking, like maybe she'll forget she has a job if I just don't talk about it, but the question's out before I can stop it: 'You're still going to be here when she has to go to the appointment? What about work?'

Rei frowns at her flip-flops. 'I told them I needed more time. They were definitely not happy about it, but they're giving me "compassionate leave".' She looks at me. 'Silverman Sayle are. So. Compassionate.' She looks down at her feet again. 'I should be grateful for all the useless new graduates who've come in recently, having meltdowns about boundaries and duvet days.'

'Sorry.'

She shrugs. 'It's just work. No one died. Anyway, I like imagining Llewellyn stabbing his desk with a fork every time I ask for an extension.'

We walk on for a few steps before I ask, 'Do you think she's lonely, living by herself?'

'Obaachan?'

I nod.

Rei thinks for a moment. 'I don't know,' she says. 'You can have everything the way you want it, by yourself.' Rei should know.

We've come to the turning off the road into the forest and I call to Hikaru, ahead of us.

'Should we wait for Ai?' I ask.

Rei shakes her head. 'She won't mind.'

The glare of the sun on the road is blinding, but within a few steps we're in heavy greenery, the light dappled and murky, and then making our way down a series of wooden staircases. The sounds are muted here, and even Hikaru is quiet, holding my hand tightly. Just as it feels like we're going to be walking downwards into forest forever, we turn a corner and the beach appears, a crescent of white sand scattered at first with pine needles, then pristine all the way to the turquoise water. The beach is loud. Gulls are hovering over the water's edge, watching for delicacies I can't see, swooping down without warning and shrieking in satisfaction. The waves rolling on to the sand, sinking in an effervescence of bubbles only to be slapped by another onslaught of water, give the impression that the sea is entertaining itself, that without the interference of human beings, the sea, the sand, the birds have been having a whale of a time. Hikaru kicks off his shoes with an exclamation of triumph and runs towards the breaking waves.

'Remember how much Mama used to swear?' I say to Rei. She nods, once, but her face doesn't move.

Rei doesn't like to talk about her. I wouldn't, either, if I believed what Rei believes. She looks out to the sea like a statue. I know what she's thinking, what she's always thinking, that she'll never say. Even when Ai is well, her fear is that Ai will go the same way she thinks Mama went. It's like Rei lives in a room with this giant black hole in the middle of it that she can't look at, or talk about.

I have a list, in my head, of things to remember about Mama. Not 'to remember' like a to-do list, or like I'm in danger of forgetting, but something to feel my way back with, when she seems out of reach. Like now, maybe, with Hikaru jumping at the edge of the water and Rei staring at the sea with her mouth in a straight line.

That she swore, all the time. This is a serious task, in Japanese, requiring ingenuity and imagination, since the vocabulary is jaw-clenchingly polite. Mama swore with the vigour and energy most people would reserve for going to war.

That she was happiest when she had a pen or a pencil in her hand and was drawing. Rei and I used to sit down to paint much more often than it interested us, just to see what she would do. She'd paint brightly coloured scenes full of funny animals, cartoons of us, flip-book pictures in the corners of books. She'd make things, too, all the time – our stuffed toys had embroidered waistcoats and crocheted hats, perfect down to the buttons she'd make from minute shells, so small even our little children's fingers couldn't work them. Rei called me once, from the Victoria and Albert Museum in London, and told me in a weird voice that she'd just been to see some old queen's doll's house collection. Not a single object, she said, was as beautiful as the things our mother used to make us out of old milk cartons and glue. Neither of us said anything for a second after that, and then Rei hung up.

When Mama died, I was only just beginning to realise how slight she was. I'd always thought of her as a giant when I was living my life around her knees, but by eleven I was only half a head shorter than her. She wore ancient smocks and strangely shaped trousers she'd patched together from old kimonos, her delicate wrists poking out of holey old jumpers, and she was so slender it looked like she meant it, a fashion statement. I remember snuggling up next to her while she was reading, stroking the inside of her arm like a comfort blanket, how soft it was.

That she had an eleven between her eyebrows to match Rei's, but when she smiled it disappeared and you could see how pretty she was, how she could still look like a young girl. The eleven made her look fierce, when really it was just from frowning with concentration, at books, recipes, the radio, at us, looking into our faces as if she were trying to read us. She seemed unapproachable, a little frightening if you didn't know her, and I liked it that way because it made her more of our secret. Only we knew how quick she could be to laugh. Her voice could be biting, almost accusing, so that when my friends heard her calling us in to eat they sat up a little straighter, their eyes widening with pity, even though the bellow didn't mean anything except that she was distracted, and if I went in she would smile and tell me to sit down quickly. The bellow was good, because it meant she was here with us, not like when she went quiet and you looked in her eyes and she just wasn't there.

She always came back, though, just like Ai will. You can't imagine it'll be winter forever.

'Do you think the tide's coming in, or going out?' Rei says suddenly.

'Hard to say.'

'We didn't learn about King Cnut, did we?'

'What?'

'King Cnut. I heard about him in England – this king who thought he could control the tides.' She puts her hands straight up in front of her like she's casting a spell.

'I don't think he was on the Japanese syllabus.'

'No.' Rei breathes out, dropping her hands to her sides.

We stay ten minutes, long enough to stand still for a short while, to walk to the end of the cove and walk back again, then straight out into the forest without discussion. Rei gives Hikaru five hundred yen as soon as we're back on the road, and lifts him up on to her shoulders, since she's strong as an ox on account of all the expensive gym-bunnying she does in London. They start up an animated conversation about the various advantages of spending it on a rubber ball, sparklers or a special eraser, and both agree that the main problem with the special eraser is that you could never actually use it.

The firework shop is tiny, barely lit, the dark wood door rattling like a terrible portent every time you open it – the same, Mama used to tell us, as it was when she was small, with the same family running it. The smell of wood mixes with scented erasers and gunpowder, an intoxicating combination. 'It's like experiencing a break in the space–time continuum,' Rei whispers reverently, sliding a glass panel across one of the square sections in the display case table in front of us and fingering an ornately painted tin box the length of her thumb. Bouncy balls shot through with glitter twinkle enticingly next to spinning tops, colour-changing pens, dioramas in matchboxes, and, behind the counter, a treasure trove of sparklers and fireworks imported from China, the coloured tissue and silver paper glistening in the gloom. Hikaru has a minor and completely understandable meltdown when faced with the choice between the ramen-shaped eraser and the one that smells of Calpis and comes in its own bottle-shaped case. The man behind the counter gazes politely at the ceiling.

'This stuff is definitely toxic,' Rei says when we eventually leave the shop, examining the tiny silver tube of semi-permanent bubble mix with its attached pink straw. Like so many other things in the shop, it's been carefully torn from a strip of identical little tubes and straws in their cardboard blister packs, the boy in the cap, a bubble obscuring his face, unchanged since we were children. The bubble set is ostensibly a present for Ai, since she loved them when she was small, and although Rei hasn't opened it, I can smell the heady solvent tang of the paste, feel the tackiness of those bubbles on my hands.

'And carcinogenic,' I agree.

'And totally non-recyclable and everything else,' Rei says.

'Are there no straightforward joys left?'

'None.'

'I reckon Ai'll be really pleased about this,' Rei says. 'She's doing so much better.' She makes this pronouncement too often. I wonder if it's what she's telling herself, or what she thinks I need to hear, a rousing lie to cheer us both on. We walk for a moment in silence.

'Did I tell you about this time when Hikaru was little,' I

ask her, 'and he randomly decided that he would only sleep if he was holding my earlobe? It was so inconvenient I cannot describe.'

Rei makes a non-committal noise and tugs on Hikaru's earlobe.

'I was so worried he was going to sleep like that forever,' I add. 'And then after, like, two weeks, he just stopped doing it.'

Rei stops walking and looks at me. 'Kiki,' she says crossly, 'I'm not a character in an HBO drama who can only operate in allegories.'

When we get back, Ai is still upstairs. I start to open my mouth to tell Rei about the period when Hikaru would only eat egg tofu and literally nothing else and I was tearing my hair out, but then think better of it.

The sound of the front door rattling open interrupts our non-conversation, and a moment later Obaachan appears at the kitchen door holding a bowl. 'Give this to Ai,' she says, the way you might order a slave to take an enemy soldier's head on a plate to his leader. She plonks it on the kitchen counter and departs abruptly.

Rei lifts the cling film to see what it is. 'It's hijiki,' she says. Sweet, loamy seaweed with fried soybean curd and edamame beans – Ai's favourite food when she was small.

Rei tuts. It's probably one of the most Japanese things about her, how she can make single noises convey so many contrasting emotions at once.

Later that evening, I go outside to take the rubbish to the bins at the end of the road. It's dusk, and lights are coming on in the houses along the street, steam and the smells of dinner wafting out of air vents and windows. I think about how when I get back to our house, Rei will be there, and I'm happy.

32

Ai

愛

I can't sleep and I feel like I'm being crushed, like the air has become really heavy, so I get up, because maybe it will feel better when I'm upright. Then I see the ladder at the end of the corridor. The loft has one window, and I slide open the paper shutter. The town below looks peaceful. For a moment, the inside of my head is quiet, too. It's like waking up after it's snowed in the night, or everyone in your house is dead.

I can't shake the feeling I've forgotten something. And then without warning it starts again, everything wrong and the ground opening up, the sound of all those voices after the quiet. It feels like something is laughing at me, so stupid to think it was gone.

It's my mind, right? Who's in charge? I don't know, but it isn't me.

I don't want anyone to know me this way. Shame runs hot up and down my skin. Nobody normal would do what I did. No wonder everyone's so horrified, so disgusted.

I try to think of all the good things in my life. There are so many of them, I know. It's like trying to hear someone talking in the roar of a train coming towards you.

I wish I could disappear without a fuss, make it so I was never here at all. If our mother taught us anything, though, it's that that doesn't work. You don't disappear; it's the exact opposite. You leave a void where you used to be that takes up a hundred times as much space as you ever did alive.

I slide open the glass, then the wooden slatted shutter. Fresh air on my face, those night-time sounds. I think about how the trees I can see, and the sea, and the clouds, don't care about me in any way at all, and it's such a relief.

33
Rei

令

In the instant I found out my mother was dead, a voice said in my head, very calmly, like a grown-up, like it was a matter of fact and just too bad, Well, that's that, then. Nothing will be all right ever again.

And then a moment later it was a wall of water, that nothing would be all right ever again, and everything breaking into a million pieces. But Ai was there, not really understanding, and wanting me to read her *Kon to Aki* about the little girl and her stuffed dog, so there was no choice. It had to be matter-of-fact and calm, nothing will be all right ever again, and on with the day.

Waking is being tipped out of a tunnel, dreaming of water, my mother, Ai as a child, picture books. Our window is wide open, enticing in the hope of a breeze, the sound of the crickets, a fat, relieved vibration. Lulled by the rhythmic percussion, my heart rate slowing, I almost close my eyes again, but then I see that Ai's futon is empty.

I scrabble for my glasses next to the pillow, press them to my face. Kiki and Hikaru sleep on.

In the dark, the house has an urgency, something it's been wanting to say but has to hide in daylight hours. If I let it, the shadows of the corridor, the corner I turn to descend the stairs, would scare me just as much as when I was Hikaru's age, as if I haven't grown up at all. I have the foolish thought that what I want is Sath here next to me, so I could hold his hand. Carefully, with the concentration it deserves, I fold up the corners of my mind the way you fold a bamboo leaf around a rice cake. It's just a house, and the people who used to live here are not ghosts.

Downstairs, only the mosquito net screen is pulled across the engawa. Under my feet, the warm grain of the tatami turns to the polished cold of the wood. I slide the screen across, and in the garden, the moss over the rocks seems to glow, eerie and unearthly. Leaves in the undergrowth catch the moonlight and glint like eyes. The star-shaped maple leaves rustle, a soft sigh. I step down on to the gravel, not admitting to the goosebumps that snake their way up my leg. The ginkgo tree slashes shadows across the ground and it's as I turn to look up at it, back towards the house, that I see her.

Ai is crouched on the sloping roof of the house, a sharp black silhouette against the moonlit sky. I remember Kiki saying she was like an egg cracked on the ground.

I open my mouth to call up to her, perched like a gargoyle, the manifestation of everything in my head I try never to look at. The sound that makes its way out is a rasp. She hasn't seen me, and I run back into the house, up the stairs, down the corridor, up the ladder, its rungs smooth with age, touching wood with every fumbling step upwards.

Ai doesn't turn her head as mine emerges from the window. She's only a foot or so below me, just out of my reach. In the half-light, in her jinbei pyjamas, she looks like a little girl.

'Ai-chan?' I whisper, like maybe she's still in bed and I'm just checking she's awake. I don't want to startle her. It's only then that she turns to me, and I think I've seen this before, imagined it exactly, but I don't know if it was her out there, or myself.

Ai looks at me like I'm someone who's distracted her from something important, like she doesn't know what I'm doing there. She doesn't look like herself: her eyebrows, the muscles around her nose, the ones that pull the sides of her mouth down, they've all contorted themselves into angles that don't make sense, that don't mirror what she's like in real life.

'Onechan,' she says, dragging the word for big sister out the way she did when she was little, when she'd had a nightmare and her eyes didn't see anything except the monsters and she was still whimpering from sleep.

'It's OK,' I tell her automatically, in the same soothing voice I used back then, even though I'm not sure it is, actually. 'What are you doing up here?' I would prefer not to venture out of the window, high above the ground, the ceramic tiles skating-smooth, but I don't know what the other option is. As I start to put my weight on the roof, to push myself up and out, my glasses slide down my nose. At the same moment, a tile a few centimetres down dislodges and goes skittering down. It shoots straight past Ai and shatters on the paving.

Ai makes no indication that she's heard.

'Ai-chan,' I say again, my voice too loud in the silence that follows the crash, 'the tiles are so slippery. Why don't you come back inside?' I push my glasses back on to my face.

'I can't sleep,' she says.

'That's OK,' I tell her. It seems like the only thing I can say now. It's OK, everything is OK. I expect something to spill out in my tone, how hard I have to try not to start screaming, but my treacherous voice is calm. 'If you come back inside, I'll sit with you.'

166

She doesn't say anything, staring out at the night like she's watching a horror film unfold.

'You know it doesn't matter what those idiots think,' I offer. Every word is a shot in the dark, a line thrown into a bottomless well. 'Everyone will have forgotten by the end of the summer, Ai.'

'Rei,' she says, and it comes out in a rush, a confession. 'Rei, I didn't mean to.' My arm reaches out towards her, pathetically short. 'I didn't mean to make everything so difficult.'

'It doesn't matter, Ai-chan.' She gives the tiniest movement, a little sigh, and the change in the angle of her head shows up the patch where it's been shaved, tufts standing up from her scalp like the nail-scissor haircuts we used to give our Licca dolls. I remember the concentration on her small round face as she did it, the pride when she showed me her handiwork. 'It's not your fault.'

It seems like an age that she says nothing. Long enough that maybe we're just going to stay up here on this roof forever, in a state of suspended animation.

'I don't know why I slept with Ichiro. Everything in my head gets in . . . such a mess.'

'Who cares about Ichiro, Ai. Literally nobody.'

I can feel something like a smile inside her. 'Literally everybody.'

'Well,' I say, and my heart soars, because she almost smiled, 'nobody who matters.'

'Rei.' She turns her head to face me. 'Why do I have to be like this?'

'I wouldn't change you,' I tell her. I've never meant anything more.

'Somebody just goes inside my head and turns out the light.'

'I know.' And I do, so well.

She puts her head down on her arms. 'What am I going to do?'

It's always the question. Sometimes you're asking it like you're looking for an answer, and sometimes it's just wondering, watching yourself like a total mystery. 'You mean, for work?' I say eventually, knowing that she doesn't, really. 'You can literally do anything, Ai. You're, like, ten. You can pick anything you want in the world and start from the beginning.' She doesn't move. 'Or just don't do anything. Me and you and Kiki can start a commune. We'll go swimming every day and make clothes out of seaweed.' I can see her relax a little, her shoulders moving down a millimetre. 'Any chance we could move this careers chat inside?'

She doesn't say anything for a while. Then, 'I'm sorry you had to be on TV,' she says eventually, still talking into her arms.

'It was a thrill,' I say. 'Come back inside.'

Ai lifts her head, staring out past the sleeping houses to the sea, black as pitch against a still, charcoal sky. Then she nods once and turns towards me.

'Careful,' I order.

As soon as I have her hand in mine, I grip it like a vice. Feeling it there, solid, alive, it's all I can do not to smack her in the face. She steps up gingerly, and I'm holding my breath until she's clambered back over the windowsill, all elbows and sharp shoulders. I don't let go of her hand and we stand there facing each other like a poster for a bad musical. Her expression is closed, hard to read, and she isn't looking at me. Frustration makes me grab her other arm, too forcefully, and I'm glad when she flinches.

'What the actual fuck, Ai. The roof?' My whole body feels

taut, painful, like everything inside it might burst out. 'If you need to take a moment, just sit in the fucking garden.'

As if I'd pressed a button, two lines of tears roll down her cheeks. My remorse is instantaneous. She scans my face, searching it. And then I can see her there, for the first time since I've been here. 'OK,' she says, and her voice is so sad. 'I'm sorry, Rei.'

'You don't have to be sorry,' I tell her. 'Just keep going. Just do that.'

34

Kiki

清美

In the middle of the night, something connects cleanly with my nose and I'm jerked into consciousness. Hikaru, blissfully unaware of his nocturnal violence, retracts his hand and folds it under one cheek, a dreaming cherub. Behind him, I see that Rei is gone.

I listen for her; for the sound of a step on the stair, a flush, insomniac TV. The house is quiet. Moving slowly enough that neither Hikaru's breathing nor Ai's next to him changes its slow, steady rising and falling, I creep from the room.

Downstairs, everything is silent. The doors to the garden have been left open like always and the air is heavy with the sweet tobacco scent of jasmine. In the moonlight, the lichen is a cascade of soft fringing and glitter, an enchanted carpet. Rei is nowhere.

Sliding open the front door and stepping out, I almost trip over Chibi. He gives me a long, filthy look, his tail lashing from side to side as if he's at the absolute limit of what he can be expected to put up with. As I close the door carefully behind me, he rushes off the step and lies proprietorially across the tarmac of the road.

'What are you doing, you crazy animal?' I ask him. 'Where's Rei?'

He tips his head back, ignoring the question, and I start off down the road. The branches of the weeping willow on the other side of the street, that we don't walk under on account of the ghosts, ripple like a greeting. The one lamp on our street casts a single pool of light, its sleepy beam forming a perfect triangle where moths dance. I take the first turning off to the right, through the stone torii gate, up the road that coils around the side of the hill.

The road is steep but smoothly tarmacked for the first hundred metres, then it ducks under another huge torii gate, vermillion wood darkened to blood red in the dark, shaped like the kanji for 'heaven' and festooned with geometric white shide streamers, glowing in the night. The tarmac ends neatly under the gate, giving way to a path of rectangular stones. I follow it to the third torii and the viewing spot just beyond, a small flat patch on the edge of the hill, fenced with imitation log balustrades. The viewing spot houses a vending machine, nestling incongruously against the greenery, glowing like some alien spacecraft. *Blend is beautiful* it declares on the side. There's a bench next to it, with two red seat cushions. I can see a plume of smoke snaking up from the other side of the machine.

Rei is sitting on the mossy ground, leaning against the machine, staring out at the dark sea. Her hair sticks up at the back and her glasses, which she never wears in the daytime, have slid down low on her nose, making her look like a child caught smoking.

'This is a terrible cliché,' I say, looking down at her.

She doesn't look up. 'No, it's not,' she says. 'I'm not a teenager at a beach party and you're not the person I've been secretly hoping will notice me all season.'

'Crushing,' I tell her. 'Why aren't you at least sitting on the bench?'

'The ground is softer,' she says, taking another long drag of her cigarette. 'And there's no danger of dog piss, unlike in London.'

'You know smoking kills, right?'

'I don't smoke,' she says without irony, reaching up to tap her ash out into the metal ashtray planted on a stick next to the machine. Her eyes are red.

'And menthol cigarettes are the worst. I heard they turn your lungs into shards of glass or something.'

She offers me one. 'Children are the pits, aren't they?' she says, like it's something we've been talking about.

'So many awful traits to choose from,' I agree, taking a cigarette and the lighter and sliding down next to her. 'Are we talking about any particular one?'

'They lull you into a false sense of security by being all round-cheeked and cute.' She takes another drag. 'Then they become teenage nightmares who ruin your life.' She doesn't even have the grace to give any indication that she doesn't mean me. 'And *then*, when you think they've finally become grown-ups and maybe they can look after themselves, it turns out that, actually, that's the moment when you can see the results of your years and years of misguided effort, and they've turned into tragic emotional disasters with zero sense of self-preservation and it's all your fault.' She goes to stub out her cigarette, changes her mind and lights another one off its still-burning end.

'Like a cake that takes forever to cook, and then doesn't rise,' I say, after a beat. And then, 'Tragic emotional disaster might be a bit harsh.'

'I just don't want her to be another victim,' Rei says eventually.

'Of what?'

'The catastrophe of the Takanawa personality.'

'Oh my god, Rei. Do you say things this rude to everybody?'

She sighs, and pushes her glasses back up her nose with the back of her hand. The lit cigarette still dangling from her mouth, she presses the nail of her forefinger into the stub of her last one, making a perfect cross.

'Your fingers are going to smell so gross,' I tell her.

Rei places the stub carefully on the ground, nudging it until it aligns perfectly with something only she can see. 'I don't know how to fix anything,' she says.

I put my hand on hers. After a second, she turns her palm up to knot her fingers through mine. We smoke for a while in silence, listening to the murmur of the crickets. I can feel her fingers twitching, never still.

Eventually, I say, 'You are such a megalomaniac. Why would you be able to fix anything?'

She laughs, a catch in her throat, but doesn't reply.

'You know that old anmitsu place on the corner past Nakamura-san's house?' I say after a while. 'The one that's been closed for ages?'

'Next to the house with the yappy dog?'

'Yeah, that one. It's reopened – apparently some dude who was trying to run a bar in Osaka gave up and has come to dedicate his life to sweet beans instead.'

'How do you know?'

'Kanagawa-san's daughter told me. I went past it yesterday, and the menu's exactly the same as it used to be.'

'Do they have zenzai?'

I nod. 'And kanten. You know there are people in the world who think a dessert culture based exclusively on seaweed and beans isn't the way forward?'

She snorts. 'Fools,' she says, and squeezes my hand so hard.

173

I don't know what time it is. Late enough to be almost early. The sky is still black, but at its bottom edge, along the stoic straight line of the horizon, it's beginning to look like a shadow lifting, like a trick of your eyes. Rei and I sit there, inhaling the teenage menthol tang, waiting for the light.

35

Ai

I've been sleeping like a baby. Like Hikaru used to when he was first born, in short snatches with a lot of crying in between. It isn't really sleep; it's waiting just underneath the surface, but that's a lot better than it was.

I'm afraid to get out of bed because I'm afraid to break the spell. Maybe if I don't draw attention to myself, pretend I'm looking the other way, sleep might stick around a bit longer, settle a bit more comfortably.

If I can't sleep, I'm stuck being me, in my head, without a break. That was the best thing about the music: that I wasn't me any more, just another instrument.

When I was small I was so afraid of living forever. It was the Bible in our piano teacher's house that gave me the idea – eternal life, never stopping, not ever – and I used to dig my fingers into my palms until they bled, shivers running from the soles of my feet to the top of my head so that my hair felt like it had been shocked.

Like the fear thought it was funny.

I wish I could climb out of my skin.

If I wasn't me, though, maybe Rei wouldn't be herself, or Kiki, or Hikaru. That isn't good to think about.

I just have to stay here and wait. Maybe if I'm still, stay under this cover not moving, life will creep back up on me and I won't scare it away. Just wait.

36

There's a tune in my head the week after I meet Rei on the roof. I think it's a Kabuki tune. The last two bars of the bridge, maybe. It feels like I've been crawling through undergrowth for a long time, and now there's a clearing, and the sound of crockery clinking, and conversation, and the smell of coffee. I suddenly remember that there'll always be coffee, that whatever happens, somewhere in the world people will be waking up to that hopeful smell, and another day. That seems like a kind of magic.

It was my idea to call us Kabuki. That thought comes into my head, and I pull away from it quickly, because thinking about Kabuki is like running my fingers along broken glass. Only it isn't, now; more like pushing on a bruise. I think again about it, about Kabuki, carefully. Sakamoto tried to tell me what the band should be called – 'Ai no Kaze,' he said. He wrote it as *Wind of Love*. I didn't mean to embarrass him – I thought he'd realised the other way of writing it – and I felt bad when I pointed out the other kanji in a big meeting. The other kanji makes it read *Ai's Headcold*. To be fair to Sakamoto, names don't seem to make a difference to how successful you are – we could be called *Funky Monkey Babys* or *BUMP OF CHICKEN*. *BUMP OF CHICKEN* is actually a translation of 'uprising of the cowards'. Don't you love that? I guess if you speak English it's easy to pull it apart, but really then you're missing the point – if nobody knows what it means, it's just beautiful sounds. I thought about having an Italian name or something, on that basis, but we went with *Kabuki* in the end, for its drama, and because I liked the way it said the band wasn't really us. We were just the players in something bigger, that was already there.

For a long time, trying to think has felt like trying to see the horizon when someone is in your face. When they're gone, you can just have a thought, that leads on to the next thing, and then you remember something, and you wonder something, and the world is so big, and so interesting.

When I remember the old man, it feels like something clearing, like a fog is lifting. I don't know why he comes into my head, the old man I saw the night I left Ichiro in the love hotel. Customers were coming out of bars and I could see the silhouettes of karaoke singers in windows ten storeys up. I wasn't even sure where I was, another neighbourhood with as much going on as an average-sized town. All those places that get swallowed into the sprawl of Tokyo. It was starting to rain, a cool mist that gave me goosebumps. I was at the top of a hill and when I looked down, I could map out my route by the skyscrapers. First I recognised one, and then another and another, lit up against the starless night sky like city constellations I could navigate by. I started to walk, and soon I was wet to the skin.

When I was waiting at a traffic light, an old man sidestepped up to me and held his umbrella over my head. The kanji for umbrella is my favourite one, 傘, literally a picture of a huge cosy umbrella sheltering all those people (人). The old man kept it there as we crossed, and he walked away before I could bow 'thank you'. He stared straight ahead the whole time. I wondered what night-shift job he must have to be walking around so neatly dressed so late.

I kept walking, and soon all I could see through the downpour was a scribble of neon on black. Sky-cars went sliding past, their lights sparkling in the rain like carriages in a psychedelic wonderland.

Thinking about the old man and the umbrella gets me up and down the stairs. I sit on the bottom step for a long time, outside the kitchen, listening to a conversation between Hikaru and Kiki.

'Mama, why aren't children in charge of anything?'

'Like what?'

'Like bus drivers are grown-ups. And the man in the firework shop. And the teachers at kindergarten.'

'Well . . . Maybe it's important for children to have enough time to play?'

'I think Kohei should be the teacher.'

'Why's that?'

'He can roll his eyes real good. Osono-sensei can't do that.'

It feels like I've been sitting in the dark by myself for a long time, me and the monsters in my head, but now somebody's opened the door a crack. I don't want to go too near, in case it closes again, but I can hear sounds on the other side, and imagine what it would feel like to step through it.

37

Kiki

清美

A few days after Rei and I enjoy our early-hours shrine hangout, Ai comes to the table at dinner. She doesn't say a lot, but she kisses Hikaru when he climbs into her lap. Rei and I say nothing, just try to pile extra food on to her plate and make life in the real world seem like the absolute best. It occurs to me that it's lucky Ai is a small half-Japanese girl and doesn't naturally stink. I'm not sure she's actually washed the whole time we've been here, and she smells of nothing, like if you left her alone for long enough she would just petrify into a small apologetic ball, or disappear altogether. Poor thing, on the one hand, having such a tenuous link to the world. On the other, for those of us who have to live with her, thank god she's not some expansive Western male with expressive sweat-ducts.

It's the day after that when Rei decides we should make our own kare-pan. Ai is curled up on the engawa like a cat, looking at one of the English-language interiors magazines Rei buys every time she goes through an airport, and the thrill of it is making Rei jittery. 'It's literally the perfect reading material,' she's whispered to me at least four times this morning. I think it's the proudest I've ever seen her.

Rei hasn't been sleeping much, I don't think – she's always up by the time I wake up, even though Hikaru considers a 6am start a waste of a good morning, and her eyes have shadows underneath. Sleep deprivation always brings out her ambitious side. I watch as she helps Hikaru slice onions for the curry, the wooden stool he's standing on the one that Mama used to use to reach the higher shelves in the kitchen, proving how much taller we are now than she was. Obaachan is sitting at the kitchen table with one of her white smocks over her clothes – this is her absolute favourite kind of activity, where she can sit in the middle of the hubbub and criticise us at every stage, preferably telling us what we've done wrong just after we've finished doing it. I notice Rei breathing deeply with her eyes closed on more than one occasion.

For the first hour or so, everyone's up for it. Once the curry's cooking on the stove, Rei helps Hikaru weigh out all the ingredients for the bread and then knead it with his hands, and Hikaru, who definitely would have given up and wandered off if it were me trying to help him, concentrates with an expression that makes him look her twin. I'm on washing-up duty, which gives me plenty of opportunity to stand by the sink holding a sponge and watching Rei and Hikaru together. Obviously you can't wish your relatives into breeding programmes just to provide your offspring with company, but I find myself thinking how nice it would be if Rei had a kid. Or three, and maybe got back with Sath, then Hikaru's family would be bigger, and everything would be marvellous. As it is, the closest relatives Hikaru has in age are Gina and Richard's children – uncles, not much older than him, which is quite a thought.

Rei thinks I don't know that she goes to see Richard sometimes. I haven't seen him since the last time he summoned us to England, like we were subjects from the other side of his empire. I don't remember him living here at all, and I don't really get anything from him as an adult – not anything good, anyway. He referred to the time he lived here as his 'Japanese

181

adventure' and once showed me a picture he had of Rei and me, when I was just born – I'm a blob on a blanket, and Rei is standing to attention in a polka-dot skirt that shows her round knees, looking at the camera like she's not sure if the person who's holding it wants her to smile or not. That's the thing that makes me want to actually murder him – that he left Rei, so small and trying so hard.

'How many kids do you reckon Richard has now?' I ask, pretending.

'I think two?' she says, guiding Hikaru's hand as they slice the bread dough into geometrically perfect diamonds.

'It's weird, right, that we have these fully foreign brothers we've never met,' I say, testing her.

'Probably blond,' she agrees, even though I know she knows. 'Like you,' she tells Hikaru, squeezing his cheeks so that his mouth pushes out into a fish pout. It disturbs me to think that he might look more like Richard's other children than he looks like me, with my dark straight hair and tanned skin. Also, that they can speak to Rei in English, and Hikaru can't.

'I don't want them in our team,' I whisper.

'Don't worry,' she whispers back. 'They will never, ever, come here.' She washes Hikaru's hands under the tap and dries them on the tea towel, kissing his palm when she's finished.

'Are you using a tea towel to dry his hands?' Obaachan asks. 'Don't you have a hand towel?' She mutters a colourful Japanese phrase, and Hikaru looks distinctly interested. I think, not for the first time, that it's not like Mama's character traits came out of the blue, is it. Or Rei's, come to think of it.

I wonder if Mama ever thought about not marrying Richard, doing it by herself instead. I hope she was happy when she found out she was pregnant. People assume that my pregnancy was a horrendous mistake and I wept all the way through like some knocked-up Lady Godiva, but the truth is, while I obviously didn't do it on purpose, it felt like winning the lottery. I hope Mama felt like that. While Rei was off over-achieving in England, sending photographs of herself with groups of blonde eggs outside ancient buildings, I wandered out of school and upped the hours on what was meant to be my summer job, working as a waitress in Tokyo, not even at a cocktail bar but a noodle one, where the highlight of my day was arranging pickles in small ceramic bowls. The nightlife was great, the men were fantastic, not living next door to my great-grandmother's opinions was a dream come true, but I'd just reached the stage where I was beginning to feel very afraid of turning into my boss, a truly lovely bloke who worked ninety-hour weeks and had three days off a month that he used to play pachinko. It is not acceptable to look at someone else's life and think, please god don't let me end up like that, especially if you don't even have an alternative suggestion, so every time I did, I had another drink to block out the thought. Thank god for getting pregnant. Just when I didn't have a clue what to do, an invitation to a life filled with purpose and company. Nothing has ever felt like more of a gift from on high.

'Now we have to wrap the curry in the bread parcels,' Rei tells Hikaru. 'Which is even less easy than it sounds. You ready?'

He nods seriously. In the light slanting in from the kitchen window, his hair glints gold where it curls around his ears.

I wonder what Hikaru's father's doing at this exact moment, a fun thought experiment I run once in a while. It isn't that easy to visualise, since I'm not actually sure which country he's in. When I found out I was pregnant, I promised myself I'd tell him about the baby, as soon as I knew who he was. Not that I particularly wanted to, and I definitely didn't expect anything from him – how much of a fool would you have to be, to set yourself up for that disappointment all over again? – but I wanted to be sure I'd ticked all the boxes and technically done the right thing. Useless as Richard may have been, it would be unfair to judge all spunk donors by his non-existent standards.

Two of the contenders were Japanese, and traceable; the Finn was the one-night stand of dreams, a nine-hour fantasy of a different life. He was a blue-eyed engineer from Helsinki, making a brief stop in Tokyo for some kind of meeting; he repeated his name three times at the bar and I never quite got it, so I just smiled and pretended I had. Possibly Mikael. Or Niko. I think there was a saint involved. Johannes, maybe. Paul? When I left his hotel room in the morning, he smiled so sweetly, putting the pillow over his head like he was embarrassed. Adorable, like a bunny. Would have driven me nuts in the long term. I'm pretty sure he said his flight out was that same day – he was going back to Finland, or possibly to America. Even with the best of intentions and the most Herculean effort, I'm not sure it would be possible to track down a nameless blond man somewhere in either Finland or America.

So when Hikaru was born, when he unfurled himself on my stomach like a tiny drunk, I was already laughing when I scooped him up to hold him for the very first time. His eyes were blue-grey, the colour of the sea on a rainy day, which meant his father must be the Finn, and Hikaru was all mine. It felt like a cosmic rebalance was taking place. We're sorry we killed off your mother early doors, but here is one fatherless son, perfectly formed.

Rei, who has been coating her bread-and-curry parcels in flour, then egg, then breadcrumbs, has grown pink with effort and frustration. 'Who the hell's idea was this?' she asks in disgust, holding up her hands, covered in dough and bread-crumbs. She blows upwards with her bottom lip in an attempt to clear her hair from her face and tuts as it falls back down over her eyes.

I go to push the hair back from Rei's face, just as Obaachan gets up and sees some of the leftover curry still in the saucepan. 'Look at your carrot chunks!' she exclaims in horror, practically crossing herself. 'They're enormous! How are you ever going to make anyone a wife with dishes like that?'

'I don't want to be a wife,' Rei says clearly. 'And there is nothing wrong with the carrots.'

Obaachan puts the saucepan down, tutting to herself.

'Japanese cooking is clearly just a plot for female subjugation,' Rei grumbles under her breath. 'Nobody can be applying for a job or thinking about the subtleties of power in the workplace if they have to make a curry from scratch, bake bread that requires three separate risings and then deep-fry something every time someone wants a snack.'

'I can't hear you, Rei!' Obaachan admonishes. 'Speak properly!'

Luckily, at that moment there's a knock at the door, which is weird, because everyone usually just lets themselves in. Rei lets out a long huff as I wipe my hands on my apron.

'Yes?' I call as I step under the noren.

The door rattles open. A man about my age is standing there, which is a surprise in itself. His face is relaxing to look at – his features even and uncomplicated, like he would be easy to draw as a manga, a series of smooth lines. Then he smiles at me, and the man is replaced with a boy I knew so well.

'Kiki,' Youta says, in a voice that's unexpectedly deep. I suddenly remember that he was the first person ever to kiss me, by the vending machine at the end of the road. He tasted of grape bubblegum.

Hikaru comes running into the corridor, his hands still dripping water from where Rei tried to rinse them, and slides to a stop just before he goes crashing over the edge of the genkan.

'You're not a delivery man,' he says matter-of-factly to Youta.

'No, I'm not,' Youta says, his eyes creasing. 'I'm sorry. Were you expecting something?'

'You don't have to be sorry,' Hikaru tells him. 'It's just if there's a man at the door, it's usually always a delivery man.'

I don't know why I feel my blush deepening. 'Hikaru, introduce yourself properly,' I admonish. 'This is Youta, our friend from when we were little.' Obediently, trained by school, Hikaru puts his hands and feet together and bows. 'It's nice to meet you,' he says.

'Youta, this is Hikaru.' My son, I don't say, because I figure it's obvious, and because saying that makes me feel like a big old fake, somehow.

Youta bows back without fanfare or irony. 'I hope our relationship going forward goes well,' he says to Hikaru, one of many official statements of introduction.

Standing up straight, he smiles at me. 'Rei said your car wasn't working,' he says. 'I was passing by, so I thought I'd come and take a look.'

Rei steps out of the kitchen, looking the way she always looks, namely flawless. Her irritation at the kare-pan has given her a rosy flush which softens her glossiness and makes her look perky and approachable. I notice that her feet are perfectly pedicured, while my toenails are chipped electric blue, the hundred-yen shop's finest, selected and applied by Hikaru.

'Thank you!' she cries, seeing Youta and stepping straight down into the genkan and her flip-flops. 'This is so kind of you. I tried everything I could – which isn't much, to be fair – but I can't make it work. Do you know a lot about cars?'

Youta laughs. 'Not all that much. But hopefully enough. I helped out at the mechanic's in Akaishi for a bit.'

'Well, don't do yourself down, then,' Rei says briskly, and it lifts my heart that my beautiful sister talks to him like a stern old nun. 'I'll show you where it is.'

They go clattering out the door. Hikaru puts his arms around my waist and pulls my T-shirt over his head, each of his feet on one of mine.

'You're a big fat alien now, Mama,' he tells me, and blows a raspberry on my stomach. I walk him back to the kitchen step by step, resisting the urge to sit him down and give him a lecture about how sexy and cool I used to be before he was born.

'Who was it?' Obaachan wants to know. She's sitting at the kitchen table cracking the stones of old salted plums with a nutcracker, to get at the bitter kernel inside.

'Youta,' I say, not expecting her to remember him.

'The one who used to follow you around like a dog?'

'Not like a *dog*, Obaachan.'

'I remember his mother. She was one of those women who didn't understand that your job as a parent is not to make your children like you.'

I'm interested to see where this is going, and make a mental note to discuss with Rei later. 'Isn't it?'

'Of course not! You have to tell them all the things they're doing wrong so they can fix them. How else are they meant to know? Nobody else is going to tell them, are they?'

While I'm thinking about this, she pushes the small bowl of kernels towards me. 'Eat these. They're good for you.' She takes one and chews it slowly. 'Youta's mother was a terrible cook,' she adds. 'And his father didn't work hard enough.'

'How do you know that? Did you ever actually taste his mother's cooking?' Youta's father was, probably still is, a good-humoured family man; his mother was busy and kind and always gave us good snacks – her cooking left no impression on me at all. I'm offended on behalf of them both. Obaachan's greatest talent is her ability to give you a hill to die on that you never even knew existed.

'I'm going to my exercise class now, Kiki,' Obaachan says grandly, ignoring the questions. 'Exercise is very important, you know.' She pushes herself back from the table and makes her straight-backed way out of the house.

Rei and Youta come back inside just as Hikaru and I have finished deep-frying the last of the kare-pan, golden and glistening on a plate lined with newspaper. Ai has gone back upstairs again.

'The car's fixed!' Rei announces triumphantly. 'Youta's a hero!'

'Look what we made,' Hikaru says to Youta before he can demur. 'Eat one. Mama says they're nicest when they're just made, but don't burn your mouth because the curry is hot.'

'Hikaru, let Youta sit down,' I chide him.

We all sit on the engawa and Youta takes a kare-pan from the plate Hikaru holds out to him.

'I've never had home-made kare-pan before,' Youta says, holding it up to the light with appreciation. I have to remind myself that is probably not because his mother is a terrible cook, but because she is a normal human being. 'This is amazing.'

It is pretty amazing, actually, the outside flaky and crispy all at once, the bread fluffy, the curry so silky smooth and spicy that nobody can speak, giving me a full fifteen seconds to admire Youta's profile in silence.

'Remember when we used to play Superman in the garden?' Rei says suddenly. Youta and I nod. Rei was Superman, obviously, and Youta and I would take turns being her sidekick, or the one who stayed home and did the cooking. Since neither Youta nor I would agree to be domestic slaves, Rei said we ran a restaurant that was popular with all the Supermen and had big queues.

'And the time we tried to build a zip wire across the garden on the washing line,' Youta says.

'You wanted to put Ai in the basket,' Rei says.

'I thought it made sense,' Youta agrees apologetically. 'Since she was the smallest.'

'You made me get in instead,' I tell Rei accusingly. 'That bruise on my butt from when the basket fell didn't go down for months.'

'Remember when we tried to dig a nuclear bunker on the beach?' Rei asks.

'Oh my god, Rei, you were so paranoid, even when you were seven.'

'So would you be, if you learnt about some city down the road being nuked!'

'We did learn it! We all did.'

Rei shrugs. 'It wasn't a very good bunker. Who knew that digging a liveable cave out of sand would be so difficult.'

'We caught those crabs, though, remember?' Youta says. 'From the rock pool next to where we were digging.'

'They were so sweet,' I say. 'What did we name them again?'

'You went crabbing?' Hikaru asks.

'Sure,' Youta says, turning to him. 'But we put them back again after a while so they could go home to their families. Have you ever tried?'

Hikaru shakes his head, and I feel oddly guilty.

'I think I might still have my net somewhere – do you want to borrow it? I can take you if you want.'

Hikaru looks up at Youta with adoration pouring out of his eyes. 'Yes please,' he says. 'Will you take me tomorrow?'

'Hikaru, tomorrow's probably a bit soon—' I say, but Youta smiles at him.

'I have to work tomorrow, but I can come the day after, if

you're free,' he says. 'But only if that works for you.' He looks up at me.

'That sounds great.'

'I wasn't paranoid,' Rei objects. 'It was actually a completely logical reaction. You should be glad I took care of you so well. Who else would have made your ice-cream orders for you because you were too stupidly shy to tell the ice-cream man what you wanted? Or let you get in my futon when you were scared, even though you farted all night?'

I cannot believe she is talking about me farting in front of Youta. 'I appreciate it,' I tell her, and keep my eyes on her, so I don't have to see his reaction.

38

The car is fixed just in time for Rei to take Obaachan to her doctor's appointment. Obaachan is so unimpressed her frown is halfway down her face, and as they drive off, she keeps herself turned pointedly away from Rei, scowling out of the window. Rei reports that at the surgery she behaves like a different human being. 'Honestly,' she says, slightly dazed, 'it was literally like she was *flirting* with the doctor.' We are both stunned into silence at the thought.

Obviously such an emotionally fraught morning has to be followed up by some intense housekeeping, so Rei decides that Ai needs a haircut. 'You can't go around looking like a failed attempt at avant-garde performance art forever,' she says. Ai doesn't react, but the fact that she consents to sit down to it is progress, I think, though she's always been pretty pliable where Rei is concerned. She'd probably consent to a trapeze workshop on her deathbed, if Rei told her to do it.

Rei's brought over Obaachan's sewing scissors, the sharpest she could find, and I'm carrying out instructions, hairdressing being one of the unexpected skills you pick up if you work in a fancy old people's home. We're sitting in the wet-room section of the bathroom, right next to the big wooden tub, Ai on the pink plastic stool, her skinny legs folded under her like a fawn's. The tiny, enclosed courtyard space outside is reflected in the mirror, a jungle of tropical potted plants that Mama used to tend. The stool's so low I have to kneel to get to a comfortable height.

'Just tidy it up a bit,' Rei directs. As I snip, tentatively at first and then with more confidence, Rei sits on the side of the bath behind me, unusually still. I sneak looks at our reflections in the mirror as I work. Rei and I used to look so similar growing up that people would mistake us for twins – although that could just have been a lack of imagination on their part, assuming we looked the same because we were the only haafus they knew. Now we don't look anything alike; apart from anything else, I'm still visibly Asian and Rei has become a chameleon – a combination of tasteful highlights and expert application of make-up, this slightly haughty way she has of holding herself, making her look so indistinguishably expensive and international that she could be Middle Eastern, South American, European, any one of a breed of put-together, high-achieving expats that come from everywhere and nowhere. Of the three of us, it's Ai who looks most like Mama, for all that she's so fair.

There was a moment when I was extremely pregnant, forty-one weeks and on birth row, propped up against the cushions in my sitting room, feeling sorry for myself and watching TV. I'd just finished googling *Has anyone ever been pregnant forever*, and made myself hyperventilate with an internet answer about a woman in India who was pregnant for seven years. The TV was showing a dubbed rerun of *Dawson's Creek* and I was crying because Joey had just had a long-anticipated teenage kiss with a guy who wasn't even that hot but who I suddenly found myself fancying, and I was old and staring at my swollen feet and shouldn't have crushes on sixteen-year-olds. There was probably something wrong with me and I was going to be an unfit mother. Which was fine because I was never going to be a mother anyway, on account of being pregnant forever. I was really giving in to the wailing, and then the channel flicked and Ai filled the screen, all dewy and sexy and age-appropriate for the cute *Dawson's Creek* sixteen-year-old. I suddenly remembered how much I'd loved ballet until we had to give it up when Mama disappeared, and I actually raised my arms in a port de bras, weeping and spherical.

After Hikaru was born, I was so impressed with my body for having created something so cute, I let it off the hook for everything else, and haven't really paid much attention to it since. What use would a delicate frame or perfectly manicured hands be anyway, for lugging buggies up staircases and grappling fully grown men in and out of bathtubs? Although it possibly isn't necessary to linger too long on our reflections side by side; my sisters, the famous tragic beauty and the immaculate, angular hotshot, and then the boring domestic one in the middle. I take a deep breath and let it out slowly, not sighing.

'Done,' I say, running my fingers through Ai's new pixie haircut.

'Thank you,' Ai says softly.

Rei looks at Ai's head critically. 'I didn't think you were going to be so good,' she says, like I was hiding something from her.

39

Rei

令

I don't actually think I'm being all that controversial, suggesting that the cemetery might not be the jolliest possible outing for a recovering depressive and a five-year-old.

'It's the first time Ai's been out since we got here,' I say.

'She doesn't have to come if she doesn't want to,' Kiki says. 'She can make tomorrow her first outing, or this afternoon. And the cemetery is basically a playground, as far as Hikaru is concerned. Don't project.'

In the end, Ai decides to stay behind. We're a little late leaving because we can't find Hikaru, who has somehow wedged himself behind the washing machine in what he considers to be the most wonderful trick of all time. By the time the three of us get outside, Obaachan is standing on the front step of the house, incensed because she's been waiting at least forty-five seconds.

'You girls were always late for everything,' she mutters furiously, struggling with the latch on her parasol. I reach over to help her, but she slaps my hand away. Kiki offers her arm without a word, and Obaachan grasps it in her iron grip. 'You never had any respect for your elders.'

'Once we've done the graves, we need to go to the greengrocer's,' she adds, managing to drag Kiki along despite her glacial pace. 'And the fishmonger's. And the post office.' She turns to Kiki. 'I know in Tokyo you never eat anything that doesn't come from a conbini, but while you're staying with me, you'll eat properly.' She turns to me. 'And you'll eat proper Japanese food, see how much better it is for your health. Not like the Western Diet you're addicted to.' The Western Diet, according to Obaachan, is responsible for all body odour, and consists solely of cheese and meat and other luxury items that demonstrate the moral laxity of the West. I widen the distance between the two of us, to avoid getting stabbed in the eye by her parasol.

The morning is grey and humid, the heat stifling, and by the time we reach the temple, a good walk around the headland and up the hill, we're drenched in sweat. Ahead of us, the road carries on climbing, eventually reaching Mani-san, the abandoned shrine that sits like a moss-covered threat at the top of a steep stone staircase. Kitsune statues, their red bibs long faded and ripped, glare out from the trees that grow up tall and unkempt on either side of the steps. There's a story that some kind of samurai battle took place on the hill where Mani-san sits, and the ghosts of the losing side still haunt the trees. Blasé as Kiki was about it as a teenager, treating it like some kind of outdoor bar, as children we would never be caught up there after sunset.

We turn off the road into the temple compound under the cypress-wood gateway, topped with a pagoda roof and pasted with small paper stickers of calligraphic script, like the Buddhist version of rock-concert toilet graffiti. Ahead of us is a paved clearing, the trees on either side so vigorous they almost touch in the middle, a fine lattice of green, crows cawing and sparrows chirping. A huge wrought-iron bowl of hot sand and burning incense, as tall as my shoulders, stands fatly in front of the temple, and an old man casually wafts the smoke towards himself for good fortune. I've always liked the temple, the way the shade cast by the roofs invites you to take shelter from the sun or the rain, the dark wood balustrades, so ornately carved along the top, the bright white of the adobe walls. We stop to pull on the giant woven bell-pull; Kiki drops some coins into the huge metal money box. As we put our hands together, I peer into what I can see of the temple hall. Dark and calm, with silks in purples and reds, sombre flowers, an altar, smoke where someone's lit an incense stick, the same as it's always been. The only thing that's different is the new stone Buddha we pass as we head back down the stairs, lying on his side on a plinth, all round belly and jolly, understanding smiles. There's a plastic chair set up in front of him, with a sign inviting you to share your woes with the Buddha of Complaints.

Behind the temple, tidy wooden shelves are stacked with wooden buckets, bamboo scoops and brooms for cleaning the graves. Kiki buys a bunch of flowers from a metal bucket, pink calla lilies and white chrysanthemums surrounded by sakaki leaves, placing the money in the old tin next to it. Obaachan fills a bucket from the tap. The paths between the graves are narrow, paved with uneven, lichen-spotted stones, and in between the graves are trees that burst into bloom in spring. The Takanawa grave is at the far end, in the shade of a huge, knobbled camphor tree, with views of the sea beyond. On one side of it is a family plot so old and weathered with age it's almost impossible to make out the name on it, and on the other, a modern gravestone made of dark-grey marble, with complicated carvings and a holder for business cards. Our grave is a stone monolith with enough names on its side to take up two full rows of text, Obaachan's name already carved there in red when her husband died, so all that needs to happen when she pegs it is for the red to be scrubbed off.

Obaachan doesn't spend even one second contemplating the grave, but pours water into the shallow depression in the ledge in front of the headstone, then splashes some over the stone using a sakaki leaf stem like a duster, frowning and efficient as if she's cleaning the fan on the ventilation unit. 'It's so hot,' she says, splashing some more. 'There you go.'

'Why are you putting water on the grave?' Hikaru wants to know.

'It's like their morning coffee,' she says, without pausing. 'Wakes them up.' She pulls a glass One Cup of sake from her handbag, opens it and puts it between the two lanterns.

'Who's that for?' Hikaru asks. This time Obaachan doesn't answer.

Nozomi's name isn't actually on the gravestone, because she was officially 'missing' rather than dead for so many years. Her Buddhist name is written on a flat bamboo stick stuck into the ground around the grave like an afterthought, the kind of marker you might use to note where you'd planted the sunflower seeds or the carrots. I don't know if I want her here – if she's squashed in with all those difficult relatives, she can never be with me in England, or with Kiki and Ai in Tokyo. I didn't even know about the bamboo stick until the first time I came back from England; Obaachan gave me a line about doing the right thing, then changed the subject.

I came here with Sath. I didn't mean to, as such, but you can't get anywhere in Ikimura without going past everything else and the day we were here was beautiful, a breeze through the cypresses and the cherry trees and the view all the way down to the bay, the water turquoise and glinting. We came all the way in, for the view, and even went right past this grave, and I didn't say a thing about it. It was one of many mysterious things I did during the course of our relationship. We broke up six months later.

197

Today, the water in the distance is a murky blue-grey, ripples of foam shivering along its surface, like the sea is brooding, and what you notice isn't how well the place is tended, but the stillness of the air, the stillness of the graves.

Sath and I – our break-up went very well. In a way. I told him we couldn't be together because it wouldn't last forever.

What had he done, he wanted to know. He asked it matter-of-factly. I just want to know if you woke up one morning and had the ick, he said.

I should have told him it was that, obviously. That would have ended it. But I couldn't bear for him to think that.

He said it so carefully: I think this is as good as it gets. If you can't see how good this is— He didn't finish his sentence.

I told him I didn't mean it like that. I told him it couldn't last forever. Because even until one of us dies – that isn't forever.

He looked at me like nobody else ever has. He said my name, and I've heard him saying it so often since. I want you for all the time we have. For as long as we get, Rei.

'Didn't we say we were going to sort out a grave for Mama?' Kiki says. 'I don't really think a stick cuts it, do you?'

'Where would we even put it?' I ask. 'We only have that one plot.' Sath is heavy on my mind. 'Maybe we should stick a headstone on a crossroads. With a stake through it.'

'Oh for god's sake, Rei,' Kiki snaps.

Before we can get into it further, there's the sound of a short shriek, and a slap. Obaachan is standing over Hikaru, next to the grave with the business cards, holding the broom, her face contorted with fury. Hikaru is clutching his hand. 'You'll be cursed for touching another family's grave!' she shouts.

Hikaru runs to Kiki. 'I was just sweeping it,' he cries, his face collapsing into tears. 'I wanted to help.'

Kiki holds him close and turns away, white-lipped. Obaachan

stumps off up the path to the wire-mesh rubbish bin, muttering to herself.

I tousle Hikaru's head, hearing Kiki whispering to him. Then I collect up the old candle stubs, the wilted flowers, and wish someone else were here, somebody we would all need to behave ourselves in front of. I think of Charlotte, forever perky and diplomatic.

She was the only person other than Sath I ever told about Nozomi; I think it might have been because her initial reaction was sympathetic but measured. Having a dead parent, by the time you're an adult, is quite sad but more like a misfortune than a tragedy. Especially if at the time of their death you were acne-ridden and bad-tempered, as opposed to round-faced and angelic-looking. Sometimes I'm grateful for the tempered reaction, the way it makes it feel normal; other times it feels like a brick wall just came down between me and the person I'm talking to. I think it was because I really liked Charlotte, and it was easier to tell her my mother had killed herself to get my point across than to shake her and say she didn't really seem to be understanding how bad it had been, and mostly still was. She looked pretty shocked. She said, like it was the answer to something, that she'd read that Japan had one of the highest suicide rates in the world. A suicide every fifteen minutes at its peak, apparently. 'Not that that makes it better,' she added hurriedly. Poor Charlotte.

My mother had an aunt in Fukuoka who'd visit sometimes, bringing tea in tins for Obaachan and biscuits for us, and after my mother died the aunt would visit just the same. She told us once, as she was handing over the biscuits, that she was sorry for what had happened, but in her opinion committing suicide was the most cowardly thing you could do. It was difficult to figure out what she was hoping to achieve with this statement – should we be grateful that our mother was no longer around to contaminate us with her cowardliness? Maybe it was designed to make us realise how forward-thinking the aunt was, for considering it cowardly to drown yourself in a giant body of water, as opposed to honourable – and I found myself in the insane situation of wanting to shout at that stupid aunt that maybe, actually, killing herself had been a *great* decision. I didn't say, even though I was thinking it, that I would always prefer to have my mother, dead, than any other mother on earth, alive, and she was so superior to all of them that the aunt didn't even have the right to be talking about her. The word for an honourable suicide is *gyokusai*, a shattered jewel, something it's better to be than a pathetic, intact tile. How unjewel-like, how embarrassing: the absent gaijin husband and the mixed-up kids. The shame of it. I knew there were people of Obaachan's age who thought that – sometimes it made me want to scream, and behead them all; other times I could not give a shit what these old strangers thought of us. The next time the aunt arrived, we ignored the doorbell and have never seen her since. Notably, Obaachan has never said a word about it.

'Let's go,' Kiki says, holding the dustpan in one hand and Hikaru's hand in the other. Hikaru is looking wanly resigned. 'Everything's done.' I nod and follow her up the path, the sky hanging low over us.

I remember Nozomi going for a walk one day, when she was well, because she wanted to go and see the light in the old station. I don't understand how you could know life so well that you see how beautiful a ray of sunshine through a high domed ceiling is, and that standing there looking at it and watching the people through it, on the way to wherever they're going, makes it worth living, and then decide that you'd rather be nowhere than here watching the light, with us.

40

Ai

When the others come back from the cemetery, the air is a bit different. Rei is making lunch and Kiki and Hikaru are trying to make origami animals, Obaachan sitting across from them writing in a notebook. On the engawa, Chibi is sitting with his paws slightly apart and his ears flat, looking at a patch of sunshine and then at us, like he's thinking about maybe lying down and relaxing but he doesn't trust anyone enough to let his guard down.

'What are you doing?' I ask Obaachan. It comes out croaky. Rei and Kiki don't look at each other secretly, the way they usually do when I talk. Sometimes they look at each other without even moving their eyes, and they're not even doing that.

'I'm writing a haiku. I like to keep my mind active. I'm not like Kanagawa-san next door, doing nothing and getting fat.'

'Obaachan,' Kiki scolds. 'Kanagawa-san has dementia.'

'She keeps forgetting she's eaten her meals and eats them again!' Obaachan says. 'She should write notes to herself, to say she's already had her lunch. It's so sloppy of her. When her children were small, they were so badly behaved.' She sighs, remembering.

Kiki's eyebrows are climbing up her forehead. She asks in

English, 'Is she holding shit against this poor demented woman from seven decades ago?'

'It's appalling, what people think they can get away with,' Obaachan continues. 'That Youta of yours' – she points her chin at Kiki – 'he could barely read as a child, and his mother kept insisting it was a condition.'

Kiki is frowning. 'He's not my Youta,' she says.

'Dyslexia,' Rei calls from the kitchen, 'is a condition.'

'Everything's a condition nowadays,' Obaachan says. 'Everyone knew she was just too lazy to make him do his homework. He was always late for juku.' She turns her attention back to her haiku. 'You'll probably struggle to find anybody else, Kiki. Most men have standards about things like divorces.' She uses the slang for it, 'strike-one', like it's a blot on your copybook.

Kiki's jaw moves. 'I'm not divorced,' she says.

'And who's prepared to take in a child that isn't theirs?' Obaachan doesn't look up from her notebook. 'But then, he comes from a very lax family, so I suppose it's to be expected. You know, Ai-chan, my haiku are often in the newspaper. I'll have to show them to you one day.'

Kiki looks like she might be suffocating on the spot but I can't figure out what to do. With no warning, Chibi rushes over to where Kiki is sitting and butts his head against her. It doesn't look like it's making Kiki feel any better.

'I'd like that,' I tell Obaachan. She looks pleased. Then she puts both of her hands on my forearm and squeezes. It's pretty painful. 'Ai-chan.' She lowers her voice, like she's about to let me in on a major secret. 'Korean pork is contaminated. It was on the news. People are dying all over the place, but there are spies everywhere so they can't recall it.'

'OK,' I say, unsure where this is going.

'And given where you live . . .' She purses her lips significantly.

'In Korea-town?' Nobody who lives there actually calls

Shin-Okubo that, even though it's full of Korean shops and restaurants, but I think Obaachan likes it when we rise to her.

She shudders. 'You could afford to move out, Ai-chan, I know you could. Or you could ask Rei to help you. The Koreans kidnap people as they're walking along the beach in Japan. Just sweep them straight off the coast and take them back to Korea as spies.'

'I like living in Korea-town, Obaachan.' I figure it's not worth telling her that I am almost definitely never going back to that share house again. I hear the whoosh and catch of the gas, as Rei lights the flame under the frying pan.

Obaachan frowns, annoyed. 'She might as well put her money to some use,' she says, letting her voice rise to a volume she knows Rei will hear, even though, really, everyone's heard everything already, 'since she abandoned her family to go and earn it.'

'You were the one who told me to do economics at university,' Rei says brightly, stabbing the chopsticks at whatever is in her mixing bowl. 'You were the one who told me anything except for economics and medicine was a waste of time.'

'She should have been a doctor,' Obaachan tells the paper in front of her. 'A doctor's a useful profession.' I see Kiki's shoulders move up and down in a silent sigh.

'Still would have taken me away from the family, though, wouldn't it?' Rei says evenly. 'You can't study medicine round here.'

'A doctor from Tokyo University,' Obaachan says firmly. 'A Japanese doctor.'

'Of course, To-dai,' Rei mutters. I hear the crackle of her throwing salt into the oil to check its temperature. Chibi snaps his head up, offended by the noise. 'Only To-dai.' Tokyo University, To-dai, is the best university in Japan. If I were

Obaachan, I wouldn't bait Rei while she's cooking with hot oil.

'Terrible things will happen to you in this life, Ai-chan,' Obaachan says, and it's not clear if the terrible thing is having a great-granddaughter who didn't go to To-dai, or what. 'Life's a difficult business – it's not about having fun, you know.' She shakes her head and points her pen at me. 'You'd better remember that. There's no rest until you get to the end of it. It won't do to think you can sing songs and shake your hair about forever.' She says it like she's not talking about me at all.

The funny thing is that I never set out to sing songs and shake my hair, I just followed the things that were interesting and that was where they went.

Then Obaachan says, 'I'll be getting my rest soon. I expect it'll be sooner than anyone thinks. The doctor said I'm getting so thin.' She looks pleased with herself.

'The doctor from yesterday called this morning,' Rei says to us over her shoulder in English. 'He says they need to do some more tests.'

'So thin,' Obaachan says again before anyone can answer Rei. 'Watanabe-san from down the road has terrible health problems, a slipped disc a few months ago and now haemorrhoids, but even she isn't as thin as I am.' She looks at me to make sure I've taken it in, so I nod seriously. 'I'll be dead before you come back again.'

Before anyone has time to say anything about that idea, there's a hiss of oil as Rei throws something into the frying pan.

'Too hot!' Obaachan snaps. She cranes round to see what Rei is doing. 'You always make the pan too hot!'

'It's fine,' Rei says. 'It makes the outsides crispy.'

'What time is it, Ai?' Obaachan asks me, ignoring Rei.

I look at Rei's phone. 'It's half past one,' I tell Obaachan. I haven't looked at a phone for a long time. I think of the entire world in there, and it seems very crazy – that I can keep it out just by not looking at this tiny rectangular object.

Obaachan lets out a squawk and reaches for the remote control. The television blasts out so loud that we all cover our ears and duck, and then Obaachan presses a button on her portable speaker, so the sound streams tinnily through that instead. On the TV, a heroine in a peasant's kimono jacket is wading through snow to a sentimental orchestral soundtrack. The title credits for *Tomorrow's Cantabile* pan across the screen.

Trying to actually understand the programme is impossible, because it's all in old Japanese, but I can follow some of the storylines, especially because Obaachan's been watching it every day. The storyline where she nods the most is the shogun, who's been dying from some really gross sword wound for about a million episodes and keeps having bedside chats where one tear runs out of the corner of his eye.

Half an hour later, Obaachan gives a huge sigh and turns off the TV, then heaves herself up and hobbles out of the room. Everyone is silent for a moment after she leaves. Hikaru has given up on the origami and is lying on his back, flying Paddington Bear through the air with sound effects.

'I reckon she'll stick around forever,' Rei says. She sets a plate of crispy hot karaage down on the low table, lemon wedges arranged around the edge. 'Just like the shogun. Dying would be conceding weakness, and she wouldn't like that.'

'Maybe,' Kiki says. She makes a very neat fold in an origami sheet and runs her nail along it hard. 'Or maybe she'll decide she's just going to wash her hands of us all and leave when it suits her, without any warning.' She seems like she's going to say something, then changes her mind. 'Remind everyone who's in charge.'

'Maybe,' Rei agrees. 'I just think she'd get such a kick out of lording it over us from her deathbed. Can you get the chopsticks?' She stretches and her T-shirt comes up so you can see her stomach, the ridges on either side of it that Kiki says make her look like Janet Jackson. 'It's actually amazing how tenacious life is. That you can be practically disembowelled and still limp on.' She sits down. 'Just think how hard our mother had to work to get rid of it.'

I expect Kiki to roll her eyes, or maybe come up with an even better punchline, but she has a look on her face that I haven't really seen before. 'I don't think she did,' she says to Rei. 'You know I think it was an accident.'

Rei looks at her quickly. There's something like grit in the air where it should be smooth between them.

'Kiki.' Rei drags the word out, like Kiki has just said something really stupid.

'Nobody knows what happened,' Kiki says. 'And we never talk about it.' It's true, that nobody knows, none of us know. My skin feels like it's crawling.

Rei looks at her for a long time. Chibi lowers his head on to one paw, the very end of his tail twitching. Hikaru is looking from Kiki to Rei. Even though they're talking in English, it isn't hard for him to figure out that something's wrong. I motion for him to come to me.

'She left her shoes together,' Rei says finally.

'I know she did.' Kiki sounds like a teacher explaining something to a really annoying kid. 'But you could leave your shoes together if you went out swimming, too. It doesn't prove anything.'

'She didn't leave any clothes,' Rei says, and she sounds sorry about it. 'No one goes for a swim with all their clothes still on.' She turns her head, as if her neck is hurting her. 'You don't know what came before.'

'Of course I know, Rei.' Kiki says the words clipped and short. 'I know she tried it before.'

Hikaru looks at me. I wonder if I should take him out, but I don't want to make Kiki or Rei look at us by standing up. I break a piece of karaage off with my fingers and hand it to him. He takes it but doesn't eat it.

'You don't need to sound so superior about it,' Rei says. She's annoyed now.

'It's not like you own her, like you're the only one who can possibly know the truth.'

Rei takes a massive breath and exhales through her nose. 'I never said that.'

'You don't even know what it's like.'

'What what's like?'

'Being a parent, how hard it is.'

'What the fuck has that got to do with anything? You think she drowned herself because of us?'

Kiki frowns and shakes her head, the way Hikaru does. 'No—' She stops, starts again, carefully. 'Parenting by yourself – some days it can make you crazy, Rei. I think she was sad, and lonely, and the situation was shit. But I don't think she did it. She wouldn't.'

'She was *sad*?' Rei says, incredulously.

'The karaage's getting cold,' I say.

'I think that other time was a cry for help,' Kiki says.

Rei makes a disbelieving sound. 'Help from who?' she asks.

'And anyway, how can you possibly be angrier at Mama than at Richard? *He's* the one who left. He's the one who turned happy families into Madame fucking Butterfly.'

Rei actually laughs then, a strangled noise. 'You know Madame Butterfly killed herself, right?'

'That's not the point,' Kiki says impatiently.

Rei doesn't say anything for a beat, and when she does, she

sounds tired, not angry. 'Because he's below contempt,' she says. 'He's so pathetic he couldn't even limp through the first rounds.'

'So Mama deserves all this, years and years of rage and blame, because she actually tried? Doesn't that sound like bullshit to you?'

'You don't remember—' Rei starts. I've never seen Rei look like she's about to cry. Stop, I want to say to Kiki. It doesn't matter, just stop. 'She left.'

Kiki stares at the table, not saying anything.

'You can believe what you want,' Rei says after a while. All the feeling has gone out of her voice. 'It doesn't make a difference.'

'It does make a difference.' Kiki drops her voice so I can barely hear her, almost like she's talking to herself. 'You're so angry you can't even see how good your life could be. You think it's fine to hate everyone because of the story you've told yourself.'

Rei laughs like the word 'ha ha'. Two short, sharp, lonely sounds like hammer blows. I think of her face, the night she came and found me on the roof, and it feels like my chest is caving in, that I could have done that to her. 'It isn't a fucking story, Kiki,' Rei says. She stands up and goes to leave the room. With one hand on the noren, she turns around. 'And you're wrong. I know exactly how shitty it is to be a parent.'

A moment later, we hear the sound of the front door closing. The karaage sits on the table between us. Kiki looks at it, her hands in her lap.

The only thing I've always known about how Nozomi died is that nobody is sure how it happened. I don't remember it, exactly, just a foggy period when Rei and Kiki were both quieter, and she wasn't there. I always thought it was funny how easy it was to talk about it, if anyone asked, because the

Japanese word for having died is the same word you can use when you've lost your keys, or something has disappeared. Our mother has been misplaced, and we've looked everywhere, and we still can't find her.

I don't know what I think about it. I've never brought it up, because I never wanted to hurt Rei or Kiki by making them talk about it. I remember the last show I played, when things were starting to fall apart. Halfway through the final song, I had such a clear picture of my mother, crouched in the corner of our kitchen, gripping her skull with both hands like she was trying to hold it together. I never even knew that was in my head.

I know that feeling. Maybe Nozomi just felt that way for a short time, the wrong short time, and there was no grown-up Rei to hold her down and tell her to wait for it to pass. But then I think: the difference between thinking of something and doing it is so big, a gap the size of your entire life, and I don't know if I think she would have. I'm not like Rei or Kiki, weighing up the evidence and remembering that day and trying to figure it out; I don't have enough. I'll never know.

41
Rei
令

The door closes behind me, and, not looking where I'm going, I almost fall straight over Nozomi's bicycle. As I grab hold of it to right myself, the metal luggage rack on the back comes off in my hand. I wish I were somewhere else.

I try to fit the luggage rack back on, but the screws that hold it down are completely rusted, the threads non-existent. I remember sitting side-saddle on that rack, when I was about twelve and we were late to meet the coach for a school trip. My suitcase was balanced on the basket in the front and Nozomi was trying to cycle and hold the suitcase down at the same time, while I clung on with my arms wrapped around her waist. We were late because Ai had taken the batteries out of the kitchen clock, and when we got to school just in time for me to run on to the coach, Nozomi was triumphant. The trip was to Tokyo, two nights in a centre that smelt of cleaning products, metal bunk beds and all our meals on trays, like a sanatorium. It was dazzling. One afternoon we were allowed to wander free, two hours to get lost in the biggest city on the planet, armed with a photocopied map. My friend Wakako and I went straight to Harajuku, of course, our mouths hanging open the entire time. Girls with blue eyes and double eyelids and glossy pink hair examined sparkly hair barrettes with the careless concentration of housewives looking at different cuts of sukiyaki beef, dark stairwells pulsating with music and lights led to caverns selling sequinned dresses and Licca-doll paraphernalia, and Western tourists pretended to be cool but really ogled as much as we did. I was so excited I could hardly breathe, like I'd found out the Alice in Wonderland hole in the tree really did exist.

I bought my mother the sparkliest hair barrette I could afford and took pictures with my crappy disposable camera. I must have known she wouldn't wear the barrette – mustn't I? – but in it was wrapped up the sudden comprehension that this Tokyo was what she dreamt of, not Harajuku itself but the people, the variety, the possibility. I started to write her a letter to tell her about it, on paper I bought in the hundred-yen shop right next to the iconic arch at the end of the street, but I never finished it, never even properly started it. I still have it, something it doesn't make any sense to keep, sitting in my bedside table in London. 'Okaasan e,' it says; 'Dear Mum,' – and then the excitement of life intervened.

I found myself in Harajuku again years later, after Nozomi had been dead for almost a decade, and it was vertigo like she'd only just gone. Nobody was keeping track of me; where I was and what I saw and did the centre of nobody's universe. I picked out barrettes for Ai and Kiki, to tell myself to get a grip, but then I left them on the counter without paying.

I have this dream where my mother's about to cross over the road, and I grab her by the crook of the arm just before she goes. She turns to me like it's no big deal and we wander down the pavement together, on my side of the street, and she's fine, happy to walk with me. I don't have to say, Please don't do it. Please, please stay with me.

42

Kiki

清美

The karaage sits on the table like a reproach until I take it to the kitchen counter and cover it with cling film. Remembering something, I lift up the drawer divider that sits under the cling film. The kitchen drawers were always lined with scrap paper that was covered in drawings that Mama had doodled. It's gone, obviously. Rei is very thorough.

The only satisfaction in the whole Richard situation is that I happen to know a reckoning is coming for him. Those chickens always come home to roost eventually – the number of residents in the home freaking out about things that were done and dusted decades ago. All I want from Richard is for him to live long enough to experience the full Lady Macbeth.

'Mama, I found a cat toy,' Hikaru tells me listlessly from where he's lying on his side, digging up the dregs of the picture-book box from the attic. I turn to look. The cat he's holding up is small and fluffy, faded now but still recognisably hot pink, with sparkly purple eyes and nylon whiskers. A raffle prize at an omatsuri, infinitely desirable, even though we were too old to want it. Rei won it and said she would sell it to me for all my pocket money, but changed her mind when she found out I only had two hundred yen. It ended with both of us clutching the kitten and screaming with all our might, and

Mama trying to keep the peace by telling us nothing was black and white. She was always saying that, most especially when we were flaming mad at each other and looking for a judge to declare a victor.

'Rei won it,' I tell Hikaru. 'She wouldn't let me have it, even though she said she would.' Sometimes I want to remind him how great it is that he's an only child and doesn't have to deal with the bullshit of siblings. He doesn't react.

It's like Mama's final joke, our not knowing; reminding us that nothing's black and white, leaving us swimming in the murkiest grey, with no clue which pole is which. She was a lot funnier when she was alive. I think of the cat picture Rei was talking about at the beginning of the summer, the one that Nozomi made up a story about. It feels like I could remember it if only I tried hard enough – it's so characteristic of Mama, and I can hear exactly the way she would have spoken to the cat, the intonations of her voice. The worst part about Mama's disappearing was – actually, that's not true; it's truly impossible to say what the worst part was – but one of the bad parts was that there wasn't ever a moment when someone said she was dead. Rei knew she was from the start and Obaachan just stopped talking about her. For a bit, I told myself this story that she was going to come back. I knew she wasn't, but I almost let myself think she might. We never saw her leave, never saw her dead.

I'm not deluded – I know that Mama had a brain like a broken radio stuck on charismatic damnation hymns with a side order of Japanese judgement. Doesn't mean it's a foregone conclusion that she did it, though.

Even when I make myself think that maybe she meant it – just imagine for a moment that she did, walked into the sea and left us behind – what then? Those are Rei's words, that she left us, not mine. Even if she did it on purpose, it wasn't that she chose to leave. She would never. It was something else. Something took her, the something that contorts Ai's face and makes Rei believe that every day is a battle where she has to get one up on life itself.

If we all reckon there isn't any getting away from the family genes one way or another, maybe what I got, even though it makes me shiver to consider it, is Obaachan's way of marching along in the reality she likes, and to hell with everyone else's. What is reality, apart from what you tell yourself, and what you believe? Please god, don't let me become quite that batshit, but who's to say what's good or bad or right or wrong, and if we're all just making it up as we go along, wouldn't I rather go with the version where things are better instead of worse? I don't think Ai and Rei choose the weeping and rending their clothes; that's just the way their world looks. Not mine. Some people reckon that's denial and delusion, and they're welcome to go hang out in their bleak and burning world, but if they could please leave me well out of it.

43

Rei

令

By the time I get back to the house, it's that bit of the after-noon when it's too late and too early to do anything. The air is muggy and close, and without the sun everything is flat and grey. From a few houses away comes the sound, hollow and honky-tonk at this distance, of someone practising the piano. Chibi is lying under the engawa yowling like some kind of deranged spirit. In the sitting room, Kiki and I studiously ignore each other. Hikaru is fractious, refusing to do anything that Kiki asks, starting activities and then abandoning them.

I pull out my laptop, even though I know exactly how poor the reception is, wanting to go back to my different life. But the company logo, when it finally rises portentously on to the screen in front of me, is disorientating. I manage to open a curt message from HR demanding an update on my return, and precisely two emails I've been copied in on, both of which are to do with very important deals I have never heard of. Out of context, they sound like exchanges in a surrealist play with extremely rude protagonists.

'I think you might be hungry,' Kiki says to Hikaru, in the slightly formal voice she's been using. 'Why don't you sit down at the table and eat this.' She holds out a plate of sliced persimmon.

Hikaru lifts his head from where he's been lying face down and looks at it. His forehead scrunches up and his mouth turns down. 'You cut it up!' he wails.

Kiki takes a deep breath. 'Yes, Hikaru, I cut it up because I don't want you slicing your fingers off with a kitchen knife and you can't eat the skin.'

Hikaru turns his head away and sobs expansively. Kiki places the plate with exaggerated care on the table. 'Hikaru,' she says, 'I think you will feel much better once you eat. Please come to the table.'

Hikaru eventually drags himself to the table, still hiccoughing. He chews on the orange slices of fruit, eyes downcast. By the time he's down to the last piece, he looks quite cheerful.

'Finished!' he announces triumphantly.

'Did you mean, Finished, thank you so much, Mama, I very much appreciate your anticipating my every need and treating me like an emperor?'

Hikaru scowls. 'No.' He starts to get up.

'Take the plate to the sink, please.'

Hikaru's eyes glitter. 'I'm too tired.'

'Hikaru, please clear up after yourself.'

'I can't. Kimchi is still licking the plate.'

'Hikaru.' Kiki's voice is dangerous. I quite admire Hikaru's balls.

Hikaru sighs deeply and looks at Kiki. Then, like he's deciding something, he curls himself up next to the table. 'No,' he says.

Kiki looks at him in disbelief. 'Are you kidding me?' When Hikaru doesn't respond, she makes a sound like someone trying to lift an extremely heavy weight. 'You are behaving like a spoilt brat,' she hisses, picking up the plate. 'I did not bring you up to behave this way.' She stomps to the sink, where she deposits the plate, then stomps on upstairs.

Hikaru stays still for a further minute, then uncurls a little, his face impassive.

Half an hour later, Hikaru has wandered off and I've achieved nothing, not even replying to HR. I'm frowning at the screen when Kiki walks in.

'Have you seen Hikaru?' she demands.

'No. Do you think I should quit my job?' The words are out of my mouth before I've realised what they're going to be.

'Obviously,' she says impatiently. 'I've looked all over the house. He must be hiding.'

I close the lid of the laptop and remind myself my beef is not with my five-year-old nephew. 'Maybe he's gone over to Obaachan's.'

'So she can smack him again?' Kiki asks.

'I'll go check,' I say.

In Obaachan's house, I remove my shoes at the genkan and slide across the freshly polished floor, rounding the corner to the sitting room. Obaachan is writing something at the little table, the television tuned to a chat show, a guest on a sofa laughing decorously into her hand. Hikaru isn't there.

The television switches over to the weather.

'There's a typhoon coming today, Rei,' Obaachan says without looking up. 'Don't go outside.'

'Have you seen Hikaru?'

'No.' She looks up suspiciously, her pen poised in mid-air. 'Have you lost him?' It's an accusation.

'Nobody has *lost* him,' I tell her, reversing out of the room. 'We're just looking for him.'

I scan the empty kitchen, immaculately clean, the tea urn drying next to the sink. The hot tap is dripping and I cross the kitchen to turn it off. As if someone turned out the lights, the sky outside darkens, a low cloud overhead. I go out on to the balcony to bring the washing in before it rains; a blue plastic pinwheel of Obaachan's child-like underclothes, neat and white, and a drying rack loaded with our cotton sundresses. I hadn't realised she'd done our washing. I'm struck by the logistics of it, having to come into our house and bring things over to hers, run the machine, hang it up. I wonder what she was thinking of while she did it. The tidy white underclothes look very small, on their rack for one, next to our gargantuan, multicoloured foreigner's clothes.

I go back into the sitting room, I don't know what for. To say thank you.

'So?' Obaachan asks, not looking up.

'Still looking,' I tell her, backing away.

'Is he here?' Kiki appears before I've heard her.

'I haven't checked the second floor yet—' But Kiki is already running up the stairs. I can hear her hurrying from room to room, calling Hikaru's name.

Kiki thunders down alone. 'I shouldn't have yelled at him, Rei.' She bites her lip. 'Where the hell is he?'

44

Kiki

清美

'The game is finished, Hikaru. Come out!' My voice sounds lower than I'm used to. I clear my throat. 'Hikaru, it isn't funny any more!'

I call his name out of Obaachan's door, but the street is quiet, giving nothing away. The silence is oppressive. I wonder if he's still upset with me, and thinking of his stubbornness makes me furious again.

Youta rounds the corner, raising his hand in greeting when he sees me; the sight of him is a shock. I'd completely forgotten that he was coming round, even though it was the first thing I thought of when I woke up this morning.

'Everything OK?' he asks, approaching.

'I'm looking for Hikaru,' I tell him briskly. 'I think he's playing hide-and-seek.'

'Do you think he's gone down the road?' Rei asks from behind me.

'He wouldn't,' I say, and it comes out too quickly. Even at home, he hasn't been out on his own yet. I glance past the house and our unassuming street doesn't look entirely friendly. All those little roads leading off from it, then others that lead off from them, roads that can eventually take you anywhere. 'I might just go and have a look.'

'I'll look this way, then,' Youta replies, like it's no big deal, and starts walking down the street away from town, towards the playground and the cemetery.

'He might have gone to the firework shop,' I hear myself saying, although surely he wouldn't go so far.

'Kiki, you stay here. He might come back,' Rei says, stepping down to the genkan, but I've already shoved my feet into her flip-flops.

As I hurry out of the door, Obaachan appears. 'Did you find him?' she asks, and behind me Rei must have shaken her head, because she continues, 'He's probably just gone to the shop. You should give him more independence, get him to help you more. He's old enough to run some errands, or take himself to school.' She tuts. 'If you let him out more in Tokyo, he'd be used to it.' She turns back into the house. 'Your generation is obsessed with crime.' I can still hear her as I start down the street: 'There's nothing to be gained from mollycoddling your children.'

'I'll stay here,' Rei calls. 'Keep your phone on; he might come back.' And as an afterthought, 'Don't worry, Kiki. I'm sure he's fine.'

I'm sure he's fine, too, but I hadn't noticed the darkening sky, and now I feel the first few raindrops on the back of my neck. Fat ones, which only give you a few seconds' warning before the heavens open. I'm sure he's fine, and it's the rain hurrying me along, so that I almost slip on the stairs down. By the time I reach the shopping arcade, my back and my hair are drenched, my flip-flops sliding on the pavement. The walkway is deserted, all the shops I pass devoid of customers. I rattle open the door to the firework shop. It's empty.

'Excuse me!' I call, and it comes out as a squeak. I take a deep breath and try again. I feel stupid; Hikaru isn't here, but, 'Have you seen a little boy? My son?' The proprietor steps out from behind the curtain, swallowing something, his face alert with recognition when he sees me.

'The little boy with the light hair?'

I nod.

'No, nobody's been in this afternoon. The weather . . .' I've turned out of the door as soon as I heard his 'no'. I hear him call after me as I leave, but I don't turn back.

Hikaru can't have gone further than this. I was crazy to come this far at all. I turn towards home, forcing myself to look into each shop I pass. He'll be waiting for me now, at the house, and he'll be soaking wet and I'll run him a bath. I check my phone for the message telling me so, but there's no signal.

As the house comes into view, I see Rei standing outside the front door, her whole body tense with waiting, and Youta approaching from the other side.

'Would he go towards the beach?' Youta asks, indicating the direction of the small cove, and, like it knows it's late to the party, all my fear and worry has suddenly rushed up inside me like ice. I shake my head no, because Hikaru is afraid of the dark and wakes me up in the night because he can't go to the toilet alone, and refuses to go down the slides even in the baby park. But Hikaru is always surprising me, changing from one day to the next, and I think how excited he was to splash in the sea when we visited the cove.

'Maybe,' I hear myself say. How long has he been gone? I hadn't seen him for half an hour before I started to look, assuming he was still sulking in the sitting room, and we must have been looking for another half. All the things that could happen in an hour. I look towards Obaachan's house, for the stoicism of her face, but she isn't there.

'Kiki, wait here,' Rei says, coming towards me, and her face has too many feelings in it. 'Wait here; I'll go with Youta.' But I've already started off. The rain is relentless, making it hard to see. Hikaru must be at the house, he must be, but we've looked everywhere and I'm running too fast past the huge torii gate, following the road along and down the hill. There are a thousand bushes and trees along the way that I've never noticed, perfect for sheltering a small fugitive. 'Hikaru, I'm here!' I call. 'Mama's here, Hikaru! Where are you?'

As I round the corner, I see the water below, gunmetal grey; it's the first day since we've been here that the sight of the sea hasn't greeted me like a friend. Just for a second, the thought of my mother falls on me. I'm looking at the same ocean, the same not-knowing.

This isn't going to be like that; he's fine, somewhere close by. We'll find him.

At the steps into the forest, I hesitate. 'He wouldn't,' I say to Youta, and I don't know if it's him I'm trying to convince, or myself.

'I'll just check,' Youta says like it's nothing, and starts down. The gaps between the steps are yawning; beneath is a tangle of greenery, a drop from the top step of thirty metres or more. I grip the banister and descend, screaming Hikaru's name into the wind the way you scream on a rollercoaster, to keep your stomach from falling out.

The sea is wild. It's morphed into something demonic, the creamy froth of the waves attacking the rocks like a pack of dogs. As my foot touches the sand at the bottom of the steps, lightning slices the landscape, the entire ocean white with light. If Hikaru's here, he'll be terrified. Another roll of thunder booms; in the second flash of lightning, all I see is the stark emptiness of the beach, the cliff rising in a straight line above us.

My mother was right here, and then gone. Hikaru can't be gone.

I turn and run straight up the steps before I can think, Youta following behind, the path through the forest so dark it's hard to see. My son is not going to disappear. When I try to say the words to Youta, though, they won't come out, only ragged breaths like the croup Hikaru had as a baby. Out of the forest, the road is straight to our house, and all of me is willing that I'll see Rei running towards me, flooded with relief, but instead there's only Ai, standing sentinel at the front door.

'Rei went to look by the shrine,' she calls, and I turn towards the torii gate. I hear someone calling Hikaru's name, the vowels stretched out, a lonely sound, and then Mama rounds the corner.

In that second it's completely unsurprising to me, that when we really needed her she would come back. She's looking at me like she knows exactly what I'm feeling, and can fix it. And then the illusion breaks and it's Rei, her hair plastered to her head with the rain. I don't know where to go. Back to the house, back to the sea. The world around me has become something viscous, the other reality that has always been there, lurking.

The sound Rei makes is hardly audible, barely even an inhalation. Her eyebrows rise fractionally and I turn to where she's looking. I make a noise like an animal, Rei says later, like Chibi when you stand on his tail.

At the end of the road, Obaachan is standing under a street lamp holding Hikaru's hand. The driving rain is lit up like a fusillade. I start to run towards them, my breath so uneven I can't move quickly enough, and Hikaru's face is crumpling as he runs towards me, holding his arms out like he did when he was tiny. Then I've got him, the warm weight of him, and he wraps himself so tightly around me I can barely speak, and I'm crying and laughing, telling him it's all right and he is in so much trouble, not able to hold him close enough. Over Hikaru's shoulder, just for a second, I catch sight of Obaachan's face, an expression I haven't seen before, and in that moment I suddenly remember what I haven't for years, that it was her who knew first that our mother was missing, her who found Nozomi's shoes on the beach.

45

Rei

令

'You found him!' As Kiki carries Hikaru back to the house, an unfamiliar voice sounds triumphantly from along the road. It's Kanagawa-san, pure joy in her smile, her feet planted a little too far apart. Her daughter is standing cautiously behind her, holding an umbrella over her mother's head. 'I was so worried,' she says. 'I'm so glad you found him.' She looks at Kiki, such a kind face, alert and understanding. 'You poor thing.' Her face changes as she looks at Hikaru. 'His leg,' she says.

We look down to see that his knee looks like it's been scalped, and his shin is soaked in blood. At the sight, Hikaru starts to cry again. 'I fell over,' he sobs. 'Chibi was too quick, I fell over.'

'Were you following Chibi?' Kiki asks him, cradling him closer. The shit she would give him for running out of the house after a cat, any other time.

Ai runs upstairs to get the first-aid kit. I look around for Kanagawa-san, but she's gone back inside. I wonder if she knew who Hikaru was, or if she thought he was somebody else, her own child or grandchild, or someone only she can remember. 'I have plasters,' Ai announces, panting. 'And disinfectant.'

'Rei, do you think it needs stitches?' Kiki asks, sitting on the genkan with Hikaru on her lap, examining the knee.

'I'll call the hospital,' Ai says before I can answer.

'I'll drive you,' Youta offers.

Obaachan brings a bowl of warm water and a clean cloth from the kitchen, and as all of us fuss and exclaim over the chubby knee, I realise that everyone's relieved to have something to do, somewhere to put the fear-fuelled energy that's still zipping through our veins. A cut on Hikaru's leg, however deep, is something we can fix, finding that the ground still holds. We all pile into the car to the hospital, except for Obaachan, who waves us off, and the mood in our group is something like euphoria.

In the rear-view mirror, I can see Hikaru sitting in Kiki's lap. He hasn't let go of her hand, and she runs her thumb over his palm as if she's reading it. He sings softly to himself like we're not here, in what Ai describes as his egg-voice, a sound like something just about to hatch. Kiki told me when he was born that she was planning on calling him Ryu, for a dragon, something to give him the strength he'd need for everything the world was going to throw at him, and also because it pleased her to know that Richard would never be able to say it. It was my idea to call him Hikaru, for light.

In the hospital waiting room, the other patients sit with their knees together, talking in hushed voices, injuries and pain no excuse for casting off politeness. I'm no good with hospitals, Japanese hospitals especially. That indefinable medical smell, sympathy tempered with efficiency and pragmatic calm. As Kiki and Hikaru are led into triage, behind a single blue curtain on a metal frame, I suddenly see what a mess we're in, soaked to the skin and variously splattered with sand and blood. I'm wondering whether I can make an excuse to leave, to go and see if Youta parked the car OK, or stay at home with Obaachan, but then Kiki and Hikaru emerge, and without seeming to notice what she's doing, Kiki takes my hand. 'They said it probably just needs a stitch or two,' she says. 'Nothing to worry about.'

A nurse appears from behind the blue curtain and looks down a list on a clipboard in front of her. 'Takanawa Hikaru,' she says. 'You're not too far down.'

We sit there side by side, not saying much. A lady whose son is waiting for a crutch presses a neatly folded Snoopy handkerchief into my hand when she sees that Hikaru's knee is still bleeding, and unobtrusively supplies him with boiled strawberry sweets. Ai smooths out the wrappers and shows Hikaru where they say, *You can have a candy because you're cute.*

The doctor who calls us in is young, and tells us seriously that Hikaru is very sweet, like it's an official opinion. The nurse takes out a picture book to show him while the doctor gets to work. I look at her regulation grey shoes and white tights, and try to get a grip, try not to cry because my nephew hurt his leg and everybody is so lovely. How are you meant to go through life making sure you don't feel too much, when at any moment a kid could lose himself chasing after a cat, and you could be reminded that the world is full of all these people? All the lovely people in the world, and the unlovely ones, who were babies once, with squidgy knees and gap teeth, who've felt guilty when they've said things they knew were unkind, and longed for sweets they haven't had since childhood, and remembered the first time the person they liked smiled back at them, and whose mothers wanted to hold them forever. You can lift the lid on an abyss, but on the other side of it there's such kindness, too, enough kindness and enough love to break anybody's heart. I try not to think of any of those things as a stranger stitches up Hikaru's leg, talking to him soothingly, four stitches, with infinite care.

46

Ai

愛

The day after Hikaru is lost, and then found again, I open my eyes and don't feel like crying.

It's such a weird feeling that at first I think something's wrong. Then I remember that Hikaru is safe, that everything is exactly the same as it was yesterday, and that that's wonderful, a miracle. I see the sunlight through the paper screen, and it doesn't feel like lying at the bottom of a well and clawing upwards. Hikaru's arms snake their way around my neck in a cross between a hug and a strangle, the buttons on Paddington's duffel coat digging into my chin. I breathe in the smell of him, clean cotton and sleep.

'Ai,' he says. You can tell by the scratchiness of his voice, not the volume, that he's trying to whisper. 'It's not sleeping time any more, it's chatting time.'

I turn around so I'm facing him. 'What do you want to chat about?' I whisper. I can see the flecks of hazel and green in his eyes, every eyelash.

He thinks, furrowing his brow, and rearranges his arms so he can twist my hair between his fingers.

'Tortoises,' he says after a while. 'They can live for years and years, and their faces are like this.' He tenses the tendons in his neck and bulges his eyes. 'And you can't make them hurry. That's the best thing about them.'

'OK,' I agree. It's the first morning of the rest of our lives. 'Let's talk about tortoises.'

Afterwards, it's always like the light has been turned up. It rains over the next few days, when I'm walking around still afraid, waiting to see if this will hold. It's that humid rain that makes everyone want to tear off their clothes and run around howling. Hikaru does that, roaring his way around the house in his pants, until Kiki decides she's taking him to the cinema, to the annual summer Doraemon movie, because there's air-conditioning. We all join in, and I don't have to go in through the back door or wear a baseball cap. There's nobody I have to be incredible in front of, or who's taking pictures. The girl at the ticket counter smiles at me in the friendly way she smiles at everyone, and I feel like I've landed on a different planet. She gives Rei promotional Doraemon handkerchiefs from a basket, and we wrap them around our heads straight away. I suddenly remember that I still have the Doraemon stickers we got with the movie the summer I was seven, because in my whole life nothing that's happened has ever seemed special enough to use them.

I half watch the film, and half watch Hikaru's face. His eyes are round with concentration all the way through, like he barely dares to close them. I feel like I've come back from somewhere far away, and I must have something to give him from my journey, something I could tell him that he could hold on to and use one day if he needs it, like a talisman. I can't figure out what it would be.

We go to eat savoury pancakes afterwards, and the pancake man, with his pink face over the griddles and his white chef's cap, is so earnest and so focused on his job that I think I probably love him. We sit at the counter and load each of the pancakes with Bull-Dog sauce and all the toppings, bonito flakes and ginger and nori, and cut them into quarters so we can share. Hikaru has okonomiyaki sauce around his mouth and Kiki and Rei have forgotten to take their headscarves off. Or maybe they haven't forgotten, and they're just choosing to eat dinner with Doraemon-patterned fabric wrapped around their heads, and if only I were religious, I would kiss the ground in thanks for all of it.

47

Rei

令

I watch Ai for days, practically following her from room to room. Her skin has changed colour, like the weather changed, which is pretty much exactly what happened. She's now going around radiating cleanliness and youth, as if she's just been away on a spa weekend rather than holed up in a depressive stupor that scared the hell out of everyone, but I don't trust it, yet. She and Hikaru make a very long, very batshit comic strip together, and a potion out of the fallen azalea and cosmos petals in the garden, and have conversations where they rank everything on earth from one to ten – the most annoying mandatory activities (Hikaru puts brushing his teeth at number one; Ai says sleeping); the best animals (Hikaru: poisonous dart frogs; Ai: those dogs whose faces look like wrinkly old-fashioned pants); food, in sub-categories of savoury, sweet and disgusting. I decide she probably has turned a corner when she starts to teach Hikaru an old Loupie Lou dance routine. She even gets Kiki to help her bleach her new pixie cut, with some stuff she gets from the conbini.

A week after Hikaru-gate, Ai says she's going out to buy snacks, and Hikaru says he'll come too. She looks at me for one second longer than strictly necessary when she says it.

'Itterasshai,' I tell her, the polite equivalent of: Off you go, then.

'Ittekimasu,' she says. I'll go and come back. She does, with iced tea for Obaachan called The Pungency, which Ai says she couldn't not buy, even though Obaachan has no idea what that means.

Tentatively at first, we start to do summer things. Holiday things. I notice that the tomatoes have started to ripen, clusters of bright-red spheres like lanterns at a festival amid the curling tendrils of the kabocha squash. Time is playing tricks – when I think of Ai in Tokyo, her tufty hair almost covering her face, I feel like I've been here forever, but every day I can think of seventy-five things I want to talk to her and Kiki about, like we haven't even properly started yet.

It's been almost four weeks since Silverman Sayle first granted me leave – about four times as long, as far as someone like Llewellyn is concerned, as you need to get over anything life could possibly throw at a person. If he knew what this particular up-chuck was, he would have expected me back at work in twenty-four hours. Things in the Takanawa household seem momentarily sufficiently functioning that I feel duty-bound to have a cursory, ineffectual look at my emails every day or so – but I'm always relieved when the internet won't play ball. One day, disappointingly, the connection holds, and I open an email from Llewellyn so impressively passive-aggressive that it elicits a reply. I write one in the voice Kiki used to resign, achingly polite and regretful about the fact that I will never have to see his face again, because I am never coming back to Silverman Sayle, and best regards to Jasper. I look at it for a moment, my heart swelling with satisfaction, before I consign it to my drafts folder and out of mind. London and my desk are so far away, and Ai and Kiki and the sea are right here.

Youta suggests a date for Uradome, inviting us to join him

and Masato and Daisuke, and it feels like we've been invited to the ball.

We're getting ready in the morning when Obaachan stomps in, allegedly to get her parasol which she left in the genkan, but in reality to tell us we shouldn't be going to the beach. She's decked out for the almost-forty-degree heat with bloomers on under her woollen dress.

'It's an inauspicious day,' she tells us for the fiftieth time, standing in the genkan and stabbing at the wall calendar with a bent finger. 'You could get kidnapped by Koreans.'

Neither Kiki nor I, standing in the hall with our hands folded together like polite security guards, asks her to elaborate.

'Or pulled out to sea by a riptide. Or attacked by jellyfish.'

'That does sound bad,' Kiki agrees, stepping into the genkan. 'Thank you for telling us.' She pats Obaachan's shoulder. Obaachan looks appalled and hurries out.

'Have a good time at your ikebana class!' Kiki calls after her. 'This will just be another grievance for her to air at the Buddha of Complaints,' she says to me. 'She told me she goes to see him most days. She'll run out of things to tell him, otherwise.'

I think how much more effective the Buddha sounds than therapy. Cheaper, and less judgemental. 'Does it make us diabolical people, to ignore our great-grandmother?' I ask Kiki doubtfully as we go back to making the tamagoyaki omelette for the lunchboxes.

'No, it's living and letting live,' Kiki says firmly.

I glance at the kitchen clock to see how long we have until Youta arrives to collect us. The comforting smell of the tamagoyaki and the bitter freshness of the grated radish are undercut by the plastic of the pool floats, already eagerly inflated by Hikaru. It's like the whole of the last fifteen years never happened, and we've been living this version of our life in this house the whole time.

'Remember that one summer when we slept over at each other's houses without a single night's break for seventeen nights?' Kiki asks. I nod. We kept count, every night another triumph. 'Remember Mikan?' she adds. Youta's toy penguin; if he slept at ours, we'd have to stop at his house first so he could get it, without any embarrassment, just like it was a fact, like brushing his teeth.

We hear the front door open, Youta's voice calling a hello.

'They're here! They're HERE!' Hikaru sounds demented with excitement.

The boys have come in Daisuke's truck, Youta and Daisuke sitting up front and Masato in the back. They look exactly the same as they did back in school, Daisuke as tall as he ever was, folding his limbs into the car, and Masato, round-faced as a Buddha. It's only when I see them, and Youta's sweet smile through the window, that I remember about Ai being Japan's very own scarlet woman. We pile into the truck, greetings called over each other, as psyched as we were on the school coach to camp. In the rear-view mirror, I see how trendy Ai looks with her new hair, someone you can totally imagine being at the centre of a sexy (kind of – I mean, not really at all, but anyway) tabloid scandal. But even though Masato blushes an impressive colour and has to cough about eight times whenever he speaks, nobody says a thing about it.

It's a half-mile walk to Uradome, along a single-file dirt track that runs through a forest of pines and then winds steeply down to the beach. The beach is almost deserted, like it always is, the walk keeping people away. The sand beneath our feet is powdery white, the sea a milky turquoise where it hits the land, deepening out to azure, cerulean and finally indigo, the water so clear that near the shore you can see glimmers of silver fish. Paradise colours, the only difference between here and some postcard tropical holiday that in place of waving palm trees, we have ancient conifers, wizened old custodians of the landscape. The beach is broken up into coves divided by stacks of sharp volcanic rock formations small enough for Hikaru to climb on, and ahead of us are the islands and arches we swim to every time we're here, rocks that rise vertically out of the water, sacred rocks, each of them lovingly encircled with braided ropes hung with tessellated paper streamers to show their status as deities. Some of them have pine trees sticking straight out of the tops and sides like over-enthusiastically planted birthday candles, or the arms of a comedy alien stuck straight up in greeting. Others are more stately, a single black cypress rising out of them, gnarled and majestic as an oracle. There's only one stack we never go near: the one with the split in the rock, an entrance just wide enough to swim through, the pitch dark of a silent cave behind it. When we were small, we used to freak out before we could even peer inside, the shadow cast by the rock on the water so absolute that we quivered even as we swam in its vicinity.

'Remember when Nozomi went swimming to the bad rock without any clothes on?' I whisper to Kiki. Nozomi brought us here a handful of times, though more often we came with friends. It's the first time we've spoken about her, since the fight.

'I died,' Kiki whispers back. 'I was so sure someone we knew was going to suddenly appear on the beach.'

Hikaru runs past, shouting to Youta that there's a small stream perfect for cooling the watermelon which Youta has brought, swinging it in a net. It suddenly occurs to me that Youta knew Nozomi. If it weren't totally socially awkward, I could probably mine Youta's memory for interactions he'd had with Nozomi that I didn't even know about, as if I were having a new encounter with her. He knew the sound of her voice, her expressions, the her-ness of her.

The sun shines so brightly that I'm squinting through my sunglasses. There's just one family further down the beach, set up with multicoloured parasols and picnic mats splashed with Sanrio characters, the mother pouring something from a thermos as a tiny person almost obscured by the rubber ring around her waist glowers at us mistrustfully.

The boys have brought beach volleyball and enlist Hikaru to help them set up. Kiki and Ai and I immediately strip down to our swimsuits and throw ourselves on to the sand. Kiki sighs with contentment, her eyes closed.

'I don't know why you don't do this all the time,' I tell her. 'If it was this hot in London, I'd quit my job and just lie in the sun all day.'

'I would literally get cast out of civilised society,' Kiki says, stretching out her limbs. 'All the women I know wear long gloves and UV sunhats from March.'

'I'm not meant to do this,' Ai says, like she's just remembered, sitting up on to her elbows. 'Did we bring an umbrella?'

'Yeah,' Kiki says, her eyes still closed. She tilts her head towards our pile of stuff.

'What do you mean, you're not meant to do this?' I ask.

Ai looks towards the umbrella, but doesn't move. 'It's in the contract.'

'The Kabuki contract?'

'The Loupie Lou contract. They never wrote a different one.' Ai lies back down, extending her arms above her head. 'It was so we had a uniform complexion.'

'Are we going to swim in the cave today?' Kiki interrupts, before I can say anything about Ai's contract.

Ai shivers. 'No way. I try to forget it's even there.'

Ai doesn't make any further move to get the umbrella, so I busy myself finding sun cream. I've brought it over from sunny England, because in Japan it's hard to find anything other than

236

very small tubes of expensive facial sunblock, doing what we're doing being unthinkable.

'Onechan, I wish we were religious,' Ai says with genuine feeling, watching the boys play volleyball.

'Do you?' I ask, spraying sun cream on her shoulders, over her tattoo of an Inari fox, one of many reasons she must never, ever show her shoulders in front of Obaachan.

'I want someone to tell me what's right and wrong, and what I'm meant to be doing all the time.'

'Is that the only thing being religious entails?' I ask, at the same time as: 'Pretty sure Rei is prepared to arrange that for you,' Kiki says. Fortunately for her, the volleyball lands on my towel before I can answer.

Youta has set up the net so it's low enough for Hikaru, and every time they score, he and Hikaru high-five, Hikaru with a little swagger that kills me. Sath turned out to be surprisingly good at volleyball, the holiday we camped in France, on a site that opened straight on to a beach with French teenagers play-ing volleyball and flirting day and night. I wonder if he'd be good with Hikaru, too. It would track.

'Those boys have got unreasonably good bodies,' Kiki observes from her towel. 'Do you think they work out?'

'How?' I ask. Sath is still on my mind, the smoothness of his torso, his appendectomy scar. 'There's no gym here. They work in construction, right?'

'Daisuke's only doing it for the summer,' says Ai. 'He said he's studying over in Kyoto – some kind of maths that I couldn't understand even a bit.'

'I guess you get pretty strong hauling sacks of cement all day, even if it's just for a few weeks,' I say.

'Evidently,' Kiki agrees admiringly.

The first time I ever saw Sath, he was kissing someone else. He was standing at the bar when this pouty, glossy-haired girl came up and put her arms around his waist, and he turned his head and kissed her without smiling, like it was just a matter of fact. I liked the lack of fuss, the confidence. Sometimes I think that was the entire reason I fell for him, because he was already in this hot relationship I couldn't screw up.

'If you want religion,' I say to Ai, booting Sath firmly out of mind, 'get Obaachan to show you. You could get up every morning to chant with her.' I spent hours as a child waiting for her to finish, the drone of her voice authoritative, our names popping up once in a while, as I waited impatiently to ask her where the biggest saucepan was, or if she had already filled in the form for the Co-op order, or whatever it was that my mother had sent me to find out.

'Buddhism is impossible,' Ai says morosely. 'You have to hold all opposite ideas in your head at the same time. And you have to have compassion for everything. Even *yourself*.' She sighs. 'I could try it, I guess. I saw an advertisement for Buddhist monks in the newspaper the other day. Do you think I'd be any good?'

I look at her to see if she's serious. She is. I have a brief image of Ai as a solemn religious adherent, deeply restricted and deeply tranquil. It makes me feel very safe.

Before I can say anything, she answers the question herself. 'I don't, either. It says you have to not be attached to anything, even people.' She blows out her lips in exasperation. 'Who can do that?'

'I thought you had religion,' I say. 'I thought the music came from the universe.'

She looks at me. 'That's not *religion*, Rei,' she says, like I'm very stupid. 'That's just the way things are.'

Hikaru has started copying the way Daisuke balances the ball in the crook of his hip, even though the ball is too big for him and his arm will barely fit around it. He's repeating the phrases he's heard, shouting, 'Out! Come on, guys.' Youta takes Hikaru just as seriously as he wants to be taken, nodding at him in agreement. It occurs to me that I've never seen Hikaru with a man before. I can see Kiki, watching them from beneath lowered eyelids, smiling at Youta with her lips closed.

'You could always join a cult,' I say to Ai.

She looks at me scornfully. 'I'm not fucking mental,' she says, but she smiles a little as she says it.

I lie back and close my eyes, the sunlight a warm orange glow. Kiki and Ai are so close on either side of me that if I reached out I could hold both their hands, like I did when they were small. I can hear the sound of the waves crashing, the lilting call of gulls, the shouts from the volleyball game. I wish I didn't have to go back to work. I think of the spoof resignation email, sitting in my drafts folder.

Kiki didn't even blink when she told me I should quit, but I know why I work at Silverman Sayle. Money gives you choices. If our mother had had more money, she could have moved to Tokyo and kept an eye on Richard, or told him to fuck off and gone to live somewhere else. Maybe she wouldn't have been as sad in a high-ceilinged apartment in Montmartre or a hippy commune in Goa, somewhere she could have rewritten her story. If Richard hadn't had money, I could never have gone to university in England, or flown home for the holidays. If I didn't work at Silverman Sayle, I couldn't have paid him back, and I wouldn't have had the deposit for a flat so quickly, a home that's all mine. I couldn't have sent money to Kiki, for roof repairs and new shoes and Ai. They say money can't buy you happiness – but I reckon it can, if you know what to buy.

'Mama!' Hikaru comes scrambling up, panting theatrically from his twenty-metre run. He grabs Kiki's knees and jumps up and down so sand goes everywhere. 'Youta says we can go get the watermelon for the suika-wari now, if you say we can.'

Bashing a watermelon blindfolded, the Japanese beach version of a piñata. By the volleyball net, Youta is shading his eyes with his hands and looking towards Kiki, his expression unreadable. Hikaru stares into Kiki's face with disarming intensity. 'Can we?'

'Sure,' Kiki smiles.

Hollering with delight, Hikaru goes rushing over to the stream. He stops dead on arrival and turns around. 'Mama,' he shouts, 'do you have an enormous baseball bat?'

'I'll just check in my pockets for the enormous baseball bat I always carry around with me,' Kiki calls back, without missing a beat. She is wearing a bikini. Hikaru looks expectant.

Later, after we've swum out to each of the islands, Hikaru a small sea monster in his green rubber ring, and eaten our obento, onigiri and tamagoyaki, and wiener sausages with their ends cut to look like octopus legs, and we've all taken turns swiping at the air and bashing the ground with a huge stick, a therapeutic activity, and Youta has successfully smashed open the watermelon so we can feast on its flesh, we're sitting back down on the towels, our skin salty, our hair in rat-tails.

'Did you know we came here with Youta when we were only a little bit bigger than you?' Kiki says to Hikaru, biting inelegantly into a hunk of watermelon. He shakes his head, pink juice running down his chin. 'Once there was a man with a camel and we all had a ride. Do you remember?' she asks me.

I nod. The irritation of the camel. 'Where did he come from? He was only here that one time.'

'And I pushed your auntie off because she didn't share the mermaid float.' I remember that, too. The grainy texture of the sand against my teeth when I hit the ground. Say what you like about Kiki, she used to be world-class at holding a grudge. She sighs with satisfaction. 'Those were the days.'

Hikaru looks up at her, still gnawing his way through his watermelon. 'No, Mama,' he says. 'These are the days.'

Basically a tiny guru in tropical swimming trunks.

Kiki looks at him for a moment, then turns to Ai and me. 'So what did you decide?' she says.

'About what?' I ask. The watermelon is so ripe its juice is sugar syrup, the flesh crunchy and soft, like snow.

'Religion. Did you find one? Shall we all convert?'

'Oh, no,' Ai says cheerfully, slurping fruit into her mouth.

'We're amoral,' I say to Kiki.

'And we can fit nowhere,' Ai agrees.

Kiki shrugs, wiping her cheek with the back of her hand. 'Figures,' she says. 'Mixed-up bastard children.'

I've reached the bottom of the watermelon, and gnaw the chlorophyll cool of the white next to the rind. 'Hey, Ai, I know what you could do.'

'What?'

'You could join a girl band that controls what you wear and what you do and what you think, every minute of your life.'

Ai throws her watermelon rind at me. 'Shut up.'

48
Kiki
清美

The sun is starting to set on what I suspect may have been the best day of Hikaru's life. We're packed up and walking away from the beach, a little sunburnt, Hikaru holding my hand in silence, he's so tired from an entire day of running around in the sun and pretending to be a man.

'Did you have fun?' I whisper to him.

He nods. 'I love Youta, Mama,' he says solemnly. 'I love Daisuke and Masato, too, but I love Youta best.'

'I know,' I say, and I wonder if I should counsel against giving your heart to someone you've only known for a fortnight, but then Youta, noticing Hikaru's exhaustion, slows up ahead of us and bends down in front of Hikaru to take him on to his back, and I suspect I might love Youta, too.

'He's heavy,' I warn him.

Youta turns and smiles at me, squinting into the sun. 'Not as heavy as you were, that time I had to carry you home from Lately's.' Lately's is one of the three bars in town, objectively the worst one, and the easiest to get into when you're fifteen. 'You wouldn't stop singing "Ganbarimashou".'

Oh my god. 'Let's Do Our Best', by SMAP in their suits with their perms. Kill me now.

'I forgot about that,' I say, concentrating on sliding Hikaru's flip-flops off his feet. I wonder how many girls have bellowed songs by Takanawa Ai while being bodily removed from bars for being too drunk.

As we make our way up the rocky path from the beach, the sun is setting with fanfare, painting the sea a thousand glittering strokes of coral and orange, our rocky islands casting long shadows on the water. Gulls glide in front of the spectacle, basking in the glow.

'It's the colour of that pink crayon in the set, remember?' Rei says, materialising next to me. Her wet hair is in a knot on her head, and with the golden light bathing her face, she looks about Hikaru's age, the eleven between her eyebrows fading.

'I could never figure out what to use it for,' I say, shading my eyes with my hand, remembering its neon lure, how that one desirable crayon remained pristine while all the others were worn down and snapped with use. It's the colour gilding the edges of the clouds as the sun makes its prima-donna exit, refracting light around it in visible rays, resplendent as some frescoed religious ceiling.

We keep walking slowly, our faces to the sun. Ahead of us, Daisuke is spinning Hikaru's rubber ring around his arm like a cabaret performer. I can see Hikaru clutching Youta's neck, slipping as he starts to fall asleep. Youta hoicks him a little higher, cradling him behind his back.

The last sliver of sun disappears below the horizon. There's a split second of something like sadness, nostalgia for the day we've had even though it's only moments past.

'Do you guys want to come back to ours for some beers?' Rei asks. It's a shock of elation, to realise I'm with adults, that we can carry the day on into the night, 6pm time for a drink rather than an argument about getting in the bath.

The boys rumble agreement, with all the polite caveats: if it isn't too much trouble, if we're sure they won't get in the way.

243

'Why would we invite you if we thought you were going to get in the way?' Rei says. 'Why are you so Japanese?'

'Let's get beers from the conbini – they'll be cold,' Ai says. 'And gyoza from the shop next door. I'm starving.'

49

Ai

愛

Hikaru is asleep with his head in my lap. Kiki said we should move him into the bedroom, but now she's had a couple of beers and she's laughing so hard at something Rei said that she's holding her cheeks to stop them from aching. I carry the gyoza from the table to my mouth with one hand cupped underneath, because I don't want to drop soy sauce and vinegar on to his perfect sleeping face.

Nobody is looking at me. I'm surrounded by my sisters and these boys I didn't know I knew but who've always been there, it turns out. I'm pretty sure that none of them care what I do next, or even what I've done before.

I accidentally brush the bottom of my beer can against Hikaru's cheek and he opens his eyes for a second. He sees me and smiles and then closes them again. He doesn't even look around for Kiki; I'm enough.

He has a very heavy head, Hikaru. I'm pinned to the ground by the weight of him, and that makes me feel like maybe this moment isn't going to slip through my fingers. Everything I want in the whole world is right here in this room. I've never said it to Rei and Kiki, that I liked it the way it was. That sounds like I'm glad Mama's dead, and that isn't what I mean. My sisters think I don't remember her. I don't have a lot of memories, but they aren't just of her holding her skull: I remember her slicing me a peach, and me spilling its juice all down my dress, a cream one with flowers on it. I looked up to see if she was cross and she was laughing, saying how delicious the peach was. I remember her holding a pencil, drawing a rabbit hopping across the page. I think I remember her reading to me, but then her voice becomes Rei's, and I don't know if I'm making it up.

When I think of being small, it's Rei I remember. Rei putting a plaster on my knee, Rei calling that dinner was ready, Rei taking me to the library and the beach. Sometimes she looked murderous, but she was solid. She was something I could throw myself against or try to run away from, and she'd curse and catch me every time. I have warm feelings towards Mama, that person who gave me a peach and a rabbit, but I never needed her.

There's this feeling I get, like someone put a balloon under my ribcage and they're inflating it a little too much. The crazy thing about it is that it's the same feeling for a rush of love and for the beginning of heartbreak, like my body didn't get the memo that those two things aren't supposed to be the same. I imagine what Rei would say, if I started having a wailing breakdown because I love everyone so much, and have another gyoza instead.

50

Rei

令

Because of Hikaru, or at least because we have him as an excuse, over the next few weeks we do the same things we used to do when we were kids. Because it's summer, and the things we're doing feel like we're on holiday together, and because we can remember each other from a time when Kiki and I sported hair elastics with sparkly heart-shaped bobbles and Youta's short shorts showed off his perpetually grazed knees, it takes almost no time for all of us to feel like we've known each other forever – which is actually true. Ai makes all the obento for our excursions, with impressive creative energy – carrots cut up to look like sunrays and scenes drawn on the rice with tiny bits of scrambled egg and nori to match whatever we're doing that day. You don't need to make penance lunches for a depression, I almost tell her, but they're delicious, so in the end I just say thank you, and eat them.

We go hiking in the hills along the coast, on trails that take us under avenues of pine trees and then burst out into views of the sea that you can't quite believe, and to visit the small dairy farm, where the milk pudding is so delicious Kiki actually gets tears in her eyes. We take a glass-bottomed boat ride around the coast, watching the jellyfish undulate through the water like luminous lilac ghosts; Kiki grabs hold of Youta when a huge, moss-covered turtle passes underneath, royally unimpressed with everything in sight.

We discover that Masato's great passion, which it takes him a while to reveal, is rakugo, traditional comic storytelling. It feels like a great honour to be allowed to go and watch him do a set in a function room off the town hall, kneeling on a floor cushion in a kimono, and we take Obaachan, too. Obaachan turns out to have a filthy laugh, which is actually totally unsurprising, and Ai laughs so hard she runs out of breath and sits there shaking silently, tears of mirth pouring down her cheeks. Masato is so pleased to see us afterwards that he turns pink like a rose, so sweet that I have to resist the urge to cuddle him.

We pick strawberries at the fruit farm, carefully holding the little cardboard carton of condensed milk they give you to dip the fruit into; Hikaru walks down the rows of fruit with one hand in Kiki's and the other in Youta's, and I really hope she isn't so dumb that she hasn't noticed Youta is as smitten with her as he has been since we were kids. Do you guys think you should hurry up and get together, I want to ask them, in all sincerity, because this life is short and unpredictable and you should probably seize the day?

Daisuke drives us over to the water park in Ogahara, a whole hour's drive during which Youta blasts out the catchiest, cheesiest J-pop and sings along to it word-perfectly with no self-consciousness whatsoever, completely unperturbed by Masato and Daisuke's disgusted ribbing. By the end of the journey, everyone is singing along and patently pretending they're in an American road trip movie. Since we've been there last, they've added bigger slides. In the whirlpool, Hikaru spins in his rubber ring until he looks like he's seeing stars.

51

I'm sitting in front of my laptop when I'm surprised to hear the hugest sigh, and realise it's me. It's been a while since I heard that sound. I'm looking at those smug cirrus clouds again, gathering up the golden crumbs of a pumpkin korokke with the end of my finger. If I keep looking at the clouds, I know what they'll steal from me – that feeling of each sunny day full of possibility, to be spent with my sisters, a team of three, all of us equal. I think it might be a first, and the idea of Silverman Sayle butting in to wreck it is deeply aggravating. My emails open, bringing the familiar pang of regret that the internet is working. I watch the number at the top of my inbox climb moment by moment, and the drafts folder sitting there treacherously in the settings bar. It's like a twitch, really, opening the drafts folder while I wait for my inbox to load, and a thought experiment, hovering over the 'send' button. I remember the time I told Sath I missed my mother's korokke and he found a recipe and cooked them, and didn't even mind when I cried and told him I couldn't eat them. Another sigh, even bigger than the first one. I hear Hikaru give a shout of laughter outside. Before I can think about it, I send the email.

I close the lid of the laptop and sit there for a moment. Out in the street, Kiki and Youta are trying to play hanetsuki with Hikaru, traditional badminton with beautifully painted wooden paddles and a shuttlecock made from a tiny, rock-hard black stone and an actual feather. I remember we used to feel compelled to play it on New Year's Day, a day when it felt necessary to be very traditional, and how impossible it was to play in our kimonos.

Maybe I wouldn't have accepted the traineeship at Silverman Sayle if it hadn't landed in my lap at the exact moment it did, like a very dubious lifebuoy. I stretch and flop backwards on to the tatami, my arms over my head. Sath and I had been living together for a few months, which it turns out was beyond my personal limit for not knowing what I'm doing with my life. Ghosts that I'd been able to ward off with a clear timetable of lectures and exams started flapping around my head, making our relationship pretty much untenable.

Sath was cooking me lovely meals and suggesting we go to the BFI together, when what I was looking for was maybe someone to tattoo directly on to my eyeballs as a distraction from the inside of my head. Silverman Sayle sounded like it might potentially offer me exactly that, and, to be fair, it has lived up to what it said on the tin. I think part of its appeal was that it was the opposite of anywhere Nozomi would ever have put herself.

'Rei!' Ai pushes aside the noren, precariously holding a huge box of eggs, a bag of sugar, another of flour. I don't think she's ever, in all her life, used a bag for shopping. 'We're going to make casutera,' she says breathlessly.

Youta and Hikaru come piling in, Kiki following, tapping her shuttlecock up and down on the hagoita paddle very carefully. 'Look!' she says triumphantly. 'I'm a hagoita master. I'll go get Obaachan. I'm sure she'll have a lot of opinions about casutera.'

'It's OK, I'll get her,' I say.

250

I wander slowly to Obaachan's house, not thinking about the email. Probably the internet's so slow here it'll time out before it sends, anyway.

'Obaachan,' I call, stepping into the sitting room. She's sitting at the zataku, reading a newspaper, and she doesn't reply. The beat of quiet is enough for me to look around the room, to notice it as it is, not an arena for battle only to be entered once you've armoured up. There isn't much stand-alone furniture, which goes for the rest of the house, too; the built-in cupboards with paper doors which line almost every wall are crammed with things hidden from view, but not much else is needed if you sit, eat and sleep on the floor. Not saying anything, not looking at me, Obaachan looks unexpectedly small in the middle of the tatami. I think of all the iterations of family that have existed across these two houses: husbands, daughters, sons-in-law, granddaughters, being born and marrying and leaving and dying, only Obaachan a constant. I wonder if it's a burden, to live so long.

'We're making casutera,' I tell her. 'Do you want to come help?'

She raises a hand imperiously, eyes not leaving her newspaper. 'I'll come in a minute.'

'I'll make a tea for you,' I volunteer. I haven't yet, this year, because I've never been able to get it right. It was Obaachan who taught me, when I was younger: exactly the right amount of powder, the water just off boiling, the movement of the whisk, starting at the top of the earthenware bowl and down in a vertical line, then round the perimeter of the bowl, tracing the letter の, fast and gentle, so the tips of the split bamboo barely touch the sides.

She nods once without expression, and while I prepare it she continues to glower at the newspaper, not looking at me. I'm kneeling while I work, something so pleasingly tidy about the image I have of myself from the outside. The tea froths up and I keep whisking; when Obaachan makes the tea, it doesn't taste of liquid at all, but the lightest foam, a suggestion of green tea, made up of a million bubbles. I whisk till there are no lumps and end the movement with the whisk in the middle of the froth, pulling it out vertically. Even though she's still pretending not to look at me, I pick up the bowl exactly as you're meant to, so its bottom sits on the outstretched fingers of my left hand, balanced neatly by my right. I turn it so the design, a view of a mountain painted with a few delicate strokes, is facing her, and bow.

Obaachan dips her head, too haughty to bend her back, and receives the bowl from me with her hands in the same position as my own, turning it so the design faces me. She lifts it to her lips, inhaling the earthy, grassy aroma of the tea. She sips.

'Disgusting,' she declares without venom, looking down at the tea matter-of-factly.

I burst out laughing.

Obaachan looks up, as if she'd forgotten I was there, and is surprised by the noise. 'You're unbelievable,' I tell her.

Her expression hovers, uncertain where to land, and I think she's going to put the tea down and carry on reading. Instead, her face suddenly creases up into a thousand smiling wrinkles, and her hand reaches out for mine. I can feel her gnarled old bones through the flesh, her poor twisted joints, but her skin, thin as tissue paper, is soft.

'You're right, Rei-chan,' she says appreciatively, and just for a moment we're looking each other in the eye. She never calls me that. 'Aren't I just.'

52

A couple of weeks after our trip to Uradome, Ai, Kiki, Hikaru and I walk to the sento one evening, one of my favourite things to do here.

'Have you put the plaster over your shoulder?' I ask, as we make our way to the entrance, the 'Hot Water' sign lit up, the smell of soap and fresh towels billowing towards us on the warm air.

'Yes,' Ai sighs, pulling down her T-shirt to show me. 'Even though I don't see why I should have to. It's not hurting anyone.'

'It hurts their eyes,' I tell her. 'It offends their sense of propriety.'

Ai has covered up her tattoo, to avoid a repeat of our last bath experience, when the three of us got into a fight with the ancient sento lady because she tried to chuck Ai out on account of it, the advantage we had in height and number possibly strengthened by the fact that we weren't dressed and she was.

We duck under the heavy navy noren. Even though we've been coming here since we were actual babies, the proprietor still sucks in her cheeks when Kiki asks for four tickets, like she's said something surprising.

The sento is old-school, one that our mother used to visit as a kid. The proprietor, who was probably here back then too, sits in a booth that straddles the ladies' changing room and the men's, peering suspiciously round into both.

'I don't think this set-up would even be legal in the UK,' I say, pulling a plastic basket out of a locker. 'Having some old lady spending her days ogling naked people.' I look at the woman, her face nudging a memory I can't reach. 'Don't you think she has kind of a neurotic face?'

Kiki glances in her direction. 'No,' she tells me. 'She just reminds you of that supply teacher you didn't like at school, the skinny one who thought everything was a cause and smelt of cupboards.'

She's right.

'We are such a herd of haafus now,' Kiki says in English as she pulls her T-shirt over her head. '*Four* of us. And in the deep countryside.'

I remember Sath telling me once about a list the girls had had at his school, ranking the boys in the class, how there was one list for the white boys and a separate list for the other boys. He said he was at the top of the separate list, though, and I started laughing, so he did too. I can't believe I just told you that, he said – we hadn't known each other long, when we had this conversation. I said it was obvious, because I thought it was, and I hadn't been laughing because he'd said it, but because of the appallingness of the lists. Then I saw that he was blushing and not smiling, and I realised he didn't know how good-looking he was. I told him that if there'd been a diversity list in my class, I'd have been at the top of it, too, since I would have been the only person on it, despite being only half diverse.

As we slide open the glass door to the baths, we're enveloped in clouds of steam, the sounds of gossiping, laughter, running water echoing off the walls. We find washing stations next to each other, perch on the little plastic stools to wash.

'I was thinking,' I say, testing the temperature of the hot water, 'that we should hang out exclusively with haafus. It would solve having to explain everything all the time.'

'Isn't this how ethnic cleansing starts?' Kiki asks with interest, squeezing soap on to her exfoliator. 'Also, we literally don't know any.' She pulls Hikaru towards her and pours water over his back. 'Although I think there are more, now. We're, like, haafu elders. I met a few when I worked in that bar in Roppongi.' She scrubs Hikaru's back. 'One of them, Lia, was half American, from Florida. She said "haafu" was a derogatory term. She said it cast me as half a person and highlighted that the only part of me that counted was the Japanese half, and actually I should call myself "daburu", like she did, since we had experiences from two cultures.'

I look at her. 'I mean, I would love to not hang out with her,' I say. 'Isn't "half" just factual?'

Kiki shrugs. 'I guess people have different feelings about it.'

'Can I go now?' Hikaru wants to know. Kiki nods.

'You're not going to wash your hair yet, are you?' she asks, turning to me. 'I wouldn't – wait till after the sauna.'

'You know that having a kid has turned you into a control freak, right?'

'You know that you're so highly strung only dogs can hear you, right?'

We tie our hair into topknots and head outside, a short set of uneven stone steps to a series of enormous onsen, the faint, familiar smell of sulphur and soap. Dense foliage surrounds the baths, verdantly green leaves dripping with condensation, and hot water pours from a bamboo tap into the pool. Ai sighs with contentment as she lowers herself into the water, opaque with herbs. All of us are silent for a minute, luxuriating in the heat and comfort.

Feeling eyes on us, I realise that a trio of teenage girls in a different bath is holding a whispered conference, stealing glances at Ai.

'I did go on a date with a haafu guy once, when Hikaru was little,' Kiki says eventually, leaning back against a giant stone and looking up at the sky. 'I thought he would be less indoctrinated into thinking I was the spawn of the devil.' I decide to ignore the girls.

'On account of having a kid?'

She nods.

'And?'

'And it was no good, because every time I thought about how hot he was, I felt like a narcissist because he looked more like me than anyone else I knew,' Kiki says. 'And when I let him kiss me, I felt like I was snogging my brother.'

'Gross. Did he look like you?'

'Well, not actually. Only as much as all white people look like each other, and all Japanese people look like each other.'

'Are those girls looking at Ai?' I ask Kiki under my breath, so Ai can't hear.

Kiki looks straight at them. 'Oh,' she says.

'Mama,' Hikaru calls from the cold tub, where he is practising swimming. 'Is the biggest rat in the world, like, this big?' He stands up and stretches out his arms as far as they go.

'Yup,' Kiki says, closing her eyes.

'How do you know? Your eyes are closed.'

'I just do.'

'Is it called Mister Kenzo Ratticus?'

'Yup.'

'Mama, can we go to the beach with Youta tomorrow?'

Kiki opens her eyes. 'Yup.'

'I know someone you could go on a date with, who isn't a haafu,' Ai says to her.

'Shut up.'

I notice that the girls across the way are looking increasingly interested. I throw subtlety to the wind, and move myself so I'm sitting with my back to them, blocking their view of Ai.

'That's quite rude,' Kiki mutters. 'A Japanese person would never do that.'

'There have to be some advantages to our mixed-up state.'

Two elderly ladies slide into the bath between us, bowing in apology. They wade over to the other side of the tub to resume their detailed analysis of one of their sons' wives.

'You know,' Kiki says in English, 'when we're old, we're probably going to have to tuck our tits into the waistband of our trousers. That's what happens at the care home.'

Ai looks at her, lip curled in disbelief. 'I'm not doing that,' she says. 'I'm going to tie them round my neck in a bow.' She rises from the tub, pink and steaming. 'Shall we go in the sauna?'

'I might fold mine up like a roll-cake and get them into a bra that way,' I say, following her. It occurs to me that it speaks excellently for her mental health that she's making plans for her old age.

Kiki stays in the bath, eyes closed and lips pursed. She looks quite a lot like Obaachan.

The sauna smells of pine and is warmly lit, with wooden steps facing an ancient television mounted into the wall. Just as we enter, there's a mass exodus of old ladies, perspiring gently, all with uniform looks of grim satisfaction. The nightly soap opera is on a commercial break.

We climb up to the top step and watch a frankfurter perform a hula dance, followed by Hugh Jackman krumping for iced tea.

'This is why I know I could never live anywhere else long-term,' Ai says seriously. 'Why don't they have sento in London?'

I try and fail to imagine my English colleagues watching

EastEnders stark naked in a darkened room with their next-door neighbours. 'I don't think it would work.'

When we're done boiling and scrubbing and drying ourselves, and have emerged outside, our cheeks rosy and hair squeaky clean, one of the teenage girls stumbles towards Ai and asks for her autograph. She's obviously been standing in wait, blushing furiously and stammering to get her words out, and I'm so surprised by the physical presence of her this close, her acne and quavering voice, that I don't intervene. I'm even more surprised by Ai's reaction, gracious, charming, mussing up her hair so that, even just out of the bath, she manages to look sultry and photogenic, smiling for the selfie with her chin angled towards the camera in a way I've never seen her do. The girl hurries back to the other two, waiting in a huddle a little way away, and the three turn to squeal at each other, jubilant.

'She seemed nice,' I say, somehow at a loss for words.

'They were mainly nice,' Ai says sagely. As the girls scurry away, the one who asked for the autograph dares to wave at Ai, and the joy and pride in her face, when she waves back, is a surge of feeling.

'Do you miss it?' I ask her. Other people around us have started looking at Ai now, alerted to her presence.

Ai considers, tousling Hikaru's hair. Some kind of possessive instinct has driven him to wrap his arms around her legs. 'Only some of it, sometimes,' she says in the end.

53

Kiki

清美

'I think I might have five children one day,' Ai says thoughtfully, as we wander down the road on our almost daily grocery round.

'Five?!'

'Or maybe seven. I like doing everything in a pack.'

We are a pack. Multi-generational, with a few generations missing. Just at that moment, the pack elder jabs me painfully in the calf with the tip of her sun parasol, toppling my happy-family dream before it can even take hold.

'Why are you walking so slowly?' She tuts. 'You are blocking my view.'

Ai is humming to herself, and doesn't seem to have heard. 'Obaachan, let's go to Maneki,' she says, taking her arm.

Obaachan sniffs. We all know she loves Maneki, the unagi restaurant which has been there since the year dot and whose menu and prices, handwritten on to wooden plaques, haven't changed since before we were born. 'Well, I have been very tired recently,' she concedes. Eel is a food for summer, its soft, melting density supposedly a cure for exhaustion brought on by heat.

Just as she's considering it, her grasp on Ai's arm tightens, whitening her knuckles. 'There's Yamamoto-san from my ikebana group,' she says, peering at an old lady with a stick hobbling around the corner away from us. 'Her daughter was always trying to run away from school. With your mother.' It's the only time she's ever mentioned Mama since she's been dead, and Rei almost stops walking. 'The teachers said they spent all their playtimes halfway up that big tree, trying to climb over the wall.' Obaachan gives a sudden cackle, remembering. 'She was never where she was meant to be, your mother, not even once.' Before any of us can say anything about Mama, she starts walking, with surprising alacrity, to accost the woman. 'Her granddaughter's a doctor in town now – you used to do ballet with her, remember? Two left feet, moved like an elephant.' Her knotted hand doesn't look like it should be able to leave the imprints on Ai's forearm that I see when she removes it.

'Oh, Yamamoto-san!' she exclaims, managing to walk straight into the old lady like it's an accident. Yamamoto-san peers up at us and smiles a warm, grandmotherly smile.

'Where are you off to, Takanawa-san?'

'These are my great-granddaughters, Yamamoto-san,' Obaachan says, too clearly, as if the old lady is ancient, or senile, and not, in fact, younger than Obaachan herself.

Yamamoto-san beams up at me from somewhere around my waist. 'What lovely girls, Takanawa-san, taking you out like this,' she says. 'I'm jealous.'

Obaachan's face is a mask, determined not to give herself away. 'Well, being a doctor is very time-consuming,' she says. 'It's no wonder your granddaughter doesn't have time for you. Or a husband.'

Yamamoto-san, either sanguine about human nature in her tenth decade of existence or just used to Takanawa-san's bullshit, is unperturbed.

Obaachan beckons Rei over, only just refraining from click-ing her fingers, pretty much the way you would flick a hand at a waiter if you were incredibly rude and wanted them to spit in your food. 'Rei works for Silverman Sayle, one of the largest financial corporations in the world,' Obaachan says to Yamamoto-san. Rei blinks. Obaachan has never, in all the years Rei's worked there, let on that she has any idea what the firm is called. 'They deal with the Queen's accounts. The Queen of England. And this one is Ai. Takanawa Ai. She's very famous.'

Yamamoto-san gazes up at Ai. 'You must be the one in the whisky advertisement! We're all so proud of you!' I wonder if Yamamoto-san knows about what happened. My guess is that even if she did, she wouldn't care much; if old people know anything, it's that nothing lasts forever and shit happens. 'My, you're even prettier in real life.' Obaachan looks as if she might pop with the effort of not crowing. Her achievements displayed, I wait for us to move on.

'And my great-great-grandson,' Obaachan finishes with a flourish, indicating Hikaru carelessly as if she might be trailing crowds of her other progeny behind her.

Yamamoto-san bends to better see Hikaru. 'How nice to meet you,' she says. 'I hope you're not finding our old town too boring.'

'It's not boring,' Hikaru says seriously. 'I like the beach and the boats and the mountains, and also it has good playgrounds.' He looks up at me. 'I wish we lived here, Mama.' Turning back to Yamamoto-san before I can respond, he tells her, 'Mama says that after lunch we can go to the one with the big slide. I'm not scared.'

Yamamoto-san's smile is enormous. 'My Junichi used to love that slide, too,' she says. 'Such a sweet boy,' she says to Obaachan.

'Of course. He's properly brought up. Kiki is a very good mother.' She manages to say it as if it's a threat. And then,

'Well, we must go,' like Yamamoto-san has been detaining her. 'They always insist on taking me all the way to Maneki's unagi restaurant.'

As we walk away, she starts up again, telling Hikaru off for yanking Kimchi's lead, and Rei for not standing up straight. It would be hard to say what it is about her that lets you know she's feeling satisfied, because her mouth is still turned down like a tortoise's. She holds her cards close to her chest. She's like Rei, I suddenly realise, and the thought makes me smile.

54

And then, before I can believe it, it's the firework display and the matsuri on the long beach, the highlight of the summer, longed for and dreaded by children, marking the almost-end of the holidays. Nobody can dissuade Hikaru from putting on his jinbei mid-afternoon and spending the next two hours alternating between opening the front door repeatedly, checking up and down the street to make the boys arrive faster, and lovingly stroking the colourful packets we bought this morning in the firework shop. Ai and Rei and I have found yukatas in the attic, maybe our mother's, maybe our grandmother's, and carefully washed and dried them in the sun. As the sun finally starts to set, we put them on, their bright colours and patterns, morning glories and anemones, as fresh as if we'd bought them brand new.

'Why is your skin so damn good?' Rei inquires crossly of Ai, peering at her in the mirror as she ties the obi around her waist, a rose-pink crêpe flecked with white. 'You eat crap all day and I've seen you go to bed without taking your make-up off.'

'Your skin was probably this good a decade ago,' Ai objects with such sincerity I know she's winding Rei up. Rei hasn't really been wearing make-up since we got here, and she looks like a teenager.

I give them both cold Asahis and kappa ebisen prawn crack-ers, and help Hikaru fill a bucket with water for the sparkler ends. The sky has gone from blue to orange to a navy that's almost black by the time the boys arrive. The sting of the heat is gone from the day but the air is still close, enveloping. I busy myself steaming edamame, adding a little fried garlic and chilli oil, slicing up cucumbers from the garden to serve with salt and dip in sweetened miso, crunchy and cold.

'You all look so nice in your yukatas,' Daisuke says bash-fully, clinking his beer against mine. Rei is standing next to him, leaning against the kitchen counter, holding a beer in one hand. I notice that for the first time this summer the fingers of her other hand aren't moving, that she's standing completely still.

'And you,' I say, and they do, Daisuke with his patterned kimono jacket, a skater-vibe fashion item that hangs stylishly on his tall frame, Masato in a jinbei that shows off his enormous calves. Youta is looking the most traditional, wearing a yukata in navy stripes with a black obi, a round uchiwa fan tucked into the back, the front falling apart a little and revealing his chest. I don't know why I have to avoid looking, when we've spent most of the summer together in swimwear.

We light the fireworks once all of us have drunk just enough that everything feels beautiful and significant. We start with the big ones, lighting them in the middle of the road in front of the house, sitting on our front steps to watch, the paving stones warm from the heat of the day. The man in the shop gave Hikaru an extra firework, and it spins like a whirling dervish, faster and faster and brighter and brighter, seeming to trip and stop just as it's about to blaze into flame. Hikaru runs forward to see what's left behind, and what was a nondescript square when we lit it has exploded into a colourful five-layer pagoda. We light little cardboard tubes three at a time, which jump into the air and shriek as they flare up, then swoop serenely down, transformed into tissue-paper parachutes. A yellow cube elongates when Youta lights it, writhing along the road in an explosion of white-hot sulphur tinged with blue, threatening to shoot across the pavement to where we're sitting, before abruptly going out, revealing a paper dragon in the smoke.

We troop back through the house and into the garden for the hand-held fireworks. The air is filled with the mysterious, acrid scent of gunpowder and the incense of mosquito coils, and the whole world shrinks down to our tiny garden, to the expectant few moments when the lighter is lit, the whoosh as it catches, the flare lighting up Hikaru's face, the smudges left by the smoke in the darkness, hiding us from each other. We light the senko hanabi, the twisted string of paper with a minute globe of a firework at the bottom, shooting out delicate, erratic sparks like someone painted them in the dark with a calligraphy brush. One jerk of the hand is enough to make it fall, and all of us are crouched on the ground, nobody risking speech or even breath, not even Hikaru. Only Youta doesn't have one, because he's holding the lighter and steadying Hikaru's, and when my globe finally falls to the ground, instantly out, I look up for a second and catch his eye.

By the time we get to the long beach, the matsuri is in full swing. Brightly painted tarpaulin stalls face the sea, selling cold beer and fizzy ramune in glass bottles, the air full of heat and fat and salt, the smell of sticky fried noodles and corn on the cob. The children are like small explosions, waiting their turn for games and sticks of candied summer fruit, pleased and self-conscious in their summer outfits. Hikaru is flushed with excitement and I queue with him for the yo-yo scoop, where coloured balloons with an elastic on the end rush by in a current of water. Hikaru, squatting next to the tank, is cross-eyed with the concentration of trying to catch one before his paper hook turns to mush. As we walk away from the stall, victorious, his face shines with elation. We catch up with the others to find them silent as children around a birthday cake, the boys eating too-hot, crispy tacoyaki, bonito flakes dancing on top, Rei and Ai absorbed in an enormous kakigori, a pyramid of pristine snow running with rivulets of strawberry syrup and condensed milk.

'Sharing is caring,' I tell them, squeezing between them and nicking Rei's straw.

'Smile, Takanawas,' Youta calls, and we all look up at the camera.

'Mm, brain freeze,' Ai says happily, her mouth full of shaved ice.

The sand is thronging with people in yukatas, children with Anpanman masks bouncing balls with lights inside them, holding bags of candyfloss aloft like trophies. I'd completely forgotten about Ai being Ai, until I see the ripple around us, the nudges and the wide eyes, the hands covering mouths, advertising surprise rather than hiding it. Ai gives what I know is an eye-roll, even though her face doesn't actually move. We walk through the throng to the water's edge and she keeps her eyes either lowered or hovering above the level of the crowd, as if she doesn't see any of it.

Rei pokes her in the ribs. 'How do you do that?'

'Do what?'

'Pretend you don't notice that everyone is staring at you.'

Ai shrugs, still radiant, a celebrity, when minutes before she was a goofy drunk scarfing sugar syrup. 'We've practised.'

It's a weird thought: my sister and a bunch of girls we don't know, conducting rehearsals for ignoring their adoring fans.

'I thought people would have forgotten about you by now,' Rei says, sounding grumpy.

'Don't worry, Rei, they will,' Ai says. 'I can't wait.'

266

'For them to forget about the scandal, or to forget about you?'

'Forget about me,' Ai says. 'Being famous is a disaster.'

Rei looks at me significantly. I'm glad Ai thinks that, too.

When it isn't just stares any more, but her name being whispered around us, and not-very-subtle photographs being taken, Rei swings Hikaru off the ground and hands him to Ai. 'Hold him over your face,' she instructs. She turns to Daisuke. 'Take off your jacket,' she says, and he obeys without question, draping it over Ai's yukata.

Ai looks at me, resigned. 'Do I get a say in this?' she wants to know.

'I doubt it,' I say. 'She thinks you're still a child. And she can tell you what to do.'

'She is still a child,' Rei says. 'And of course I can tell her what to do. How can we concentrate on the fireworks when we know everyone's staring at you? Hide your face.'

Ai complies, Hikaru giggling.

We make our way to a patch of beach where we can sit squashed together in a row, Ai keeping Hikaru in her lap. When the first firework shoots up into the sky with a sound like a gunshot, we're all children again, mesmerised by the spectacle. The Japanese word for fireworks is 花火, hana-bi, flower-fire, and they bloom in the darkness with all the bombastic self-assurance of hothouse flora, each whistling explosion a triumph of light against darkness. Everyone's face is tilted up, smiling slightly, the reflection of the colours on the water like floating in a dreamland.

'This is the best,' Ai sighs, holding Hikaru.

'I love fireworks the most of everything in the whole world,' Hikaru agrees, and seeing him sitting there, the sea in front of him, I think about what he said to Yamamoto-san, about wishing we lived here.

By the time the pyrotechnics have come to their screaming finale, leaving a ghostly trail of grey smoke and the image of giant neon chrysanthemums imprinted on our retinas, my neck is cricked from staring up for so long. All around us people are dusting themselves off, chattering contentedly.

'Let's wait for the crowds to thin,' Rei says, stretching. 'Keep the tabloid scandal under wraps.'

'I need to pee, though,' Ai complains.

Rei looks at her pointedly. 'I told you you were a child.'

'I'll take Hikaru, for cover.'

'I'll come with you,' Daisuke says, and they disappear into the crowd.

The rest of us get up slowly, savouring the night. I can see Masato and Rei ahead of me as a gaggle of girls pushes between us, giggling about how cute the guy at the mizuame stall was.

'Want a beer for the road?' Youta asks.

'Always,' I say, and while I'm waiting for him, I suddenly, awkwardly, notice I have butterflies in my stomach, just because he's going to come back.

The others have gone on ahead by the time Youta and I are out of the crowds and walking home. Halfway up the hill, I stop and turn, to see the lights of the matsuri by the water. The echoes of the taiko drums and the flutes coming from the makeshift stage are muted. From the beach, I follow the sky upwards, and above us the constellations are bright and clear. To save my neck, I lie down in the middle of the road, the tarmac warm on my back.

'That looks comfortable,' Youta says, and lies down next to me, his bottle clinking against mine as he puts it down.

The sky is so bright with stars that for a moment I feel like I'm going to fall into it.

'God, we're so small,' I say.

Youta laughs. 'Yeah.'

'It's been such a good summer,' I say.

'Can I take you out on a date?' He says it like it's just the next thing to say.

'Me?'

'No, the other girl lying on the tarmac there.'

I can feel a smile about to burst out of me. 'Did my grandmother put you up to this?'

'Your grandmother? I haven't really spoken to her since we were ten.'

I feel him turn his head to look at me, and even in the dark my cheeks are suddenly hot.

'I'm not glamorous like Ai,' I say, and curse myself.

I think he's going to laugh but he doesn't say anything. 'You're a lot of things not like Ai,' he says. 'Not like anybody.'

'But I'm a single mother,' I say.

'I had noticed.'

An energetic shout rises above the low hubbub of the matsuri, followed by raucous laughter. 'We can't go on a date,' I say.

'Oh.'

'We're already married, remember?' In the split-second pause, I'm hit with a tidal wave of embarrassment. 'You probably don't. I wouldn't have, either, except Rei reminded me.'

He turns his head so he's looking up at the sky again. 'Of course I remember. I had such a crush on you I was scared to talk.'

'That is not true.'

'It is. And then I kissed you by the vending machine and spent the next fifteen years wondering if I had coffee breath.'

I start laughing, too high and too long from nervous excitement and disbelief. I think of Hikaru trying to be cool.

'I don't think Hikaru will like it.'

'He won't?' He sounds crushed.

'No. Because he'll want to come too.'

'Oh.' I can feel the smile in his voice. 'Well, he can come if he wants. But only sometimes.' He moves his hand, so that the edge of it is touching mine.

You can never count your chickens, obviously. That's what Rei would say, and Obaachan. But it feels like the beginning of something good.

55

Rei

令

It's Watanabe-san who comes to tell us, early in the morning. Ai is still upstairs, and Kiki and Hikaru are in the garden. I've just put toast on for Hikaru when I hear Watanabe-san's voice. I know what it is as soon as I turn the corner, from the way she walks towards me, staying in the genkan with her shoes on but coming right up to the edge of it. She takes both of my hands in hers. 'Rei-chan,' she says, looking me straight in the eyes, 'Obaachan's died.'

The first thing I feel is the hugest relief. 'Thank you,' I say. I mean, Thank you for making it so clear, but then I'm embarrassed, because even though it's less weird in Japanese than in English, it still isn't the right thing to say. Watanabe-san seems to understand; she squeezes my hands, and I'm so glad it's her who's told me. Kind, sympathetic Watanabe-san who will nevertheless be forever referred to as Watanabe-san-with-haemorrhoids. 'I called round for her so we could go to our exercise class. She went in her sleep,' she says.

I'm glad she was found so quickly by someone else, proving what a good life she had when we weren't here, that people looked out for her and cared, that she can't have been lonely.

'I've called the doctor. I'm going to go next door and wait for them. You and your sisters can come over when you're ready.'

She shakes my hands with hers. 'Don't you worry. Everyone will help you.'

If I cried now, it would be completely appropriate. Still, I do my best to hold it in. 'Thank you,' I tell her again. I stand there for a few moments after she's left, sliding the door shut carefully behind her, just the way Obaachan showed us.

I hear the bedroom door open, and I turn around to see Ai pad downstairs. She looks at me.

'It's Obaachan, isn't it?'

★

I'm sitting on the engawa later, trying not to think that the garden seems to be looking especially radiant today, like it's a particular shame for her to be missing it, when Ai comes creeping up like a cat. 'I'm glad it was while she was sleeping,' she says, leaning her head against me. Her eyes are red, but dry. 'I hope she was dreaming something lovely.'

I nod.

'And we avoided the deathbed scene issue, thank god,' Ai says. 'I wonder what she would have said.'

I think about it for a moment. '"It's so typical of a Westerner to wear a skirt like that to a deathbed."'

I can feel Ai smiling into my shoulder. '"I'm so much sicker than Watanabe-san from down the road."'

'I'm glad she was so old,' I say, and it's true. It's also true that she wasn't old enough for it to be OK. Nobody ever will be. You'll always wish you could have seen them just one more time, looking unimpressed and saying something critical. Just once more. 'I just don't want to think I won't see her again.'

Ai lifts her head from my shoulder and looks at me like I've lost my mind. 'Why won't you? I saw her this morning. That's how I knew she was dead.'

I look at her, wondering if she's screwing with me. She isn't.

'She walked across the garden. She told us not to forget to water the plants. That you probably would, because you're so distracted.'

'Me, specifically? The first thing she said in the afterlife was to slag me off?'

Ai shrugs guiltily. 'Sorry.'

Sometimes I forget how Japanese they are, my sisters.

56

Kiki

清美

She was difficult, stubborn, arguably a bona fide racist; she never gave the reaction you needed; she was no replacement for our mother. But somehow it still feels like the roof was just blown off our house.

Ai and Rei are arguing about ghosts. 'Stop being so damn foreign,' Rei says to Ai, looking disturbed.

Ai is nonplussed. 'I'm not foreign. You're the foreigner, with your weird ideas about Marmite and salt-and-vinegar and your total narrow-mindedness when it comes to anything you can't see. Don't forget which country you're in, please.'

Sensing a moment he's missing out on, Hikaru wanders out on to the engawa and squeezes himself between Ai and me. I wonder, for an insane moment, if I can get away with not telling him. We have a *Where's Wally?* book with a page of jolly-looking identikit vampires carting coffins about, and for the longest time I used to try to skip over it, dreading the moment when he'd ask what the human-sized boxes are for. I don't think he's ever asked, and, like so many other things I don't want him to know, the information reached him via the small-children's network, or school, or osmosis.

'Hikaru . . .' I say, and he looks at me expectantly. I take one of his hands and hold it, then say it quickly, like ripping off a plaster. 'Obaachan died.'

Hikaru is quiet for a moment, looking at me like he's trying to work something out. At last he says, 'Where has she gone?'

'I don't know, Hikaru,' I say, and I hate letting him down. 'Nobody knows.'

He climbs into my lap, fingering the sleeve of my T-shirt. 'Can't we see her again?'

'No.' Even as I say it, it seems absurd.

'Will we get a new Obaachan, like Kohei got a new cat when Pooh-chan died?' I'd forgotten that Hikaru had come into contact with the Grim Reaper already.

'I don't think so,' I tell him, running my fingers through his hair where it curls just around his ears. He's looking out at the garden, but he turns to study me, like he's trying to figure out if I'm lying.

'I don't want to die,' he says finally, like it's the answer to something.

'No.' I don't want him even to say it. 'You won't die for at least another hundred years.'

'Promise?'

'Promise,' without hesitation.

'But what happens when people die?' he persists.

'Well . . . people believe different things,' I try. I think about what sounds the most feasible, or at least the most benign. 'You're part of the universe, so all the energy that went into making you will go into something else.' I link my fingers through his. 'Maybe you'll become a lovely flower.'

Hikaru is horrified. 'I don't want to be a lovely flower!'

'You don't have to be a lovely flower,' I backtrack. 'That was just a suggestion. Perhaps Obaachan will become a lovely flower. You could look right out into this garden and see her!'

His face is starting to crumple.

275

I cast around in my mind quickly. 'Maybe you'll come back as a different person.' Chibi stalks on to the engawa, looking superior. 'Or an animal.'

'An animal? Like a mouse?'

'Yes, like a mouse. And some people say that maybe the people you knew in this life will be with you again in the next one.'

'So you could still be my mummy mouse in the next life?'

'Exactly.'

Chibi stretches luxuriously in the sun, performatively blissful. 'Hikaru,' Ai ventures, coming to my rescue, 'do you want to do some drawing?'

'Mama, I don't want to be a mouse.'

'That's a good idea, Hikaru,' I tell him. 'Shall I get out your new colouring book?'

'Or a different person.'

'I saw it had some really good pictures of fire engines in it,' Ai says.

'I just want to be Hikaru, and I just want you to be my mama.'

'I know, my love,' I tell him in English, because Japanese has no endearments. 'I know.'

57

Ai

愛

She was so old, and she had a good life. I think she was ready to go. Tired enough. Sometimes I feel like I'm so world-weary and haggard, but now I can feel how tight my hold on life is.

I think of when we couldn't find Hikaru, just those few hours. I don't know how she lived through everything she lost, how she stayed whole enough to carry on. I never really asked her about it, because there wasn't a right time, and I couldn't have found the words.

Even now, even though I'm wishing I could see her one more time, it's not like I'd use that time to ask her profound questions. I'd just link her skinny arm through mine, and we could take another walk around the block.

58

Apparently, Obaachan's death is pretty much a walk in the park, admin-wise. Every single important thing we need to know is in a plastic folder in the first drawer Rei opens, in the big cupboard in the sitting room next to the ceramics cabinet.

'My respect for her has gone through the roof,' Rei marvels, looking at the neatly handwritten paper.

'And think about it – there's no employer to tell, no internet to cancel, no social media accounts to worry about, no subscriptions, no landlord, no mobile phone, no credit card, no loans, no mortgage, no nothing,' Kiki says.

'How do you have so much death admin in your head?' Rei asks.

'It's another great skill you pick up working in care homes,' Kiki says. 'It's the job that keeps giving.'

'I suppose she might have a library card,' Rei says. 'But I don't think anything bad is going to happen if we don't manage to cancel it. I guess we can just tell the tofu guy to give us less tofu the next time he comes round. And she only has one bank account. That's it. Tofu and a bank account.'

'You don't know,' I tell them. 'Obaachan might have huge secret gambling debts to the yakuza. It might all come out when you talk to her bank manager.'

'Or have been running the Ikimura drug cartel, so well hidden nobody has ever heard of it,' Kiki agrees. 'That would be kind of great, right?'

'What are we going to do with all her stuff?' I ask.

Rei makes the sound in her throat that Chibi makes when you've stroked him for too long. 'One thing at a time,' she says.

We don't even have to call anyone about the funeral arrangements, because Watanabe-san's daughter lives next door to the funeral director. The priest turns up that same afternoon to wash Obaachan. He dresses her in her white pilgrim's robes with her kimono folded right over left, the way all of us have dressed ourselves sometimes by mistake, before some shocked older person quickly corrected us. He sets up a little table at her head, with a paper screen and incense and a candle, so Obaachan won't get lost, and a bowl of rice with the chopsticks stabbed down vertically. Obaachan has already chosen every part of the funeral and paid for it, in instalments that finished fifteen years ago. Which was impressive forward planning, and good for a lot of reasons, like now we definitely don't have to feel guilty that we didn't get her the shooting star memorial service, which I thought we might have to, when I first read about it in the funeral home leaflet. It said you send your loved one's remains into orbit, where you can track them on your phone, and then in a few months or years, they will re-enter the atmosphere as a shooting star. I told Rei I'd like that please, and she said a) she is categorically not going to be around to organise my funeral and b) if so, I'd better start saving now. So now I'm thinking maybe my great-grandchildren can just tie my ashes to a firework instead.

Before we've made a single call, people start turning up to Obaachan's house. They come the next day, too, and the one after that. They bring food: home-made potato salads and miso stir-fries in Tupperware, and also cream puffs and daifuku mochi from Marusho. All the three of us have to do is make caffeinated drinks and carry sweet things on trays, which I'm pretty sure Obaachan would think was lax of us. The visitors are from her ikebana group, and her classical music appreciation, and her exercise class, and the temple, and her haiku writing, and a choir we didn't even know about because they're on summer break. Everyone seems to know us, even though we've never met any of them. They all give us condolence money in white envelopes – used notes, to show how unexpected the death was, and that they didn't plan for it by getting new notes out of the bank ahead of time. That's a nice touch, isn't it, given that she was nearly a hundred. She has a new name now, a death name, a really long one that Rei says must have been unbelievably expensive, since you have to pay the temple for each letter. I keep walking into rooms to find people discussing us, like we're characters in a book. They don't even care if we hear them – they just raise their eyebrows and carry on talking. The good thing about everyone Obaachan knew is that they're really old, so they've either never heard of Kabuki and don't care who the singer slept with, or they have, and it compares favourably to other things they've dealt with, like the atom bomb.

It's still sunny, and too hot, which Obaachan would be annoyed about.

'Totally disrespectful weather,' Rei says, arranging dorayaki on a plate. She's cut each one in half and balanced them on top of each other at angles, like she's maybe designing a display in a shop window.

'Do you remember that time we were going for a picnic in the meadows up by the strawberry farm, and it got rained off? And she told us off, because we hadn't tried hard enough to change the weather with our minds?' I ask Rei, pouring more sencha leaves into the teapot. 'It's kind of flattering, isn't it, that she had that much faith in our abilities.'

'Yes,' Rei says. 'Or clinically deranged.'

Obaachan has her staff and her six coins ready to cross the river of death and give them hell, and a white cloth over her face. The cloth partly makes me think of the ghost cartoons we used to watch when we were little, and partly makes me think she's playing some weird game of hide-and-seek involving table napkins, which isn't really in keeping with what she's like. Under the cloth, she's wearing lipstick in a colour she probably wouldn't have chosen, because in order to enter a new world you have to look your best but also least like yourself. She's on dry ice, given how hot it is, and I imagine scattering just a little bit of water around the sides of her, so the dry ice smokes up, and how impressed Hikaru would be.

On the third day, like a parody of a Bible story, Obaachan's ready to be cremated. Since we know it's what she'd like, we all go to the formal-wear shop, where you can buy or hire wedding and bridesmaid's dresses that make Princess Diana's look like she didn't make an effort, or outfits for a yakuza funeral. Even with so many dresses to choose from, Rei says there's only one acceptable option: a fitted dress with little capped sleeves, sale only, naturally.

We all squeeze into one changing room to try it on.

'Won't it be kind of weird for us to wear matching dresses?' I ask.

'Less weird than us turning up in full-length ball gowns,' she says.

'I could wear the tutu dress with the veil,' I suggest, as I zip up Rei's dress of choice. 'I don't really want to own this.'

'It's an investment,' Rei says. 'If you wear this in public, people will assume you've had a lobotomy and all your troubles will be over.'

'It's really uncomfortable,' I say.

'And hot,' Kiki agrees, buttoning up Hikaru's suit as he makes strangled noises.

Bubble writing on the mirror tells us, *You look so gramolous!* We buy the dresses.

We've all been to wakes and funeral after-parties before ('Can you call them that?' Rei says. 'Like getting pissed when a gig's over?' 'That's literally exactly what they are,' Kiki tells her), but this is the first time we've been to a Japanese funeral all the way through. In the temple, the air smells of the incense Rei told me she keeps in her apartment in London, just so she can light it sometimes and feel like she's home, and there are so many flowers on the altar it reminds me of an awards ceremony. A framed photograph of Obaachan is nestled among them, and Obaachan-in-the-photo is smiling a little, the way Jesus smiles in those pictures where there's light behind his head. She never looked that way in real life, but that's the one she chose.

'Do you think that's how Obaachan saw herself?' I whisper to Kiki as we walk to our positions at the front of the temple, our hands folded in front of us.

'Maybe,' Kiki says, looking at the picture. 'That's her ultimate outside face.'

We kneel on the tatami matting, Rei, Kiki and I at the front. Youta is sitting with Hikaru at the back, so they can make a quiet exit and tear around the cemetery when Hikaru's best behaviour runs out. Rei closes her eyes as we start to chant from the booklets we're given. I check the number of pages as subtly as I can – sixty. Two pages in, my legs are dying of pins and needles and my mouth is dry, but it's cosy, all of us droning monotonously together, Kiki on one side of me and Rei on the other. Occasionally the priest smacks the massive gong to tell us there's a pause, and we all inhale together, like characters in a pantomime.

You can dress it up with chanting and sheets, but you can't really pretend that cremation isn't sticking someone in a giant oven. Since she's the eldest, Rei is invited to push the button that starts the fire going, and she does it with a straight back, like always. But I can see how thin her lips go, the millisecond pause before she places her finger firmly on the button. We never had a funeral for our mother, since no one ever found her. Years later, people started asking if we wanted a certificate of death, or if she should just be marked 'missing'. That was when Rei decided to go to England, which was quite an extreme way of avoiding admin, but understandable.

In the crematorium waiting room, nobody says anything for more than an hour. Just when I've started trying to find a rhythm in Kiki's blinking, the undertaker appears, and ushers us into a different room. Obaachan has been turned into a baking tray of bones. I try not to act surprised, but I was expecting ashes. The undertaker produces an urn and hands each of us a set of gold-tipped chopsticks – one made of wood, one made of bamboo – Rei first, obviously. She bows when she receives them and says nothing, so I do too, even though I'm really concerned about the fact that the man who's just cooked our grandmother is handing us cutlery. The undertaker says something to Rei I can't hear. Without reacting, Rei picks up a bone from the tray with the chopsticks and drops it in the urn. Then it's Kiki's turn, and, like a dream, mine, and the bone I choose is too big to pick up elegantly so it falls, and I find myself scrabbling around on the floor searching for the bone of my dead grandmother.

Then we all get truly pissed. The crematorium is halfway up a hillside, like almost everything in Ikimura, and we troop into a tatamied hall next to it that only does funerals, lined with shoji along one side and windows on the other, with views out to the sea. Two long, low tables are already laid with these beautiful arrangements of food: sashimi served in a bowl made of actual ice, tempura in a basket of woven leaves, miso soup with clams. Obaachan-in-the-urn is set at the head of the table, in front of her own place, and served all the magnificent food, and loads of sake in tiny earthenware cups.

'Did Obaachan really choose this menu?' Kiki asks incredulously, picking up a radish carved into the shape of a chrysanthemum. 'I thought she would have a fit about food this luxurious.'

Ladies in kimonos are waiting on everybody, and toasts are going up every five seconds, and since we're all sitting on the floor anyway, it really doesn't take that long before people are literally rolling around drunk. The nice waitresses make a fuss over Hikaru and he helps them serve, mainly by crawling round the table topping up everyone's sake cups.

'Well, that was fun,' Kiki says in English, when she's done being polite to the relative we don't know sitting next to her. 'I knew about the bones, but it was still kind of a shock. I guess I had Granny's funeral in mind.'

'A hymn and an egg sandwich,' says Rei.

'You know what's good about this, though?' I ask, trying to light the little flame in front of me to cook the bean curd. 'There's been a massive fuss. We've seen the bones. That lady is definitely dead.'

'One hundred per cent, no question, definitely dead,' Kiki agrees, pouring out more sake.

'To no limbo,' Rei says, raising her cup.

We drink. The volume in the room is growing louder, and the other toasts are getting more garbled. Two ladies appear as if by magic, to light the cooking flame and take away our empty plates and refill our drinks all in one movement, smiling the whole time.

'They're like waitresses and therapists and goddesses combined,' says Kiki, squinting after them. 'What a job.'

'To Obaachan, for putting up with us,' Rei says. We drink.

'And for pointing out all our faults,' Kiki adds. We drink again.

'To proper goodbyes,' Kiki says, when our cups have been refilled, gesturing vaguely and spilling some of her sake.

'To Mama,' says Rei, and because none of us are expecting it, we're all looking at each other in the second it comes out of her mouth. The word hangs in the air. Her laugh, the cool of her hand against your skin. This once, I'm so sure we're all thinking of her the same way.

There's an eruption of laughter somewhere along the table, a group of rowdy uncles shouting to get the karaoke out. We down our drinks and smile at each other, Rei's and Kiki's matching secret smiles, with only one side of their mouths. I wonder if I look that way, too.

'So, are you going to sing us something?' Rei wants to know.

And I'm so drunk, and so far away from caring what anyone thinks, that I do. I take the karaoke mic and sing my favourite Kabuki song with all my heart, and the staff come out of the kitchens and the waitresses take pictures and all the people who came to Obaachan's funeral smile and look proud, and Rei and Kiki dance with Hikaru, and the whole thing is brilliant.

59

Kiki

清美

I never expected Rei to say it. It's a few days after the funeral, when we're hanging the laundry in the garden and she's looking up, squinting into the sunlight shining through the white of a sheet. 'Maybe we should put her name on the grave.'

I'm so surprised that for a second all I do is look at her, a pillowcase wilting in my hands. At last, I say: 'Mama's?'

Rei nods, frowning against the sun.

'I thought you said it wasn't fair to put her somewhere she was going to be told off by Obaachan for all eternity.'

Rei secures the sheet to the washing line and shrugs. 'Maybe that's not actually so bad.' She smooths out the sheet. 'Maybe her parents miss her, even though they didn't want to let her do anything.' She reaches into the laundry basket for another pillowcase. 'Probably they were just trying their best.'

I don't know what to say.

'It's a good time to do it,' Rei says. 'Makes sense to get all the death-based admin out of the way in one go. Can you pass me the clothes pegs?'

The peg bag is a fabric cone with a circular hole in it. As I hold it out to Rei, I notice that it's made from a cream fabric covered in sprigs of flowers, the fabric of matching skirts that

Mama made for the three of us when we were small. I guess Rei couldn't get rid of everything she made.

After more than a decade of putting it off, getting her name on the grave only involves a single phone call. Since our headstone is already a work in progress, they say they can get it done in three days. They ask us if we want a priest, blessings, sutras, but we don't.

On the morning we head out to visit the cemetery, the sky is cornflower blue and a breeze drifts inland off the water. I imagine our journey is going to be significant, maybe a little subdued, especially given that Obaachan was with us last time we made this trip, but as soon as we've set off, Hikaru pipes up, as if he's been waiting for exactly this moment to open the conversation. 'Youta says his cat has kittens in its tummy. How did they get in there? And how are they going to come out?'

Ai and Rei look at me. 'You tell him,' I say to Rei.

'Why?'

'You're much more scientific than I am.'

'I don't think this is about being scientific, Kiki.' She turns to Ai. 'You tell him.'

'Why?!'

'Cos I had to tell you, and Kiki has to tell him loads of stuff. This can be your contribution.'

So Ai tells him. She holds his hand as we walk down the street and does a pretty decent job of being factual and just about vague enough. When she's finished, she looks down to see Hikaru staring at her with distaste. He doesn't say anything for a moment. Then he says, very gently: 'I don't think so, Ai.' He reaches into his pocket and hands her a misshapen piece of wire. 'You can have this. I found the wire in the bin and made it into a heart.'

As soon as we turn into the cemetery, Hikaru runs up to high-five the Buddha of Complaints, which seems somehow sacrilegious, even though that jolly old Buddha looks totally fine with it. He's smiling, one hand under one generous cheek, his ear cocked, listening. In my mind's eye I can see Obaachan sitting on the chair in her sunhat, her stick in front of her, aggrieved and chatty. How much she must have had to tell.

Rei fills a pail with water, Ai buys some flowers from the bucket, and I collect a broom. If our mother hadn't died, or if Obaachan had been a more maternal kind of relative, or even if Richard had done something, literally anything at all, I would probably have stuck at school, and maybe gone to university, or training college. Maybe I would have moved to England, like Rei. In any of those scenarios, there's no way I would have been in a random drum-and-bass club at 1am on a Tuesday, and I really don't think there's any other way I could have met Hikaru's father. And without him, there'd have been no Hikaru – all those souls zinging about, and I could have just missed him. So I suppose I can't regret anything in my life, not the tragedies, not the people whose behaviour has been objectively inadequate, not even my own stupid failure to do better. I feel Hikaru's hand reaching up for mine, small and warm.

The grave looks almost the same as it did the last time we came with Obaachan, her name still in red because the urn of her ashes has to hang out at home with us for forty-nine days before she's buried. The new engraving looks crisp and clean, putting its best foot forward. It's been a long time since I saw Mama's name written down. I always forget her kanji – it means 'long hoped for'.

We exchange the flowers and replace the candles and put down the One Cup of sake, and then Hikaru sweeps the grave and helps me weed it, careful not to touch the graves on either side. It's only after he's run down the path towards the clearing in front of the temple, Ai chasing him, that Rei squats on her heels, and looks straight at Mama's name.

'I'm sorry about the argument,' she says. It takes me a beat to figure out what she's talking about. It feels like a lifetime ago. I remember shouting at her, and I feel myself shrivel. It was never Rei's fault that Obaachan thought she was destined for the best university in Japan and my only realistic life plan was to throw myself at any man with standards low enough to have me. 'I'm sorry I said it was shitty to be a parent,' she says before I can say anything. She's still looking at the grave. 'I don't know why I said that.'

'Probably because it's an amazingly annoying activity that involves you giving up your entire life for the sake of ungrateful people who don't care how much you suffer,' I offer. 'Also a lot of laundry and wiping.'

She smiles. 'Maybe.'

Rei was there right from the very first half-hour of Hikaru's life. She came to the hospital all the way from London. I didn't know she was coming because I'd turned off my phone a week before, when a colleague texted me to tell me she was bored of waiting for the baby. Rei was in a towering rage because she hadn't been able to get through to me and hadn't known when to come, and had only figured out where the hospital was by breaking into my apartment and going through all my post. Also, she told me, because she hadn't known whether I was dead or not. Then Ai came rushing in, too, and I handed the baby to Rei and none of us said a thing, just looked at him lying there with his eyes tight shut, brand newly here from who knows where and exhausted by the journey.

'I'm sorry I said you hated everything,' I say. 'I didn't mean it.'

She picks a fallen camellia petal off the headstone. 'Not *everything*,' she says, smiling a little. 'But it's not like it was entirely inaccurate.' She lays the petal in the palm of her hand, heart-shaped and perfect. 'It made me so angry,' she says to the petal. 'She never gave us a chance to say thank you.'

I grab hold of her little finger. She lets me have it, looking at our hands swinging. Then, 'I know you think I shouldn't see Richard.'

'You should see him if you want, Rei. He's your dad.'

She snorts. 'I mean, he really isn't. It was just – he made her so happy sometimes.' She looks at me. 'Do you remember?' I shake my head. I wish I did. 'Sometimes I felt like if I could see him, maybe he could remind me of her, when she was happy.' She says it like it's just an observation, no big deal, but there's no breath in her voice. 'He never did, though,' she says, conversationally, after a while. 'He only ever made me think what a useless dickhead he was.'

She smiles at me sideways, rolling the petal gently between her thumb and forefinger. She opens her mouth and closes it again.

'Just say it,' I tell her.

She stands up, still not looking at me. 'Do you really, honest-ly think it was an accident?'

I don't say anything for a long time. I think a lot of things. Ever since Hikaru was born, all I can think is how much she did for us, putting herself aside and aside, all the time. Some-times, especially when I see how broken Ai can be, I think the way we feel has been passed down in our blood and there's no getting away, a cage we were born into. Me with Nozomi's straight black hair but our boring father's boring temperament, and the other two with some of the sadness she carried in her bones. I think she loved us so much we took it for granted that we were the centre of her universe. In a way, that's Rei's tragedy. She's left wondering how Nozomi could have left us, how she could have done that to us, because she can't imagine her doing something that had nothing to do with us at all.

In the end, I say, 'Whichever way I look at it, it doesn't change what I think of her.'

Rei looks at the petal in her hand, runs a finger along its velvet softness.

'I think she went out swimming and something happened, and she was trying to come back to us but she couldn't.'

Rei doesn't say anything.

In the other version, too, she was trying so hard to come back to us, but she couldn't.

60

Rei

令

A familiar black tail whips behind a headstone a few rows away, its owner slinking out of sight.

'Is that Chibi?' I ask Kiki. 'Isn't this really far away from home for him?'

'I guess not, if Hikaru followed him all the way to Mani-san,' Kiki says. 'Did I tell you that's what he said?' She considers. 'Although I always figured he'd made that up.'

It suddenly comes to me as a fully formed memory. 'The cat drawing,' I say. 'The one that Nozomi talked to about the waistcoat and the birthday party. It wasn't you who drew it at all. It was me.'

'I told you!' Kiki says.

I start laughing a little. Kiki couldn't remember it because she wasn't there, not because she didn't care or pay enough attention.

A small group of people is coming down the path towards us. It's only when they've almost reached us that I look more carefully and realise it's Youta, Masato and Daisuke. Youta is holding flowers.

'Kiki told me you put your mum's name on the grave,' he says. 'These are for her.' He holds out a bouquet of flame-coloured spider lilies, the curl and dance of their petals like the fireworks on the beach.

It takes me a second to get the words out. 'These were her favourites.'

'I know,' Youta says.

'How?'

'She told me. When we were little.'

Youta puts the flowers down carefully. I thought that I couldn't bear to see her name on the headstone, but there it is, and here I am, still standing, OK. Hikaru comes running, dust flying at his heels, Ai following behind. Seven people feels like a proper crowd in the tiny dirt lane. I think I imagined, when I thought of her headstone, that I would be standing here alone, and now I'm ashamed to have thought that.

Youta takes a lighter from his pocket and cups a hand around the incense, releasing its woody, calming smell, the smell of home. It's Hikaru who claps his hands together first, and bows his head.

61

When we get home from the cemetery, I open my laptop for the first time since I resigned, death admin having left no time or headspace for life admin. My inbox finally loads, to a series of officious messages from HR about passwords and laptops, and a terse one from Llewellyn. It's the kind of tone that would have made my soul shrink, once upon a time, and now I delete it, revelling in the digital thud made by the 'delete' button. I also find an email from Arisa, from Loupie Lou. God knows how she got my address, but she asks me to tell Ai that they found Coco the hamster, sitting in the middle of the floor in Ai's room. Arisa says she's looking after him, and has attached a photo. I close the laptop and go to tell Kiki, who is watering the garden with yesterday's bathwater hauled out by the bucket-load.

'Do you think Arisa was the one who sold the head-shaving video to the TV network?' Kiki asks.

'Could have been,' I agree.

'Should we hate her?' Kiki says. 'I'm not sure I can be bothered.'

'Let's not bother,' I say. 'I'm glad she's looking after Coco.'

I hold my watering can over the chirpy faces of a cluster of irises. 'Doesn't it feel like all the summer admin is done?'

Kiki looks at me. 'I literally never in my life thought I would hear you say admin was finished,' she says. 'Was Obaachan dying also on your to-do list? Is that something you can tick off, too?'

'I quit my job,' I tell her, without meaning to.

Kiki only looks surprised for half a second. 'That is just the best thing,' she says, genuinely delighted. And then, suspiciously, 'Wait, is it because you have another terrible corporate job waiting in the wings?'

'No,' I say, tutting.

'I'm so proud of you. Congratulations.'

'Don't be so patronising,' I say. 'If I'd known you were going to think it was this much of an achievement for me to get myself unemployed and directionless, I would have done it ages ago.'

She snorts. 'No, you wouldn't.' I turn away from her, to water the vegetable patch, which has gone feral and produced so many tomatoes and cucumbers we can't keep up. 'You can't talk, anyway. I know you've been looking at job websites.'

'Bossy *and* nosy,' she mutters at me, but she doesn't deny it. 'I was mainly going online to check out what people are saying about Ai, anyway.'

'And?'

'As predicted, the media terriers are yapping about something else now. Specifically, a multi-layered shit fight about a too-sexy K-pop music video.'

'Was there anything about Ai?'

'Not really.' Kiki picks a single tomato, the colour of a London double-decker bus, off the plant. 'An article that said the recent Kabuki shows were kind of boring.'

'Excellent news. See, the world is ready for us to come out of hiding. We can't just hang out here forever.'

Kiki frowns. 'I don't see why not. This is a real place, you know. People do actually live here.'

They do. On our way back from the cemetery yesterday, we passed a group of schoolchildren with their randoseru, making their way home from early-bird school, getting ready for the new term. I could practically smell the purposeful, sharpened-pencil vibes of September.

Coming from two places is what I imagine it must be like to be the child of divorced parents: all the advantages of having two of all the good things, more to love, more places to call home, and all the disadvantages of never being in one place without missing the other, never feeling like anything is quite enough – not the places themselves, not you in them. And watching power struggles, and changing your own allegiances, and finding things that drive you mad but also being prepared to defend the perpetrator of the madness to the death.

I knew from my arrival here that the moment would come when my time was up and I needed to leave. When I go to the bad conbini, to pay Obaachan's final electricity and gas bills, the girl behind the till gives me the flustered look. I get the amounts mixed up because I'm thinking about Sath and the policeman. When Sath and I were here, we went for a walk one evening, and a police car followed us from a little way behind. When I confronted the policeman, he seemed genuinely bemused that I would question him checking out the actions of the only brown foreigner the region had ever seen. Sath invited him to get out of the car and walk with us, which the guy understood, even though I refused to translate, and he did, parking his car carefully by the side of the road. He turned out to be nice, which was not actually that surprising. It was always Sath's gut reaction, to be interested and extend a hand, where mine was to attack. By the time we broke up, all I wanted was to set fire to everything just to get a rise out of him. One of a few slightly regrettable reactions, looking back.

The girl in the conbini swallows and reads the titles of the bills out to me very clearly, even trying her best to translate them into English. It's kind of her, and I consider it a sign of maturity and life experience that I can see she's only trying to be helpful, and don't swear at her.

It would be pretty ridiculous to say I booked my flight back to London because the girl in the conbini looked at me funny. Kiki would have a fit. And yet. The first morning I ever woke up in London, the day after Sath and I moved into our studio flat, it was to the competing sounds of a man in a kilt playing the bagpipes on the pavement, an impassioned argument in Spanish and the call to prayer from the mosque on the corner. Prince Fancy Goods' wig shop vied for space with a Swedish bakery and a dumpling takeaway set up inside an old printing press; people who dressed like they were homeless swaggered with a cool bordering on arrogance. The Afghan owner of the corner shop, the Sri Lankan proprietor of our favourite restaurant and the Polish bagel baker all treated me with the same baseline contempt they had for everyone. I could behave very well or I could go off the rails in ways I didn't even have the imagination to conceive of; nobody gave a shit either way and slightly suspected it was more likely to be the latter.

I never noticed, when I was small, that we change the air here, my sisters and I, as soon as we walk into a place – how could I notice, when I couldn't live outside of my self? It was only when I'd been in London for a while that I could feel it – that in the countryside, it's impossible to blend into the background. We make a place a bit less itself just by existing. Which particularly sucks when you love a place exactly as it is.

I book the plane ticket on my phone, standing right on the pavement outside the conbini, piggybacking off the Wi-Fi from the bookshop next door. I book it for ten days away, and tell myself I can always change it if I need to.

62

I wake up the next morning surprised that Sath isn't there. This is old news; at the beginning it was almost every day, as if I have the memory of a goldfish, but it didn't fade as much over the years as one is led to believe these things do. It's fine to feel disorientated, I try to tell myself; a lot has happened recently. Of everything I've tried, talking to myself nicely is new, and disturbing.

I roll over and close my eyes. In my mind's eye is a picture I've seen who knows where, of Sath and the girlfriend after me. Sath in the picture looked older, leaner, and the girl in his arms looked so happy. She had expensive-looking hair, white teeth, an open smile. I could imagine her in a kitchen with an island, laughing with their kids. I wonder what happened to her.

I wasn't jealous when I saw the picture and now, half asleep, the back of my mind – a tenebrous, treacherous place I mainly try to ignore – tells me why. They could be married, his delightful wife and him, and have children, and live their entire lives together, and still, in my insane heart of hearts, I'd think he belonged to me, and I belonged to him, and the unfortunate fact of who we spent our lives with was irrelevant. A brilliant little fantasy that has no need of anything to happen in real life to prove or disprove it, like whole-heartedly believing God is a marshmallow and when we die, we turn into sugar puffs in a parallel universe. I open my eyes, thinking that I really need to forget I ever thought that. The exact sound of his voice comes back to me: 'This is bollocks, Rei.' That might have been the last thing he ever said to me.

Before the incident at the wedding. Which I am absolutely not thinking about.

I make Japanese breakfast to compensate for my out-of-line thoughts.

'Obaachan would be so proud of you,' Kiki says when she comes downstairs, lured by the smell of the fish grilling.

'That is the biggest lie you've ever told me,' I say. 'Grated radish is too watery,' I tell her, pointing at it. 'Wrong brand of natto.'

'Too much miso in the soup.'

'Tamagoyaki layers too thick. And a *salad* on the side.'

'*Raw vegetables!*' Kiki agrees in horror. 'No effort whatsoever. We're not *rabbits.*'

'So what are you going to do now?' I ask Ai when we're sitting down, cracking an egg into my rice.

'Do you mean, like, today, or in life?' Kiki asks. 'Don't those kind of questions need build-up?'

'I thought we might finally have moved past the small talk stage.'

'Open a tattoo parlour,' Ai says, like it's obvious. 'I'm sure if I shave my head and change my name, nobody will know who I am.'

'What will you change it to?' Kiki asks with interest.

'Angelica Peaseblossom,' Ai says without hesitation.

'It's no wonder you and Hikaru get on so well,' Kiki observes. 'Hikaru, if you put that much mustard with your natto, you're going to blow your head off.'

'That will be a katakana nightmare,' I tell her.

299

Ai shrugs. 'Or maybe I'll start a funk band in a different country. I'm not Monica Lewinsky. I'm only big in Japan.'

Hikaru eats his too-mustardy natto and sits there stoically, his eyes watering.

'I've booked my ticket back,' I say, as we all watch him with interest.

Kiki doesn't react. Ai sighs heavily. 'When?' she asks.

'Next Friday.' It's like breaking a spell, naming the day.

'I'll come,' Ai says, like she's agreeing to go to the supermarket with me. 'London might be quite a good place to start my tattooing career, anyway.'

London with Ai. I think of all the things she'll love there.

'Are you serious?'

'Yes,' says Ai. 'Can I stay at yours, just at the beginning?'

'So I'm just meant to stay here and hold the fort?' Kiki objects before I can answer, her chopsticks halfway to her mouth.

'Come too,' I say.

'She doesn't want to,' Ai says. 'She fancies Youta so much it's like Adam Levine in music videos, where your brain gets scrambled and you start to think everything he's doing is hot, even the things that are objectively weird, or probably criminal.'

'For god's sake,' Kiki says. 'Youta is objectively not weird. Or a criminal.' I notice she doesn't disagree about the brain-scrambling.

'You should stay here,' I tell her. 'You and Hikaru can be like landed gentry, spreading yourself out across two properties. For free.'

'You're so bossy,' Kiki mutters, but she looks at Hikaru, now sucking on an entire salted plum, and I can tell she's thinking about it.

300

63

Couldn't I stay here, too? Convince Ai to? The three of us in the same place, happy forever? Couldn't I get over being the odd one out, the way that Kiki has; appreciate the undeniably myriad beauties and charms of Ikimura?

Well.

It's the smell of the rice cooking, a glutinous, warm, round smell. One evening, a couple of days later, I've just taken the washing off the line in the garden, when it hits me. I don't know who put the rice on today, if it was Kiki or Ai. Someone who is making it their work to feed us all. The smell of every evening meal of our childhood, as we came bickering in from the dusk, the food on the table without question. I bury my face in the washing so nobody can see my face. It smells of fresh air, and the cotton of Hikaru's pyjamas is very soft.

Someone rounds the corner and stops abruptly when they see me, crouched on the floor like a lunatic with my face buried in a pile of clothing.

'Onechan?' Ai's voice is hesitant, and I really don't want her to talk or I'm going to cry. 'Are you OK?'

'Mm.'

'What's wrong?'

'Nothing's wrong. It's the smell of the rice cooking.' The last word doesn't really come out because it's stuck in my throat.

'Oh,' she says softly, and I love her best because I feel her sit down next to me, but she doesn't touch me, or say anything else.

In London, there are no smells of sticky rice, no patterns on futons, no sounds of the glass wind-chimes she loved, to take me unawares. When I do think of Nozomi, I imagine her living on a houseboat, painting like she means it and exhibiting her work in cafés and galleries, all those art-filled cafés and galleries that don't exist in this town. Or shacking up with a successful writer and having dinner parties in some boho house covered in abstract art and ethnic rugs, or even returning to her Japanese roots and setting up tidy home in Golders Green, enjoying early-morning walks in Golders Hill Park with her Orthodox Jewish neighbours. Alive, in all scenarios. I think of how much she would have loved it, how her shameful life with her half-breed children would have raised no eyebrows at all, how nobody would have pitied her because everyone had bigger fish to fry. In London, my dead Japanese mother is happier to me, and I can think of her on my terms. There are no corners I can turn where she's suddenly there; no break in the constant vigilance required against the hubbub and filth that's big enough for her ghost to squeeze into. London is too busy, too noisy, too bad-tempered for melancholia; I think that's why it's home.

64

Early one morning, just before I leave, I drive to Uradome alone. Even at this time, it's so hot the sky is hazy, and when I open my eyes under the turquoise water, I can see all the way down to the sand at the bottom. It'll be Obon soon, when the dead come home for three days; Obaachan would tell us not to swim, if she were here, for fear of their dragging us down. This year, I guess we'll listen, and Ai and Kiki won't swim, out of something like respect, or maybe superstition. Anyway, Obon brings the jellyfish with it. I wonder where Obaachan's gone, and if she'll be back, too.

It's knowing that I'm leaving, I think, that pulls me towards the cave. It gets deeper as I swim closer, the bottom too far away to see in the inky shade cast by the rock. I have a sudden picture of my legs from beneath, kicking away. Everything that's in my head, the whole world I carry around with me, and it's all so small. With nobody to hear me, I laugh, a manic sound, then stop immediately.

I edge slowly towards the entrance. The cold of the cave seems to be breathing, damp and alive. All the nightmares of my childhood fizz on the edges of my brain; one part of me laughs at myself, while the other is convinced beyond reason that the cave is going to swallow me whole. Just when

I think I have to back out, I see a pool of light before me.

As soon as I've seen it, my eyes adjust. A hole in the roof of the rock is streaming sunlight into the cave, turning it into a natural chapel, flecks of light dancing on the water like watching the sound of a harp being played. My feet find themselves on sand, coarse between my toes, and the residue of my fear runs down my arms. I can hear the lazy lapping of the waves against the stone.

The expanse of sea outside is huge and unbroken, the stuff of dreams and nightmares. I think of King Cnut, trying to hold back the tide. I kick off to float on the water and watch the light.

65

Kiki

清美

Ai brings me the newspaper, smirking. I think maybe she's been publicly exonerated and they're going to make Ichiro walk around with a scarlet letter on his head, but it's an article about North Koreans.

'What is this?' I ask.

'Some people have come out of North Korea, saying they're Japanese. They were kidnapped from the beaches twenty years ago and have been trained to be spies.'

'You're taking the piss,' I say.

She isn't. I take the paper and read.

'Just imagine how justified Obaachan would feel,' says Ai. 'We have to put a cutting on the butsudan.' She reaches into her pocket and pulls out a carefully folded newspaper clipping. 'I found some of her haiku, too. When I was clearing out the cupboard in her room. There were a few, but I like this one the best.'

I take the paper. There's the end of an article about changes to voting regulations in local government, and, underneath, a column about different ways to use your empty PET bottles rather than throwing them away (they make very useful muscle massagers, apparently). Obaachan's haiku is next to that.

> I want them to come
> I long for them to depart
> Summer granddaughters.

I look at Ai, and now I'm smirking, too.

'Dying to get rid of us,' I say.

'I'm going to frame it. You have to give it pride of place in the sitting room.'

Ai's ticket to London is booked for a month away. Before she goes, and before I start my new job as a carer at the home attached to the hospital, we're going to Tokyo to pack up my and Hikaru's stuff, and fetch the hamster. I guess it was on my mind a lot, even before Rei suggested it. There is literally nobody around here who looks like Hikaru; on the other hand, everyone around here looks out for him, and not paying rent means I can work less, be with him more. In the end, it was Hikaru himself who decided it, that we should stay here. He went running around the engawa with joy when I suggested it, shouting about the beach and the garden and Chibi and Youta. I tried to convince him that Youta wasn't that much of a factor, but when I told Youta about that, he told me he was offended that he wasn't. We've seen him every day since.

'I'm glad Rei's not going back to London by herself,' I say.

'Well,' says Ai, 'somebody's got to look after her, haven't they?'

66

'I'll miss you,' Rei tells us as she gets into the taxi, the same one that brought us here when we arrived almost three months ago. It's morning, and we haven't had time to clear away the breakfast dishes yet. Rei's coffee is still on the table, still warm. Ai stands beside me, barefoot on the street.

Just as the taxi is about to leave, Rei rolls down her window. 'I think I would actually be dead if there was no you,' she says.

'Apparently, I wouldn't even exist if there was no you,' I tell her. I indicate Ai. 'Probably she wouldn't, either.'

Rei smiles.

She waves out of the window until the taxi turns the corner, out of sight.

I know she can't stay, even though I wish she would. There are too many demons here. At the same time as getting it, though, I hate her for it – doesn't she know that she'll go back to England and think of us in Japan, and I'll stay here and think of her in England, and when we're together, that's home, and as good as it's going to get. I'm glad she's leaving, if she doesn't know that. Idiot.

Hikaru starts to sing to himself. '*The oni's pants are good pants, they're strong; Granny can wear them, and Auntie, and Grandpa. Rei likes that song.*'

'She does?'

'Yes. She knew all the words.'

Why the hell does she know all the words to a children's song about monster pants? Another thing to ask her, next time.

67

Ai

愛

The street feels quiet after the taxi has gone. I sit down on the front step and Hikaru crawls on to my lap.

I think of him telling Kiki he doesn't want to be anybody else. I don't, either. Not anyone. In all the world, in all its iterations throughout all of time, I only want this life, this family. This difficult, batshit group. That's it.

I always knew I wouldn't make a very good Buddhist.

'Your cheeks are wet,' Hikaru tells me.

'Are they?'

'I'll dry them for you, Ai. It's OK.'

68

Rei

Five minutes after I get through the departure gate, it feels like I'm underwater and I've just torn off one of my own limbs. I buy an English magazine, sit, gather myself. It feels like I've spent the whole summer spread out, not at all fighting fit; I gather it all into a ball, tight and rolled up, holding everything precious on the inside. By the time I'm on the plane, where there are Caucasian stewardesses, I can see myself through other people's eyes again, leaning up to put my bag in the overhead locker, efficient, polite. I watch a not-very-good American comedy with the subtitles off, and choose a too-cold sandwich, something it's impossible to get sentimental about.

I think of the first flight I took to England alone, on my way to university, feeling so many things that in the end I felt nothing. Term started a few days after I arrived, and the first weeks were so overwhelmingly filled with admin and new people that I didn't have a second to wonder what the hell I was doing. I realised I was happy about a month in, moments before I spoke to Sath for the very first time. I was completely alone in one of the morgue-cold stacks of the university library, wearing cut-off-finger gloves with no irony, and I was shivering as I cursed my way through the shelves. The book I was trying to find was about some historical addendum to an economic forum, and I was planning on writing an essay about it that probably wouldn't be very coherent, and also on going to the arty cinema or the ancient pub down the road, with Charlotte or blissfully alone. Thoughts of my mother and responsibility for my sisters had lifted off my shoulders and, every morning when I woke up, I was confused by my lightness. I think now of Ai, this summer, sitting in the glass-bottomed boat, running her fingers through the clear water, and the image of her smile is an ache that makes me feel bad forever having been glad to be somewhere she wasn't. But the reality is that when Sath walked into the stack, I was happy, so I was singing to myself and possibly even tapping out a rhythm on the shelves with my fingers, so he had a completely incorrect impression of me off the bat.

When it's time to go through Arrivals, I walk quickly, arranging my features to convey how sorry I am that I'm not the person anyone is waiting for.

My flat is as clean and ordered as it was when I left it, and bloody freezing, even though it's apparently still summer. I unpack quickly, tipping all the sand I find in the bottom of the suitcase into the bath. It creates a tiny golden dune next to the plug, and I wash it away quickly.

The next morning, I go for a run along the canal, breathing deeply and choosing to find the build-up of rubbish and abandoned shopping trolleys, something you would never see in Japan, an enervating sign of a liberated society. I shower and put on a wash and sit down to make a plan.

Two and a half hours later, I've swapped around the first two sections of my CV, learnt from LinkedIn that Jasper is now either heading up Silverman Sayle or taking positive language to whole new levels, and am wondering if I should move to Totnes and sell temporary tattoos. Or I could start a mail-order business of things currently only available in Japan.

Even though the idea doesn't appeal on any level, I spend the next two hours researching trans-Pacific shipping methods. As I'm closing the laptop, my hand brushes against the AirDrop button. The screen thinks for a moment before declaring its verdict:

No people found.
There is no one nearby to share with.

I laugh a little too loud and too long.

For dinner I eat crackers and a tin of sardines standing up on the balcony, watching a man sitting in his car with the engine on, fiddling with his phone. It begins to rain, inevitably, drops hitting the windscreen like an act of spite.

69

He's standing there when I open the front door the next morning. I don't see him because I'm checking for my keys as I step out into the street, and I almost walk straight into him; he's so close that even before I look up, the smell of him has made my foolish heart beat faster, clocking on before my brain has caught up. Broad-shouldered, with his face in shadow; a familiar stranger. I step backwards just as the door swings shut, so that I smash my head straight into it and swear.

'Sorry,' Sath says, frowning. 'Are you OK? I – sorry.'

I didn't know he knew where I lived.

'I wanted to give you this,' he says, when I don't say anything. He hands me an envelope with two hands, strangely formal. 'I didn't know you'd be here. I thought you were still away.'

'Thank you,' I say, although I don't know what I'm thanking him for. For an insane moment, I wonder if it's some kind of legal document, if he's suing me for something diabolical I didn't even know I'd done. Never knowingly relaxed, or guilt-free. I accept the envelope with both hands, too, as if I haven't left Japan at all.

'It's your earring,' he clarifies. 'It was . . . I found it in my stuff.'

I feel heat rising up my neck. 'Thank you,' I say again, my voice gravelly. 'My sisters gave them to me.'

'I know.'

I look at him then, like a normal person, like we're having a normal doorstep conversation. He was clean-shaven at the wedding; now black stubble accentuates the line of his jaw and the smoothness of his throat. I see the movement of his Adam's apple as he swallows. I almost put my hand up to run my finger along the back of his ear, down his neck. I place it on top of the envelope instead, like an evangelical preacher in the pulpit.

'I was going to get coffee,' I say. 'I just got back; there's nothing in the flat.' He says nothing for all of one second. 'Do you want to come?' I hear the words, and hate myself.

'I'm going to the airport,' he says, and indicates the duffel bag on his shoulder.

'Oh, right.' I am a calm black hole. Obviously I never wanted him to come with me, disturbing the peace and making everything complicated.

He frowns and checks his watch, the same watch he's worn forever, a wind-up metal Casio from the seventies that his dad gave him. 'I probably have a little time,' he says. 'Maybe, like, half an hour.'

'Don't do me any favours,' I tell him automatically, and for a second he looks stung. Then his face relaxes and he smiles like he just saw someone he recognised in the street.

'I'm not doing you a favour,' he says.

The pavement is still slick with last night's rain, but sunshine is breaking through the clouds. The major disadvantage of where I live immediately becomes clear – there are cafés every-where, three within a thirty-second radius. Sath says nothing as we pass them all, so I don't either. Each time we come to a street lamp, cast-iron black and emblazoned with ER or GR, like the monarchs of England placed them there personally, we separate and I think about him gamely accompanying me, wishing he didn't have to humour a mad spinster before getting on a plane. Then he steps towards me again, closing the gap so our shoulders are almost touching, and I think, I'm happy now, at least I have this moment. I wish I'd never asked him to come, and I wish we could carry on walking down this street forever.

We turn on to the high street, and I realise I'd forgotten it's Saturday. The outdoor tables are full of couples self-medicating with orange juice and brunch menus, taking tentative first steps into a morning after the night before. In the reflection of a bookshop window, above a display of paperbacks about rewilding, I catch sight again of Sath's duffel bag.

'You're going to America,' I say. I only realise I knew as the words come out of my mouth. 'Today.'

'Yes.' That expression again, closed.

I stop in front of a café with a takeaway window under a striped awning. 'Here's good,' I say, so I don't have to engage with America. 'How was your summer?' It comes out like the start of an interrogation, unfriendly.

'Good,' he says, with that little nod and the familiar expression of anyone who's ever been asked. Like the question has really made them consider for the first time, and they are surprised to discover that it was good, actually. 'Yours?'

'Good. I was in Japan.' My sister fell into a depression and became a national disgrace. My great-grandmother died. But it was good – fantastic, actually.

The barista, who looks like she has either already been for a run or is still high from last night's drugs, takes our orders and starts up a flirtatious conversation with Sath. I idly open the envelope. Tucked in next to the earring is a photograph of the two of us, the one he used to keep in his room at home. We look unashamedly ecstatic, and about twelve.

Sath hands me the coffee, and I shove the envelope into my bag.

'That night,' he says as we're walking away, and I'm not ready for it. I want to tell him to stop so I'm not standing there with a lip covered in coffee froth, and can remind myself I don't care before I have to hear what he's about to say. 'I'm sorry about the morning. I screwed up. I had a girlfriend.'

I swallow. 'No worries.' The coffee burns my throat as it goes down.

'It was wrong of me,' he says, so formally that I hate him. 'I'm sorry.'

'I said it's fine.' My voice is sharp. I stop walking. 'What time's your flight? Don't you need to go?'

'Probably.'

We're standing on a corner by a pub, the curved plate-glass window so old I can see drips in the glass. I squint with great concentration at the shine of the lettering on the window, picked out in gold. Sath sits down on the wooden bench in front of it.

'I couldn't get in touch with you,' he says, looking at his coffee cup. 'After the wedding.' He makes a shucking sound through his teeth. 'I don't have your number.' I perch carefully on the bench, leaving enough space for a very wide person to sit between us. 'I tried social media, but you were never there. So I got your number off Charlotte, in the end, but it didn't work.'

'Nothing works in Japan.' Our own little island nation, safe from gaijin intruders.

He hesitates, then says, 'I called you at work. But they said you'd left. So I asked her for your address. Charlotte. I had to message her three times. I told her I wanted to send you a post-card. I think she thought I wanted to kidnap you or something. I could practically hear her discussing it with Ben.'

I look up at the pub front. 'That's a lot of effort to go to,' I say, 'just to explain you had a girlfriend.' The queen's head on the sign sneers at me, smug beneath her crown. 'You didn't need to.'

'I wasn't calling to apologise. We broke up.'

A single heartbeat bangs at my chest. 'Oh.'

Don't go. I imagine saying it: Don't go to America, stay here with me, even though I'm unemployed and have a personality like a giant spike and we broke up years ago. I imagine telling Kiki I said it, and smile to myself.

A toddler being cajoled up the road decides she's had enough and falls to her knees, wailing inconsolably. Hikaru would be proud. Sath smiles at me, a rueful smile, and we stand up. I take all his words and fold them away, to look at again later, when he's gone.

'Do you know what you're going to do next?' he asks. 'Work-wise?'

'No,' I say, and I'm almost impatient, because it seems so irrelevant. 'I might dabble in psychedelics. Maybe check out your brother's merchandise.'

He smiles and frowns all at once. 'I thought you loved your job.'

'I didn't love it,' I say. 'I just gave it all my attention.' I think about it for a moment. 'I was waiting for it to give me freedom.' I almost start laughing. At myself. And my stupid, stupid life.

'I didn't think you'd be there,' Sath says, looking straight ahead, his hands in his pockets. 'At your place. I don't even know why I came. I thought maybe you were going to stay in Japan.' He looks up, to the flats above the line of shops, at a girl opening a window. 'I thought after I moved to America, I'd probably never see you again.' He says it like it's a problem he's admitting to. 'It's just that I couldn't stop thinking about you.' He looks at me. 'I haven't ever not thought of you.'

All the words I never said crowd into the space between us.

'That's why I came back,' I hear myself say, and it's like letting out a breath I didn't know I was holding. 'For you.'

There are flecks of gold in his eyes, near the pupils, that I hadn't forgotten, but that I didn't let myself remember.

'I should go,' he says. 'I'm going to miss my plane.'

But he doesn't move.

70

Okaasan e,

I'm not angry with you any more. I don't know if I was ever really angry. Maybe I just told myself I was, because it hurt so much less than thinking how much I missed you.

I wonder if you've met up with Obaachan. Ai would reckon that you have, and you're cavorting around in white dresses or something. Or maybe she doesn't really think that. If anything, I reckon Obaachan'll be giving you an earful – rather you than me.

I think Ai got your artistic genes (well, obviously). I don't know if she remembers your drawings, but you might have heard that her new plan is to ink designs directly on to people's skin. I bet she'll be pretty good – maybe I'll get her to do me one. I think Kiki's going to get together with Youta – the boy she married in first grade, if you remember. He'll be the best dad. They might even live together by the sea, the first functional couple the house has ever seen. That would be a result, wouldn't it? Ai's coming to London soon, and Kiki says she's going to visit next year, because she wants to eat scones, and also take Hikaru on a train trip around Europe. Why not, right?

I've been thinking about the way things pan out. I hadn't

thought about it, till Kiki said to me this summer that if you'd stuck around, there would probably be no Hikaru. We never could have had you both. I haven't figured out what to do with that yet.

I'm so sorry for how much it must have hurt. To live. Don't you feel like some people make it look so easy?

I have to go now. Sath is waiting for me. It turns out he'd been waiting a while, actually. I miss you. God, I miss you. I'll never stop. I have to go.

71

It's raining again when I take a photo from the balcony. The street light suffuses the picture with gold, and behind the blur of rain is a roofscape of chimneypots and lit-up windows. I send the picture to Kiki. Hello from a whole new world, I write.

Instantly, I can see Kiki typing, then a new number is added to the chat.

Ai got a new phone! Kiki types. Be honoured, we are the only two people in the world who have Takanawa Ai's number.

The group icon changes to a picture of the giant kakigori we ate at the summer matsuri. I can just make out Ai's eyes behind it, wide with anticipation. The kakigori looks bigger than her face.

WHAT have you been doing for the last three days??? Kiki writes. We thought maybe your plane crash-landed in a jungle and it was a Survivor situation

That would surely be on the news, I write back.

Not what Obaachan would have us believe

From the kitchen behind me, I hear the gentle sizzle of something hitting the frying pan. The air is rich with the smell of garlic.

I can see Ai typing, and then the name of the group chat changes. Kakigori summer, it says.

'Rei,' Sath calls from the kitchen, 'this is really important. Do you have all the ingredients for a negroni?'

'What do you take me for?' I ask him. 'Obviously. Give me a sec; I'll get them.'

I like the icon, I write.

So you can always remember true deliciousness, Ai says.

And matcha syrup and adzuki beans. The essence of a happy life.

And how you can get all that out of FROZEN WATER. Then she sends a picture of her and Kiki pouting exaggeratedly at the camera, dressed from top to toe in Obaachan's old clothes. They look mad, and possibly quite trendy. Vintage gold. Do you think she'd like it?

Absolutely not, I write.

But then I pause, and delete that, and write instead

Maybe

And rows and rows of hearts.

72

Ai

愛

I'm wondering what I'll do now, what's next, but not in the way I did at the beginning of the summer, when I knew the bomb had landed but couldn't see the destruction. I can see it now, and it isn't destruction at all. It's more like someone cleared the area out, ready for something new to be planted.

It was that evening when we were on the way back from the onsen that it suddenly came. That joy that winds you out of nowhere and wraps you up; life reminding you it's still got it, an unreliable lover you moon over for decades because the good times were just so good.

We'd bought cold drinks from the vending machine in the changing room, sweet iced coffees for us and milk for Hikaru, in glass bottles with waxed-paper lids. 'I think we're meant to return these,' Rei said, helping Hikaru get the lid off his, condensation trailing down the side.

'Hikaru and me can take them back tomorrow,' said Kiki, taking his hand. He was quiet, absorbed with the cold, clean taste of the milk, and Kiki's face, just looking at him, was something to hold on to forever.

It wasn't remarkable. We were just walking down a quiet back street, freshly bathed, sipping our drinks. My sisters and the baby. Two high-school boys cycled past laughing about something, the brass buttons on their uniforms gleaming, their hair recently buzz-cut for the summer heat. I remembered Rei teaching me to ride, how many times I fell off, the way her thumb would rub my palm when she picked me up, all the things she was telling me that she never needed to say. I thought of our mother, how she must have walked down this road, too, listening to the crows crooning at the dusk. She didn't just leave us her sadness; she gave us everything else, too.

Sometimes it comes in a rush, too much feeling, like I'm mostly asleep, but once in a while I wake up and there the world is, in all its glory. The sky was a grey-blue so pale it tricked your eyes, the pinks and lilacs above the buildings the colour of a dream chiffon prom dress, and just looking at it made me feel like any soul I might have was singing.

Look, I wanted to say to her. Look at us all, still here, how far we've come.

How can life be at once so short and so long? So flimsy it can disappear like a trick of the light, and so generous that you can grieve for decades and still have it left to live.

73

There's no ending to a story, just like there isn't any beginning. There's only where you choose to start telling it, and where you decide to stop. The thing that goes on, and on, and on, is life, in all its grimness and sorrow, and pockets of beauty and love so spectacular they're almost too bright to see.

Obaachan told me once that that was the thing that annoyed her the most about dying, not knowing what was going to happen next. Like not being able to watch the next episode of *Tomorrow's Cantabile*, she said. Although, come to think of it, she might actually have meant that was the most annoying thing about death, and it wasn't an analogy at all.

You could say that this summer was when the story of Kiki and Hikaru and Youta started. Maybe, though, it started when Hikaru was born, which means it began the night Kiki met Hikaru's dad, whoever he was. Or maybe it started the very first time Youta and Rei narrowed eyes at each other across the school playground. And on and on, and back and back and back.

So here we are, making plans, and we don't know if things will work out, or heartbreak is round the corner, or if any of us are going to be able to keep the show on the road long-term. There's the part of me that's freaking out, thinking of this as an interlude, an island haven that we'll look back at one day, and say to ourselves, 'Did we know how happy we were?' I wish we could hold on to it, the blasted elusive moment, but the harder I grasp, the more it slips away, like trying to hold a shaft of sunlight in your hand.

Then there's the other part of me, that's started to hear songs in the breeze again, that managed to believe that this too shall pass, and is watching Hikaru try with all his might to slide further across the floor on his stomach than he did the last time because that's the most important thing on earth at this moment. That part of me is pretty sure we all know exactly how happy we are, and that some day in the dim and mysterious future, we'll call each other up and say, 'Remember the time . . .?' and that's as tightly as you can ever hold on to anything. To live isn't scary at all, said nobody ever, and the more there is to love, the higher the stakes. But you only get to play once, and game over is the inevitable ending, so what can you say, apart from 'bring it on'? And then I have to touch wood because it is all so fucking frightening, but on I go with the tiny little bit I can do. One step in front of another.

I know the thing I want to tell Hikaru now, the thing that might come in useful one day. There'll be days when the way things are will make you weep, and the fact of the world is too heavy to get out from underneath. And then other days, when you can't believe you're here, with people you love in a world that contains barley tea and kakigori and sun after rain, watermelons and grumpy cats and this front door. Hikaru runs through it, in such a rush he barely has time to get his shoes on, roaring at me that it's time to go. Sunshine catches one half of his face, and the only thing I want to tell him is to keep his face turned towards it. The light, always the light.

Acknowledgements

Hugest thanks to my stellar editors, Francesca Main and Katherine Nintzel. Working with you both has officially been the privilege of my life – I cannot tell you how happy I've been, sitting at the kitchen table on a rainy morning, reading through your notes on the manuscript, not really able to believe my luck. Thank you for your wisdom, humour and kindness.

Thank you also to the rest of the fantastic team behind the book: my agent Kirsty McLachlan; Alice Graham at Phoenix Books; Charlotte Abrams-Simpson and Heike Schussler for the dreamy English cover; Sarah Fortune and Eleanor Updegraff for being so extremely on it with the copy edits; Tara Hiatt, Ben Fowler and Marie Henckel, foreign rights geniuses (genii??); Emily Cary-Elwes and Ellie Nightingale for the publicity and marketing.

I'm so grateful to Mariner for giving *Kakigori Summer* a home in the US, especially to Mumtaz Mustafa and Hirouki Izutsu for that glorious blue cover, to Nicole Angeloro, Ellie Anderson and Erin Merlo.

Thank you to Irene, most wonderful first reader and one-woman PR campaign. To Marley, in a book about aunts and nephews, for rocking up and casually being perfect. To Rocka and Takasan and all the Yamamotos, for all those summers that felt like home. To Tim, for making me laugh, and tea, and for putting up with my very occasional bullshit. To Jijibaba, for the UN-approved supplies and the shed, amongst a small number of other things. To Sebastian Kenji Sessions and Joshua Jun Sessions, with apologies for all the times I haven't heard you because I was frowning at a screen – presumably it won't help to hear that in so many ways this inaccessible book with no spies, no ninjas and no supernatural events at all, is for you. And to Naomi, obviously.